Ten Days

Ten Days

Janet Gilsdorf

KENSINGTON BOOKS
www.kensingtonbooks.com

KENSINGTON BOOKS are published by
Kensington Publishing Corp.
119 West 40th Street
New York, NY 10018

All Kensington titles, imprints, and distributed lines are available at special quantity discounts for bulk purchases for sales promotion, premiums, fund-raising, educational or institutional use.

Special book excerpts or customized printings can also be created to fit specific needs. For details, write or phone the office of the Kensington Special Sales Manager: Kensington Publishing Corp., 119 West 40th Street, New York, NY 10018. Attn. Special Sales Department. Phone: 1-800-221-2647.

ISBN-13: 978-0-7582-6944-7
ISBN-10: 0-7582-6944-7

First Kensington Trade Paperback Printing: October 2012

10 9 8 7 6 5 4 3 2 1

Printed in the United States of America

To Jim, as always

Acknowledgments

With deepest gratitude, I thank Marty Calvert, Emmy Holman, Jane Johnson, Danielle Lavaque-Manty, Don Lystra, and Margaret Nesse for their enduring patience, Lauren Kuczala for her amazing editing skills, Cynthia Manson for her persistence and never-ending optimism, and John Scognamiglio for making it all happen.

Chapter 1

Anna

The car rounded the turn and she spotted the bridge. From that distance it was tiny, a faraway cobweb stretched over the foggy Straits between St. Ignace on her side and Mackinaw City on the other.

Her fingers gripped the steering wheel. "Who's going to drive over?"

"You don't want to?" her husband asked.

"No."

"Think of it as a highway."

She turned toward him, bit her lip, and shrugged. She hated the bridge.

"Okay, okay," Jake said. "I'll drive."

Before her, the Mackinac Bridge—graceful, majestic, enduring—spanned the waves, its far end lost in the morning mist. The support cables that looped from the concrete stanchions moored deep into the lake bed grew greener, thicker as she drew near.

"Hey, are we going on that bridge?" Chris called from his car seat in the back.

"Yes, Daddy's going to drive." Anna glanced in the rearview mirror at her son. His arm, cloaked in his favorite blanket, stretched toward the front seat. His finger pointed at the windshield.

Three days earlier, on the way to her cousin's wedding, they had also crossed this bridge, going the other direction. But it had been dark then, and she and the children had slept while Jake drove. She had been awakened by the bump of the tires rolling from the bridge bed to the highway.

"Where are we?" She had yawned. Rocks and pine trees lined the road on her side of the car. A few lights dotted the empty spaces.

"St. Ignace. It's two hours to Grand Marais. Go back to sleep."

Now they were at the bridge again, going home. She dreaded the ride over it—too long, too high, too slippery. It was always windy at the Straits, often rainy. And the water below—far, far below—was very, very deep, very cold.

"Can I walk on it?" Chris asked, referring to the bridge.

"No," Jake said. "It's only for driving." He reached into the backseat and ran his fingers into the baby's diaper. "Eddie needs clean britches and Chris needs to run off steam. Let's switch drivers at the rest stop."

"Good idea," Anna said. She stared at the highway and the bridge ahead, at the cars in the opposite lane rolling toward her. One by one, they all had made it safely across.

"Good idea," echoed Chris.

She steered the car onto the next exit ramp and Chris started coughing. "Put it in your elbow," she said over her shoulder. On top of everything else, he was sick.

At the rest stop, she swept dirty popcorn from the picnic table, sat down, and blew her nose. She'd caught Chris's cold, had coughed all night and gone through half a packet of Kleenex. Even through her stuffy nose, though, she could smell the marine odor in the air, watery and fishy, with an industrial overlay of exhaust off the bridge.

Lake Huron spread to her left, Lake Michigan, beyond the

horizon, to the right. A wall of northern pines rose behind her above the escarpment. Next to her foot, a green dandelion poked through the yellow thatch of last year's grass, a promise of the spring to come. She squinted sideways at the bridge, at the cars, trucks, campers, and motorcycles that sped on and off its deck. Soon she, too, would be on the bridge.

Chris was racing along the water's edge, and Jake, with Eddie in the carrier, followed at a slow stroll. The boy skidded to a stop and scooped a handful of pebbles from the shore. He leaned back and tossed several stones at the gulls that swooped and squawked overhead. The birds turned and, in perfect unison, dived toward him. His eyes grew wide. He raced to his father's side. Jake laughed as he patted him on the head and Chris took off again.

Her son was growing up too fast, loved his freedom too much. He was spunky and curious, loving and smart. She wanted him to stay a little boy for a bit longer.

She turned her face into the wind, breathed the hint of spring. The past winter had been tough. Long nights. Gloomy days. What she remembered most were the snowsuit struggles with Eddie every time they left the house and the endless wait while Chris, at his insistence, pulled on his jacket, hat, and boots himself.

"Slow down, buddy," Jake called to their son. Chris spun around and faced his father, his mouth in a pout.

She didn't like pout. Or defiance. Where did that come from?

Yesterday was her cousin's wedding. As the guests filed into the pews, a groomsman had ushered her parents down the aisle and seated them in the first row, in front of Jake, herself, and the kids. She thought of her mother as stylish, in a matronly sort of way, with her beige lace dress and black leather pumps. When she fanned her face with the program, her fluttery hand motions emphasized the matronly part. Her father, trussed in his winter suit, tugged at his tie and smoothed the hair at his temples—ever the proper businessman. With a flourish, Chris had pointed to her cousin at the back of the church and yelled,

"There's the bride." His voice, usually smooth and soprano, was raspy from his cold.

"Shhh," she had said, embarrassed at his outburst. But, he was only a little boy. With muscles tight and cheeks aflame from excitement, he gripped her knee. A strip of moisture—a left-over from his runny nose—glistened on his upper lip.

She elbowed Jake. "Nose wipe needed," she said, nodding toward Chris.

"I see Aunt Jennifer back there," Chris called again. She cringed, reached for his arm.

Anna's father turned in his chair. Face-to-face with his grandson, he set a finger on his lips. Often during her childhood she had seen that finger, now crooked with age, rise to his mouth. "Keep it quiet," the gesture said.

The slit-eyed glance that she sent toward Jake begged for help, a signal that meant it's best not to bother my father. Jake smiled knowingly and pulled Chris into his lap. Together they folded the program in half and then in half again, Jake's large fingers guiding Chris's small ones. She watched as they concentrated on their project. Both had the same tall forehead, the same sandy hair—although Jake's was two shades darker than Chris's—the same furrow between their eyes. Soon, the paper program had become an airplane.

During the ceremony, she had been struck with her cousin's serenity as she walked—step, pause, step—down the aisle. Jennifer's shoulders were square, her chin raised. Her eyes seemed peaceful as they moved from face to face, stopping briefly with a nod and a smile. The chapel lights sparkled off the cream-colored beads on the bodice of her gown, adding elegance to Jennifer's already splendid presence, and her hair—the penny-colored curls that Anna had brushed into French rolls when they were young—flowed free as spring rain over her shoulders. No veil, no tiara, nothing to tame that wonderfully wild hair.

The night before her own wedding, she had had choking doubts. Did she want to be married? Was Jake the right man? What if she met the real Mr. Right the next year?

"Mom," she had sobbed, "I can't go through with it."

"Of course you can," her mother had said.

"I'm not sure I want to."

"Every bride has the jitters, honey," her mother had said while glancing over her shoulder as she made a last-minute phone call to the florist. "It'll be okay." Her mother then reminded her of the months of planning, the expensive tuxedos and dresses, the catered dinner, the flowers, the out-of-town guests stowed in three different hotels.

At two o'clock in the morning, unable to sleep, she had kneeled over the toilet bowl, vomiting. A half hour before the ceremony, she downed a beer, hoping to quell her churning stomach and realign her ragged nerves. Through it all, her head throbbed as if squeezed in a vise.

She picked up a dead leaf from the top of the picnic table, smoothed it against her knee, heard the hum of the traffic on the bridge, and watched Jake trudge toward her. She tried to remember her marriage ceremony, the walk down the aisle as a single woman, the words of the minister, the recitation of the vows, the walk back up the aisle as a married woman. The details were vague.

Now, most days she moved from early morning to late evening without ever thinking about her marriage. It was a state of being that became lost in the crush of her responsibilities, the cooking, vacuuming, grocery shopping, dropping off and picking up the kids at Rose Marie's, hunting for parking spots at the community college, devising lesson plans, corralling her students' attention. Through it all, she rarely thought about the man—the real person—who was her husband and was walking toward her.

"Here," Jake said as he set Eddie in her arms. "I'll keep chasing Chris."

"Where is he?"

"Around here somewhere."

She shifted Eddie to her shoulder, stood up, and squinted at the horizon. "Look, Jake, you can't just let a three-and-a-half-year-old go off on his own." She scanned the water's edge, the parking lot of the rest stop. "There are a thousand dangers . . ."

"Honey, he's fine. Just exploring."

She passed Eddie back to her husband. "What do you mean 'he's fine'? You have no idea where he is. He could have drowned, could have been run over by a truck . . ." She headed toward the parking lot.

"Okay, okay. I'll get him. You stay here with the baby." He handed Eddie back to her.

Why couldn't he be more careful? she wondered. He was too willing to take stupid chances with his children. She watched him disappear behind the visitors' center. The breeze carried his calls. "Chri—is. Hey, Chrissss."

She stood beside the picnic table, rocking Eddie, patting his back. Where could Chris have gone? She examined the spaces between every car in the parking lot, searched the trees of the dog run, surveyed the water's edge. Her arms tightened around Eddie and she rocked him faster. What was the matter with Jake? She knew he loved his children. Sometimes he just didn't think. Farther out, beyond the rest stop, cars and pick-ups and semitrailer trucks bumped over the edge of the bridge deck.

"Found him." Jake's voice cut through the sound of the waves and the wind and the traffic. "I'll take him potty."

This time it was fine. This time Chris was safe. How about next time? she wondered.

She sat on the seat of the picnic table and kissed the top of Eddie's head. He smelled of baby sweat and fabric softener. He had Jake's wide, blue eyes, her own pointy chin and puckery mouth. He was growing fast. Soon he would grow out of the infant Pampers.

She knew it was unfair to her children to make comparisons, but their differences were astonishing. Eddie was only six months old but was obviously the placid one, satisfied to let the earth turn at its usual, gentle pace. He seemed curious, but in a quiet, contemplative way. On the other hand, Chris had always wanted—and still wanted—to shove the world forward on his own commanding terms, to upend everything until he figured it out. Jake said he was exploring. That was Chris, all right. Always exploring, under every rock, behind every mountain.

Earlier that morning, she had just finished brushing her teeth when she heard the *kerthunk. Kerthunk. Kerthunk.*

"Don't let him do that," she had called, loud enough for her voice to carry into the bedroom.

"Hey, it's a motel." Jake had sounded playful.

She stepped from the bathroom and saw Chris suspended midair, arms flung wide, golden hair flying, ankles eight inches above the mattress. "Quit it," she called as he dropped to the bedspread. "Get off."

Jake twisted his upper lip and shrugged his shoulders. Once again, their son catapulted up from the mattress and again his bare feet kicked the air. He shot a glance at Jake and then at her. He was weighing his father's indifference against her directive.

"I told you to get off."

"Do as your mother says."

The boy leaped into the air one more time. His legs shot forward and he landed butt down on the bed.

Jake grabbed his arm and pulled him to the floor. Chris squirmed like a skewered worm. Jake tickled him in the armpits. Chris shrieked with laughter and folded into a heap on the carpet.

Why do these confrontations always end this way? she wondered. She had to lay down the law and Jake followed up with the fun.

She waited for Jake and Chris to return from the men's room—all rest stop bathrooms were grungy and this one would be no exception. She hoped Jake had helped Chris wash his hands. Would the bathroom have a soap dispenser? Paper towels? It turned her stomach to think of her son urinating into a filthy toilet.

She rocked Eddie to the rhythm of the waves, felt him wiggle against her. It was his hungry wiggle. She put him to her breast. The twitch of her baby's lips and the lap of his tongue against her nipple drew her milk into his mouth, into his body. Again, she watched the steady flow of the traffic on the bridge. Coming. Leaving.

Someday her boys would do that, would leave her. In some ways, Chris seemed to have already left. And Eddie? As of today he could roll from front to back and from back to front and had just started to sit alone. Next he would cruise and then, in a gesture of extreme daring, would let go of her fingers and stagger forward by himself. In the future he would run from her, would disappear behind the trees in their backyard, would climb into the maw of a noisy school bus, and finally would vanish into the bunker—foreign, inaccessible—of his own life. But for now, he clung to her breast. For now his supple body still fit easily into the pocket between her chest and bent arm.

Chris dashed ahead of Jake and skidded to a stop at her side. His cheeks were flushed. He started coughing.

"Remember . . . in the elbow," she said.

He reached under the flannel blanket that covered his brother, poked him in the tummy with his finger, and sang, "The itsy, bitsy spider climbed up the water spout . . ."

Eddie drew his knees to his chest and chortled.

"Down came the rain and—"

"Ready to go over the bridge?" Jake asked.

"Yeah," Chris yelled and danced in a circle on the dry grass.

"We'll refill the water bottles while you finish feeding Eddie," Jake said.

His face looked dispassionate, its profile stolid against the cloudless sky. His clean-shaven jaw, the knob on his nose from a hockey mishap, his shaggy eyebrows. These features—his entire body—were as familiar to her as breathing. Yet who was he? Why could he let Chris get lost? At this moment he was a stranger. At his core he was unknowable to her.

Hand in hand, Jake and Chris walked to the water fountain.

Had she married him because he was funny? Honest and loyal? Kind to his mother? Smart and good-looking? True, he was all of those things. He also was incapable of remembering her birthday. And, in the mornings, he stumbled from the bed to the bathroom without uttering a civil word and stayed crabby until he finished his cereal. The rare times he used the dish rag, he never rinsed it out, but tossed the milk- or coffee- or juice-soaked cloth into the corner of the sink to molder until she retrieved it. Maybe her attachment to him was little more than habit, as automatic as conjuring up the words to the Lord's Prayer she had recited at Jennifer's wedding.

During the service, the best man had read a poem, something about time and rivers and journeys. She had squeezed Jake's fingers. When he returned the gesture, she had grown teary-eyed and swallowed hard to dampen the sob that had been building inside her. He had smiled at her, a loving smile, a smile of understanding.

Now she watched the waves of Lake Huron pound the rocks along the shore, again and again, rhythmic and organic as a beating heart. She found the water petulant and fierce at one moment, soothing as silk at another—rising, falling, giving, taking. Sort of like her marriage, she decided.

As they walked back toward the car, the sunshine warmed her face and seeped through her hair to her scalp. Chris rocketed forward on the path to the parking lot. With each step, the soles of his shoes blinked cranberry-colored light as if propelled by a missile's afterburners.

"Slow down, mister," she called.

"He's okay." Jake patted her on the fanny. "You can't see it but he has an invisible leash that's about twenty-five feet long. He never strays beyond that."

"How about when he disappeared behind the visitors' center?"

"Well . . . that was just a tad over twenty-five feet." He grinned. It was one of his sweet-as-rhubarb-pie grins.

She straggled behind them, feeling as if, once again, she had lost a minor skirmish. Should she send a dart back Jake's way? No. There was no point in escalating this little kerfuffle. She could never win. As always, he would charm his way to victory.

Ahead, Chris bent over and picked something up. Then another thing. And a third.

"What're you doing?" she called.

"See . . ." Chris opened his fist. On his palm lay three acorns.

She stooped at the base of an oak tree and found an acorn for herself. She turned it over, ran her finger along the rough shell and the smooth nut. She looked up into the bare branches overhead at the network of leafless twigs tipped by buds. This huge tree had grown from a similar, tiny seed.

Jake took the acorn from her hand and rolled it between his fingers. "Think I can hit the lake?" he asked.

"Yeah," Chris yelled. "Throw it."

Jake took a step backward and flung the acorn toward the water. It sailed into the sky, then nicked a low-hanging tree branch and tumbled down a rocky embankment. It bounced off a boulder, skipped over a patch of weeds, hit another boulder, and continued down the steep slope until it bumped against the knobby root of a tree. There it stopped. Short of its target.

"You missed," Chris said.

Jake laughed.

Was there was enough dirt along that tree root for it to germinate, enough water on that steep incline? she wondered.

She slid into the passenger side of the car. Jake strapped the kids into their seats. As he turned the key and started the engine, she leaned against the headrest.

"I sure hope you don't get this," she said and blew her nose.

"Me, too. Monday's a big knee day—two arthroscopies and two total joint replacements. Can't be sick during those."

She blew her nose again.

"Have you taken something?" he asked.

"Sudafed. Doesn't help."

Within minutes, their car rolled onto the bed of the bridge. "I think we should go on the inner lane," she said.

"It's too rumbly."

"I know, but there's better traction on the grate than on the wet pavement."

"It's not raining."

"The pavement's always wet up here."

Jake changed lanes. The tires hummed as they rolled over the perforations of the grate. The steel blue water of the Straits of Mackinac swirled one hundred fifty feet below.

"Remember that lady who went over the side?" she asked.

"It's not a good idea to think about that right now," he said.

She couldn't erase the image from her mind. Young woman in a Yugo. Stormy day. Running late to meet her boyfriend in the Upper Peninsula. Speeding. Apparently the car skidded and raced toward the side. The flea-weight auto, boosted by the wind, climbed over the tiered barriers at the bridge's edge.

Every time they drove to the UP, she thought of the lady inside that car as it dove toward the water. Maybe she unbuckled her seat belt in a futile attempt to escape. Maybe she just stared through the windshield at the approaching waves, an endless moment of unmitigated terror. The car would have hit with terrible force. Maybe she was killed instantly from the impact. Or, maybe she watched the water grow darker as the car sank. Probably the lake water seeped in along the edges of the doors and eventually filled the car. Maybe the lady ran out of air before she drowned.

The Bridge Authority pamphlet said the bridge could sway up to thirty feet during high winds. She couldn't feel the sway but knew it was moving, knew that several forces, all going in different directions, were acting on their car: its forward movement, the sideways sway of the bridge, the oblique push of the wind. When it was too windy and wet, the Authority closed the bridge. They were only halfway across.

Off to her right and far below, a Great Lakes freighter cleared the bottom of the deck as it chugged through the Straits on its way to, maybe, the Port of Chicago or to Milwaukee or Green Bay. To her left across the water was Mackinac Island, the Grand Hotel a white fleck against the dark of the trees. The waves seemed decorated with silver sequins. These were familiar sights. They helped to ground her during the long, worried journey over the bridge.

Then they were on the other side. Jake drove through Mackinaw City, past rows of cheap motels and franchise restaurants, and headed south on I-75.

"Want to drive again?" he asked.

"You're doing fine," she said.

Chapter 2

Jake

His knees ached from kneeling all afternoon on the basement floor. Jake dipped his trowel once again into the glue pail and slapped a wad of adhesive on the concrete. The notched edges of the trowel drew wobbly stripes in the glue, reminding him of the windrows that marked his uncle's fields during harvest. Those rows had been amber colored, these were ash gray; those were made of alfalfa, these of gooey glue.

Black and white was what Anna meant when they chose the tile. She had, though, described the flooring in her usual, lyrical way, "Tweedy charcoal and creamy eggshell."

He preferred brighter colors. Last week at the flooring store, he asked, "How about this?" The sample in his hand was as teal as a mallard's head, without the iridescence.

But Anna had her mind set on a checkerboard floor and she wanted it black and white. He thought it would make the basement look like a saloon. She disagreed. "Crisp, dramatic, clean," she had said, tossing her hair away from her face and raising her eyes toward the ceiling. "You'll see . . . it'll be wonderful." He understood from her posture that the issue wasn't negotiable.

Cartons of tiles sat on the bare concrete beside him. He pulled a white square from the nearest box and wedged it into the lap of a black L. Adhesive oozed from the seams and then disappeared with a swipe of his sticky wiping rag. He then pulled a square from a box of black tiles and wedged it into a white L. Something didn't look right. The corner was off square. He wiggled the new tile tighter against its neighbors. "There," he said out loud.

He sat back on his heels and admired his work. He should have known her project would be classy. That was Anna—maven of high style. Just last week she had hauled an armful of old dresses to the garage. "Outdated," she had said, wrinkling her nose as she stuffed them into the sack for The Salvation Army. She fussed over her appearance more than he thought necessary. She tweezed stray hairs from her eyebrows, painted her toenails dull red, smeared creams over her face twice a day—the greasy stuff that smelled like balsam at night and the pink-tinged, shiny stuff in the morning. He thought she was beautiful as she was. He liked the way she looked while asleep—calm, relaxed—or immediately upon waking—breezy, distracted, natural. When she walked, she reminded him of a young doe, strong and fluid, trim and confident.

He placed a white tile into a black L. The idea for this project had begun a month ago. They were driving home from the hardware store, a new space heater for the basement stowed in the rear of the van.

"Wish we could fix it up," Anna had said.

"Fix up what?" He had no idea what she was talking about.

"The basement."

"What's the matter with it?"

His wife had stared out the car window, a disturbed look on her face. "It's so dull down there."

"That's not very specific."

"Well, for starters, it's too dark and a cement floor isn't very interesting."

"I could paint the floor," he suggested.

"Ummm . . ." She straightened her back and her eyes began to dance. "How about tile?"

From deciding on tile for the floor, they went on to an area rug, insulated drapes for the walk-out door, a hutch to store toys and books, and a hide-a-bed sofa for guests.

"The pull-out couch in the family room isn't very private," Anna said.

"This will all take time," he warned, knowing his wife liked instant results.

"Of course," she said with a shrug. "There's no hurry."

Now, while he wedged the tiles into the black and white Ls, she was working upstairs on a sketch for the hutch. She and her friend Elizabeth had found a monster of a pine cabinet at a thrift shop and were going to paint it to look like a pile of stones covered with ivy. His preference was to scrape off the old paint and give it a coat or two of urethane. But Anna, the director of design for the new basement, insisted on trompe l'oeil.

Time for a bathroom break. Upstairs, he found Anna hunched over her drawings, a deep frown on her face. She attacked the paper with an art gum eraser, furiously rubbing away the penciled lines.

"This's driving me nuts," she said as she swept the shreds of rubber onto the family room carpet.

"What's the problem?" He patted her shoulder and gazed at the shadows of the former drawing.

"These leaves. They're ugly. Look more like holly than ivy." She stood back from the sketchbook, her arms crossed over her chest. "They're too long and the points are too spiky."

"Looks okay to me." He headed into the bathroom.

They had disagreed, too, about the color of those walls. He wanted beige, she orange. In the end, he had painted them the color of ripe mangos and she applied pale green fleur-de-lis. Now, his eyes followed the stenciled flowers from ceiling to floor. The rows were parallel—precisely vertical, plumb-line straight—with the corners of the walls. She had borrowed his carpenter's level to prevent slanted rows.

The bathroom had turned out nicer than he expected. The orange walls didn't induce claustrophobia. The fleur-de-lis didn't look like seaweed. And the sconces she had found at a second-hand store didn't overwhelm the mirror. He had to admit his wife had a flair for decorating.

On his way back toward the basement, he stopped again beside her.

"Nice," he said, referring to the drawing.

"No, horrid."

Why did she make herself so miserable over what should be a satisfying project? he wondered. Nobody would care what the ivy leaves looked like. No one would notice. The cabinet would be in the basement, for God's sake. He shook his head as he trudged down the cellar stairs, thinking of Anna's reaction to the tie problem at Jennifer's wedding. Shortly before they were to leave the motel for the ceremony, Eddie had burped milk on his necktie.

"For Pete's sake," Anna had groaned. "Where can we get a new one?"

He dabbed the stain with a wet washcloth. The milk smear was barely visible against the brown and ivory swirls printed on the fabric. "It's coming off," he said.

"You can't go with a goobery tie."

"It isn't badly goobery. It's fine."

But she had insisted cleaning the tie wouldn't work, seemed angry he hadn't packed an extra one, paged through the phone book for a store that might sell them. Finally, she had marched down the hall to her parents' room and borrowed one from her father.

He laid another black tile into a white L and wiped away the adhesive. Footsteps started down the wooden stairs and echoed off the cinderblock walls. He watched first Anna's brown clogs, then her jeans, then her flannel shirt, and finally her face—serious, unsmiling, scowly eyed—descend the steps. She must still be mad about the ivy leaves.

"Okay," she said, coming to a stop at the edge of the bare concrete. "Three choices for dinner." She wasn't mad, was being, instead, coy. "Number one is"—she tapped her right pointer finger against the left—"hamburgers. Number two is macaroni and cheese—out of a box. Number three is KFC."

"Chicken."

"Extra crispy or original or all dark meat or what?"

"I don't care." He laid a white tile into a black L.

"Jake . . ." Her voice faltered. She was quiet for a moment. "You should have used the level. The tiles are crooked."

He dropped the trowel onto the concrete floor and sat back on his heels. He didn't see anything wrong.

"There by your knee. They're crooked."

He stared at the tiles. Then at the wall and back at the tiles.

"Look at that wall." He pointed behind him. "The tiles are aligned along the bottom. See that? And look over here." He jabbed his finger toward the opposite wall and said, his voice growing louder with each word, "They're not perfectly aligned because the walls aren't perfectly square. The builder should have used your damn level, not me."

"Okay, okay, settle down."

He had had it with her nit-picking. "For Christ's sake, I've spent all afternoon down here laying your frickin' floor and all you can do is criticize."

She stared at him, lifted her chin briefly. It was her obstinate look. Then her face softened, her shoulders relaxed.

"I appreciate this. I really do. I just spotted a little irregularity, but it's okay. I'm off to get dinner. Be back in a sec. I'll take Chris. Eddie just fell asleep."

The upstairs door banged shut. He combed another patch of adhesive and jammed a black tile into a white L.

Why couldn't Anna lighten up a little? She saw the dark side of everything. Those leaves painted on the toy cabinet were fine as they were, pointed or not pointed. It didn't matter. The tie event at Jennifer's wedding was beyond ridiculous. Compared to what he dealt with day after day—fractured legs, infected bones, twisted backs, worn-out joints—a stain on a necktie was nothing.

He slid a white tile against a black L. Life with Monica wouldn't be like this, he thought. Back then, Monica didn't rag on him, didn't carp, didn't dump disapproval on him as if emptying a bedpan over his head. There were no slamming doors. When she left, the door just stayed shut—silently shut.

It had been at least eight years since he last saw her. He wiped the adhesive. He could almost sense her standing beside him, could hear her laugh, smell her soap, feel her northwoods wholesomeness, her easygoing manner. Last weekend, at the wedding in the Upper Peninsula, he had thought of her. Twice. It wasn't exactly a thought—more like a shadowy, regretful urge.

While Anna had fussed about the milk on the tie, he remembered the day he and Monica stood in the parking lot at the bottom of a ski lift. Monica asked about heavy stockings. It was snowing and she'd forgotten to bring hers.

He found a spare pair of hunting socks balled up in the trunk of his car but they were caked with dry mud. She had reached for the socks, sized them up for a moment, and then whapped them against the car door. The largest of the dirt clods fell to the asphalt. She whapped them twice more and picked the last of the mud scales from the wool. Then she pulled them on over her knee-highs.

Later they locked themselves out of the hotel room and much later his condom broke. On the way home, the car had sputtered to a stop—out of gas. She had laughed, in her hearty, full-throated chuckle, through it all.

He also thought of her at the rest stop beside the Mackinac Bridge when he'd tossed an acorn toward the lake. It had hit a tree branch and tumbled down the bank. An acorn with a lot of potential that landed on the rocks. That was the story of Monica.

He fitted a black tile into a white L, mopped the seams with his rag, and straightened his sore back. In the end, all he had was her silence, her leaving, and the bottomless void.

Six months after Monica left, he had met Anna. He hadn't been on the lookout for a woman, had sworn off them, in fact. He had buried himself in neuroanatomy, biochemistry, and physiology homework and lived the life of a monk—slept in a narrow bed in a tiny basement cubbyhole at Ella Schwartz's rooming house; ate boring, cheap food wherever he could get it; organized his days according to his class and study schedules; occasionally drank a beer and played a hand of poker; but dated no women.

Then he saw her through the foggy window of the E-Z Wash. She was sitting in one of the plastic chairs at the end of the dryers, reading a magazine. She was gorgeous, like no one he had ever seen. He had been on his way to the library, but took a one-hundred-eighty-degree turn and raced back to Mrs. Schwartz's. He ripped the sheets off his bed, grabbed his pajama bottoms from the floor, and with the dirty laundry heaped in his arms, dashed back to the Laundromat. On the way, he wondered if he had enough quarters. He'd forgotten the detergent—hopefully the dispenser had some. Would she still be there?

Outside, thirty feet from the door, he slowed to a walk. He needed to catch his breath. Couldn't have her see him gasping for air. Inside, the chairs near the dryers were all empty. Where was she? Had she gone? He wandered down the aisle of washers. At the end, he turned and spotted her stacking linen at the folding table. As he walked past her, she turned—a pair of turquoise lace panties in her hands—and smiled. He nodded a silent greeting, tried to appear interested but not too interested. She kept smiling and followed him with her eyes. He stuffed the sheets and pajama bottoms into the first open washer and headed for the vending machine. A hand-printed, cardboard sign was taped to the front. OUT OF ORDER.

He leaned his elbow against the dispenser and called to her, "Hey, do you by any chance have any detergent? The machine's on the fritz."

She chuckled and said, "You're in luck." She walked over to him, her body moving like a waterfall, and held out a box of Tide. "Take what you need."

"Thanks a lot. Cup of coffee for payment?"

She hesitated a moment. Then she nodded.

While his laundry sloshed in the washer, they walked across the street to the coffee shop. Anna slid into a booth and folded her hands on the tabletop, waiting for him to speak.

"Black? Cream and sugar? Latte? Whatever's your pleasure," he said. Instantly he wished he could retract those words. Had he really said, "your pleasure"? Too sappy.

But, she smiled, the most generous, beautiful smile he'd seen in a long while.

"Cream and sugar will be fine," she said.

He couldn't believe he was sitting across the table from the most amazing woman in town. They talked about the Georgia congressman Newt Gingrich, about Ronald Reagan's Alzheimer's disease and the invasion of Chechnya, about his classes, her work.

"I teach English as a second language," she said. "The students are great. For the most part, they really want to learn and are pretty funny." An hour later, they exchanged phone numbers.

The next week he learned that *Forrest Gump* was playing at the State Theater. He wanted to see it with Anna. Would she go with him? He debated with himself for three days and finally, his finger quaking, dialed her number.

"Hi, Anna. This is Jake Campbell." He tried to sound calm.

"Jake. Good to hear from you." She sounded excited; her voice rang like a crystal bell.

They held hands during the show, laughed together at the silly parts. Anna dabbed her eyes during the sad parts and he put his arm around her shoulders. Comforting her seemed as natural as the sunshine, seemed as if it had been ordained since the dawn of time. Her tense back softened against his arm.

The weekend after that they attended a jazz concert together, rocked in their seats to the music, clapped with the staccato beat. From then on, they were pretty much a couple.

* * *

"Chicken's here." Anna's voice coiled down the basement stairs.

"Daddy, come an' eat," Chris added. His son's words sounded like a muffled wind chime.

The table was set with their stoneware dishes. Anna had arranged the chicken pieces on a platter and the potatoes and coleslaw were heaped in serving bowls. Instead of the KFC plastic forks and paper napkins, a stainless fork and knife lay on a cloth napkin beside each plate. In spite of his irritation with her, he had to chuckle. She liked fancy table settings, wasn't satisfied with the cheap stuff, was willing to spend a little extra time making a routine meal into something special. For him and the boys.

"I figure I'm about halfway done," he said as he slid a chicken thigh onto his plate.

"Good. It looks nice," Anna said.

Apparently she wasn't focused on the crooked tiles anymore. True to form, she didn't hang on to a grudge for very long. The emotional thunderstorms that hung over them from time to time dissipated fairly quickly.

She cradled Eddie in the bend of her left arm and nursed him as she ate with her right hand. He found the sight of his wife going about her routines with a child attached to her breast to be very satisfying. She was a good mother, in spite of her fastidiousness. She was patient with the children, seemed to enjoy helping them master the myriad skills they learned every day.

"The coleslaw," she said, pointing her fork at Chris's plate. "It'll make you grow strong like your daddy."

"I don't like it," Chris whined.

"Makes hair grow on your chest, buddy," Jake said. "See what eating salads does for me?" He pulled up his shirt, baring the fuzz between his nipples.

Chris giggled and shoveled several shreds of cabbage into his mouth.

"Good job," Anna said. "Now, two more just like that."

*   *   *

"Here." Chris waved a white tile toward Jake. They had just finished dinner.

"Whoa, buddy." Jake eyed the grease from the fried chicken on his son's hands and, then, the oily smudges on the tiles. "Run back upstairs and wash your mitts."

Through doleful eyes Chris stared at his hands. He turned them palm up, palm down, palm up. Then he coughed, snorted through his stuffy nose, and coughed again.

Poor kid, Jake thought. He wants to help. Just like every other little boy. As a child, he and his father, together with his brothers, had built bookcases, shelves for the garage, a sewing table for their mother. Since he was the oldest, he was the first to learn how to hold the hammer—"At the end of the handle, Jakey, not near the head"—and how to pull the saw—"In slow, firm, even draws. Stuttery little jerks tear the wood."

Chris, too, was the oldest and would be the first to do everything, while Eddie would be the forever tagalong—eagerly, desperately trying to live up to his bigger brother. Chris would be the first to go to school, to read, to drive, to date. At least, most likely the first to date. He was such a social little guy; he shouldn't have any trouble attracting the girls.

Eddie was too young for Jake to get a bead on his personality yet. But, already, it was clear he was a mellower baby than his turbocharged brother had been. Eddie seemed to take the more philosophical view. He batted his fists against the mobile toys that dangled over his crib seemingly forever, at least for much longer than Chris had. He tolerated Bullet's sandpaper cat-kisses better than his brother. Even wet diapers didn't seem to bother him. At that age, Chris used to holler at the first hint of discomfort. They had learned the drill with their oldest son: Change the diaper, offer the breast, roll him over, wrap him in his favorite blanket, unwrap him, rock him, sing to him. They had applied each comfort measure in turn until he finally settled down. Eddie—quiet, playful, congenitally satisfied—knew how to settle himself.

"*Mom.*" Chris called for Anna as he traveled through several rooms upstairs. "*Mom.*" He was only three and still depended on Anna for so much. And, willingly, earnestly, she always complied. Chris stopped calling and yelled, "Lift me up." The water ran and then stopped. Chris's shoes slapped on the basement stairs, their clatter interrupted twice by his hacking cough.

He skidded to a stop beside his father and held out his hands. Drops of water glistened on his knuckles, a streak of soap foam lined his right wrist.

"Rub them on your pants." Jake swiped his hands against his thighs. "Like this."

Chris mimicked his father.

"Okay, buddy. That's much better. Hand me a white tile."

Chapter 3

Rose Marie

Rose Marie stepped out to the porch and closed the front door behind her. She didn't want the chilly air in her living room. From the top of the stairs, she called to the little boy who sauntered down the driveway. "Chris, your blanket's getting dirty." The boy—the back pocket of his jeans bulging with the plastic egg he'd brought from home that morning—kept walking.

"Pick it up, honey," she called again.

Without missing a step, Chris spooled the ragged blanket around his arm; the trailing edge fluttered an inch above the gravel. She watched as Anna opened the rear door of the car, hoisted Chris into his car seat, secured his seat belt, and then waved. Rose Marie couldn't see the baby. He must be asleep in his infant seat beside Chris.

Anna was sick, had stayed home from work that morning. "Could I bring Chris to your house this afternoon?" she had asked earlier on the phone, her voice muffled from her cold. "I'll keep Eddie with me."

The mud-spattered Subaru rolled backward down the driveway, crawled up the street, and turned the corner. Chris was the last to leave for the day. All the children were finally gone, off to their real homes with their real mommies.

She smiled at the thought of Chris chattering about his day to his mother in his high-octane, galloping way—lunch, nap, afternoon story, the cupcakes they decorated, the broken lightbulb, the lack of hot water.

Halfway over the threshold into the living room, she stopped and backed up a step. The name plate was crooked, its letters heading downhill as if they might tumble onto the porch floor. Anna had painted it, a Christmas gift last year. A string of twisted branches and flower blossoms framed her last name, Lustov. She straightened the board. "Strange name," she said out loud. Lustov was Roger's name. She had accepted it as hers over forty years ago, but sometimes, especially since his death, it seemed foreign, as if it didn't belong to her.

She paused a moment longer to feel the fresh, spring breeze against her forehead, the rays from the setting sun against her cheeks. The rhythm of the day, a hectic throb that started with the morning greeting and ended with the afternoon parting, now slowed to a peaceful hum. She needed the quiet. It was hard work for a sixty-three-year-old woman to chase after young children from morning to night.

Her house was toasty inside. She closed the front door against the chilly air, straightened the crumpled rag rug on the floor with her toe. Some days she wanted to quit this work, to escape to a warm, sunny place where pansies bloomed all winter and no one knew what a snow shovel was, a place where she could go on long walks every afternoon—year round—wearing a wrap no heavier than a sweater. Still, child care was a good job for her. She could work in her home, wear comfortable clothes, be her own boss. She'd learned a lot about kids when her girls were growing up—raising them had been her higher education.

Maybe hot water was no longer a problem. She turned the spigot on the sink, let it run for a moment, thrust her hand under the stream. Still cold. Since yesterday the hot water had gradually become cooler, and by earlier this afternoon, it was downright frigid. This morning she'd boiled water in her stock pot to add to the lukewarm water in the tub for her bath and, then again this afternoon, to wash up after the kids.

She couldn't figure out what was wrong, had tested all the faucets: kitchen sink, bathroom sink, bathtub. All cold. Must be the water heater. When had they last replaced it, anyway? The girls were young, then—maybe thirty years ago.

She switched on the basement light, stepped down the stairs, walked around the furnace. Then she saw it. A puddle. It ran from the water heater to the storage shelves and on toward the washing machine. Her box of canning jars was soaked. So were an old suitcase and the bag of oatmeal cartons she had been saving to make building blocks with the children. A new water heater would cost a lot of money.

Back in the kitchen, she began to thumb through the yellow pages. What would it be under? Plumbing? Water heater? Maybe she should just call Sears. She shut the book. Couldn't deal with it right now.

"Beefeater," she called, her hand on the refrigerator door. "Where are you? Time for our constitutional."

The hot dogs in the meat keeper were for lunch tomorrow, the large, orange brick of cheddar for grilled cheese sandwiches the day after. On the bottom shelf, lime Jell-O shimmered in her CorningWare casserole dish. She moved a package of carrots to get to the bottle of white zinfandel, half full and angled against the ketchup. Every evening she had a glass of wine before dinner. Just one.

How much would a new water heater cost? Four hundred dollars? Six hundred dollars? More? And someone would have to install it. Last time it broke, Roger and his buddy from work spent the day swearing and drinking beer but somehow managed to hook up the new tank. Another two hundred dollars to install it? Delivery fee? Maybe one hundred dollars more. Where would she get that kind of money? She'd think about it later, after the constitutional.

Reaching into the fridge for the wine, she spotted a baby bottle. Its milk looked at least several days old and was probably bad. She swirled the bottle, searched the bluish white liquid for clots. *EDDIE C* was printed in blue magic marker block letters on the strip of masking tape that curled along one side.

No date. She shook her head slowly and made a tsk-tsk sound. A name but no date. She had a rule about that—food brought by parents had to be dated. It was enough trouble to keep track of her own stuff, let alone everyone else's. Anna followed the rules, but Jake had labeled this bottle, using large, bold letters that demanded immediate attention. Anna's writing was dainty, almost floral, and often in red ballpoint.

She could imagine Jake writing Eddie's name in his lighthearted, casual manner. He was always steady, confident, never let on that he was in a hurry. To his face, she always said, "Dr. Campbell." She wasn't comfortable calling a doctor—any doctor, even the father of one of the kids—by his first name. But in her thoughts, he became Jake, the name Anna used for him.

She unscrewed the lid of the baby bottle. The milk inside smelled like a blend of dairy product and sour feet. She dumped it down the drain. There was plenty more where that came from. Anna—skinny, flat-chested Anna—brought in more milk than she thought possible.

"Come on, Beefeater," she called again. Roger had named the dog, a tribute to his favorite gin. Rose Marie thought it was kind of cute. Reminded her of those humorless British soldiers that guarded Buckingham Palace. The name fit the dog's poker face.

"If you're on my bed, you'd better get off. Now." Her voice jutted into every room of her small house. She scolded the dog every evening about the bed but didn't really mean it. She liked him to be comfortable. When Beefeater had his fill of torture from the kids, he took refuge on her water bed, where he would paw a nest for himself in her feather-and-down—mostly feather—quilt.

She pulled a dirty wineglass from the dishwasher, rinsed it in the still-cold water from the faucet, and filled it three-fourths full with the white zinfandel. She always drank her nightly constitutional in a wineglass—no wine in a SpongeBob juice glass for her. Kid stuff was fine during the day, but in the evenings, on her time, she was committed to being grown up.

She liked adulthood, liked being mature. Over the years, she had been lots of things: the daughter of poor Ukrainian immigrants, a pregnant teenage bride, a tired mother to Julie and Sarah, a lapsed Russian Orthodox, a cranky housewife, a grieving widow, a long-distance grandmother to Julie's five-year-old daughter, a Republican, a babysitter.

The frosty, pale pink of the wine was the same color as the petunias she planted every spring. In about a month, she would load two flats of seedlings from Walmart into the back of her car. At home she would dig a row of holes beside her front sidewalk and, one by one, jam each plant into a hole. If she waited until after Memorial Day, the plants would be marked down and, if she shopped early in that week, they wouldn't be too leggy yet.

She poured a splash of the wine into a cereal bowl and called once again, "Beefeater, come here. Wine time." She set the bowl on the floor in front of the stove. *Click, click, click.* His toenails tapped across the wooden dining room floor.

"Atta boy." She stroked the smooth hair over his knobby backbone as he lapped the wine, his pointy Jack Russell terrier ears quivering with each swallow. Now that he was old, he was a good companion—even tempered, undemanding, loyal, cheap to feed. He needed only half a scoop of dry dog food a day, in addition to the crackers and bread crusts, Oreo cookies, and orange wedges the children dropped to him.

She opened the back door and took a deep breath. The muddy part of spring was gone, soon to be replaced by the blossomy part. In the distance, the thrum of truck tires on the freeway's pocked concrete reminded her of connections to the wider world: the mailman, the phone repairman, the cable guy, the plumber. She set the wineglass on the patio table, unhooked an empty bird feeder, and filled it with thistle seed.

The wine had a magical, settling effect on her. After the first sip or two, her shoulders loosened as if someone had pulled a

plug and sent the tightness in her muscles swirling down a
drain. Then her forehead relaxed. And the back of her neck.
Evenings were like stepping into another universe, a more predictable one with no interruptions, no surprises, no yelling
kids, no aches. Retirement might be like this all day, every day,
especially if she didn't have a broken appliance to worry about.

She picked at the loose paint on the arm of her lawn chair.
That was the trouble with Michigan winters—hard on yard furniture as well as on highways and gardens. She took another sip
from the white zinfandel. The inside of her mouth prickled
with the wine's sweet astringency as she wondered about the
cost of a quart of paint. That on top of one thousand dollars for
the water heater.

In the corner of the patio, behind an empty clay planter, lay
the GO BLUE pennant that Meghan had carried last week in
Chris's parade. Chris had been his usual take-charge self,
prancing like a drum major while he yelled, "March. Come on,
Sawyer. March." Meghan had obviously forgotten to put the
pennant away. Rose Marie had a rule about toys. No child left
her house until everything had been returned to where it belonged. LEGOs in the LEGO can. Blocks in the block box.
Crayons in the carton on the shelf. Big wheels lined up beside
the fence. Dress-up clothes in the trunk—that's where the pennant belonged. She took another sip of wine. She had more to
be upset about than a misplaced toy.

When she finished her wine, she returned to the kitchen and
confronted the yellow pages again. Water coolers. Water damage emergency service. Water gardens. Water heater dealers.
The Building Center ad said, "Same-day installation. Complete
ordering with one call. Low prices, guaranteed." That's what
she needed. Surely she could arrange a monthly payment plan.
She dialed the number.

Chapter 4

Anna

Evening settled over their house and the lengthening shadows promised an end to her miserable day. Back and forth she paced across the family room, round and round between the piano and the toy box. Eddie's head nestled on the crook of her left elbow and his legs were tucked beneath her right arm. The warmth of his body seeped through her shirt as he squirmed against her chest. With each step she twisted at the waist, rocking him as she walked.

Surrounded by quiet, she hummed a nonsense tune. Note after note, her song climbed the scale, then hovered at the high tone for a long moment and finally tumbled down to the bottom of her register. Eddie seemed heavier than usual that night. His weight tugged against her arms as if she were carrying a bag of bricks.

Every fifth or sixth round, she pulled a sheet of Kleenex from her sweater pocket and dabbed her nose. This was the fourth day of her cold—maybe tomorrow she would feel better. But first, she had to get beyond the rest of today.

Through the family room window she watched the evening

sun float like a fireball above the treetops. Its rays backlit the clouds in wavering shades of orange and purple. Earlier in the day she caught the smell of spring—fresh and crisp as young parsley—while it rode the breeze, a welcome hint of warmer weather to come. The days had grown longer and the air had finally lost its winter bite; patches of emerald dotted the straw-colored lawn. She was eager for summer, for lilacs and irises and daylilies and tomatoes off the vine.

"Mommy, why's Eddie so crabby?" asked Chris. His question echoed her question, earlier in the afternoon, of him. "Why are you so crabby today?" she had asked. His words often reflected hers, reverberated back her observations, her wonderings, her impatience. Chris's legs stretched into a wide V on the family room floor and his back rested against the toy box, against the field of violets she had painted on that pine chest when he was a baby. At this moment, he was sanguine, easygoing, focused on play. One after another, he fitted LEGO pieces together. He was building a fire station.

"I don't know," she said. Sometimes she answered his questions that way, just to stop the constant inquiry. He could go on forever, asking her to explain a seemingly endless, and random, litany of things. What's a breeze? Why doesn't that bird fall down from the sky? Where does hair come from? Do snakes poop? Does it hurt when he's dead? he asked after Gordy, his pet gerbil, had died.

But this time she really didn't know the answer to his question. Eddie was an ordinarily happy baby, smiley and bubbly and quick to charm everyone who met him. When he was hungry, he'd fuss for a moment and then, as she nursed him, he'd settle down immediately, nuzzling at her breast like a satisfied puppy. She'd rate his contentedness a 9.5, while, some days, Chris barely made a 7.

But tonight Eddie was whiny and restless. Earlier, when she laid him in his crib, he cried until she picked him up again. She'd fed him, then changed his diaper. He'd never been like this. Maybe he was getting sick, too. He hadn't been ill at all, not even a cold, in the six months since he was born.

"Time to put the toys away and head to bed," she announced.

"I want a story." Chris stared at her through commanding, hazel eyes identical in color to her own. A high-energy child who demanded action, he liked to sing very loud, to play miniature golf using three balls, to blow soap bubbles at his baby brother's face.

"Not tonight. We can read two stories tomorrow night." She wanted both boys to go to sleep so she could take a bath and go to bed herself. She would lounge in the tub, her head propped against a folded towel—a good end to this long, unpleasant day. The warm water would lick her weary skin and soothe her achy muscles, and the steamy bathroom air would clear her congested sinuses. As a treat, she would even dump in a handful of her new aromatherapy salts—her cousin Jennifer's gift to the wedding guests. Thinking of the bath, she could almost smell the pungent lavender-scented vapor and feel the silky water.

"*Please?*" Chris whined. "Read *Melanie's Walk.*"

In so many ways, he was like Jake—persistent, emphatic, self-assured, with a take-charge demeanor. No matter what Chris did in his adult life, she could already tell he would be a leader. Last week, when she picked up the boys from Rose Marie's, Chris had organized a parade, had appointed himself as the grand marshal. His best friend Davey was assigned to pull the wagon filled with stuffed animals. Sawyer rode the trike, with Beefeater, Rose Marie's old dog, tethered to the handlebars by a dirty piece of rope. Meghan, and then Amanda, brought up the rear, one waving a pennant that said, Go Blue, and the other banging pot lids like cymbals.

She sighed and considered Chris's request for a story. "Okay. Just one." She was too tired to talk him out of it. "Sit here while I feed Eddie."

Chris's fluid body wiggled and molded itself into the narrow space between her hip and the arm of the easy chair. His dewy skin felt like chamois against her elbow. She took a deep breath and, in spite of her clogged nose, could smell his scent—earthy, dense, fresh like ripe pears.

Sometimes Chris could be loveable, in his sweet, determined way, as he was right now. And yet, earlier, at dinner, he had begged for chocolate milk rather than 2 percent. She refused. He begged. She refused again. He begged again.

Finally, she spun around, grabbed his elbow, and yelled, "I said no. Quit begging. I can't stand a beggar."

His eyes had flashed fear. He glared at her, drove a look of hurt and loathing into her heart. Tears flooded his lashes. She held firm and poured white milk into his glass, with a promise they would have chocolate pudding for dessert.

She unsnapped the left flap of her nursing bra and coaxed Eddie to her breast. He was slow to take it, but after she brushed the nipple against the corner of his lips, he finally latched on. Usually he ate with relentless vigor, the skin over his temples pulsing as he worked his sucking muscles. Tonight, he dabbled at her breast and swallowed very little. What was wrong?

She opened Chris's book to page one and began coughing.

"Read," Chris yelled.

"Soon as I quit coughing," she gasped. She took a deep breath, held it, let it out slowly. Then she began to read.

The rhyme and rhythm of her voice seemed to hold Chris in a trance. He had already learned the letters that spelled "Chris," "mom," and "dad," and before long, he would be able to read the words in his books himself.

Usually she treasured their evening routine of snuggling and reading, knowing that years hence she would ache to have him young and dependent and near her again. Since the moment of his birth, he seemed hell-bent to leave, seemed fearless of the road ahead. He yearned to understand everything about the world and to race away, toward its farthest reaches. She longed to keep him close for as long as possible, but right now, she wanted to skip the story.

The throbbing behind her eyes felt as if her face would fall off. She flipped two pages at once.

"Hey," Chris yelled. "You forgot the part where Melanie gives the apple to the horse."

"Okay. Okay." She sighed and turned back a page.

* * *

After another story, a glass of water, and two trips to the bathroom, Chris was finally asleep. Eddie began to whimper again. His weak, wrenlike sounds rattled in the back of his throat. He must have caught her cold. Why else would he be like this? She held him against her shoulder and lowered herself into the rocking chair. Back and forth, over and over, they rode the rocker. Still Eddie whimpered. Worry crept over her. Was he sicker than just a cold?

Most days she saw utter purity and unending beauty in Eddie's face. It was angelic in its innocence: tiny, puckery, perfect lips and lively, glistening eyes. But now, his face was twisted and grotesque. She rocked and hummed and wished her lovely, good-natured baby would return. Or at least wished the crying would stop so she could take her bath and go to bed. She needed to sleep, wanted this day to end. As bad as today had been, or maybe *because* it was so bad, she was sure tomorrow would be better—her headache would be gone, Eddie wouldn't be so fussy anymore, and she could enjoy Chris again.

The worry had grown to deep concern. What if Eddie was really sick? Should she take him to the ER?

At times like this she wished her husband had a different job. Usually she could handle the long evenings with only children for company. She enjoyed the quiet time after they went to sleep, when she could read and tidy up the house and listen to Mendelssohn or Brahms and gather her wits. This night, though, she felt terrible and needed relief. Jake would help her if he were home. But he was at work. If he were an insurance salesman or an accountant or a biology teacher, he would be here and she would be in bed. Instead, he was taking care of other people's sick wives and children.

It was four hours since the last dose. She carried Eddie into the kitchen and, balancing him against her hip, swallowed two Tylenol caplets and a glassful of water. Then she squirted a half dropper of Tylenol drops into the corner of Eddie's mouth. He sputtered for a moment and smacked his lips. She held her breath, hoped the medicine would stay in. Then he swallowed with a gulp. He seemed looser than usual. Almost limp.

She glanced at the oven clock—7:45. She'd call Jake. He'd know what to do with a sick baby. She dialed the hospital paging service.

As she waited for Jake to answer, she leaned against the sink and stared out the window into their backyard. Her heart was racing. What could be wrong with Eddie? Chris had never acted like this. Even when he'd had roseola. Maybe that was it. Maybe Eddie would break out in a rash tomorrow and the fever would go away. Or, maybe not.

The remaining daylight, faint orange along the horizon, glowed behind the slats of the patio railing. The swing set was barely visible, its ropes and wooden scaffold a shadowy skeleton intertwined with the bony branches of the sweet gum tree. She tipped her head to view the swing set and gum tree from a different angle. She bent forward and muffled a cough in the terry cloth that covered Eddie's warm, damp belly.

After what seemed an eternity, a female voice spoke quickly, mechanically. "Answering for Dr. Campbell. He's scrubbed."

She felt the twitch in the left corner of her mouth. It was her irritation twitch. She knew Jake couldn't do anything to help her while he was at work, but she didn't want to be alone with a sick baby. If she had to be miserable—had to make decisions about an ill child—he was going to help. They were his kids, too.

"Please have him call home when the case is over," she told the nurse.

She returned to the rocking chair. Eddie was quiet for the moment. She needed to think about something else. What did Jake have for dinner? Anything? Sometimes when he was on call he forgot to eat. He'd lost weight over the past year—gone from size thirty-six to thirty-four pants. Definitely he didn't get enough sleep. Often, on the nights he was home, he was so tired that both he and Chris would drift off during their reading time. She would pluck the book from Jake's lap and carry

Chris to bed. Later, Jake would jerk awake in the easy chair, announce with a yawn that he was "going to hit the sack," and stumble up the stairs to their bedroom.

Eddie curled his legs against his tummy and whimpered again. She rocked and waited. What was taking Jake so long to answer her call?

It was only twenty-four hours ago that Jake had sat in the easy chair with Chris sprawled across his lap, reading *Mister Mulvaney*. He had used a different voice for each character—gruff for Mulvaney, dreamy for his wife, falsetto for the little boy, and whispery for the old lady. When he read about the dog, he made barking noises, and when the boy found the cow, he interrupted the falsetto voice with a deep-throated, "Moooo, moooo." Chris had bounced against Jake's thighs to the rhythm of the words. Even Eddie, who had been nursing, seemed to listen to the story. Whenever Jake's voice hit the high tones, Eddie let go of the nipple and a thin stream of milk drooled from his mouth and trickled down his neck.

But now, Eddie continued to whimper, and his body radiated heat through the nap of his sleeper as if he were on fire. It had been over a half hour since she gave him the Tylenol. She couldn't remember how long until it was supposed to work. Twenty minutes? Thirty? Forty? Pumping the rocking chair back and forth, she began to chant, "Sing a song of sixpence, a pocket full . . ." When she reached the end, she repeated it. And then repeated it again. Each time she varied the tune and the rhythm—sometimes 4/4 time, sometimes 3/4, sometimes syncopated, sometimes waltzy. What was Jake doing? Had the nurse forgotten to give him her message? She'd wait another fifteen minutes and then page him again.

Eddie was finally quiet. Her eyes closed, her sinuses flooded, and her hair matted against the chair's headrest, she continued to rock and wait for Jake's call. Back and forth. Back and forth. Back and forth again.

She sang, "Four and twenty blackbirds baked . . ."

The phone was ringing. As she eased herself from the chair, Eddie's eyes fluttered open. He began to whimper again.

"Hi. What's up?" Jake asked.

She trapped the receiver between her right ear and shoulder and swayed from side to side in gentle arcs, trying to settle Eddie back to sleep. "Eddie's real fussy and has a fever. I don't know what's wrong with him."

Jake sounded distracted. She heard a quiet, repeated peck in the background, the sound of something tapping.

"Are you listening?" she asked. Sometimes he tuned her out, didn't seem to pay attention when she was speaking.

"Sure." The pecking stopped.

She described Eddie's fever, his weak suck, his listlessness. "Can you hear him whimpering? He's never been like this."

Jake said, "I bet he has your cold. I'll take a look at him when I get home tomorrow." An icy quiet filled the space between them. She didn't want to wait one more day. She needed Jake to help her tonight. What if Eddie was really sick? What if he had pneumonia?

"It'll be fine, Anna," he said. "Remember how you worried about Chris when he was a baby?"

She shifted Eddie in her arms. He had quieted down. Maybe Jake was right about her worry. When Chris was younger, she had fussed over every sniffle, had called the pediatrician each time his temperature went over ninety-nine degrees. She had been sure each cough was tuberculosis, each patch of heat rash was scarlet fever. When he had an ear infection and a swollen lymph node in his neck, she lay awake three nights in a row, convinced he had cancer.

Tonight she hoped Jake would take her worries seriously. The least he could do was say something kind—a few directly sympathetic words such as, "I know this is tough for you," or, "You're a good mom and I appreciate your shouldering all the work of a sick child." But he said nothing like that. He told her to call the pediatrician. Finally, her voice thick with sarcasm, she said, "We'll be waiting for you to come home."

After another half hour of rocking and singing, Eddie stopped fidgeting. She sat awhile longer, cuddled him close, brushed her lips across the top of his feverish head.

When she needed to cough, she tried to let the air out in gentle little spurts so it wouldn't disturb him. Fatigue, raw and insistent, clawed at her shoulders, wringing the last bits of energy from her muscles. Her eyes still throbbed.

When she finally laid Eddie in his crib, he straightened his left arm, kicked his right leg, turned his head toward the wall, and whimpered again.

"Please, please, please, don't wake up," she whispered as she stroked his silky hair with her lightest touch.

She lay in bed and stared at the swirls etched in the ceiling plaster, the half circles that bumped against each other—none of them complete, none of them leading anywhere. Should she call the pediatrician? It was late, almost ten thirty. He would say it was just a virus, would tell her to give Eddie another dose of Tylenol and bring him to the office in the morning.

She had had that conversation with Dr. Elliott often and she knew the routine. Chris was only three months old when she went back to work and he had been sick a lot. Runny nose. Diarrhea. Cough, runny nose again. Every virus that drifted through the day care seemed to land on Chris. Even though Rose Marie's house was immaculate and she ran the plastic toys through the dishwasher every night, Chris still had gotten sick. Often.

She had watched the other children cough and sneeze all over Chris, and reminded herself, glumly, that that's what kids did when they played. Chris sometimes snatched toys from other children's spitty hands, sometimes shoved his head against other children's snotty-nosed faces to get their attention. The kids at Rose Marie's shared lots of things . . . secrets, cookies, wishes, blocks, hats, and viruses. After Eddie was born, she had waited five months before going back to work. She wanted him to be older before she left him in the cesspool of Rose Marie's house.

Her achy muscles lay limp against the inside of her nightgown. She had skipped the bath. Fatigue sent her to bed as
soon as Eddie fell asleep. She imagined her body going
through the motions of calling Dr. Elliott. Throw back the covers, sit up, slide first one leg and then the other over the edge
of the mattress, open the drawer, pull out the phone book . . .
So much effort merely so he could reassure her that Eddie had
a cold. Before turning off the lamp, she rubbed a dollop of
Vaseline on the patch of raw skin beneath her nose.

Chapter 5

Jake

The clock in the radiology suite hung high on the wall, its round, institutional face skewed ten degrees to the right, its stark, simple hands splayed to forty-five degrees. At first glance, the clock read 10:05. Adjusting for the tilt of its face, he saw it was actually 8:55. The night was still young and anything could yet happen—he might be awake until dawn or he might be able to catch a nap or two. It wasn't likely he'd sleep straight through to morning. That almost never happened.

He flipped the toggle switch on the alternator. For a moment, the fluorescent bulbs behind the lower view boxes flickered—half on, then off. Half on, then off again. Finally they lit. He was looking for the Durban kid's knee films, first name Mike. Or Matt. Or maybe Mark. One of those *m* names.

As the toe of his running shoe pushed against the alternator pedal, rows of radiographs, four films abreast, rumbled down over the translucent backlights and disappeared into the lower reaches of the machine. Row thirty-one. Row thirty-two. Row thirty-three. He released his toe, leaned forward, and stared at the films on row thirty-four. They were knees, the left knee on one film and the right knee on another. The two bent joints leered at each other as if frozen in a face-off. The identification plates in the corners of the films read MATTHEW DURBAN. "That's him," he muttered out loud.

Earlier in the evening, the boy had been admitted to the hospital with a swollen right knee. Questioning his mother, Jake tried to pin down the cause of the swelling.

"Any injuries?"

"Let's see . . ." She looked as if her mind were scrolling down a list of Matt's activities over the past few days. She turned to her son, who was perched on the edge of the examining table, tying the hem of his hospital gown into a knot. "Did you fall on that knee? Or bump it?"

"No," he said.

"Wait," she called. "You ran up the porch steps yesterday afternoon and stumbled. Remember, honey? You dropped your ice cream cone when you fell."

The boy had shrugged.

Except for the ghostly glare from the alternator, the room was dark, like night deep inside night. Everything around him—the carpet, his scrubs, the telephone on the alternator shelf, the stack of X-ray jackets beside the phone—was the color of a shadow. That's the way it was in radiology reading rooms. Black-and-white films, gray everything else. And quiet. Dead quiet now that the day crew had gone home.

Suddenly, a muffled *thunk* bumped into the silence of the reading room. He started at the sound, a minor noise that would have gone unnoticed in the din of the day. The clock's hour hand had jumped forward, creating the thunk. Jake did the calculations. It looked as if it were 10:10 but was really 9:00 PM.

Shifting in his chair, he stared at the images on the X-ray films. His gaze traced the smooth edges of the chalky bones. He saw no periosteal elevation. The fat lines around the sore knee were distorted, showed swelling in the soft tissues. He figured there were four possibilities—osteomyelitis, septic arthritis, toxic synovitis, fracture.

When his pager sounded, he was studying the trabeculae of

the bones, looking for a disruption in their structure. Without removing his eyes from the images of Matt's knees, he unclipped the pager from his waistband and held it in front of his face. The message read "5-7512," the black, dashed numerals stark against the eerie, luminescent blue light of the pager screen. It was the OR.

"Campbell, here," he muttered when the nurse answered.

"Dr. Campbell, I forgot to tell you to call your wife. She paged you during that last case. Sorry about that."

Now what? He sighed as he clipped the pager back to his waistband. It wasn't that he didn't want to talk to Anna. Rather, he couldn't do anything about her problem, whatever it was. And the calls were always about problems. She never interrupted him just to chat; she knew he was too busy for that. Last week, the day before they left for the Upper Peninsula, Bullet had climbed the sweet gum tree and Anna had worried he couldn't get down.

"That cat will come down when he gets hungry," he had said, shaking his head at the silliness of her concern. The week before that she had locked her keys inside the car.

He dialed and continued to study Matt's films while the phone rang. Earlier in the evening he had examined the knee. It was red and swollen and obviously sore—the boy had winced and then cried when he tried to straighten it. He couldn't be sure from his exam whether the boy had a fracture or an infection.

Anna answered the phone.

"What's up?" He lifted a paper clip from the alternator desk and rotated it between his fingertips. He stared at Matt's bones. Then he began clicking the paper clip against the metal shelf.

She said Eddie was sick and had a fever.

She told him to stop making the noise. He palmed the paper clip.

"How high's the fever?" he asked.

"Don't know. Chris dropped the thermometer yesterday, smashed it to smithereens."

"Did you give him any Tylenol?" He ran his fingertip along

the edge of Matt's tibia, eying the cortex ahead of his finger to make sure he hadn't missed a break.

"Yeah. Didn't help much." She went on to say he wasn't nursing well, although he did a little better with the last feeding.

He told her Eddie had the same cold she had. The line was silent. He knew Anna was pissed off, but he couldn't do anything about it, neither about the baby's fever nor about her being mad. The paper clip twirled between his fingertips.

"Remember how you worried every time Chris had a runny nose?" he said as he gazed at the metal fastener. He admired the bend of the wire with its satisfying lack of symmetry, its look of a spiral that someone had stepped on. "It'll be fine, Anna."

She didn't say anything.

"Look, honey, if you're worried about Eddie, call Dr. Elliott." He pulled the bottom of the film away from the light box to put a different tilt on the image.

Her response was a deep sigh.

His fingers curled around the clip. "Okay. See you tomorrow afternoon. I'll try to be home by three."

Her final words were, "We'll be waiting for you to come home."

As he set the receiver back on the cradle, he sucked on the narrow end of the paper clip. For Anna, badness lurked behind every corner and blew in with every breeze. Things that were minor disruptions to most people were major dangers to her. "Look at this . . ." she'd say, pointing to a scratch on Chris's cheek. "Is that okay?" she'd ask, picking at a minuscule scaly patch on his neck. She lived like a cartoon character—a woman with a thundercloud permanently installed above her forehead.

He stared at the Durban kid's films, searching once again the bony trabeculae of the kid's knee for a crack line.

He hooked the paper clip to his wedding band and spiraled them against each other until the clip slipped off. Wedding. Bride. Last week. Upper Peninsula. Six years previously. Baltimore. Another bride. Anna's walk down the aisle at their wedding, her hand resting on her father's arm.

He hoped this memory would never grow dim. As she strode toward him, her milky satin gown had twisted over her breasts and hips like a whisper, its fabric writhing to the rhythm of the processional. Watching her move nearer, he was incredulous that the most beautiful creature on Earth was about to become his wife. Even now she was beautiful, but in a different way. Less ingenue. More responsible.

She had nervously whispered, "With this ring as a symbol of my love, I pledge to . . ." He couldn't remember the exact words, even though he had uttered the same phrase as he slid an identical ring onto her trembling finger. Something about being faithful. At the time, they had spent hours weighing every word while they wrote and rewrote their vows. It was as if the ceremony were a cosmic phenomenon that hinged on using absolutely correct language. He remembered that they agreed "obedient" would not be in their nuptial contract. Now, over half a decade, a large mortgage, and two kids later, the exact wording seemed deadeningly unimportant. But, he remained committed to the idea of the whole thing.

He checked the clock on the wall—9:15—and wondered where the intern had gone. He typed a paging message into the computer, "I'm in radar—call 72025. Campbell," and sat back to wait for the phone to ring.

Thank goodness Chris had a brother. There was something lonely—almost tragic—about only children like Anna. Their singleness deprived them of the tough, but irreplaceable life lessons that siblings could teach each other: how to negotiate for equal treatment from Mom and Dad; how to win and lose a fight; how to share a brownie and a bedroom and a can of orange Crush and the limited territory in the backseat of Dad's Chevy. Not only did she have no siblings, Anna had only one cousin, Jennifer.

His family was different, full of kids, full of fun. As children, he and his two brothers and whichever boy cousins happened to be around would swipe jugs of 7Up from Uncle Allen's basement, empty them as fast as possible in huge, slurpy gulps, and then hold burping contests. On cool misty afternoons, they drank creek water from their cupped hands and wiped their chins with the tails of their plaid flannel shirts. When they helped their grandfather feed the sheep, their stiff Carhartts— miniature versions of the overalls their dads wore—kept out the muck and the frigid winter wind.

And now, an echo through the generations, his son imitated him. He found it cute that Chris fished pickled pigs' feet from the jar with his fingers and ate them sandwiched between Ritz Crackers; that he insisted on wearing the bill of his Detroit Tigers baseball cap—its plastic clasp was cinched as tight as it could go—low on his forehead; the way he drummed his fingers on the kitchen table in a syncopated, tappity-tap cadence while waiting for breakfast. Once Chris had patted Anna on the fanny as she walked past. She spun around and yelled at him to never do that again. But then yesterday, when Chris spilled a glass of orange juice and shouted, "Goddammit," Anna had smothered a laugh and said, "Honey, that sounds just like you."

Unlike Anna, he knew all about children. As a boy, he had been recruited to walk his younger cousins in the stroller, to push them on the swing in the park, to play horsey. He had learned how to change a diaper and mop up baby vomit before he was six.

He'd been impatient with Anna when Chris was a baby. She'd been terrified she would make a horrible mistake and wreck her child forever. She seemed to turn what could be very easy into something very, very hard—often. She worried about food allergies and buying the right toys, about Chris eating from Bullet's bowl or falling headfirst into the toilet or tripping down the step between the kitchen and the family room. He, on the other hand, had always viewed kids as resilient and knew the important things about them: that eating cat food doesn't hurt anybody; that kids are close to the ground—with bones as forgiving as Slinkies—and tumbles rarely produce serious damage; that the best toys for three-year-olds were cardboard cartons, tablets of plain paper, and boxes of crayons.

Yet, Anna was a good mother. Her worry was grounded in the deepest, most profound love for her children. Who could fault her for that?

In the silence of the reading room, he pushed aside his thoughts of Anna and tried to concentrate on Matthew Durban's knees. He tapped the paper clip on the metal shelf of the alternator, creating a noise to perturb the quiet, to spring him back to the real world.

His pager sounded again. "ADMISSION—6N. NURSING HOME HIP FRACTURE," read the message. He sighed. First, he'd do an arthrocentesis on Matt's knee. Most likely the boy had a septic joint. Then he'd go see the old person with the broken hip. He twirled the paper clip between his fingers twice and slipped it into his pants pocket.

Chapter 6

Anna

Outside the bedroom window, first light tinted the inky sky with a tangerine blush. Alone in her bed, she coughed and a glimmer of awareness edged into her sleeping mind. She didn't fully realize yet it was morning. Her back had pressed against the mattress for too long and needed a new position. She folded her pillow and rolled onto her side, curling her spine into a comma. With that turn, her left foot slipped into a place on the sheet, now cool and empty, where Jake usually slept. She withdrew her foot, nestled into the warmth of her half of the bed, and pulled the covers over her shoulder. She coughed again. Her mind began to unfold. Simple thoughts replaced sleep. Cozy. Snug. Secure. Bathroom. It's so comfortable here.

Soon her neck felt stiff. She rolled onto her stomach. Pain. Searing pain. In her chest. She rolled back onto her side. Her groggy mind cleared even further. Her breasts ached into her armpits. Now her mind was fully free of sleep. Her breasts were tense, too full, sore as boils.

She opened her eyes to the peachy halo around the clouds

that dotted the dawn outside the window. Why hadn't she heard Eddie cry for his middle-of-the-night feeding?

As she stepped into his bedroom, she looked through the crib rails. He was asleep and still. She often crept into his room to watch him breathe, to observe her baby deep in the innocence of sleep, in that dreamy world that was his alone, a place she could never enter. She wanted to be sure he was still alive. Whenever she did this, she felt silly. Of course he was alive.

This morning, like every other morning, he was safe in his crib, breathing in and out, a peaceful rocking motion. She folded her arms under her heavy breasts to ease the pull on her chest. It was the most comforting sight imaginable—her baby quietly, gently breathing.

But as she drew closer to Eddie, she saw that his breaths were not even, were not the usual, steady to and fro. Instead, they blew out of him in jerks and stutters. With each breath, he uttered a soft grunting noise—an airy, mournful whimper. What was wrong with his face? It looked like chalk. "Eddie," she called. "Eddie." She pulled her baby from the crib. "Are you okay?"

He didn't stir, but lay motionless in her arms. She jostled him, kissed him on the forehead. His skin was clammy. He still didn't move. Why was he like this? Something was terribly wrong.

Thought fragments stumbled through her mind as she rushed him into the bathroom. He'll be okay. He just needs a little tussling. Hot water. Jake. He's got to be okay. Police. Cold water. 911. Of course he'll be okay.

She turned the handle on the cold water faucet and sat on the open toilet seat, clutching him to her throbbing breasts. His head hung limp over her elbow; his arms and legs dangled against her belly. Forward and then backward, driving, driving, again and again, she rocked as if the intensity of her movements would bring color to his ashen face.

"No," she called out loud. "No. Jake, why can't you be home?"

Thought piled upon thought. Her heart galloped. Her breaths—deep gulps of air—came in quick jerks. Her body prepared to flee, she was ready to run. She could jump straight up; she could leap from rock to rock; she could cover a half mile in no time; she could run away. She had to get him to the emergency room.

She laid him on her bed and pulled a plaid, cotton shift from the closet. She tugged it over her head, down over her nightgown, and slid her bare feet into her clogs. Gathering Eddie in her arms, she ran into Chris's room.

"Wake up," she shouted. "We're taking Eddie to the hospital." Chris wiggled under the covers and was then still.

"Now," she called again. "Get up."

He scrambled to the floor and stared at her with glassy eyes. The early-morning sunlight streamed through the window and sparkled off the patch of golden hair kinked above his ear. "I can't go in my jammies." His voice was thick and whiny.

"Yes, you can." She grabbed at him.

"No." He twisted out of her reach.

She stooped down, eye to eye with him. Her voice trembled. "Honey, Eddie's really sick. We have to go now. Nobody will care if you're in your jammies." She dug her fingertips into his sleeve and dragged him down the hallway.

Her Subaru swerved around the corner into the emergency room driveway. EMTs were unloading an ambulance parked at the entrance. They pulled a stretcher from its rear door, set it on the pavement, and snapped the clasp that raised the bed to waist level. The patient was wrapped from chin to toes in a dark-colored blanket. She saw its head—a genderless face framed in gray hair and pitted with the creases of old age.

Her foot stomped on the brake. The car jerked to a stop behind the ambulance. A strange, gurgling sound rumbled from behind her. She listened. It came again—from the backseat.

"Mommy, Eddie looks funny," Chris called.

"Funny, how?" She twisted her shoulder toward Chris and glanced backward. She winced as her seat belt dug into her aching breast.

"His eyes are rolling around."

"Oh, God," she gasped. She clambered out of the car. The soles of her clogs sank into an oily puddle. A man in a scrub suit stood in the hospital's entryway. She screamed at him, "My baby's having a seizure. Please help me."

Inside, the damp, heavy air seemed to part in front of her as she ran after the man who carried Eddie. Smells of sour breath, disinfectant, fluorescent lights, rubbing alcohol, and old meat floated in sickening waves around her. Occasional electronic beeps punctuated the clatter of distant conversation.

A nurse—her name tag said MARY—laid Eddie on the scale. She wrapped a tiny cuff around his upper arm, pumped it up, and let it deflate. She stuck a thermometer into his armpit and, holding his elbow against his side, trapped it in the folds of his skin. She placed a stethoscope against his chest, stared at the clock on the wall, and bobbed her head to the beat of his heart.

In the boxes on the ER record, the nurse wrote, *10.1 kg, 65/40, 40.8° C, 80,* and *120.*

Anna didn't know what these numbers meant, other than readings from Eddie's body.

"Is that okay?" she asked. "Are those numbers normal?"

"High fever," Mary answered, her voice pulsing with urgency.

Anna's thoughts raced in forty directions yet went nowhere as they tried to grab the moment, tried to keep her far away, tried to bring her close, tried to convince her this wasn't happening.

Mary carried Eddie into the nearest alcove.

Anna followed with Chris in tow.

"My husband is Dr. Campbell," she said. "He's here at the hospital. Could someone page him?"

She stared at her baby lying on the gurney. He looked like a rag doll. His eyes were shut, his knees bent, his lips slightly parted, his face pasty. Against the long, smooth sheet, he seemed very, very small. She shook her head, thinking he must be someone else's child. This wasn't the laughing baby that belonged to her. But those were Eddie's clothes. The cotton sleeper with the rabbit embroidered on the front was a gift from her cousin, Jennifer. Last Christmas, she thought. No, the Christmas before. No, Eddie wasn't born then. It was last Christmas. She shook her head again, trying to untangle the scrambled thoughts inside.

A doctor, tongue blades and ink pens stuffed in her breast pocket and a stethoscope dangling from her neck, slipped into the alcove and introduced herself.

A harsh light glared overhead. The walls seemed to move inward. Anna felt as if she were being crushed. She stared at the middle-aged, black-haired doctor, seeing and yet not seeing her. This woman, this stranger in the white coat, had stepped boldly forward to take care of her sick baby. She would help Eddie. The plastic ID badge pinned to the doctor's pocket read DR. JUNE EASTERDAY.

"He looks dead," Anna whispered. "Is he dead?"

The doctor slowly shook her head as she leaned over Eddie, caressing his soft spot. She cradled his head in her hands, moved it up and down as if weighing a melon. She pulled the wrapping off one of her tongue blades and tossed the rumpled paper toward the end of the gurney.

Anna watched it bounce off the sheet and fall to the linoleum. She stooped to retrieve it, but stopped midcrouch— it didn't matter that the paper wrapper was on the floor.

Dr. Easterday edged the tongue blade between Eddie's lips and shined her penlight into the back of his throat. She worked quickly and confidently, laying the head of her stethoscope over the left and then the right side of his tiny chest. She tucked her fingertips into each armpit and moved them along each clavicle. She bent and then straightened his elbows and knees. She rolled him over, ran her fingertips over his back, and then turned him frontward again. She prodded his belly, tapped below his kneecaps with the rim of her stethoscope, pushed a finger into the skin over his shin. Her eyes, steady and deep in their sockets, never left Eddie. She seemed to be studying every breath, every heartbeat, every inch of him.

Dr. Easterday stood up straight and turned to her. "Mrs. Campbell," she said, the snap of authority cutting her voice,

"Eddie's a very sick baby." She paused a moment, shifted her weight to the other foot, and then continued speaking. Her voice was like velvet, softened by a Southern accent. "I'm worried about meningitis. That's an infection of the tissues surrounding his brain."

Anna's head throbbed. The light overhead seemed to dance in circles, shining, flickering, turning. Bright spots floated like glitter before her eyes, sparkles that didn't disappear when she closed her lids. She reached for Chris's shoulder. He buried his face in the folds of the shift that covered her nightgown and began to wail. The doctor's voice sounded wobbly, far away— like an echo ricocheting through a long, narrow, empty space. This wasn't real. It was a bad dream. She wasn't standing in the ER with Eddie on the gurney. Any minute now it would all evaporate.

". . . very serious infection," the doctor continued. Her words filled the air, drowned Chris's sobs. She spoke of a spinal tap, of sending specimens to the lab, of starting antibiotics.

"Okay," Anna whispered. She didn't understand what the doctor had just said or what she had agreed to. It didn't matter, as long as Eddie would be all right.

She lifted Chris and straddled him on her hip. He laid his face against her shoulder, and his fingers, probing like pincers, picked at her hair. She felt an arm slide across her shoulders.

"You and your older son may wait in the lounge," Mary said. "It will only take a few minutes and then you can come back."

Anna stood firm as the nurse pushed against her shoulders. She couldn't leave. Eddie couldn't stay here alone.

"We'll take good care of him." Mary nodded toward the gurney. "Your older son won't want to watch this procedure. It'll take only a moment."

She didn't know what to do. Eddie needed her to stay. Chris needed her to take him to the lounge. Eddie. Chris. Which son would she pick? Why did she have to choose one and leave the other?

Guided by Mary, she carried Chris to the waiting room. A breath of chilly air brushed against her arm. She stood, shivering, beside a giant aquarium. A school of angelfish glided to one end of the tank, turned in unison, and glided back to the other end. Back and forth. Over and over. Their rhythmic movements—monotonous, hypnotic, synchronous—filled her mind.

After what seemed a very long time, she felt someone at her side. She turned. It was Jake. A white lab coat covered his wrinkled scrub shirt and pants. Scabs of dried blood dotted the paper booties over his shoes and his hair was stuffed beneath a gauzy green cap.

"What happened?" he asked.

She tried to explain. "He was limp, hardly moved. He had a seizure." The words spilled from her in jerks. "The doctor thinks he has meningitis."

"Jesus Christ," Jake groaned. He wrapped his arms around her and Chris, leaned his cheek against the top of her head. He was strong. Now everything would be okay.

She set Chris on the floor.

"Daddy?" Chris leaned against Jake and pulled on the hem of his scrub shirt. "Daddy?"

Jake sank into the nearest chair. A tortured grimace, its creases carved into the shadow of beard stubble, spread over his face.

"Mommy made me come in my jammies."

Jake patted Chris's hair. "It's okay, Son. It's okay." Then he pulled him into his lap.

Chapter 7

Rose Marie

Steam rose like a ghost from the teakettle, floated across the kitchen, and settled on the window. Rose Marie watched the children smear finger paint on the pages of yesterday's newspaper. Sawyer plunged his palm into the bowl of red paint and slapped it on the photo of a goalie. Meghan, a smudge of blue on her cheek, dipped a fingertip into the purple paint and drew circles diagonally across the page. Amanda printed a string of green x's on the want ads. In the meanwhile, a bead of condensed mist loosened its grip on the windowpane, skittered down the glass, and puddled on the sill.

This was her third mug of tea for the morning. She smiled at the orange fist prints Davey had made and said, "Good job." When she looked sideways at his picture, she saw a row of pumpkins against the black and white and gray of the newsprint. His mother, who wore oversized jewelry and tie-dyed caftans, would especially enjoy receiving her Mother's Day gift wrapped in this wildly colored paper.

"Where's Chris?" Sawyer asked.

"I don't know," she answered. "Probably he and his mommy are still sick."

The clock on the stove read 9:35. Chris and Eddie hadn't come yet and their mother hadn't called. It was unlike Anna to be negligent. She had never failed to call before if the boys weren't coming.

She didn't want to charge Anna for today, especially if she was ill, but the rules were clear—no-shows had to pay. Even if Anna was still sick, their father could figure out how to get the boys to day care, couldn't he? Or, at least, to call?

Time for the morning snack. "Anybody hungr—" she asked and, before she finished the question, Davey yelled, "Me."

"Wash the paint off your hands." She set the dishpan, with soapy water warmed in the teakettle, on the center of the table. "And here're the paper towels. When your hands are dry, you may get a muffin from the sideboard."

As the children scrambled away from the kitchen table, she called, "One. One muffin each."

Ten o'clock. Still no word about Eddie and Chris. She dialed the Campbells' home phone number and heard Anna speaking from the answering machine. She left a message.

After the paints were put away, after the morning snack, after she had taped the damp, handprint-filled pages of newsprint to the back door to dry, she set up the second activity of the morning. She enjoyed helping the children with their projects, marveled at their movements, their patience, their tenacity, the speed with which they learned new skills. Their brains were like little blotters, soaking up everything that hit the surface. New songs? They sang like choirboys. A French poem? Twice through and they sounded as if they were born in Paris. Now, Meghan, Amanda, Davey, and Sawyer gathered, elbow to elbow, around the kitchen table while she showed them how to string Cheerios onto pieces of twine.

"Moisten it to a point." She drew the end of the string over her tongue. "Hold it close to the tip—otherwise it'll flop over. Then stick it through the hole."

They were making necklaces for Mother's Day presents. Chris would feel terrible if he didn't have a necklace to give to Anna. He didn't like to be left out of anything. She dumped two handfuls of cereal into a plastic bag and laid a hank of twine on top. Next time Chris came, he could either work on the necklace or take the packet home.

The children's legs dangled like tassels beneath the kitchen table. Beefeater wandered from chair to chair, his nose surveying the linoleum, his tongue gobbling up stray pieces of cereal as soon as they hit the floor. He was a perfect day care dog, loyal, gentle, tolerant of kids and their foibles.

"Come here, Beefeater," she called. The points of his ears, usually turned down, now stood straight up, and he lifted his nose into the kitchen's air. "Here, boy . . ." He padded across the floor to his mistress. "Good dog." She held out a half-eaten muffin.

She turned back to the children. "Hey, Sawyer." She tapped the boy's chubby hand as it palmed another fist full of *o*'s into his mouth. "No more eating or you might not have enough Cheerios to finish the necklace. Keep stringing."

Chapter 8

Jake

Chris lay curled like a lynx in Jake's lap. His son's right ankle dangled between his calves, the pajama leg pushed up past the scratches on his knee, the result of a disagreement with Bullet. Chris, still asleep, squirmed and his fingers clawed at the uppermost scratch. He caught his son's hand, clamped it against his chest.

Anna slouched in a chair in the corner of the waiting room, the hem of her nightgown taut against her knee, her eyes hidden behind her hands. Maybe she was asleep or maybe she had retreated into her own world. He couldn't tell which.

Something about the lighting—the olive green glow from the plastic seat cushions, the electric blue glare from the fluorescent lights, the dark blond striations of Anna's uncombed hair, the apricot tint of her cheeks—made her look old. As people walked in and out of the room, their shadows, eerie shades of gray, wafted ominously across her forehead.

"Excuse me, Dr. Campbell." The papers in the young man's hands quivered, his voice was tentative. "My name's Sunil Patel and I'm the med student in the ER today." He picked up a *Na-*

tional Geographic and set one of the papers, askew, on the cover for support. "Your son needs a spinal tap and Dr. Easterday sent me to get the consent form signed." He pointed to the sheet of paper on the magazine.

Jake didn't read it. He knew what it said: The possible complications of a spinal tap include bleeding or pain at the needle's insertion site, post-spinal headache, nerve damage, hematoma, paralysis, and herniation of the brain stem into the foramen magnum.

Foramen magnum. Big hole. It was the drain hole at the bottom of the skull. He winced, shook his head, tried to banish the images that raced through his mind. Brain stem herniation. Eddie's soft little brain stem, the command center for his breathing and his heartbeat, could jam through the drain hole during the spinal tap, shoved downward by the pressure inside his head. A near instant killer.

He shook his head again. The risk of herniation was minuscule; Eddie's open fontanel would protect him.

Chris wiggled. Jake stroked his leg. Was Eddie's fontanel still open? He couldn't remember the last time he'd felt his baby's soft spot. No matter, the risk was tiny, the rest of the complications relatively minor.

He pulled a pen from his scrub shirt pocket, turned the form to fit squarely over the magazine cover, and scribbled his signature on the line at the bottom.

"Date?" he muttered.

Sunil glanced at his watch. "Um . . . April fifteen, I believe."

Jake wrote the date on the next line. He stared at what he had written. "Jacob S. Campbell, MD." The trailer "MD"—medical doctor, the signature of a physician—was scrawled beyond recognition. He wrote those two letters behind his name a hundred times a week—on insurance forms and prescriptions, on medication orders and X-ray requisitions. Sometimes, at home, when he wasn't paying attention, he wrote them on checks to Detroit Edison or on the income tax return. Last week he had written it on a birthday card Anna had passed in front of him, her finger pointing to the white space beneath the greeting.

Here, his signature, Jacob S. Campbell, MD, was on the consent form for his son's spinal tap. It seemed very wrong, an error of colossal proportions. Something had gone badly awry.

He knew what was happening on the other side of the door to the patient area—he'd done maybe ten spinal taps himself, back when he was a medical student. Eddie would be lying on a gurney. One of the nurses would be holding Eddie, his body folded into a C, against the sheet. One of her hands would be clamped on the back of his neck and the other would hold his knees as close to his chin as she could bend him. Would he wiggle? Was he well enough to fight her grasp? Another nurse would paint his lower back with Betadyne, drawing concentric brown circles with the sponge. Then she would cover him with a sterile green sheet, placing the eyehole over the brown antiseptic.

He knew the drill—doctor pulls on sterile latex gloves, snaps the fingers until they fit evenly, palpates the iliac crest with one forefinger to orient herself to Eddie's anatomy and, with the forefinger on the other hand, locates the L3–4 lumbar space on Eddie's backbone. Like a well-rehearsed dance.

He wiped his forehead with his palm. Would it go well? Would the ER doc hit it right? She would advance the needle slowly into Eddie's back until she felt the pop, the signal the needle's tip had stabbed the dura. Then she would remove the stylet from the needle.

The details of the spinal tap played over and over through his head. In one version, fluid clear as water dripped from the hub of the needle—normal spinal fluid. In another, the fluid was cloudy, looked like diluted skim milk. That would be bad, would mean meningitis. In a third version, the fluid was bright red because the doctor had hit a blood vessel with the needle tip. The blood in the specimen would obscure the lab results; they might not be able to tell if he had meningitis or not.

He wanted to be in the cubicle, to watch the tap, to send mental telepathic instructions that would guide that needle into the right place. No blood. No complications. Quick.

No, that wouldn't be a good idea. He didn't want to be there if the sample was cloudy or even bloody. Didn't want to be in the room if things didn't go well, if the doc had to stick Eddie's back several times, if she grew frustrated and impatient and sloppy, if the needle couldn't be coaxed smoothly into the subdural space.

Anna seemed to be still asleep, tucked into the corner of the green chair. What had happened last night? Yesterday, when he left for the hospital, he had kissed Eddie's head as it lay propped against her arm, her nipple in the baby's mouth. His son's skin hadn't seemed feverish. But his nose was stuffy, and clear snot had bubbled out one nostril. Eddie had a cold. Same cold as Anna, which she probably caught from Chris. She had called him last evening, said something about Eddie having a fever. From what she told him, the baby didn't seem very sick. She said he was still nursing, hadn't said anything about vomiting. What happened?

The questions hammered inside his head. What had she done? Or not done? Why hadn't she recognized he was so ill?

Had he missed a clue when she called? It didn't sound too bad, baby with a fever and a cold. Happened all the time. Why hadn't he questioned her more carefully? If he had understood how ill Eddie was, he would have told Anna to get the baby to the ER last night. How could this be happening to them?

Chapter 9

Anna

"What was going on with Eddie last night, Anna?"
She heard Jake's voice over the drone of the ER waiting room. Then a woman's cry rose above the noise, replaced by a man's grunt. A phone rang, a baby screamed, wheels rolled over linoleum, something metallic fell with a clang.

She stared at his pale, whiskery face, at his tired eyes. "He was sick."

"Honey, what happened after we talked on the phone?"

It was chilly in the waiting room. She wrapped her arms around her chest, folded them under her breasts—her achy breasts. "I rocked him for a little while."

"Was he nursing?"

"Not very well. But he took a little bit. Jake, I'm so scared. Is he going to be all right?"

"I don't know." He wiped his forehead. "Was he crying? Or whimpering?"

"He was fussy, eventually he fell asleep."

Then she remembered. She had begged Eddie not to wake

up when she laid him in the crib. And then he didn't. She couldn't tell Jake about that.

She pulled a piece of Kleenex from her pocket and blew her nose. "Then I put him in his crib."

She was cold. She kicked off her clogs, folded her legs up into the chair, and gathered her shift around her bare feet.

"Then what?"

"Then it was morning."

"And?"

She didn't know how to describe it. "Eddie didn't wake me up for his middle-of-the-night feeding."

"And then what?"

Jake was accusing her of something. Of not taking care of Eddie. "This sounds like a criminal interrogation," she said.

"No, no. I'm just trying to figure out what happened last night. Did you call Dr. Elliott?"

"No."

"I told you to do that if you were worried about him."

He wouldn't stop. He kept pounding her with questions. "Do you think Eddie was crying in the middle of the night and you didn't hear him?

"Did you take a sleeping pill or something?

"What time did you wake up this morning, anyway?"

She didn't answer. Finally he quit asking.

He rose, set Chris in the seat of his chair, and stepped toward her. At her side, he stooped, laid his hand on her knee, and stroked her hair. "Please tell me about last night. I just need to know what happened."

"Well, I don't know what happened. When I went into his room this morning, he was pale and barely breathing." She hid her face behind her palms, made Jake disappear.

"Okay. Enough questions. I think I get the picture." He returned to his chair and pulled Chris back into his lap.

The white band of cloth—the bottom of her nightgown—hung beneath the green and blue plaid hem of her shift. She ran her fingers over the knit fabric, folded it, folded it again, and folded it yet again. Then she unfolded it, and slowly refolded it once more.

Eddie was still in the treatment area. What was taking so long? He seemed so far away and she was stuck in the waiting room, the place where people idly lingered. Some paced from wall to wall, as Jake had done in ten-minute cycles. Some paged through dog-eared magazines. Others just sat. For her, time was strings of empty seconds tied together like foam buoys along an endless rope—dangling, twirling, bobbing, swaying, but going nowhere.

Waiting. Waiting. Waiting until she could see Eddie again, could learn what was wrong with him. Was he still alive? The possibility of good news tugged against the probability of bad news; the unknown made her head ache. He'll be just fine, she told herself. He's going to die, she told herself a minute later. She ran her fingers through her hair, combing it back away from her face. She wanted the suspense to end. And yet, at the end of the waiting, could she deal with what came next?

She wanted to make the time go faster. She didn't want to read. Didn't want to talk. Didn't want to answer Jake's probing questions. Didn't want a cup of the stale coffee from the urn across the room. She couldn't sleep while sitting up in the chair, couldn't consider sleeping while Eddie was trapped in the other room. What were they doing to him, anyway? She shifted her weight to her right hip. What was taking so very long? Then she shifted her weight back to the left.

It seemed as if she spent her life waiting for something to happen: She had waited for her wedding, waited for Jake to finish medical school, for Chris to be born, for Eddie to be born. On a more mundane, day-to-day scale, she waited for Jake to come home in the evenings, for Chris's birthday, for the trip up north next time Jake had a full weekend off, for the blue linen jacket with the bone buttons she had ordered from the Talbots' catalog, for the next semester of new students who spoke three or four or six different languages but not English.

Now, she was waiting to hold Eddie in her arms, to rub her

hands against his skin. He'd be scared without her, back in that room, would know something was missing—would know *she* was missing, that he was being hurt and the usual comforts, her smell, her kisses, her singing, her warm, sweet milk, weren't there. He'd look around the cubicle, stare at those ugly curtains and wonder where she was. If he could wonder. Can a six-month-old baby wonder? Her fingertips smoothed the hem of her nightgown against her shin, patted out the wrinkles. Surely he'd wonder why she wasn't there with him.

It was her third visit to this emergency room. Last summer, on the Fourth of July, Chris had a fever and scratchy voice. She thought it must be strep throat. Turned out to be an ear infection. The summer before he had had a fever, then a bright red rash.

"Probably baby rash," Jake had said.

"Maybe scarlet fever or measles," she said.

"Not measles. He's been vaccinated against that."

The rash turned out to be roseola, an innocuous virus.

During those other visits she stayed in the cubicle with her sick child, hadn't been banished to the waiting room while they examined him or drew a blood sample from him. Everything else was the same, the waiting for the tests to come back, the flickering fluorescent lights, the moans and shouts of the other patients, the confusing smells that seemed both antiseptic and rotten. Only, this time was worse.

She knew what they were doing to Eddie—sticking needles into him. Taking blood samples. Doing a spinal tap. Why didn't someone tell her what was going on? She stared at the vacant door that led to the hallway that led to the room of cubicles that led to the gurney where Eddie lay.

"What's taking so long?" she asked.

Jake rearranged Chris on his lap. "They're probably starting an IV, drawing blood, doing the lumbar puncture, infusing his antibiotics."

She folded the hem of her nightgown yet again, and then unfolded it. "Is he all right?"

"I hope so."

His voice sounded thin. He seemed to be on the moon and yet he was slumped in his chair, Chris snuggled in his lap, merely six feet to her left. She stood up—couldn't stand to sit any longer—and wandered into a hallway.

A sign with a large arrow pointing to the right said CAFETERIA. The thought of food made her stomach lurch. She turned to the left, away from the cafeteria, and walked down the hallway among the clutter of empty gurneys, wheelchairs, IV poles, and cribs. First a man and then two women, all three dressed in wrinkled green scrubs, zigzagged through the maze of equipment, their arms loaded with boxes, stacks of linen, coils of tubing, plastic bags filled with clear fluid. She had been waiting and waiting and waiting. They were busy.

Of course Eddie would be okay. The soles of her clogs padded against the floor to the rhythm of her thoughts. Would be okay, would be okay, would be okay. He has to be okay. He's had a little spell, a snit from his cold. Most certainly he had a virus that would soon pass and they could all go home.

Ahead was a crossroads in the hallway. An arrow that said X-RAY pointed to the left; one that said GIFT SHOP pointed to the right. One that said CHAPEL pointed straight ahead.

She could pray. She stepped inside the doorway. Rows of benches led to the altar. A white beam from somewhere—the ceiling? somewhere else?—lit the altar. A cross and a Star of David glowed in the pool of eerie light.

She didn't know what to pray for. Forgiveness for not calling Dr. Elliott? Absolution for sleeping through the night? For Eddie to be okay? She didn't know how to pray, except to repeat the Lord's Prayer she had spoken by rote in Sunday School when she was a little girl. Worship wouldn't help Eddie. It was the doctors who would make him better. She turned around and walked back the way she had come.

The seat of her chair in the waiting room was cool. She wished she had worn a sweater. Her old brown cardigan lay draped over the chair in her bedroom. Why hadn't she thought to bring it? If Chris were nestled in her lap, he would keep her warm, but he clung to Jake's shirt like a baby monkey to his mother monkey's hairy front. He seemed to be asleep, hidden from the world behind closed eyes. Suddenly his arm jerked. He uttered a smothered yelp, grabbed at Jake's shirt again, and snuggled back against his dad's chest.

Jake looked like a pile of wrinkled laundry in his chair. The legs of his scrub pants twisted around his knees. His puffy eyes showed his weariness, his tangled hair his discombobulation. The stubble on his jaw was a leftover from his long night on call. If he'd been home last night, he would have shaved by now, his clothes would have been pressed.

If he'd been home last night, none of this would have happened. He would have taken care of Eddie and Eddie wouldn't have had the seizure, wouldn't be so sick. On the phone he'd said Eddie was fine, said he merely had a cold. If Jake had been there, he would have known what was happening to their baby. He wouldn't have said everything was fine, wouldn't have misled her.

She wanted to be warm, tried to remember what it was like to be warm. She coughed into a Kleenex, curled her feet against the cushion beneath her bottom, and waited. She closed her eyes and tried to remember the warmth of the Upper Peninsula sun against her face.

"Mr. Abrams?" a nurse called. "Is Mr. Abrams here?" The old man in the corner struggled to his feet, grasped his cane, and, with a woman's lumpy purse dangling from his arm, tottered out the door behind the nurse.

She spotted the tuft of caramel-colored hair that peeked from the V neck of Jake's scrub shirt. She wanted to poke the tuft back inside his clothes. She leaned forward, about to rise from her chair, and then sat back. Let it be, she thought.

"Mrs. Campbell?"

She turned toward the voice. A young man in a short white lab jacket—the medical student who had asked Jake to sign a permit for the spinal tap—stood before her.

She jolted upright in her chair. "What's happened?" she asked. "Is he okay? Can I see him?"

"Um . . . Dr. Easterday is with him now, and . . ."

"Honey, they'll tell us when they're done," Jake said.

"So, Mrs. Campbell, my name is Sunil and I'm a med student working in the ER today. I met your husband earlier." Sunil turned toward Jake, smiled briefly, and turned back to her. "I have a few questions about Eddie."

"What?" she said.

"I said, I have a few questions . . ."

"I know. What questions?"

Sunil squatted beside her chair. A clipboard rested on his knees. He pulled a card from his pocket and a pen from another pocket.

He stared at the list of words on the card. "When was Eddie born?"

"October eleventh, six months ago."

She watched him write *DOB: 10/11/00.* "What's DOB?" she asked.

"Date of birth. October 11, 2000." Sunil glanced at Anna and then back to his paper. "How much did he weigh when he was born?"

"Eight pounds, one ounce."

"How many pregnancies have you had?"

"Two."

The student continued down the list. Any complications with the pregnancies? Any medications during the pregnancy with Eddie? Any problems during Eddie's birth?

"Apgar scores were 8 and 9," Jake interrupted.

Sunil looked over at him.

Jake added, "I think it was one off each for color and tone at one minute and one off for color at five minutes."

"Thanks." Sunil jotted down the numbers. "I usually don't get that kind of detail from parents." He shot a momentary smile toward Jake and then returned to his cue card.

Coal-colored hair tumbled over Sunil's forehead and brushed against his eyebrows. As he spoke, his fingers swept through the hair, pushing it away from his face. His skin, the color of freshly brewed tea, made her think of warmth. His chin was pointed and his lips were thin and dry, which, for her, downgraded the warmth to tepid. The crust of a cold sore stippled the corner of his mouth.

She rubbed her fingers against the hem of her nightgown. These questions irritated her. Eddie's birth was six long months ago and had nothing to do with what had happened overnight. The only important thing now was that the doctors make her baby better, and these questions wouldn't get them closer to that goal. Besides, Sunil seemed nervous; he stumbled over words as if unsure of their pronunciation. He was very young, inexperienced, an amateur. If she had to talk to him, at least he could know what he was doing.

"Which baby shots has Eddie had?" Sunil asked.

"All of them."

"Even hepatitis B, the one he should have had right after he was born?"

"I don't remember exactly which ones." She felt exhausted. Her arms and legs ached. She was too tired to think. Her head throbbed, her chest hurt. She pressed her knuckles against her temples and coughed. "He's had everything he was supposed to have."

Sunil flipped his card over and stared at the chart on the back. He sucked on the end of his pen and then said, "Well, at age six months, he should have gotten the third hepatitis B shot, the third DTaP, the third polio, the third Hib . . ."

She twisted in her chair, straightened her legs, and then coughed again. "I said I don't remember." She closed her eyes. "Does this really matter right now?"

Jake stood, once again set Chris in the corner of his vacated seat, and stepped toward her. Chris scrambled off the chair and bolted after his father. "Daddy," he screamed. "Daddy."

Jake's fingers—warm even through the layers of her nightgown and shift—kneaded her shoulder. "Honey, they need all of Eddie's medical information . . ."

She shrugged his hand away, wanted the student to leave her alone. "Then you tell him."

"I wasn't there for his well-baby visits. I don't know for sure which shots he's gotten."

"Well, I don't remember right now and I'm tired of these stupid questions."

She slouched back into her chair. "Just make him better. Just let me go in there."

Sunil slowly backed toward the door. "Dr. Easterday, uh, will be out in a minute."

Jake returned to his seat and scooped Chris into his arms. "Sunil and the rest of the doctors need to know everything about Eddie's health."

She felt tears run down her cheeks. "I was very tired. After I put him in his crib, I went to bed."

"It's okay, honey."

"He didn't cry at night to nurse. When I woke up, my breasts were sore and he looked dead. But, Jake . . ." She couldn't read the look on his face. What was he thinking? "He wasn't dead, just limp. And pale."

Jake nodded. "It's okay."

Chris wiggled in Jake's lap, opened his eyes, and stared into his father's face. "Mommy made me come in my jammies."

She glanced at her watch. Only two hours until class time. She'd need to arrange for a substitute. Cell phone. Where was her cell phone? In the charger on her dresser.

Sub. She had to get a sub for her class. She slipped a quarter into the pay phone at the end of the waiting room.

The phone rang twice, three times, four times. A sense of panic clawed at Anna. What if Elizabeth doesn't answer? She couldn't think of another way to arrange for a sub, didn't have the phone numbers of the community college or the program coordinator in her purse. Please, Elizabeth, answer the phone.

She could depend on Elizabeth. They traded babysitting occasionally and carpooled together to faculty meetings on the main campus. Last summer, before Eddie was born, they had refinished an old dresser for the silent auction at the linguistics department. The memory of that day threaded through her tired mind. After applying the primer, they had painted the background, had smeared on layers of deep sapphire-colored enamel. Then Anna had tole-painted maroon and pink roses on the fronts of the drawers, had dabbed thorns on the stems and shadowed the edges of the petals and leaves in deep green.

At the beginning of the seventh ring, her friend answered the phone.

"Elizabeth, I'll need a sub this morning."

The seat of the chair at the pay phone was sticky, as if Kool-Aid had dried into the upholstery. She shifted her bottom to the edge of the cushion, tried to avoid the spill.

"What's wrong?" Elizabeth sounded alarmed.

She didn't know what to say, where to begin. What's wrong? No one had done anything bad. What's wrong? Everything. "Eddie's in the hospital. In the ER."

"Oh, no," Elizabeth gasped. "Wh-What happened?"

She began to explain. Her chest tightened as if it were wedged in a clamp and the screw were slowly turning. She breathed in short little pants and her words were mixed with air. She clutched the handle of the pay phone.

"Anna, where are you?" Elizabeth asked. "Are you alone? Where's Jake?"

"He's here."

"Are you at the hospital?"

"Yes, in the emergency room."

Speaking was becoming easier. The clamp around her chest loosened and she took a deep breath.

"I'll call Rob to line up a sub." Elizabeth's voice sounded settled, in control. "Bonita—that's your aide's name, right?—should be able to help. How independent is she, do you think? If nothing else, I'll take over your class. Does the office have lesson plans?"

"We've been working on business skills—writing checks, filling out rental agreements and citizenship forms, that kind of thing. Bonita can be a big help. The kids seem to like her, especially the Spanish speakers."

Anna pulled the moist Kleenex from her pocket, found a dry corner, and wiped at her nose. For a moment, she was back in her real life, a world of languages and students and workbooks and pronunciation exercises. Scenes from her class tumbled through her mind. Elena's new haircut. The birthday card Ismael and Huang had made for her. Maria's platform shoes and polka-dotted socks. Tran's high, squeaky voice begging, "Mrs. Campbell, show me how," repeatedly: how to say "hamburger" and "French fries" in English, how to make "mailman" into a plural word, how to give someone forty-three cents in change.

"We'll arrange subs until you tell us not to," Elizabeth said, just before hanging up. "You take care of Eddie and yourself and we'll take care of your class."

Then Elizabeth was gone. All that remained was the empty thrum of the dial tone. A sub would take over her class. All she had to worry about now was Eddie.

"Dr. Campbell. Mrs. Campbell." The nurse touched her shoulder. "Dr. Easterday decided to intubate Eddie"—she felt the pat on her arm as the nurse continued—"to help him breathe more easily. We're ready to move him to the ICU. Just waiting for them to prepare a bed." The nurse's hand pulled away from her shoulder. "You can go see Eddie now."

She scrambled out of her chair and dashed through the doorway into the hall. She heard Jake's footsteps behind her.

When they reached Eddie's cubicle, she heard Chris call, "I wanna go home."

"We'll go home in a little while," Jake said.

There he was on the gurney, unmoving as if asleep, but his body lay at all the wrong angles. His pudgy legs splayed like a bloated frog's against the sheet, and his arms, L shaped and unmoving, seemed locked in surrender. A saucer-sized yellow-brown circle stained the sheet beside his waist. His hair was arrayed in a halo around his head. She ran her fingers along their tips. Silky and fine as cobwebs—same as usual.

She felt Jake behind her and leaned back against him. She closed her eyes to escape this sight, but then opened them again. She couldn't bear to see her baby like this but couldn't bear not to see him. Plastic tubes ran into him from bags of fluid overhead. One, two, three. One to his right hand. One to his groin. One to his left wrist, limp beside a dime-sized spot of blood on the sheet. A tube, protruding from his mouth like a thin, hideously long, ivory-colored plastic tongue, was attached to a coil that ran to a machine humming beside the gurney.

She stretched her hand toward Eddie, but it hovered midair like a storm-tossed bird. "Is he alive?" she asked in a whisper.

"Yes," Jake said. "The ventilator's helping him breathe. You can touch him. Just don't pull anything out—the tubes and stuff."

She ran her fingers slowly, tentatively over the pale skin on Eddie's shin. What if she hurt him? A tear tracked down her cheek. Then another. Her breaths came out in little sputters.

"Anna, I'm going to find Dr. Easterday," Jake said. "I'll take Chris, you stay here with Eddie."

She felt the edge of the chair against the back of her legs. She perched on the seat, rested her head on the gurney, and stroked her baby's foot.

Chapter 10

Jake

Jake leaned against the edge of the table. An EKG strip, anchored by a half-full bottle of Diet Pepsi, looped over its side and coiled toward the floor. He cradled Chris in his left arm. The boy seemed to be asleep. On the far wall, a hand-printed sign read:

Foreign bodies found in vaginas and rectums:

Beer Can		Cookie
	Candle	
Cell Phone		Pencil
	Baby bootie, hand knit	

The last time he read this sign, he had found it funny. The objects and the body cavities were comically incongruent, the

way things were in the ER. Now, it wasn't funny at all. He now
considered the dissonance to be ugly, a violation of something
he couldn't quite describe.

The phone beside him rang. The receiver lay upside down
on its cradle, signaling that someone had placed a page to this
number.

"ER. Staff room, Campbell speaking," he said. He looked
around the room. "Not here," he said and replaced the receiver
on its cradle.

The door opened and June Easterday walked in. Jake stood
up. She gave him an uncomfortable smile.

"I wish this hadn't happened to your son." She peeled off
her surgical gloves and tossed them at the trash can. One
landed inside the can; the other hit the metal rim, slid off, and
puddled on the floor, its fingers twisted against the linoleum
like a grotesquely deformed hand.

Jake nodded. "I don't know what happened last night. When
I talked to my wife about nine o'clock, she said Eddie had a
fever. They both had colds and, as she described it, he didn't
sound particularly ill to me." He swayed from side to side and
patted the brightly colored balloons printed on Chris's pajama
top. "Any of the labs back yet?"

Sunil looked up from the computer screen. "The spinal tap
results just came in."

Dr. Easterday peered over Sunil's shoulder. "Let's see," she
said. She tapped the tip of a pen against the screen as the lab
values scrolled up. "CSF white count is forty-three hundred and
the red cell count is thirty." She slid the pen back into her
breast pocket, nestling it beside the tongue blades and her
flashlight. "Um . . ." The letters and numbers rolled off the top
of the screen as soon as new ones appeared from below. "Diff
on that is ninety percent segs."

He leaned his cheek against the top of Chris's head. The
white count said it all—too many cells, almost all neutrophils.
Meningitis. He closed his eyes, envisioned the oceans of pus
that were swirling over Eddie's brain, strangling its cells, un-

wiring its neural networks. He might not survive, ran a fair chance of not being normal. Several former patients who had meningitis, now shadowy, nameless figures, marched through his head. He remembered the brain-damaged ones, those with uncontrollable seizures, severe mental retardation, twisted limbs, empty minds. Eddie could join their ranks.

"Gram stain?" he asked. He wanted more details, more medical information. Yet, he knew all he needed to know. Eddie had meningitis.

Sunil continued scrolling the electronic pages.

"Here it is." Dr. Easterday jammed a fingernail against the screen as if to trap the words before they disappeared. " 'Numerous polys present.' 'Moderate Gram positive cocci in pairs.' "

"That's the end of the report," Sunil said. "Glucose and protein are still pending."

"I'd guess pneumococcus," she said. "That, as you know, can be a nasty bug. But we won't bet the ranch on the Gram smear. We've started both ceftriaxone and Vanco."

Jake patted Chris's top again. "What's the risk to Chris?" he said.

"No risk if it's *Strep pneumo,* because that isn't contagious. You're right, though, about other bacteria. Meningococcus, for example, may spread from person to person."

"But you don't know for sure yet that he has pneumococcus," he said.

"Right, again. We won't know that for a day or so. But, the bacteria are Gram positive—and the Gram stain is usually correct—so they would be *S. pneumo.*"

He hugged Chris. At least this son was safe. Or, likely safe.

"Here's his chest X-ray." She pointed to a film on the view box. "Normal."

He looked at the radiograph, at the ladders of ribs that ran up the sides of his son's chest. The alabaster blob in the center was his heart. Little Eddie's little heart. He couldn't see it beat on the X-ray, but obviously it was still beating. Between the ribs were the charcoal-colored lungs. Whitish bone, blackish air—

Eddie in varying shades of gray. His son's insides had been captured by the zap of an X-ray beam, his baby reduced to a static, colorless, two-dimensional image with no apparent depth.

Jake followed Dr. Easterday back to Eddie's cubicle. She pulled aside the curtain. Anna sat curled into a chair beside the gurney, her head resting on the sheet next to Eddie's shoulder, her hand on his thigh. She seemed to have tied herself into the smallest possible knot. Maybe she wanted no one to see her. Or, maybe she wished to be an insignificant dot that had no relationship to the surrounding events. She might be willing herself to a place far, far away. Sometimes she did that . . . bundled up her feelings and disappeared. Like the time she went for a long walk, alone, after learning her grandmother had died. She said she didn't want to talk about it.

He sat on the remaining chair beside the gurney and laid his hand on Eddie's foot. It was cool. The skin was pale, almost gray. Poor perfusion. He wrapped his fingers around Eddie's toes, trying to warm them. Chris held on to Jake's shirt like a burr.

"We have the results from the spinal tap . . ." Dr. Easterday began.

Anna lifted her head.

"It shows many, many white blood cells, meaning he has meningitis."

Anna groaned. She closed her eyes. When she opened them, they wore the glaze of desperation, the blur of terror. She stared into Dr. Easterday's face, then into his, then back at Dr. Easterday.

The doctor continued. "We also know the fluid has Gram-positive cocci in pairs . . ."

"What's that?" Anna's voice was hoarse.

His wife wouldn't understand medical terms. "That means they see bacteria in his spinal fluid," he said.

"Most likely the germ causing his meningitis is *Strep pneumo,*" Dr. Easterday added.

"Is that bad?" Anna whispered.

"Well, he has a very serious infection." Dr. Easterday paused a moment.

Jake recognized the carefully chosen words. She wanted to convey information to Anna without confusing or unduly scaring her. But Anna was already maximally scared.

Then Dr. Easterday continued. "He's already received the first doses of the antibiotics we use to treat this infection. He got them in his IV." Then she turned away from Anna, back to him. "So far, his vital signs are fairly stable."

"What do you mean, 'so far'?" Anna asked. Her voice was like poison.

"We hope his vital signs will stay stable forever," Dr. Easterday answered, "but this is a serious infection and—"

"Anna, look," he interrupted. "Eddie's very, very sick. He may even die. We have to be prepared for that." He heard his voice waver. He looked to the floor.

Anna was sobbing now. She sucked in great gulps of air and clawed at her cheeks. Then she buried her face against Eddie's leg and whispered, "Don't die, Eddie. Please don't die."

Chapter 11

Rose Marie

The phone rang. It must be Anna. Finally she'd learn what had happened to the Campbell kids.

"Hi, Rose Marie. This is Jake Campbell."

She moved the phone receiver from her left to her right—her better—ear. It was odd for the boys' father to be calling. Anna must be really sick. "Is An—" she began.

"We have bad news about Eddie," he said.

Her body froze but her brain galloped. Was he dead? Hurt? Lost? She gripped the phone receiver against her ear, held her breath.

"We've been in the emergency room since six this morning." He made a deep, stuttery sound, halfway between a choke and a cough. "Eddie has meningitis."

"Oh, God." She sagged into the rocking chair. "Gosh, Dr. Campbell." She couldn't think of the right words. "That . . . that's awful. I'm so sorry. How is he? Is he okay?" She didn't know exactly what meningitis was, but it sounded bad. Dr. Campbell sounded bad.

The phone was quiet for a moment. Then he said, "Well, he's very sick—on his way up to intensive care."

His voice was thinner, rougher than usual; it sounded as if he were speaking into a pillow. Occasionally, when he picked up the boys, he looked tired with baggy eyes, slumped shoulders, a weak smile. Sometimes he needed a haircut, when his hay-colored hair curled, cockamamie, down his neck. He must look like that now.

She scratched her ear. "How's Anna?"

"She's pretty upset." His words were so quiet she could hardly hear them.

"This's awful. Just awful. How'd little Eddie get something like that?"

"We don't know."

She tried to remember what she knew about meningitis. She'd read something a couple weeks ago but, at the time, paid little attention. Maybe in *Newsweek*. Probably in the *Free Press*. It was some kind of infection, as she recalled, and it was bad. She combed her fingers through her hair, trying to arrange her thoughts. Certainly worse than strep throat, or pneumonia. As bad as rabies? How about Ebola? Or AIDS?

"Dr. Campbell," she said slowly, stumbling to find the right words. "Meningitis is . . . uh . . . meningitis isn't catching or anything, is it? I mean . . ." She paused and dug her fingernail deep into the groove in the rocking chair's arm where the wood had split. "I really hate to ask this but . . . will the other children get it?"

He didn't answer immediately. Silence, heavy and awkward, hung between them. Finally he said, "I don't think so."

From the corner of her eye, she could see Sawyer eating the Cheerios again. She waved her hand at him, shook her head, and mouthed the words, "No. Quit. Now."

"Rose Marie, I have a huge favor to ask. I'd like to bring Chris over in about a half hour. Could he spend the rest of the afternoon at your house?"

She twisted the phone cord around her finger two turns and

then answered, "Sure." She had planned to go to the grocery store. She'd go later. Also, she still didn't have hot water. She'd heat more on the stove. "Absolutely," she added. "Of course he can."

"He's here at the hospital with me. I have a bit of work to finish and Anna won't leave Eddie to go home with Chris."

"He can stay here as long as necessary," she said. "He could even stay overnight. Whatever works best for you, Dr. Campbell."

"Thanks a lot. We really appreciate this." After a moment, he added, "Figure out how much we owe you for the extra time and add it to this month's bill."

She was relieved to hear about the payment. With Eddie so sick, it would have been crass to discuss money.

"One more thing," he said. "Are any of Chris's clothes at your place? He's still in his pajamas and is pretty mad about that."

"Oh, I think we can find something for him to wear."

The doorbell rang. Before unlocking the latch, she peered out the window. Jake, pale, looking bewildered, dressed in rumpled hospital clothes, stood on the porch. Chris, in his pajamas, snuggled in his father's arms.

"Come in," she said as the door swung open. "Come right in." She gave her voice a lighthearted, falsetto lilt. She wanted Chris to see her as a carefree, happy person.

"Thanks again, Rose Marie."

"How's Eddie?" She lifted Chris from Jake's arms and sat down on the sofa. She cuddled him against her chest and slowly rocked from side to side. Chris was uncharacteristically quiet.

"Well, he's holding his own," Jake said. "He's breathing with the help of a ventilator. His heart seems strong."

"You're just in time for lunch, Chris," she cooed, patting his back. "We're having hot dogs and lime Jell-O." She looked up at Jake. "Would you like a bite to eat, Dr. Campbell? You're probably starved. We have plenty."

"Oh, no, but thanks. I have to get back to the hospital. I'll try to pick him up by seven o'clock." He bent over and kissed his son's forehead. "Good-bye, buddy. See you later."

Chris's head nodded against her bosom. "Bye, Daddy," he mumbled.

"As I said, he can stay here tonight if that'll help."

Jake shook his head. "I'll take him home."

After Jake left, she carried Chris to the rocking chair in the kitchen and cradled him on her lap. The other children were eating lunch. She rocked to familiar sounds, the scrape of spoons against plates, the soft thud of a milk glass being set on the table, the low murmur of kid talk. Chris needed cuddle time.

He squirmed off her lap and whined. "My mommy made me wear my jammies."

"Well, that's kind of strange, isn't it?" she said as she twisted her mouth and narrowed her eyes, trying to give Chris a whimsical, "how odd" look. "Let's find some regular clothes for you."

After lunch, while the children rested on their nap pads, she brooded. The rockers of her chair rumbled against the kitchen linoleum. What had she read about meningitis? Her mind sifted through the memories. She was sure she had read about it in the newspaper. Students from Michigan State. Or was it Wayne State? Or both? Kids in Detroit? Helen Keller had it and that's why she was deaf and blind.

"For Pete's sake," she said to no one, "why can I remember the Helen Keller part but not what meningitis is?"

Even when Beefeater stepped on her feet on his way across the kitchen floor to the last of the fallen Cheerios, she kept the chair in motion. The rhythm of the rocking—insistent, repetitive, monotonous—helped organize her thinking.

Sarah would know about meningitis; she kept track of things like that. She dialed her daughter's cell phone number.

It was a relief to hear Sarah's voice. She was always calm, logical. "Honey, I need help," she said and explained that Eddie was in the hospital, that he had a bad infection. Quoting word for word what Jake had said, she tried to describe meningitis.

"Jeez, Mom, that's awful. Is Eddie going to be okay?"

"Well, Dr. Campbell says he's in intensive care. Said his heart was strong."

"That's good . . ."

"I asked him if the other kids could catch it and he said he didn't think so, but I'm not so sure. I remember reading about college kids. Something about it spreading in the dorm. Or, maybe they worried it would spread in the dorm. I can't exactly remember. I hope my other children can't get it."

"I don't know anything about that. Let's see . . ."

She pictured Sarah in thought. Her daughter's fawn eyes would be staring upward and to the left and her broad, fleshy chin would be jutting forward.

Beefeater pawed at something trapped under the sideboard and made a high-pitched, screechy noise. A Cheerio? A fragment of dog biscuit? A mouse—Heaven forbid? She grabbed him by the collar, shoved him into the pantry, and closed the door.

"I'll get on the Internet and see what I can find. In the meanwhile, I think you should just stay cool."

She could barely hear her daughter's words over Beefeater's howling and the scritch-scratching of his paws on the pantry door. She rapped on the wall, hoping to keep him quiet. "I don't think that's possible."

"Sure it is." Sarah hung up the phone.

She couldn't stop fretting about poor Anna with a terribly sick baby. Among the mothers of her current flock of children, Anna was the most careful. She had surveyed the house meticulously before letting Chris stay there, inspected the electrical outlets for safety plugs, looked under the kitchen sink for poisons, checked the integrity of the fence latch. Eddie was always spotless when he arrived at her house, sunny highlights twinkling off his wispy hair, clean fingernails, dry diaper, and sleeper smelling of Downy. How could such a hygienic baby get such a bad infection?

She heard a cough. Then another cough. Must be Chris. She

started across the kitchen floor, stopped to listen, heard nothing, and then returned to her rocking chair. The kids were all still asleep.

Where was the Webster's? She needed to learn about meningitis. Roger had used it every night to look up words as he worked the crossword puzzle in the *Free Press*. The book was old, but the meaning of that word wouldn't have changed much.

The dictionary wasn't in her bedside cabinet or on the shelves beside the fireplace. Finally she found it in the kitchen, wedged between the *Betty Crocker Cookbook* and a tattered, paperback copy of *Hawaii*.

> **Meningitis:** *n. Pathol. Inflammation of the meninges, esp. of the pia mater and arachnoid, caused by a bacterial or viral infection and characterized by high fever, severe headache, and stiff neck or back muscles.*

So, she was right—it was an infection—but what did the rest of that mean? When Eddie was last at her house, he had no fever and his neck and back didn't seem stiff. How on earth would you tell if a baby had a headache?

The phone rang. It was Sarah's friend, Barbara, the talkative pediatrician.

"What kind of meningitis does he have?"

"I don't know." She found the question puzzling. "What kinds are there?"

"Well, several. It's an infection of the brain and is caused by different types of germs," Barbara explained.

She grimaced at the words "infection of the brain." Poor Eddie. Infection sounded like pus. Did Eddie have pus in his brain?

Barbara continued. "Most cases caused by viruses are benign and require no treatment. Those caused by bacteria are more serious. And there are several different bacteria that can cause meningitis. Some are contagious, some are not. Antibiotics are used to treat the bacterial kind." Barbara then asked when

Eddie had last come to her house, and about the kids' vaccinations.

"Their vaccinations are fine," she answered, almost before Barbara finished the question.

In reality, though, she wasn't certain. The parents had filled out the health forms when the children first enrolled in her day care home, but she couldn't remember what they had written. She didn't want Barbara, or Sarah, to know she hadn't paid closer attention to that. Besides, she wanted information, not inquiries.

Finally, Barbara said, "I'm sorry, Mrs. Lustov, but without more details, it's impossible to know if the other children are at risk of getting what Eddie has. You need to discuss this with the pediatrician who advises your day care. He, or she, can talk to Eddie's doctors and help figure out what to do."

Outside the kitchen window, two blue jays fought for a foothold at the bird feeder, and four chickadees were lined up in the trees, waiting for the jays to move on. She closed her eyes and shook her head at the memory of Barbara's comments. She'd never had a "pediatrician who advises your day care." None of the other day care ladies that she knew had a pediatrician advisor, either. They had never needed one.

When she applied for her day care license, she had typed up a health policy, copying, exactly, the example in the pamphlet from the State Health Department. Besides providing the wording for a health policy, the booklet described what to do if a child had diarrhea, a fever, a rash, or strep throat. It also suggested rules for giving medicines at the day care, tips for serving meals, and techniques for changing, and discarding, diapers. She couldn't remember it saying anything about meningitis.

After the children awoke from their naps, she herded them into the backyard. The breeze, as fresh as clean sheets, blew from beyond the fence and rustled the canary-colored blossoms on the forsythia branches. Overhead, clouds floated like wads of white insulation.

Amanda yelled at Sawyer to get off the tricycle. A hank of her hair blew into her open mouth. Her face was stiff with determination as she grabbed the hair and hooked it behind her ear. "Get off the trike, Sawyer, or I'll tell Rose Marie," she yelled again. Meghan and Davey headed for the sandbox and Chris leaped, spread eagle, against the chain link fence. The toes of his shoes jammed into the metal mesh, his fingers clutched the steel wire. He looked like a spider hanging on its web.

Such lively children, she thought, watching them romp across the grass. So innocent. So protected. So unaware of the trouble with Eddie. Even if she told them about his illness, which she hadn't done yet but would do later, they would shrug it off.

"Oh—kay," Meghan would sing in her melodic, sunny voice. She was unable to understand adversity. Everything she saw streamed through her prism of cheerfulness.

"Poor Eddie, he'th thick," Sawyer would lisp and then race toward his next idea.

She sighed as she compared the simplicity of their lives to the complexity of her own. They didn't know about dead husbands or credit card debt or broken water heaters. Or about intensive care units. In the wonderfully naïve world of these children, sick didn't get any worse than paper cuts or bloody noses or tummy aches.

"No climbing on the fence," she called. She needed to help them focus their energies. "Let's see who can build the tallest sand tower." She stepped into the kitchen to prepare their snack. "Remember to keep the sand in the box," she called out the sliding glass door.

How had Eddie been on Friday, the last time he was at her house? She struggled to recall that day. He hadn't been particularly fussy, took his nap as usual, ate like a starving baby Hun.

She looked up to see Chris racing toward her. "Rose Marie," he called, trying to catch his breath. "I need a Band-Aid." He leaned into the kitchen, his fingers gripping either side of the door frame, his torso arching forward like a sail full of the wind.

"What happened?"

"I got hurt." He stepped into the house and laid his elbow in her palm.

"Where?"

"Here." He pointed to a faint, pink line.

She kissed her fingertips and touched the skin beside the barely visible scratch. "All better."

"No," he whined. "I need a Band-Aid."

"That's too little for a Band-Aid, Chris. It isn't even bleeding."

"No," he whined, louder. "It hurts."

She stared into his face, searched his sullen, pleading eyes, tried to understand. It was his third request for a Band-Aid that afternoon. True, he was at the Band-Aid age. True, he was trying to reassure himself that assaults of all sorts could be fixed with a piece of pink adhesive. She shook her head at the irony . . . Eddie in the ICU, Chris demanding Band-Aids.

"Okay. Come with me." She led him into the bathroom, pulled the Band-Aid box from the medicine cabinet. A little strip of flesh-colored plastic would heal Chris's medical problem. How about Eddie's? What would it take to heal meningitis? Poor Anna. How would Anna ever cope with her baby being so sick?

Chapter 12

Anna

"Where were you born?"

"Baltimore," Anna said.

"New Baltimore? New Baltimore, Michigan?"

"No." She spoke louder, drawing out the syllables. "Baltimore, Maryland."

The admitting clerk furrowed her brow, tapped the delete button on her keyboard, and began typing again. "What's your mother's maiden name?"

She didn't answer immediately. Her eyes drifted to the bulletin board behind the clerk's head to the poster of the pregnant woman to the NO SMOKING sign to the patients' bill of rights in print too small to read. Her mother's maiden name? She was too tired to think. The question sounded like a trick.

The clerk's fingernails clicked against the counter beside her keyboard, steady, rhythmic, impatient. "These are security questions, ma'am. To protect your child from being kidnapped."

Kidnapped? Eddie already had meningitis. How many bad things could happen to a child? All she wanted to do was get to the ICU.

"I want to see my baby," she said.

The clerk's face softened a bit. "Let's get him registered into the hospital first. Your mother's maiden name?"

She rubbed her palm against her nose and tried to sort through the family. Her own maiden name was Baxter. Her mother's maiden name was . . . Her grandparents' last name was . . . "Feldy."

"Spell it, please."

"F-E-L-D-Y."

The woman sighed and continued to type. "Occupation?"

"My occupation? Or Eddie's?"

"Eddie's a baby, right? We would like your occupation."

"Linguist."

"Again?" The clerk looked up from the keyboard.

"Linguist. L-I-N-G-U-I-S-T. I teach English as a second language."

The clerk nodded and kept typing. "Employer?"

"LaSalle Community College."

"The child's father—what's his occupation?"

"Physician."

"Employer?"

"Here. He works here."

The clerk asked about their insurance, about emergency phone numbers, about religious preference.

"Okay, Mrs. Campbell." The printer beside the clerk's elbow started to rumble. "We have all the information we need." She smiled at Anna. It was a slow, sultry smile. Her thick, ruby lips parted to reveal a wide gap between her front teeth. "It'll take just a minute to process and then you may go."

Anna stepped into the lounge adjacent to the registration desk. Suddenly, dots of light skittered above the seat cushions, over the magazines on the tables, across the carpet. Wherever she looked, bits of glitter—pink, yellow, pale green, lapis blue—danced in the air. She shut her eyes. The glitter still sparkled, now against an empty, black nothing.

She sank into the nearest chair and laid her head on her bent elbow against the back cushion. Deep breaths, she told herself. Take slow, deep breaths. She hadn't eaten anything since last evening. Maybe that's why she was light-headed. With her eyes closed, she unzipped her purse and ran her hand along the inside pouch until she felt the candy. Two chocolate mints. Leftovers from the hotel in the Upper Peninsula. Her fingers trembled as they unwrapped the cellophane. The candies were gooey. She ate them anyway.

Her forehead felt damp and clammy, her arms cold. Darkness deep as midnight surrounded her. The warm, bright world was far away and its sounds—now muffled—echoed in the distance.

By the time she swallowed the second mint, the glittery dots had begun to fade and, one by one, the room noises moved toward her, out of the rattle of the background. A phone rang. A tiny voice called, "Grammy." Sharp heels clicked against the floor tiles. Nearby, a woman's voice spoke in Spanish—lyrical words that sputtered like a bow bouncing on violin strings. The voice spoke of someone named Romero who would take a bus somewhere. *Mañana*. Tomorrow.

When she opened her eyes, she squinted against the light. Sunshine streamed through the window and outlined the figure before her. The young woman, seated in an armchair, leaned forward, nose to nose with a brown-skinned baby propped in a stroller. Shiny ebony hair fell across her face. While the woman talked into a cell phone, she nudged a spoonful of pureed food against her baby's pursed lips, her own mouth falling open. *"Mi hija. Mi hija."* The woman sang, *"Abre la boca."* Open your mouth. She tapped the baby's chin with the edge of the spoon. *"Por favor, mi hija?"* Please, little one?

The flashing spots had gone and her thoughts were clearer. That other mother was as normal as daisies while she coaxed her child to eat, relying on the baby's instincts of imitation to get the job done. Anna, on the other hand, wasn't normal. She was the mother of a baby in the intensive care unit, trapped in a limp and unmoving body. A knot tightened in Anna's stomach.

She spotted a shiny new penny on the floor beside her left clog.

This must be an omen, she thought as she stared at the coin. A good omen. A sign that Eddie would be okay.

Like her lost earring. Another omen. A week before the trip to the Upper Peninsula, as she stood in the shower combing her fingers through the tangle of hair and shampoo foam, she had sensed something wrong, something out of balance. She had rubbed her hands along the sides of her face. The gold hoop was no longer hanging from her left earlobe. Those earrings had been her first anniversary gift from Jake.

She had dropped to her knees to search the tub's drain. Not there. Not on the bathroom floor or the counter. She shook the bed sheets and pillowcases. Nothing. Finally, she gave up, unhooked the other hoop and put it in the drawer. What do you do with one orphan earring? she wondered as a wave of sadness rolled over her.

Then, an hour before leaving for the drive up north, she found the missing gold hoop. It lay on the carpet between their bed and the nightstand.

Luck always comes in sets of three. First, the earring, then the penny, and next would be Eddie. It was a sure sign Eddie would get better.

She picked up the penny and then slumped against the back of her chair. The Spanish-speaking lady and her baby in the stroller were gone. The clerk was still working on the admission papers. Chris was set. Her class was set. Jake was set. Suddenly, she jolted upright. Eddie. He was upstairs. In this hospital. He might die. A silent scream folded over her, wrapped its gnarly fingers around her neck.

Her heart raced faster and faster, pounding against the inside of her chest. She leaped from the chair, ready to run, as if she could outsprint the unspeakable, as if she could outrace the unthinkable. Her baby was desperately ill. He might die. This was really, really, really happening.

Before she actually started across the reception room floor, she stopped and dropped back into the chair. With shaking hands, she buried her face, once again, in her soggy tissue.

* * *

Anna followed the nurse through the sliding glass door, down a short hallway, past the sign that said PEDIATRIC INTENSIVE CARE UNIT. They turned a corner.

"He's in here, Mrs. Campbell." The nurse motioned toward one of the cubicles.

She stopped, twelve inches from the crib. It was a stainless steel cage, cold and metallic. The sides were raised, the mattress was waist high. Inside was a tiny person.

"Is that Eddie?" she whispered.

"Yes, hon," answered the nurse. "The machine there"—she pointed to a gray box beside the crib—"is helping him breathe. We put his medicines into his IV—his antibiotics, his anti-seizure drugs, his blood pressure meds."

A monitor, like a television screen, hung above the crib. Numbers flashed in red, others in blue. 148. 30. 64. What did it all mean? Was he okay? Was he alive? Square boxes with dials and toggle switches were stacked like building blocks on the poles near the head of the crib. Clear plastic tubes snaked from the boxes, looped over the bed rails, coiled into a tangle, then disappeared under the flannel receiving blanket that covered the baby.

She stepped to the side of the crib. Eddie lay on his back, his arms and legs still, his face unmoving. She wanted to touch him but didn't dare. His skin was as pale as snow. Would it feel icy? His straight, fine, corn-silk hair lay crumpled against the mattress and looked as if it might send off an electric spark if she stroked it.

The thin, tooth-colored tube, still protruding from his mouth, was anchored to his face with strips of tape and connected to the breathing machine by a springy, ribbed pipe. She stared at the pipe. A ribbed, springy pipe. It seemed familiar. Then she recognized it. A miniature dryer vent hose.

"Do you have any questions, Mrs. Campbell?" the nurse asked.

She shook her head, her achy, empty, overloaded, adrift, throbbing head. No, she couldn't think of any questions.

Wait. She did have a question. "How can he eat with that tube in his mouth?" she asked.

"He gets sugar water and minerals in his IV," the nurse answered. "If he needs the breathing tube for several more days, he'll get hyperal—that's elemental proteins and fats—in his IV. We'll be sure he gets enough nutrition."

Anna nodded.

"Ask us to explain everything to you. But right now, we'll have you wait in the waiting room. You may return in about fifteen minutes."

Leave him again? She didn't want to leave him.

"What're you going to do to him?" Likely they would hurt him again, stick other things into him.

"Well, we'll draw some blood, empty his urine bag. Dr. Farley wants him to have another art line, so we'll put a tiny tube into his radial artery . . . there on his left wrist. You'll be more comfortable in the waiting room while we do these things."

"Mom, this is Anna." She leaned her head against the wall of the phone closet in the visitors' lounge.

"Something awful has happened." Clutching a Kleenex in her free hand, she bent over the phone receiver. "Eddie's in the intensive care unit."

Sobs and half breaths interrupted her sentences. She was a little girl again, a little girl in trouble. Terrified. Alone.

She told her story as best she could. She explained that Eddie had meningitis, said that Jake had taken Chris to Rose Marie's. Would she understand?

Her mother's words came like an echo from long ago. "Listen to me, Anna. It'll be okay, honey. I'm sure of it."

Suddenly she was back to the time when she had poison ivy all over her arms, when she thought she had flunked her first algebra test, when her horse sprained his ankle skidding around the barrels.

"He's so sick, Mom."

"Darling, your dad will check the flight schedules to see what we can get. I'll call as soon as we have reservations." Her mother paused and then said, "Where will you be? Where should I call? Honey, we love you. Eddie's going to be okay."

Chapter 13

Jake

His pager chimed. He grimaced at its sound, at the repetitive electronic noise that snapped like a jackal for his attention. Someone needed something from him, yet again. During the three hours since he had taken Chris to Rose Marie's, the pager had rung fourteen times. Its business—those constant interruptions, nonstop demands, incessant questions, forever trouble—never stopped. He wanted to go home but still had several orders to sign and three dictations to complete. Before leaving, though, he needed to see how Anna was doing and, of course, check on Eddie.

As he turned a corner in the hallway deep in the basement of the hospital near the morgue, the ceiling lights cast serial shadows of his body on the walls, one overlapping the other, that overlapping the next. The shadows followed him along the corridor as if they were phantom tails. A pain stabbed in the right-lower quadrant of his abdomen. He rubbed his side. Must be a replay of the original conditioned-response experiment— ring the bell and Ivan Pavlov's dog salivated; sound the pager and Jake Campbell's gut churned. Some days he was tempted to dump it, batteries, holster, and all, into a toilet. Today, especially today, he wanted peace.

Maybe the ER needed him to see a kid with a fracture. Maybe the OR had, yet again, rearranged the schedule for tomorrow morning. Maybe 9 North was requesting more pain meds for Mr. Minette. "Fix it yourself," he muttered, bitterly, to no one.

The pager chimed again. Two short beeps, a reminder that he hadn't responded to the earlier page. It might be Rose Marie with a question about Chris, except she never called him. Whenever she needed to reach them, she called Anna. It might be Anna, except Anna wasn't home. She was in the ICU waiting room.

Had something happened to Eddie? He was intubated and on a ventilator, so the call couldn't be a notice he had stopped breathing—the machine took care of that. Maybe he was seizing again. Maybe his heart had stopped beating.

He tried to remember the patients from his pediatric ICU rotation during medical school. What kinds of trouble could happen to a kid with meningitis, especially after going on the ventilator? Bleeding? Not likely. Increased intracranial pressure? Possibly. Maybe the neurosurgeons wanted permission to insert an intracranial bolt. That was an ugly thought—a trocar shoved through his baby's skull.

His fingers trembled as he unhooked the pager from the waistband of his scrub pants. The overhead lights reflected off its ghost-blue screen and dimmed the message. He tilted the pager and squinted his eyes. "Call 79100, Dr. Dunwoody's office."

The chief of orthopedic surgery. Now what?

He stopped at a hallway phone.

"Good afternoon, Dr. Dunwoody's office." The secretary spoke in a singsongy, flight-attendant voice. Didn't she understand that, at this moment, some people in this building were critically ill? Some were dying. Some were already dead. Don't give me an empty-headed, chirpy greeting, he thought.

"Campbell," he said. "Someone paged."

"Oh, yes, Dr. Campbell. Dr. Dunwoody would like to see you. In his office."

Three junior residents walked down the hall toward him, two men and a woman. They were laughing. One guy patted the other on the back. Jake didn't want to see them. He turned his face toward the wall.

"Okay," he told the secretary. What the hell does the Old Man want? He shook his head in disbelief.

"Is now a good time?" she asked.

A good time? Is there ever a good time to be summoned to the chief's office? Had any time been good for anything in the last two days?

"Yes," he said.

He replaced the receiver and glanced at his watch. Four o'clock in the afternoon. He wanted to go home. He didn't want to deal with this . . . whatever it was. He stuffed his hands deep into the pockets of his clinical coat and headed toward the elevator.

This was the office of one of the most powerful men in the hospital—the chairman of the Orthopedic Surgery Department, the vice president of the Medical Center. Jake had been there several times in the past: when he interviewed for his residency position, when he signed his annual evaluation papers. Those were easy visits. He was sure this one—no matter what it was about—wouldn't be easy.

"I'm Dr. Campbell." He took a deep breath. "Dr. Dunwoody wants to see me."

"Oh, yes." The secretary peered over the rims of her reading glasses and then looked down at the phone console on her desk. "Dr. Dunwoody is on a long-distance call. He'll be with you in a moment."

Jake took a seat. Maybe someone had complained, possibly one of the clinic staff, likely Olivia, the extremely unpleasant head nurse. She had no sense of humor and took everything far too seriously. When the doctors remarked among themselves about a patient's weight—"so and so's eating herself into a knee replacement"—or about a patient's lack of intelligence—"so and so's dumb as a brick"—Olivia would get huffy. Maybe she had filed an incident report.

Or maybe one of the attending physicians didn't like his work. That didn't seem possible. Just two weeks earlier he met with the residency program director and his evaluations were in the four to five out of five range. Maybe one of the patients had had misplaced expectations or an unfortunate experience or a bad outcome and had filed a lawsuit. Just what he needed—Eddie in the ICU, Anna worried sick, and now this, whatever it was.

He stared at the covey of framed documents—there must have been at least forty of them—hanging on the wall. The Gothic letters on the yellowing parchments mapped the road to Dr. Dunwoody's professional success: Teacher of the Year, the Murphy Award, Master of the Order of the Bone, The Hammer and the Saw Award. Transparent as ice, a crystal statue of a twisted femur balanced awkwardly on a waist-high oak pedestal. Its brass plaque, dimmed with tarnish and dust, read DR. DAVID DUNWOODY, PRESIDENT, AMERICAN COLLEGE OF ORTHOPEDIC SURGEONS, 1994–96.

Jake scratched his neck, realized that he needed a haircut. His stomach rumbled. When had he last eaten? Not today. Sometime yesterday. Sometime before Anna had called last night.

He didn't want to think about that phone call. What was Eddie really like last night, lying there, sick, in Anna's arms? She should have told him how ill Eddie was. He would have told her to take him to the ER immediately. Eddie could have gotten the antibiotics earlier. Why didn't she realize he was so sick? If Anna didn't panic about every little thing, he would have taken her call more seriously.

Slowly he shook his head. Food. He should focus on food.

Maybe his son had gotten sicker and sicker while he and Anna chatted on the phone last night. How was Eddie breathing then? Smooth as usual? Gasping? Maybe he should have asked her more questions, should have insisted she call the pediatrician. Why didn't she do that on her own? She seemed to walk away from her responsibility as a mother. Not him. Physicians didn't walk away from sick people.

But Anna was a good mother. Yes, she worried about the boys. That was normal. Admirable. She hadn't neglected Eddie. She got him to the ER as soon as she could. In fact, if she had called 911 and waited for the EMS team, Eddie may have been even sicker by the time he arrived in the ER. What would Dr. Elliott have done if she had called him last night? Maybe nothing except tell her to do what she already did. Maybe he would have told her to take Eddie to the ER then. So many unanswerable questions.

His stomach grumbled again. His last meal was that Snickers bar at noon yesterday. Hungry as he was, he couldn't imagine putting anything into his churning gut.

He glanced at his watch. He'd been waiting in Dunwoody's reception area only a few minutes. Seemed like an hour. He stared across the room. In the center of the wall hung a huge aerial photograph of the Medical Center, its authoritative white stone exterior aglow against a backdrop of roiling, blue-green thunder clouds. Looks like today, he thought as he stared at the picture. Gloomy.

Wait. In truth, although it felt like a stormy day, the weather had been beautiful—clear and warm and cloudless—when he drove Chris to Rose Marie's. His gaze rested on the upper-left corner of the building in the photo. The PICU. That's where Eddie was, on the other side of the third or fourth window on the fifth floor.

"Dr. Dunwoody can see you now, Dr. Campbell." The secretary rose from her chair and opened the door to the chairman's office.

The afternoon sunlight shone through the Venetian blinds, casting stripes on Dunwoody's silver hair, along the shoulders of his white coat, and over the papers scattered across his massive desk. As he pulled himself to his feet, the chairman waved his open hand toward the sofa. "Please sit."

Jake sat. Dunwoody shuffled around the desk and took a seat

beside him. The chairman had a limp. Who would do the hip replacement on the Old Man? Who'd have the courage? Jake wondered.

"Jake," he said. "Heard about your son." Dunwoody settled into the sofa's cushions and adjusted his pant leg. His socks didn't match. Both were brown but one had a faint herringbone pattern and was darker than the other.

"Terrible," the chairman added.

"Yes, sir, it is," Jake said. Maybe Olivia hadn't issued a complaint after all. Maybe this wasn't a dressing down in any way.

"Tell me what happened and how he's doing."

"Um . . ." It would be difficult to tell their story to this imposing man with steel blue eyes and strong hands tempered by thousands of surgical scrub brushes. "Well, Eddie has bacterial meningitis, probably *Strep pneumo*. At least that's what the Gram stain suggests. The culture hasn't grown anything yet, but it's only been seven or eight hours since it went to the lab." Tears began to blur his vision. Oh, God, no, he thought. Not here. He took a deep breath, held it until his lips ceased quivering. Then he continued speaking.

"They couldn't control his seizures, even with Ativan and phenobarb, so they intubated him in the ER. He's on the vent with pretty heavy pressor support. I think his systolic pressure is now in the fifties, which is okay for a kid his age." As long as he stuck to the medical stuff, he'd be all right.

"I haven't thought about meningitis for many years, but he sounds pretty sick," said Dunwoody.

"Yes, sir. It's not good."

"How's your wife holding up?"

"She's upset, naturally. And tired. And feeling guilty." Lots of guilt, he thought. Hers. His. Yet, no one was really to blame. Bad things happen to good people, like Anna. Like him.

He felt the tears rise up again. He took another deep breath and blinked hard to keep them from spilling over his lids.

The Life Flight helicopter landed on the roof of the adjacent wing of the building and the *whap-whap-whap* of propeller blades filled the room. He stared at the floor. The sound of the helicopter faded, replaced by the hum of a fan.

"Jake, I know how miserable this is for you." Dunwoody crossed his legs, lifting his left knee with both hands. "My oldest son drowned when he was three years old."

Silence, huge and throbbing, filled the room.

"He fell into a pond. But those details don't matter now. It's the worst thing that ever happened to me. The absolute worst."

Jake looked at Dunwoody, at the tilt of his lips, at the wrinkles beside his eyes. In a near whisper, he said, "I'm sorry, sir."

"Michael didn't die right away. After several months in the hospital, we took him home. He aspirated about a year later and then died."

The room was silent again. Dunwoody rubbed his hands together impatiently, as if washing out a stain. "I didn't intend to be so morbid, Jake. Hopefully, your son will come through this just fine. But it might be a long, tough, unpleasant journey."

"Yes. Thank you, sir."

"Has . . . What's his name? . . . The chief resident . . . Hanson. Has Hanson been able to work with the schedule so you can have a little time with your family?"

"Well, I was on call last night so my next call night will be Wednesday . . ."

"I'll tell him to give you a break. You look as if you haven't slept for a month."

"Yeah, this's pretty exhausting."

"Hanson and I will figure something out."

"Thank you, sir." He stood up.

"One more thing, Jake." Dunwoody's eyes had softened. They looked almost gentle. "Physicians usually do very badly as patients and even worse as parents of patients. They can't keep their hands off the throttle, so to speak."

His voice had softened as well. "Your son has many fine doctors here who will make the right medical decisions, but he has only one father. Don't neglect being the dad."

Chapter 14

Anna

If time could speak, it would be a backward, then forward twisting sound that roared like thunder at some moments, shrank into a sigh at others. As the hours stretched before her, they seemed an endless highway running for miles and miles into the unknown. And yet, sometimes those hours piled on top of each other, becoming stacks of important events—lab results, proclamations from the doctors, vital sign changes, new X-ray findings—that crowded at the top of the pile, crushing those that languished beneath.

Sometimes the hours twirled and roiled in nauseating swells. Sometimes they sailed onward as smooth as glass. No, she corrected her thought. They were rarely smooth, never slick as glass. She could hardly remember back when time had been normal, when days had mornings, noons, afternoons, and evenings, when night was night—the quiet, sacred time of sleep that gently folded itself around her and carried her to a peaceful place. When had they come to the hospital? A month ago? A week ago? She thought for a moment. Only a day ago. Yesterday.

Now, the only time that mattered was the fifteen minutes out of every hour she was allowed at Eddie's bedside. Expectantly, cautiously, she clung to the brief moments when the doctors explained Eddie's progress—or lack of progress. Her son's blood pressure went up, his blood pressure went down. He breathed on his own for a short while, he no longer breathed on his own. His temperature was 38.8° C, his temperature was 36.1° C. His sodium was 128 and they slowed down his IV, his sodium was 141 and they turned up his IV. They lightened his paralyzing meds and he had a seizure; they increased his anti-convulsants and ordered a CT scan. She didn't understand what it all meant, when it would end, how it would end.

Anna had staked her territory in one corner of the lounge. To her, the room was a refugee camp, teeming with others who were also displaced from their regular lives. Even now, during the daytime, some of the other parents slept on the shabby sofas. Their bodies were wrapped in flannel sheets, their scuffed shoes dangling from one end, their drawn faces and oily hair protruding from the other. A sea of remains—paper cups, crumpled Wendy's sacks, French fry cartons, sandwich wrappers—spilled from the wastebasket.

This was her home now, her base of operations. A blanket, the gray scratchy one Jake had brought from the backseat of his car, lay folded over the arm of the chair. A pillow in a polka-dotted case was wedged against its back. The bruised banana and a foam cup half full of cold coffee—the detritus of lunch—rested on the table beside her. She settled into the chair and waited for . . . She wasn't sure what she was waiting for, other than a miracle.

Somebody's diaper bag sagged open, at ankle level, to her right. Inside she could see talismans—security deposits on promises that the sick babies would be well again, soon: a rattle to scare off evil karma, lotion to erase a witch's spell, powder to sprinkle like moon dust, wipes to remove the dirt. It was all about hope, she concluded. Would that hope be rewarded or would it be dashed? Who could believe in such empty magic?

She shuddered, realizing that she, too, had made such

promises. She'd said to a deity she didn't believe in, "I'll stay awake all night; I'll keep Eddie's teddy bear—the one with the blue *M* on the maize sweater and the missing left eye—nearby; I'll be the most attentive, adoring, even-tempered, responsible, prepared mother of all times, if you'll let Eddie be healthy again."

But these deals were fleeting and she knew deep in her soul that such promises wouldn't do any good.

The room was too hot. The light was too stark. Her neck itched. The skin on her legs had become scaly. A mix of odors—dirty socks, hamburger grease, stale sweat, ketchup—seemed to float past the lamp shades and coatracks to her chair. The muggy and fetid air was beginning to suffocate her. Every time she inhaled, she felt a germy puff sweep into her nose and spread, like a tea stain, across her throat and deep into her chest. Every square inch of the air in this room had flowed in and out of other people's lungs—down into their insides, then out, and down into her insides.

The painting on the far wall mocked their children. It was obscene in this place. None of the parents here would want to stare at the dewy face of a toddler who giggled as she blew the fuzz off a dandelion head. The sign on the door commanded, in foreboding, black letters, NO CELLULAR PHONES. Beneath, an apology in smaller, light blue letters read THEY MAY INTERFERE WITH THE ELECTRONIC EQUIPMENT. She hated the carpet, the windows, the pale urine color of the ceiling tiles. This is what prison must be like, she decided. Mindless restrictions. Arbitrary schedules. Absence of privacy. Lights on all night.

"Anna, I'm headed to the cafeteria. Want something?"

She turned toward Charlotte, toward the sad and tattered face that wore an eternal smile. It was the mask of serenity, the façade of contentment. Charlotte was the mother of a seventeen-year-old cheerleader with brain cancer. "Thanks. I'm not hungry."

"You sure?" Charlotte's daughter had had her third operation yesterday. "I could bring coffee from the Starbucks stand?"

This was the sixth week of the daughter's stay in the ICU. Charlotte had appointed herself dorm mother to the rest of the parents, had earned the position by dint of longevity. She explained the rules, gave directions to the chapel, loaned quarters for the vending machines, interpreted the routines.

Slowly Anna shook her head. She wasn't thirsty, wasn't hungry. She wanted nothing, at least nothing to eat.

"Maybe a latte?" Charlotte's lips, thin and cracked, moved in a pained, crooked curl when she spoke. They were determined lips that belonged to a woman committed to making life better for people in the lounge. Maybe Charlotte thought her service to the others would be rewarded by miracles for her daughter.

"No, thanks. Maybe later."

Anna settled into her chair and closed her eyes. Her swollen breasts ached. Her head hurt. She listened to the hum of conversation around her and opened her eyes to the stirring of the room. Sleep was impossible.

She paged through a *Cosmopolitan* magazine, pausing at an article about older men who marry younger women. She scanned the first column. ". . . second and third marriages . . . midlife crisis . . . sense of stability . . . fatherhood at fifty (or sixty) . . ."

Men. She knew about men, at least a couple of them. Jake, for one. Her father, for another. And little men, like Chris. Like Eddie. She shut the magazine. Half the people in the room were men, fathers of the patients. The twenty-something-year-old beside her, with a white buffalo tattooed on one arm and a blue chameleon on the other, had spent the last two hours cradling his head in his hands. The man across the room, in the UAW jacket that smelled of stale cigarettes and heating oil, picked at a scratch on his forehead as he pleaded with his wife to quit worrying.

"Just forget about it," he said.

"I can't," she sobbed. "He's my son."

"He's my son, too. You're making yourself sick."

"I don't care."

The jowly man with a salt-and-pepper pompadour and emerald green jogging suit held hands with a woman about a third his age. Maybe he had a sick-child crisis on top of a midlife crisis.

She picked up another magazine—last December's issue of *House Beautiful.* A blue Christmas tree with silver balls sparkled on the cover. Christmas. What would next Christmas be like? Two days ago she had expected Eddie to be walking by mid-December, to be pulling the decorations off the lowest branches of the tree and tearing the wrapping paper off the gifts. Now she couldn't imagine what their next Christmas would be like. She tossed the magazine back onto the table.

Another father walked into the lounge, a straight-backed man dressed in desert camouflage. The tag on his shirt read EVANS. A military man. If Eddie had to get sick, she supposed she should be grateful that her child's father was a doctor. He could explain the procedures, the lab results, the medicines to her. He could tell if Eddie's nurses and doctors were doing the right things, could pry useful information from the staff about Eddie's status. All Evans could do was fret, helplessly.

These other fathers might be teachers, bankers, mechanics, cooks. They might even have been home when their children first became ill. Maybe these fathers took their child's temperature, called the pediatrician, measured out the Tylenol. Each had probably believed his wife when she told him their child was sick.

Time was so slow. It seemed a decade ago that she was the mother of a healthy six-month-old boy. Way back then, in her naiveté and innocence, she had hardly noticed the miracles of Eddie's normalcy, his bounciness, the way he turned his head toward Chris's voice while nursing, stretching her breast into a long, narrow cone; the way her milk drizzled out of his mouth when he smiled up at her, his eyes bright and glistening.

He was a contented baby, satisfied to lie on a blanket on the carpet while he followed her with his eyes as she dusted the bookshelves, or tolerated incessant tickling from his overeager brother. When he giggled—which was often—his eyes sparkled like jewels as his arms waved and his legs kicked. Her favorite picture of him was while he giggled. Jake had snapped the photo at the best possible instant and had caught the pure essence of Eddie.

She wished she had paid more attention to his sweet babyness. He would be little for such a short time and then the baby part of him would be gone forever. Maybe that's why she was in the waiting room and he was imprisoned in the ICU . . . because she hadn't noticed everything about him that a good mother would see.

Her breasts, heavy with milk, throbbed against the inside of her bra. As it had been programmed to do for the past six months, her body was prepared to feed him. It didn't understand that Eddie couldn't nurse right now. A moist stain blossomed on the front of the clean blouse Jake had brought.

She stared at the growing shadow of the stain. Since they arrived at the hospital, she had been kneading her breasts, emptying them into the nearest bathroom sinks. At first she thought she should try to find baby bottles to fill. But, that was senseless—a flashback to her old way of thinking. The reality was, he couldn't swallow with that tube jammed down his throat.

Maybe she should stop expressing. If she did, the pressure from the milk that backed up in her breasts would shut down its production and she'd quit leaking. But then she wouldn't have any milk for him when he was better.

She closed her eyes. Would he get better? Would that breathing tube go away so he could nurse again? So he could cry?

When she opened her eyes, Jake was threading his way through the crowd that hovered around the waiting room door. She was glad to see someone who belonged to her, weary of being alone in a room full of anxious, chatty strangers.

She gauged how her son was doing by reading her husband's face. When Jake's eyes sagged with sadness or grew wide with desperation, when his head bowed and his shoulders stooped, when he avoided her glance, Eddie wasn't doing well. When he flashed that whimsical smile of his, parting his lips to show his upper-left front tooth that overlapped slightly the one beside it, she knew Eddie was making headway. Now his face was quiet, a blank page she couldn't read.

He sat in the chair beside hers.

"Were you in there?" she asked, tipping her head toward the patient area.

He nodded and picked up a dog-eared copy of *Better Homes and Gardens*.

"What's happening?" she asked.

"Nothing new. Vince Farley showed me the CT scan they did this morning. It was the same as the earlier one." He paused, and then added, "He probably explained that to you already."

"Yes." Dr. Farley had shown her the scan. She had no idea what the pictures meant.

She laid her left hand on Jake's knee. The warmth of his body seeped through his thin, cotton scrub pants. He set his hand on top of hers. With the tip of his finger, he flicked the diamond in her engagement ring, twisting it first to the left and then to the right. Over and over, flick to the left, flick to the right. Since shortly after giving it to her, whenever he held her left hand, he absentmindedly flicked her ring. She hadn't completely understood the meaning of his restless twirling of the diamond. Now she saw it as a nervous tic—flick to the left, flick to the right—that echoed the cadence of his impatience.

She didn't want him picking at the stone in her ring. Rather, she wanted him to be gentle with her, to take care of her, to make the badness go away. If only he would erase her worry, her irritability, her cold, her fatigue, her leaky, achy breasts, just as he had replaced the torn screen in the back door last month. But, he couldn't mend any of the things that bothered her now. She stared into his face, into his faraway eyes. He might be able to fix other people's broken bones and wrenched backs and smashed hands, but he couldn't fix her and he couldn't fix Eddie.

"Is he breathing on his own at all?" She was searching for something positive, a tiny piece of good news that could grow into a bigger piece of good news.

"I don't think they've tried him off the vent yet." With a pensive shrug, he began paging through the magazine, from back to front.

"Are they going to?" As she spoke, she pulled the front edges of her sweater together and fastened the middle three buttons to hide the expanding milk stain. "They won't know if he can breathe on his own unless they unhook him every once in a while."

He stared silently at her as she buttoned the sweater. Then he shut the magazine and set it in his lap. "Looks like you'll need another clean shirt. And underwear."

She stretched the front of the sweater away from her damp blouse, letting in the warm, germy air to dry the milk spot. The stain was embarrassing. She hoped no one else noticed. Breast milk was like urine or vomit—too personal for public viewing.

"Better yet"—his voice was quiet but hopeful—"why don't you go home and change? And get a decent night's sleep."

"No, Jake. I can't." She pulled a tissue from her pocket, blew her nose, and watched as he opened the magazine again and leafed through it, flipping past the ads on the back page and then forward to the buying guide and recipes for chili and lobster rolls. His right calf bounced rhythmically on his left knee.

"My parents finally booked a flight," she said. "They arrive tomorrow morning. They'll rent a car at the airport and be at our house by noon." She tucked the tissue back into her pocket. "Will you be able to pick Chris up at Rose Marie's tonight?"

Jake turned another page and glanced at his watch. "Yeah, I'll get him. You should come home tonight. Chris wants to see you."

Her body stiffened. "No, I'm staying here. I can't leave when Eddie's so sick. You or my parents can bring Chris up here."

A young doctor, his white coat hanging off his narrow shoulders, his stethoscope dangling from his long neck, leaned through the doorway. The room was instantly silent. Anna froze and stared fearfully, expectantly at him. "Is anyone from the Quam family here?" he asked, surveying each face for a response. His eyes swept past her eyes, past Jake's eyes. No one answered. "Quam?" he repeated. The silence resounded through the room. "Quam?" He then turned and walked out the lounge door.

Jake pulled an orange from the basket of fruit beside her chair.

"May I have one?" He pulled off the peel and separated the sections. "Where'd they come from?"

"Elizabeth sent them." She leaned over and ran her fingertips along the plaid yellow bow. "It's from the linguistic staff at the college."

He tossed the orange peel into the bed of burger wrappers in the wastebasket, picked up the *Better Homes and Gardens* again, and began turning the pages.

"Jake, that drives me nuts."

He looked over the top of the magazine at her. "What?"

"Reading from the back to the front."

He snickered. "Why do you care how I read?"

"Because it's very weird and makes you look illiterate."

"That's a pile of baloney." He continued to page forward.

She stared at a bare spot on the wall. Why did he have to be like that? If he cared about her, he wouldn't do these unappealing things that bothered her so much.

He laid the magazine on his lap, set his head against the back of his chair, and closed his eyes. He was tired. Of course he was tired. Likely he had had no more sleep than she had. In his profile—the velvety eyelids, the bushy brows, the bumpy nose, his resolute mouth—she saw the man who remembered every joke he ever heard, who left the stove burners on after the food was cooked, who ate dill pickles for breakfast, who sang Mariah Carey songs in the shower. She saw the man she had fallen so hopelessly in love with seven years ago.

After Jake left, Anna curled in her chair and pulled the gray scratchy blanket over her head to shield her eyes from the lights. Still, the glare of the overhead bulbs seemed to shine through both the blanket and her eyelids. Voices ebbed and flowed around her, like waves that crawl to the shore, spread across the sand, and finally dissolve into nothingness. Someone chuckled. She pulled the blanket tighter and muttered into the wool, "There's nothing to laugh about here. It's night. Go to bed." A phone rang. Something hit the floor with a thud. A book? A purse? A person?

Fingers gripped her shoulder. She shrugged them away.

"Anna," a voice said. The hand grasped her sleeve. "Anna."

She opened her eyes. A blurry face hovered six inches from her nose. She blinked several times. The face said, "Anna, you have a phone call." Now awake, she sat up. It was Charlotte's face.

She stumbled into the phone closet beside the visitors' lounge. On the message board, blue, forehanded script read *Quam family: check with your son's nurse,* and in black, backhanded script, *281-555-7499.*

She stooped for the receiver that dangled, at the end of its metal-wrapped cord, six inches from the floor. "Hello?"

"On my way home . . ." It was Jake. "I thought of something . . . a question I don't know the answer to."

"What?"

"Did Eddie get the pneumococcal vaccine?"

"The what?"

"The pneumococcal vaccine. It's one of the immunizations infants should get."

"God, Jake, I don't know. You mean his baby shots? I can't keep them all straight." She shook her head, trying to clear away the sleep and to connect with Jake's question. "He's had everything he was supposed to get."

"It's sometimes called the pneumonia shot." He paused a moment and added as if he were reading from a textbook, "It's sometimes called Prevnar. Did he get it?"

She took a deep breath. He was pressing her, using his patronizing I'm-the-big-smart-doctor voice.

He continued, "Babies are supposed to get it at two and four and six months and then a booster when they're about a year old. So, Eddie should have had two or three, depending on whether or not you took him for his six-month visit."

She stiffened. His words cut deep. He was questioning whether she had taken Eddie for his shots in a timely manner, whether she had done her job as a mother.

"I don't know. Is it important . . . now?"

"Yes, it is, because those are the shots that should protect him from the kind of infection he has."

She gripped her temples with her free hand and squeezed her eyes shut. Now he was accusing her of making Eddie sick, suggesting she had neglected Eddie's baby shots and that was why he had this terrible infection. How could he think she would do that to her precious son? Jake was the one, after all, who'd assured her Eddie only had a little cold.

"Do you have his immunization record somewhere?" he asked.

She paused, then finally spoke. "In the top drawer . . . of the desk . . . in the kitchen."

She was sick to her stomach. She might vomit. What if, somehow, she had missed some of his shots? As clear as day, she remembered the routine of setting up the well-baby appointments. The first had been made before she'd left the hospital after Eddie was born. The second was made at the end of the first one, as she leaned against the reception counter at the clinic, Eddie squalling against her shoulder after his shot, the diaper bag banging against her hip, Chris pulling at her jacket. Eddie's six-month birthday was four days before he got sick. He must have another appointment any day now.

She could hear Jake pawing through the drawer. "It's in an envelope—a greeting card kind of envelope," she said. She wanted to help him find that record—to vindicate herself. "It has 'Eddie's immunizations,' or something like that, written on it."

And yet, what if she had forgotten an appointment?

"Got it." He sounded triumphant, as if he had won a marathon or a game of checkers. Then he was silent.

She couldn't read meaning into his silence. "What does it say?"

"I can't hear you. Speak louder."

She cleared her throat. "I said, 'What does it say?' "

"He's had the first two Prevnar shots and should get the third in about a week."

She leaned her forehead against the wall of the phone closet and wiped her tears from her cheeks. At least she hadn't done that wrong. She couldn't live with herself if Eddie had gotten sick because she'd missed his shots.

"Are you okay?"

She nodded.

"Anna, are you still there?"

"Yes," she sobbed.

"Eddie's had all the shots he was supposed to have. Listen to me, Anna, it's okay."

"But, you think I didn't pay attention to Eddie, that it's my fault he got sick. You think I'm a terrible mother."

"No, honey. You did everything right, had him vaccinated, kept the records, got him to the ER. We need to know if he got the shots and still got the infection."

"Well, he did. What does that mean?"

"I'm not sure. Dr. Farley will have to sort that all out. It might mean, though, that his immune system doesn't make antibodies to the vaccine."

She shut her eyes, leaned her head against the wall of the phone closet, sobbed. The bad news just kept coming, like a monster lurching, repeatedly, from a muddy lagoon.

"Honey, I'm coming to bring you home for tonight. Eddie'll be fine. A nurse is always at his bedside. He needs you to get some rest. I'll be there in about twenty minutes."

"No." She stood up straight, away from the wall. "I'm all right. Really I am. I need to stay here."

Chapter 15

Rose Marie

"I'm trying to reach Anna Campbell." Rose Marie straightened her shoulders and pulled at her lower lip.

"Hang on a sec while I get her."

The person who answered the phone—a woman—spoke with a thorny East Coast accent. Maybe from Boston. Maybe New Jersey. She couldn't tell; she'd never been east of Ohio.

Strange noises sputtered over the phone line—voices echoing in the distance, furniture scratching across a tile floor, a cough, something tapping against the receiver.

"Hello?"

"Hi. Anna? It's Rose Marie."

"Is Chris okay?" Anna sounded curt, worried.

"Yeah. He's here at the table with the other kids." She smiled at Chris, at the sunglasses he insisted on wearing today, even in the house. "Actually, that's why I called. I really hate to bother you, but I think he would like to talk to his mom. Is that okay?"

"Please put him on the phone." Anna sounded as if she was weeping.

Rose Marie handed the receiver to Chris. "Honey, your mom wants to talk with you."

His eyes grew large and he clapped the phone to his ear. At first he didn't say anything. Then he nodded. Then he was quiet again. "When are you coming?" he asked.

Rose Marie couldn't hear what Anna was saying. Chris nodded again. "Come today." He started whimpering and handed the phone to Rose Marie.

Anna was sobbing. "He wants me to take him home. I can't leave Eddie."

"Oh, dear," Rose Marie said. "I didn't mean to upset both of you. Chris'll be fine, Anna. I'll let him spend extra time on my lap this afternoon."

"Thanks," Anna said. "I'm glad you called and let me talk with him." Her voice was thin, tired.

"The kids are sewing together pages for their photo albums," Rose Marie said. "Chris's back at the table with them. I think he'll be fine now." She wedged the receiver between her ear and her shoulder and then retied a knot in the shoelace Davey was stringing through the punch holes.

"I'm also wondering about Eddie. How's his appetite?" She wanted to be pleasant, to let Anna know she'd been thinking about him. "He's such a great little eater."

"He's unconscious, Rose Marie." Anna had stopped weeping. "He doesn't eat right now. Or cry. Or open his eyes."

Unconscious? Can't cry? Can't open his eyes? She couldn't imagine what he was like. "Is he in a coma, then?"

"Yes, a kind of coma."

She didn't dare ask the next question—when will he wake up? Or the question after that—ever? She'd never heard of a baby that sick. "Is there anything I can do for you?"

"Thanks. Watching Chris is a big help." Someone laughed in the background, a raucous guffaw that buried Anna's last syllable. "My parents are flying in today. They should get to our house early afternoon. My dad will probably pick Chris up at

your house after that. I assume Jake told you they'd stay home
with Chris tomorrow."

No, Dr. Campbell hadn't said anything about Chris's grandparents, but there was no need to tell Anna that. Instead, she
merely said, "Okay. Take care of yourself, Anna. Give Eddie a
kiss for me."

After hanging up the phone, Rose Marie returned to the
photo album project.

"Good idea. We'll get the cameras as soon as we clean up this
mess."

She handed a camera—the disposable kind—to each child.
Their names were printed in purple magic marker across the
backs of the cameras. Davey, Amanda, Meghan, Chris, Sawyer.
Eddie didn't have one. He was too little.

"Today we'll take two pictures. Two. No more or we'll run
out of film." She ushered the children outside. "Davey, what're
you going to take?"

"The tree," he said, pointing to the maple in the middle of
the yard.

Meghan took a picture of the trucks in the sandbox. Sawyer
aimed his camera at her, Rose Marie. She put on her most loving smile. He clicked the shutter. She relaxed.

"And you?" She turned toward Chris. He seemed brighter
since talking with his mother. "What picture are you going to
take?"

"My feet."

"What?"

"My feet."

She shrugged. "Okay." She cradled his hands around the
camera and curled his pointer finger over the shutter button.
Chris's digits were less than half the size of her own, his skin
like dewy suede. She peered through the lens and aimed it at
his shoes. Chris always chose the odd things; she thought of
him as Mr. Unexpected.

As she felt the warmth of his hands, she wondered what was
going on inside his head. He obviously wanted to see his
mother. He'd recovered pretty quickly after the phone call.

Hearing her voice was good for him. And, surely, he was worried, like everyone else, about his baby brother, but he didn't talk about Eddie at all. After he clicked his two pictures, he leaned against her legs and looked up at her face. His eyes seemed to be pleading, as if he wanted something, desperately, and couldn't figure out how to ask.

She gave him a hug and held the embrace extra long. She wanted him to understand, without words, that it was going to be okay. That he was okay.

Soon he burst away from her and headed for the bathroom. "Gotta go pee."

"That's fine. Aim carefully. Into the pot," she called after him.

Amanda looked like a lonely orphan girl on the porch steps. "What picture are you going to take?" Rose Marie asked. She brushed the hair out of the little girl's eyes.

Amanda was silent.

"What picture, honey?"

Amanda whined a meaningless sound.

"What's the matter?"

She laid her head in Rose Marie's lap and shook her head. She wasn't her usual spunky self today. Rather, she seemed to be tucked into a faraway pocket. "Don't you feel well?" She ran her fingers over Amanda's forehead. Not too warm.

"We can skip your pictures today, honey. Would you like some juice?"

Amanda, her head now buried deeper into Rose Marie's lap, nodded. She must be tired. Soon it would be nap time.

Shortly after lunch, the doorbell rang.

"Mrs. Lustov," the gray-haired man said. "Jim Baxter. I'm Anna Campbell's father. Hopefully either my daughter or Jake explained that I would pick Chris up."

He was a good-looking man. She wouldn't expect anything different from Anna's dad. The resemblance was there, the pointed chin, the narrow-set eyes.

"Please come in," Rose Marie said.

The children wandered into the living room from the kitchen. "Grandpa," Chris shouted and dashed into Mr. Baxter's arms.

"How are you, little fellow?" Mr. Baxter asked, hugging his grandson.

"Eddie's sick. My mommy's at the hospital."

"Yes, I know. That's why Grandma and I came, to help you and your daddy and mommy until Eddie gets better."

Later, after the children had gone, she stepped out onto the patio. High above her neighbor's roof, an airplane—a dot followed by a trail of white exhaust—moved in silence through the clear evening sky. She watched the smoky exhaust. Its length didn't change—the back end widened into nothingness at the same rate that the plane moved forward, laying down new exhaust.

Moving forward at the front, dissipating at the back. As she watched the plane's contrail, she knew—not so much the kind of knowing she could explain but, rather, the sneaky kind that dwelled deep in her bones and made her underarms clammy— that the goings-on around her weren't like the steady-state plane exhaust. Everything was topsy-turvy—for Eddie, for Dr. Campbell, for Anna, for Chris. Definitely for Chris, since he couldn't understand what was happening.

A pair of dragonflies, stuck together in insect passion, flitted in tandem over the patio railing and down into the cotoneaster. Beyond, a row of daffodils—their dusty green leaves and tight buds waved in the breeze against the dark green backdrop of junipers—had emerged from the dirt for yet another year. At least they were predictable, unaffected by the unknowns around her.

In spite of all the familiar, ordinary things—dragonflies, April flowers, airplane contrails—the potentially expectant, wonderfully hopeful mood of early spring evaded her, replaced by achy unease.

Chapter 16

Jake

From the outside, their house looked like most of the others on the block—two-story colonial skirted by leggy evergreens and framed by mature oak trees and the lilac bushes Anna loved so much and the ash sapling he planted last year. Terracotta red bricks faced the lower level in the front—an awkward attempt to lend a sense of strength to the structure—and, above, the wooden siding was painted the color of vanilla ice cream.

He pulled into the driveway and parked his van beside a shiny new Taurus. Must be his in-laws' rental car. He set the gear shift in park and pulled the keys from the ignition. The shingles on the corner of the garage were curled. The whole roof would need replacing in a year or two, an expensive fact he tried to ignore. At least the grass was healthy and the garden easy to maintain.

While the outside looked like the neighbors' houses, the inside was very different. Not in appearance—they all had similar floor plans, with living room, dining room, family room, and half bath down, three bedrooms and two baths up—but in attitude. The darkness that now hovered over his house seemed to suffocate Jake. Slowly he walked from the driveway to the back door, stopping to kick a dead oak twig that had fallen on the concrete. The stick flew into the nearest forsythia bush, zigzagged through the yellow blossoms, and finally landed on the dirt. None of the children in the other houses were critically ill.

He stepped into the back entry and briefly studied his face—its exaggerated creases, its swollen eyes—in the mirror. He shook his head, took a deep breath, and called, "Hi, everyone, I'm home."

Chris rocketed around the corner from the kitchen and leaped into his arms. "Daddy," he screamed.

"Whoa, tiger," Jake moaned, hobbling backward to keep from falling. "You're sure full of vinegar." He tried to sound upbeat, to hide his misery from Chris, but the lilting swing in his voice rang hollow and insincere to even his own ears. He set his son on the floor.

"Grandma and Grandpa are here, but Mommy's not," Chris said.

"Yeah, I know. Mommy's still at the hospital with Eddie. She misses you a lot." They walked into the kitchen. "We'll call her in a few minutes."

"Hi, Jake. This is all so terrible." Anna's mother stood at the stove, one of her daughter's aprons tied around her waist. She looked ten years older than when Jake last saw her, just a week ago.

"We're so glad you could come, Eleanor," he said and brushed her cheek with a kiss. She bore the same scent as his wife, something like gardenias with a touch of cinnamon.

"Hi, Jim," Jake said, walking to the kitchen table.

His father-in-law lowered his newspaper and held out his hand. "So sorry. I wish our visit were under more pleasant circumstances."

Jake told them what had happened, explained meningitis, described how Eddie needed a ventilator to breathe. He was vague about the future.

Chris tugged at his father's arm. "Come on," he whined, pulling him toward the family room.

"You two rest for a while. We'll call you when dinner's ready. About a half hour," Eleanor said.

He settled into the La-Z-Boy. Chris clambered into his lap. Along with the smell of simmering onions and garlic, tomatoes and chicken, his mother-in-law's voice, a lower and slower version of his wife's, drifted from the kitchen. It carried the same clipped rhythm, the same practical message, the same reverberant tone. For a fleeting moment, he thought it was Anna cooking dinner. Then he remembered.

Ordinarily, he would have been ravenous after a long day at work, would have savored a good meal. Tonight, however, the odors, the clanging pans, the din of the television, even his mother-in-law's efficient helpfulness, seemed intrusive and wildly irritating. They battered his senses and yanked him from where he wanted to be.

He shrugged off the unwelcome interruptions—they were yet more of today's many annoyances—and called toward the kitchen, "Smells great."

His father-in-law leaned against the door frame between the kitchen and family room. "Chris and I spent the late afternoon in the garden, pulling weeds. I tried to teach him the difference between dandelions and daisies. Poor little guy got bored . . ." The clatter of dishes and the *ding-ding-ding-ding* from the microwave oven hid the last of Jim's words as he returned to the kitchen.

Jake laid his head against the back of the La-Z-Boy and let the familiarity of the room glide over him. The overflowing toy box. The LEGOs scattered on the floor. The coffee table heaped with Chris's books, Anna's decorating magazines, and his orthopedic surgery journals, the flotsam of their family life. Against the back wall stood the piano that Anna played when she was moody. "Beethoven Sonata number five," she would sing out right before her fingers hit the keys. He never understood who the announcement was for. Certainly not for him.

An old cotton diaper, wrinkled and tinted ivory with dried

milk stains, hung over the arm of the rocking chair. It seemed like a memorial to his wife and their baby. Anna used that cloth to mop up when she fed and burped Eddie. Spitting up milk may have been the last normal thing Eddie had done. He adjusted the back of the La-Z-Boy to the recline position and arranged Chris on his chest.

Although it seemed like two and a half decades, it had been only two and a half days since Eddie had gotten sick. That night, Anna would have been here in the family room. She would have used the phone just around the corner in the kitchen when she called him. He closed his eyes. Imprinted against the black, he saw a shadowy image of Anna with Eddie in her arms, speaking on the phone.

He leaned his cheek against the top of Chris's head. If only he could rewind time to three days ago, he'd play that evening over again with a different script, one in which Anna would recognize how sick Eddie really was. He'd ask Anna more questions about Eddie, would try to get a better sense for how he was acting. Is he nursing okay? he would ask. Does he seem to hurt anywhere? Is he playful? Can you make him laugh?

Maybe he shouldn't have reassured her that Eddie was okay. But, based on what she'd told him, he sounded fine. And, there was the issue of Anna's never-ending anxiety about the boys. There was no way he could have known what was really going on. If only he'd been home. If only he'd asked more questions. If only Anna had communicated more accurately how Eddie was acting. If only. If only.

He looked down at Chris, now sprawled across his belly like a rag doll, a limp arm here, a languid leg there. Tiny blood vessels branched like winter dogwood over his closed eyelids. The words "University of Michigan" emblazoned on his T-shirt moved with his breathing. Chris was sucking his thumb.

"Tell me what you and Grandpa did today," Jake whispered.

Chris slowly shook his head, his eyes still clamped shut, his thumb still hooked inside his mouth.

The poor guy, he thought. The poor, poor, poor little guy.

Chris had stopped sucking his thumb almost two years ago. Last night he'd even wet the bed and had woken up shrieking.

He felt the tickle of Chris's hair against his arm. Too much change. Mom gone. Baby brother gone. Dad a wreck. Grandparents, nearly strangers, here. He hadn't even been to Rose Marie's house on his usual schedule.

He wished Anna would come home. Chris needs her so much, he thought. More than Eddie, right now. First she failed to see Eddie's illness and now she has abandoned Chris. He clinched his jaw. Anna abandon one of her children? No, she would never do that. Everything was just so screwed up.

They sat around the kitchen table, his mother-in-law in Anna's seat, his father-in-law across from Chris. The serving dishes were passed in silence. Even Chris was quiet.

The room seemed hollow, the emptiness enormous. He felt as if he were deep inside a cave and its walls wavered around him.

"Tell Grandma how much you liked the chicken," Jake said.

Chris said nothing.

"Didn't you like your dinner?" Jim asked, leaning toward his grandson.

Eleanor laid down her fork. "Look, the poor little fellow doesn't want to talk right now. I think that's just fine."

Jake agreed.

While Anna's parents loaded the dinnerware into the dishwasher, Jake called to Chris, "Let's phone Mom."

He dialed the number to the visitors' lounge and waited for someone to find Anna.

"Hello?" Her voice was wooden.

"Hi. Chris wants to talk to you." He held the phone to Chris's ear. His son wiggled in his lap and then suddenly quieted.

"Mommy?" he whispered.

Jake tipped the receiver toward his own ear so they could both hear.

"Yes, honey." Anna was crying. "Chrisy, I love you very much," she said. "I'll be home soon."

His son's head nodded as if someone had offered him a Popsicle. He chased Chris's ear with the receiver to keep it in listening range.

Finally, Jake said, "We should let Mommy rest now. Tell her good-bye."

"Bye."

Jake set Chris on the floor. "Honey," he said to Anna, "I hope you have a good night. Maybe tomorrow night you can sleep here."

It was a long time before Anna spoke. "Not if Eddie's still in the ICU. He's too sick. I can't leave him." He heard the rumblings of the lounge in the background. Finally, she whispered, "Good-bye, Jake."

"Do you have any decaf?" Anna's mother called from the kitchen after they had finally gotten Chris to bed.

"Yes, in the cupboard above the microwave," Jake answered. "Want some?"

"Sure. Thanks."

Some evenings Anna would slip off to the living room, where he would find her, seated here on the sofa, her legs folded under her bottom, a book resting on her lap, her eyes staring into the wallpaper.

"What're you thinking about?" he would ask when he found her like that.

"Nothing," she would say with a sigh.

The living room was Anna's place, free from the clutter of the family room. The lamp with the gold braid on the shade was a wedding gift from his medical school roommate; the clay pot was a souvenir—more expensive than he thought was reasonable—from their trip to Mexico; the sofa, with its puke green floral upholstery, had belonged to Anna's parents. He built the bookshelves last summer to her specifications and painted them Navaho white to match the walls. To him this room wasn't comfortable. Its stiff formality reminded him of rose bushes.

Anna's mother set a cup of coffee in his hands. "Here you go. Now that Chris isn't around, tell us more about Eddie." Her face was grim, echoing that of Anna's dad.

How could he explain it to them? He sipped his decaf and answered their questions as best he could. "He needs the ventilator because he doesn't take breaths on his own. The machine pushes air into his lungs.

"No, we don't know how long he'll be in the ICU.

"Yes, there's still hope." He wasn't sure what they meant by hope. Anna's mother sobbed into a handkerchief. Her father dabbed at his eyes with his fingertips. Jake didn't tell them that, if he survived, Eddie stood a good chance of having neurologic residua. Now wasn't a good time for them to learn that Eddie might end up blind or deaf or mentally retarded.

Later, his eyes half closed, his brain half asleep, he leaned over the bathroom sink and scraped his toothbrush over his teeth. Why did this have to happen? He yearned for the time when their lives were comfortably on an even keel.

Robotically he stepped into the faded aqua scrub pants he used as pajama bottoms and crawled into bed. Until two nights ago, he had never slept in this room alone, except the night after Anna delivered Eddie. Anna often slept here alone— every third or fourth night, while he was on call. He nuzzled his face into her pillow and caught the faint spicy scent that usually lay buried deep in her hair.

The room seemed to throb with her presence, which only heightened her absence. She had sewn the bedspread, choosing fabric to match the painting she bought at the art fair. She had found the four handmade felt dolls at a yard sale and mounted them in the shadow boxes that hung over their dresser. She had rescued the oak chair from a secondhand store and refinished it. So much of her was here, yet the important part—the real part—was missing, more than the furniture she chose to decorate the place, more than the pictures and bed linens. Her spirit was missing, the way she laughed at the jokes he brought home from the operating room, the way her fingers stroked his bare back, her gentle, knowing smile.

Light from the hallway filtered into the bedroom and splayed over the table beside her pillow, dimly illuminating the book she was currently reading. A sheet of Kleenex, folded in half, protruded from between the pages. Her slippers lay, one crossed on top of the other in an X, under the desk where she would have kicked them. Her white satin robe, limp and ghostly, was draped over the door to the bathroom. If only she would walk into the room right now, would sit on the bed beside him, would set her hand on his cheek. If only. If only.

He stared at the ceiling, at the swirls in the plaster. How could someone who was so uncommonly observant not see that something was badly wrong with her baby? She always knew where he left his keys, his checkbook, his Visa card, his hammer. Whenever he was low on deodorant, she bought a couple cans for him. She knew when Bullet's kitty litter needed changing, when they were nearly out of milk. She had even spotted a patch of morel mushrooms that sprouted in the mulch beside the back fence last summer. This was different, not minor little managerial duties. This was the most important thing in their lives, the well-being of their child, and they had both missed the ominous signs that threatened Eddie's existence.

Jake turned on his side, dragging the sheet and blanket as he rolled. Ordinarily Anna's body would have anchored the covers. The room was unbearably solemn.

An hour later, he was still awake. Every minute of the last three days had played through his head, with answers to none of the many questions that nagged him. He tossed back the bed covers and wandered, bare feet padding on the carpet, down the hallway past the open door to Chris's room. He stopped at the doorway to Eddie's room. His father-in-law's snoring burbled from the hide-a-bed downstairs.

He didn't switch on the light in Eddie's room, didn't need to see the details. The crib rails, the footboard, a knit blanket wadded in the corner as if it were tossed in a storm—no different than last week, yet very different from last week. By day, the foam diamonds, squares, rectangles, and circles of the mobile that dangled over the mattress were bright crayon colors. Now they were shades of gray, seemingly suspended by cobwebs and eerily still, except for the diamond that, caught in the current of his movements, twisted almost imperceptibly to the left. It was here that Anna had found their baby nearly lifeless. He imagined the look on her face when she spotted Eddie lying there—her eyes wide and disbelieving, her lips parted in terror. He could hear the shriek that surely sputtered from deep inside her.

If he had been home, he would have seen the first stages of the chalky color sick babies get, would have felt the weak tone of his muscles and heard the change in his cry. If he had been home, they would have taken Eddie to the hospital that night; the antibiotic would have been started at least eight hours earlier than it had been. Eight hours is merely a heartbeat in a lifetime, but it's the difference between life or death, damaged or normal, in a baby with meningitis.

But, he hadn't been home the night it all happened. Because of that, and because Anna hadn't recognized the extent of his illness, Eddie might die. Or, worse in many ways, be terribly handicapped. During his pediatric rotation as a medical student, he had started an IV on Marcus, a kid with microcephaly from a congenital infection. The little guy's virus-wracked brain didn't grow, so his head didn't grow, either. He looked like a monkey, with big ears, a forehead that slowly sloped back from his dull, blue eyes, and a bewildered, uncomprehending look on his face. In another era, the boy could have been the pinhead in a sideshow. Eddie might end up like that, a ten-year-old unable to walk or talk, a boy with a feeding tube dangling from the side of his abdomen into which he and Anna would squirt thick, milky formula.

If only he had asked Anna the right questions, had taken her phone call seriously. It had been, after all, a call for help. He tried to imagine a son with no language, no way to express pleasure, no ability to relate to other human beings in meaningful ways. He had heard parents speak in dreamy tones about the joy their handicapped children brought to their lives. He could see no joy whatsoever in Eddie being a vegetable.

With a bad neurologic outcome, Eddie would grow bigger and more difficult to handle. And then, he would go through puberty and be a baby in the body of a teenager, with facial hair and pubic hair and a man's penis—a useless, pitiable member. His grunts and groans, uttered in a deep, adult voice, would sound like a jungle animal. All because Jake hadn't been home that night, because he hadn't understood that his son was terribly ill.

As he left Eddie's room, he passed the easy chair, lost in the shadows, where Anna used to sit and nurse Eddie in the middle of the night. It was empty. Everything, the chair, Eddie's room, their bed, his life, seemed indescribably empty.

Chapter 17

Anna

The nurse, pen in hand, stepped toward Eddie. She pulled a scrap of paper from her pocket, smoothed the folds, read the lab report, and wrote on the bedside chart, *WBC 9,400; 61 polys, 4 bands, 31 lymphs, 1 mono.*

Anna watched as the nurse printed the letters. It was a foreign language, strange words that, as the nurse had explained, meant different kinds of white blood cells. She wanted to understand these numbers, as they seemed to be a key to Eddie's improvement. The WBC number from yesterday morning was 10,300 and by evening was 11,200.

"It's going up. Is that bad?" she had asked Dr. Farley. He explained that numbers like that weren't really different.

"How much do you weigh?" he asked. "About one thirty or so?"

"Close enough," she answered.

"It's like your weight—one thirty or one thirty-two or one twenty-eight. No difference," he said. "You go up or down by a couple pounds every day. Same with Eddie's white count. A thousand or two either way doesn't mean anything."

The nurse folded the paper with Eddie's numbers and

slipped it back into her pocket. "Eddie has a visitor," she said. "Do you want to see her now?"

"Who is it?" Maybe her mother. She had spoken to her parents briefly when they first arrived, but she didn't want to see either of them yet. She wasn't ready to answer their questions— the ones about what happened to Eddie. Why didn't you call the pediatrician? they would wonder. It would have been the easy, logical thing to do. Why didn't Jake come home when you and Eddie were ill? How could you sleep through the night without checking on a sick baby? She had no explanations they would accept.

She could lie. She could tell them Eddie had been fine when she put him to bed, had taken his last feeding with no trouble, hadn't had a fever, had smiled and gurgled as she laid him in his crib. But, eventually, they would find out what really happened. Besides, lies wouldn't change anything that mattered. If only she could live that night all over again, with the lies becoming the truth the second time through, with Eddie still healthy.

Why did Jake have to be at the hospital that night? She remembered the afternoon at the rest stop near the Mackinac Bridge. He had lost Chris then. Now they would lose Eddie because of Jake. Lose Eddie? Lose her baby? She closed her eyes against the thought, stared into the darkness. Chris had been found. Eddie wouldn't be lost, either.

"Her name is Elizabeth Tucker." The nurse hung the bedside chart on the end of his crib. "Says she works with you."

"Oh, yes. Elizabeth. Sure. Let her in."

She watched Elizabeth walk past the nurses' station, past Charlotte's moaning teenaged daughter in the corner bed. Elizabeth seemed to be a mirage, a page from a Talbots' catalog in her tweed pantsuit and maroon neck scarf. Yet here she was in the ICU, her shining black hair pulled away from her face, her eyes framed by mascara. Elizabeth belonged in the other world, the one that seemed a million years ago, a million miles away.

She glanced at her watch. Elizabeth had come directly from work, was still dressed in her teaching clothes. She looked at her own lap, at the wrinkles in her pants, at the grease smudge from a packet of French fries. She wished away her rumpled, grimy clothes and oily, straggly hair.

"Anna, honey." Elizabeth slipped her arm around her shoulders and pulled her close.

She had never felt Elizabeth's body. It was soft and warm, even through her business attire. Touching Elizabeth, feeling her humanness, was like walking in a dream.

"This is unbelievably horrible. I don't know what to say." Elizabeth continued to hold her and together their bodies swayed—a bit to the left, a bit to the right.

She stepped back from the crib, leaving Elizabeth at the metal rail. Her friend leaned toward Eddie. "Poor baby," she murmured as she wiped a tear from her eye. The scent of Elizabeth's hand lotion, like a field of waving lavender, rose from the fingers that patted the flannel blanket covering Eddie's legs. She stroked the patch of cheek between the strips of tape that held his breathing tube in place. She didn't back away from him, didn't think he was too freaky to touch.

Elizabeth—neat, organized—seemed terribly out of place here, didn't belong among blood stains and tracheal secretions and urine bags. Rather, she and Elizabeth should be together at the school, planning field trips for their students, logging grades into the computer, assisting nervous youths as they practiced making telephone appointments in English.

"What's happening to my class?" Anna tried to grab a distant memory. "Are the kids okay?" She couldn't name a single student right now.

"Well . . ." Elizabeth paused as she reached for Anna's hand and laced their fingers together. Her skin was smooth as lamb's leather. "Bonita has stepped up to the plate nicely—I understand she's working well with the subs. It's not the same without you, but it's satisfactory. Maybe a C plus." Elizabeth dropped Anna's hand and then straightened her scarf. "Don't worry about them. They'll limp along until you get back. You need to focus on Eddie. And yourself."

Anna sank into the chair beside the crib. She and Elizabeth

seemed to be acting in a mind-twister movie. Nothing was real. Everything was distorted. Irregular. Out of sync.

"And, how's Chris?" Elizabeth asked. "This must be hard on him."

Anna wrapped her arms around her chest. If only she could wrap them around Chris. He was only three, not much more than a baby himself. He needed her, too. "Well, yes, it's hard on him." She shook her head, hoping to rid her mind of the bad-mother thoughts. "My parents are here. He begs for me to come home, but I can't leave Eddie."

"Can he visit here?"

"They don't allow kids his age in the ICU. Besides, I think he shouldn't see Eddie like this. It'd scare him too much."

Elizabeth patted Anna on the shoulder. "Maybe he can visit later."

"Yes, later. I miss him so much. I wish I could hack myself down the middle . . . one side for Eddie and one for Chris."

"Ugh, that's pretty gruesome." Elizabeth twisted her mouth and wiped her hand across her eyes. "Soon, I bet, you'll figure out how to halve your time between them, not halve yourself."

"I hope so."

"I brought you something." Elizabeth handed her a package wrapped in brown paper with a huge, floppy bow of lacy ribbon. "Here's something to distract your thoughts for a while. When Eddie goes home, we'll work on some of these."

Anna's hands trembled as she untied the bow. With her finger-nail, she slit the Scotch tape that held the wrapping paper together. Inside was a craft magazine, its cover decorated with pictures of brightly painted chairs—one was cobalt blue with clouds across the backrest, another was rainbow colors, the third was ink black with a white and yellow daisy on the seat.

"Great." She strained to sound cheerful. This woman, beautiful, thoughtful Elizabeth, was a friend and yet a stranger. Did she know her? Had they ever laughed together? Whispered secrets? Figured out projects? She felt herself float up into the corner of the room where she could peer down on the two of them sitting shoulder to shoulder beside Eddie's crib.

"See . . ." Elizabeth rubbed her fingertips over the rainbow chair. "I thought we could do something like this to that ugly thing in your basement." They called it the Old King Cole chair, the huge wooden throne Jake had found in the back reaches of their basement after they moved in.

Anna nodded. Maybe someday she could paint furniture again.

Now Elizabeth had gone, carrying the dream of the other world with her. Anna curled up in the chair beside the crib. Outside, the sun had set, leaving a tangerine halo that outlined the building across the street. The light in one of the building's windows flicked out. Someone was leaving work for the day.

Soon Eddie was going to be dead. She pictured him, pale and lifeless, inside the toy-box-turned-coffin that was covered with the nodding violets. She had decorated the box to hold her children's toys. It would be the perfect size for him.

Or maybe they would make him a real casket. Jake could build it and she could paint Eddie's favorite things on the lid— a stack of graham crackers, his one-eyed teddy bear, the mobile that dangled over his crib at home. She'd put the teddy bear in the casket with him. The bottom would be hard. He needed something to cushion his body from the wooden floor. The blanket Jake's mother had knit would be good for that, a nice soft bed for her dead baby. Where was that blanket, the one Eddie liked to suck on? Probably still in his crib. What outfit would he wear? She tried to think of the clothes in his drawers, but could remember only the little suits Chris had had as a baby. Didn't Eddie have any clothes of his own? Poor, second-born Eddie with his secondhand wardrobe.

First-born Chris. That had been a long pregnancy. She had been nauseated, exhausted, weepy for months and months and months. With each passing day, the baby grew, her belly bloated, her ankles and hands swelled. She ended up starting her maternity leave three weeks earlier than originally scheduled. Her pregnancy with Eddie had been completely different. She had more energy, gained less weight, worked until two days before he was born. Boisterous Chris had been hard on her from the moment of his conception. Placid Eddie, even as a fetus, was an unending joy.

Something was happening on her left; something was moving. She turned her head. It was Eddie. He was jerking. His legs kicked at the air and his arms shook as if he were working a pump handle.

She leaped from her chair and grabbed his flailing hands. "He's having another seizure," she screamed. Where was his nurse? She held Eddie's arms, trying to quell the spasms. "Another seizure," she screamed again.

The nurse rounded the corner. "Dr. Farley," she shouted.

In three breaths, he was at her side. "Let's give him . . ."

Anna couldn't hear the rest of his words. Another nurse was guiding her toward the visitors' lounge.

"Why don't you wait out there? You can come back as soon as things settle down. It'll only be a few minutes."

"No." Anna stopped. She felt the nudge of the nurse's arm. She didn't want to languish in the lounge. "Please let me stay."

"Mrs. Campbell, you know what these seizures are like. They aren't fun to watch. We're giving him more meds to stop this one. When it's under control, we'll come for you."

She looked back at his crib but couldn't see Eddie. All she saw were the back sides of one nurse and two doctors.

In the lounge, she edged into her chair, the one with the pillow and the blanket Jake had brought. Another seizure. The drugs they had given him didn't stop the seizures. What was going to happen to him? What was the infection doing to his brain? What happens to a baby without a brain?

She drew her fingers through her hair. Maybe they should just throw him away, like a bruised tomato or an ear of corn with a borer stuck between the kernels. Eddie was a cull. She didn't want him anymore. She and Jake could make a new baby, a perfect one. She stared at her wedding ring, at the way it circled her finger, and began sobbing. How could she think that? Eddie was her precious baby. How could she want to make him go away?

His smile was precious, as was the way he gurgled when he heard her voice. His little hands were precious in the way they wrapped around her finger and grabbed at her hair and palmed Cheerios from the high chair tray. The first time he rolled over, he scared himself. After he flopped on his back, his eyes grew huge and he gasped, seemingly in terror. But then his body relaxed and he seemed proud as a prince at his new trick. No, he couldn't go away. He needed to stay with her, to stay her precious little baby.

She wrapped her blanket around her head, leaned against the arm of the chair, and wept.

Chapter 18

Jake

The resemblance was uncanny—the slow twist of her hands as she spoke, the sultry tilt of her head when she laughed, the silky sweep of her hair, the button at the tip of her nose. A wave of melancholy washed over him, alternately drawing him to her, then pulling him away. It was as if Monica were here in the hospital cafeteria, sitting across the table from him.

It had been less than a decade since he last saw Monica, but it seemed like a millennium. He blinked his eyes and stared out the window. A cardinal flew away from the roof and into the sunset. He tried to erase the image of Monica in front of him. It wouldn't go away.

The woman at the table wasn't Monica, though. Her identification badge read BETSY BLOOM, MD.

"Jake," one of the other doctors said. "Meet Betsy, the new surgery intern."

This woman, Dr. Betsy Bloom, was about the same age as Monica, back then. When she spoke, her voice bounced with the optimism of youth. Its tone, while discussing her patients, was competent, alluring: "Mr. Thornton's hemoglobin is seven point two . . . And his chest X-ray shows heart failure . . . So I ordered one unit of packed red cells and forty of Lasix . . ." Everything about her was familiar in a distant, aching, haunting way. When he looked at her, he felt a fragrant autumn breeze blow across his face. He couldn't take his eyes off her.

How old would Monica be now? He calculated in his head: She was almost twenty-four when they first met. That was eight years ago. The effects of age would have changed her, deepened the lines along her nose, drawn delicate crow's feet beside her eyes, nudged the flesh beneath her chin southward. Her skin had been soft as velvet. It would be even softer now.

"Where'd you say you're from?" he asked. It was a dumb question, but maybe she was related to Monica.

"I didn't say," Betsy answered. "I'm from Oregon—graduated from med school in Portland, grew up in Pendleton."

"Well, you remind me of a person I knew from the Thumb. Thought maybe you're a cousin, or something."

"Nope, no relatives in the Thumb or anywhere near Michigan, for that matter."

He shrugged, raising only his right shoulder. How could two unrelated people be so similar?

He reached for the salt, she for a napkin. His hand, gripping the shaker, brushed against her wrist. The warmth of her skin lingered on his knuckles.

The other doctors at the table excused themselves. The second-year surgery resident gathered his empty food containers and then paused for a moment beside him.

"How're things with your son? Off the ventilator yet?"

"Not yet, but he's making progress in that direction." Jake shoveled another forkful of lasagna into his mouth.

"Your son is ill?" Betsy Bloom asked. Her eyebrows were knit into her question just as Monica's had been when she was wondering. "He's on a ventilator?"

He stared at her, trying to anticipate her reaction to the story of Eddie and his illness. She wasn't Monica. This was a woman he didn't know at all, even though she seemed like a clone of Monica.

"Yeah, he has meningitis." His fingers twirled a paper clip inside his pants pocket. She isn't Monica, he told himself, again.

When he finished his dinner, he shoved his chair away from the table. "We'd better get back to work."

Later that evening, he lay on the call room bed in his scrubs and stared at the slit of light from beneath the bathroom door. Soon the on-call OR crew would arrive and he would have to do an internal fixation on a man with a broken hip.

He wondered where Monica was, now. Last he heard, she was working for an HMO in Maine. At this very moment, somewhere out there, she might be wondering about him. The telepathy between them had been eerie. At times it seemed as if they were wired through the same fuse box. Maybe that connection, long idle, was still operating. Maybe she, too, yearned for the old days. Regrets about him might haunt her, cloud her reason, overwhelm her in the middle of the night when she couldn't sleep.

He could try to find her. What was her name now? Was she still Monica Daley? Maybe she had a married name. He hadn't tried to find her before—had decided the Book of Monica was closed forever, never to be opened again. But, things had changed. Eddie was desperately sick. Anna was going crazy. Monica could, as she had at one time, soothe every one of his raw nerves, could rub away the pain.

He shook his head against the pillow and turned onto his side. His knees nearly met his chest. Keeping the Book of Monica closed seemed a good idea. He was married, was a father. He had made a commitment to Anna and to the boys and he intended to keep it. Now, he needed to get whatever sleep he could before the OR crew arrived. He turned to his other side.

And yet, the touch of Betsy's wrist still seared his hand. If only, somehow and somewhere safe, he could see Monica again, could bury his face in the willowy scent of her hair, could fold himself into the warm softness of her body.

They had been classmates in medical school, anatomy lab

partners during their freshman year. He had first spoken to her as they pulled the waxy canvas off the stiff, naked body of their cadaver.

"I'll take that," he had said, referring to the smelly, heavy canvas she held in her hands.

For a long time, they had joked about those words. Monica had thought he meant something quite different, something more personal to her that he would take. "You're right," he had said many times, "I didn't mean that stinky, formaldehyde-soaked tarp at all."

Compared to the girlfriends he had had in college, Monica was completely different. The other girls were goals—rings on the merry-go-round of college life that he might successfully snatch if he was lucky enough, fast enough, tried hard enough, leaned over far enough.

Monica, on the other hand, wasn't a distant target; she had been a part of him. In biochemistry class as they learned about DNA—two threads of nucleotides twisted together, building the scaffold upon which all manner of life emerged—he had thought, That's us. The two of them seemed to be strings of organic mutuality, growing and swaying and turning, the dance of living. He considered them to be useless apart, capable of wonderful, amazing results together.

He rolled onto his back, straightened his knees. If Monica were here now, he could tell her about Eddie. She would understand. He wouldn't have to explain the lab results or the medical lingo the doctors and nurses used. Unlike talking to Anna, he could talk to Monica about Eddie's illness without being an interpreter.

That fall, on sunny Sundays, he and Monica took study breaks in Gallup Park. Hand in hand they wandered the paths along the Huron River, stopping on the footbridges to watch the water—it was the color of gunmetal—pitch and swirl and glide as it flowed relentlessly toward Lake Erie.

He told her about the toboggan slide he and his brothers rode during winter afternoons, about his love of rabbit hunting as a kid. She told him about her parents' house in Bad Axe, about the Pointe aux Barques lighthouse near the tip of the Thumb. They imagined themselves as the doctors they would become, possessing the skills to heal people.

They imitated the squawks of the Canada geese that lived in the park, watched a gaggle of the smoke-colored, arrogant birds waddle away indignantly.

"What do you suppose we said to them?" he asked, slipping an arm around her shoulders.

"I think . . ." She leaned her body into his. "I think we said, 'You're losers.' "

For the first time in his life, he noticed wildflowers as she pointed to the yellow-as-an-egg-yolk goldenrod, the periwinkle chicory blossoms, the white umbrellas of Queen Anne's lace. Together they watched the hawthorn leaves turn from kelly green to straw to brown before dropping to the ground. They saw the crimson fruit that dangled like Christmas tree ornaments from the leafless branches of the high bush cranberry trees. When he was with her, the crows suddenly seemed blacker than black and the egrets whiter than white.

Although at the time he didn't think consciously about permanence, he had assumed in an abstract way that the sense of wholeness between them would go on forever. It was like the developmental milestones of childhood. When kids have gained the neural and motor connections to walk, they walk and never stop walking. Same thing with talking. He figured loving worked the same way and he had finally gotten there.

Then it began to unravel. He wasn't sure what happened. In looking back, he thought it might have started when Monica failed the final exam in gross anatomy. He had scored the third-highest grade in the class. She refused to discuss the test, but he learned about her failure from another classmate. Gradually, in little ebbs and swells, she turned away from him. When her father's colon cancer relapsed, she didn't want to talk about it. She said he'd surely respond to the chemotherapy, so there was no point in saying anything more.

On a Wednesday shortly after the beginning of the second semester, she didn't come to class. Same on Thursday. That night he took a six-pack of 7Up and a bag of popcorn to her apartment, assuming she was sick.

He knocked on her door, using the syncopated rap they had invented. From behind the door he heard movement and then the click of the dead bolt sliding back. The door opened a crack, enough for him to see the pink patches on her face and her red, swollen eyes.

"What's wrong?"

"Nothing." Her voice was a whisper.

"What do you mean 'nothing'? You look awful." He pushed against the door, tried to open it wider. It didn't budge. "Are you sick?"

Silence. She tried to shut the door, but he had wedged his boot against the frame.

"Can I come in?" On top of his confusion, he was now becoming frightened.

"No."

He set the 7Up on the porch rail to free up one hand. "Monica, something is very wrong. Tell me."

She pulled a Kleenex from her pocket and blew her nose. "I need a break from school. Need to figure a few things out. Please go away."

He pulled his boot from the doorway and the heavy wooden door slammed shut. He sat on the porch steps, his head in both hands. She was on the other side of the door but seemed light-years beyond his reach. What was going on?

Later, she didn't answer his phone calls, nor the doorbell, nor his impassioned letters. She had vanished like a shadow into the fog. Finally he called her parents. "Monica's fine," her mother said, "please don't call her again."

Permanent gloom enveloped him as if he'd been dunked in a pool of dirty oil. He couldn't sleep, lay awake night after night and wondered where she was, what she was doing, what he could have done to help her, why she refused to talk to him.

He felt like half a person, as if someone had torn off one leg and one arm, leaving him bleeding and unbalanced and alone. He wandered the paths of Gallup Park and secretly hoped she'd step out of the bushes. He no longer saw the birds or the flowers or the leaves. He saw only gray. The ripples in the Huron River no longer danced along the surface, but now seemed to drill downward, ever deeper into the murky water. Away. Always moving away.

He mentioned her to his brother.

"She's pretty special, huh?" Luke had said.

"She is. And she's pretty gone right now."

Luke must have told their grandmother, because she sent him a flowery card, with a note in her wobbly script that read: *Jakey, girls are like streetcars . . . if you miss one, keep waiting at the corner, because another one will be coming down the tracks in just a little while.*

He turned over on the call room bed. The plastic mattress cover crunched as if he had rolled on a mound of foam pellets. He looked at his watch. What was taking the OR crew so long to get things set up?

And where was Monica now? Several years after she left, he learned she had returned to medical school in Ohio, had completed her studies, and entered a pediatric residency in Boston. Was she still in Massachusetts?

His pager rang. Its jangle jolted him awake, the sound first lurching forward, then tumbling backward. Maybe it would go away. He rolled over. The pager rang again. He sat up in bed, pressed the answer button, pressed the light button, read the message. "READY IN THE OR IN TEN MINUTES. IS THE PERMIT SIGNED?"

He leaned back against the pillow, his mind aching for more sleep.

His pager rang yet again. Again, he fumbled to read the screen. This time it said, "YOUR SON HAD A SEIZURE. YOUR WIFE NEEDS TO SPEAK WITH YOU."

He shoved the pager back into its holster. Sitting on the edge of the mattress, he clutched his head and then rubbed his ears. He didn't want to talk to her. She'd be a basket case, wouldn't listen to what he said, wouldn't believe him if she did. He trudged out the call room door. First he'd stop in the pediatric ICU to check on Eddie, then he'd head to the OR.

"And, yes," he called into the empty hallway. "Yes, the goddamned permit has been signed."

Chapter 19

Rose Marie

An island of sanity in a sea of craziness. That was how each weekend was for her, uninterrupted quiet, just right for letting her thoughts tumble against each other as they sorted themselves into some kind of sense. Today was a good day to be Friday. She would be ready for a break tomorrow.

Only three kids came today, an easygoing transition to the weekend. Poor little Eddie was still in the hospital. Even after talking with Anna, she couldn't imagine what he looked like, too sick to eat, needed a machine to breathe. Chris was at home with Anna's parents; he'd soon drive them nuts with a hundred questions and a million schemes.

And, now, Amanda was sick.

Last night, after she returned home from a run to the grocery store for peanut butter and Swiss cheese, the message light on the answering machine was blinking.

"She has a fever and vomited her dinner." Amanda's mother had sounded tired, or exasperated, on the recording. "I'll stay home from work in the morning to take her to the doctor."

Rose Marie replayed the answering machine message twice to be sure she heard it right, that Amanda had been vomiting.

Food poisoning? Had she fed something bad to Amanda? She reviewed the menu from yesterday. Chili. It didn't fizz when the can opener broke through the lid. Had she sliced hot dogs into the chili? No. The Oreo cookies were from a freshly opened package and the apple juice was pasteurized and only two days old. She herself had drunk a glassful and it was fine. Even the milk had been from a new carton. The other kids weren't ill, so whatever made Amanda sick must not have come from her house.

The idea hit her like a splash of ice water. What about meningitis? Could Amanda have that? Jake told her meningitis wasn't catching. At least, he thought it wasn't. She checked Roger's dictionary again and the description of "meningitis" was as she remembered. Nothing about vomiting. It talked about fever and headache and stiff neck, but not vomiting. She decided Amanda must have some kind of stomach flu.

She tried to call Amanda's mother earlier this morning, but no one answered. Maybe they were at the doctor's.

Now Davey was working on a construction project in the sandbox. He liked to build sand cities, with towers and roads and little escape tunnels. Sawyer was running a toy dump truck up and down the sand hills Davey built. Meghan was tying leaves into Beefeater's collar. She got the wet ones to stay under his chain but the dry ones crumbled in her hands. Soon enough the grass would be green as Ireland and Meghan could string a dandelion necklace for the dog. Maybe, later this summer, they could make hollyhock dolls, as her daughters had when they were little girls. She didn't remember exactly how, except that she would need a fully opened flower and a bulging bud and then somehow would attach them together. It would come to her again when she had the flowers in her hands. In August.

She was still bothered by Amanda. But the other kids, romping around her backyard, were healthy as could be. Should she call the mothers of the other children? What would she tell them? She had no idea what was wrong with Amanda. She'd try to call Amanda's mother again in another hour or so to see how she was doing.

Now Sawyer was driving the dump truck up the bark of the maple tree. The toes of his sneakers dug into the dirt and he held the truck as far above his head as his three-year-old arms would reach. He was murmuring, "Brrrr," his version of motor noise.

She picked at the loose webbing on the lawn chair and surveyed the sky. Giant clouds, almost pewter in the middle and fading to light gray on the edges, tracked from west to east. Looked like rain. The chimelike calls of the blue jays and the twitters of the house sparrows broke the muggy morning air. They seemed more urgent than usual, as if the birds were spreading bad news from treetop to treetop. What could they be nervous about? There were plenty of worms and seeds in the world, no mortgage payments on nests.

Lunch was easy with only three kids. Today would be tuna sandwiches and, for color and vitamins, carrot sticks. For dessert, they'd have leftover Oreo cookies.

While the kids ate, she called Amanda's mother again. Still no answer. It couldn't be too bad if she hadn't heard anything yet.

She set a plate of Oreos on the table. The kids scrambled for the cookies as if they hadn't eaten in a month.

"Hey, use your polite manners," she said with a giggle.

They were good children, safe in her care and yet free to explore her backyard, at least the area inside the fence. She still had the playhouse Roger had built for Sarah and Julie. On the hot summer days to come, she'd drag the plastic wading pool out from the garage. In the fall, she'd have the kids rake the dead maple leaves into a big pile and then let them jump off a lawn chair into the crispy, tobacco-colored heap.

She didn't believe in propping children in front of the television set all day. That would lead to brain rot. She wanted the kids to play outside, to stretch their imaginations, to follow their curiosities, to figure out for themselves how to get along. Her grandmother had it right when, in rapid-fire Ukrainian, she had waved the hem of her apron at Rose Marie and her cousins, calling, "Shoo. Shoo. Go outside. Get the stink blown off you."

The phone rang. She hoped it was Amanda's mother. Or, maybe Sarah. She needed more information about meningitis. The conversation the other night with Sarah's friend—Barbara was her name—hadn't completely settled her worries about the other children.

She picked up the phone.

Instead of Sarah's businesswoman voice or Amanda's mother's high-pitched, pixy chirp, she heard words that soon became lost in the roar of the cement mixer rolling past her house. The sounds toppled together as if spoken by a chorus of mumblers.

Then the voice—a man—said, clear as day, "I understand Edward Campbell and Amanda Goodman attend your day care center. Is that correct?"

She took a deep breath and straightened her shoulders. "Who's calling?" she finally asked.

"As I said, Mrs. Lustov, I'm David Morris from the *Detroit News*. I'm writing a story about the cases of meningitis. These kids attend your day care center, right?"

Detroit News. Why was he calling? Cases of meningitis? Plural? More than one? She perched against the edge of a kitchen chair. "Why do you want to know?" she said.

"Well, since Edward and Amanda are both in the hospital with meningitis, we thought you could tell us a bit about them."

She grabbed the back of her chair to steady herself. Amanda in the hospital, too? With meningitis? What was going on?

"I don't know anything about that," she said and hung up.

She wanted to forget the phone call but it stuck in her head like a rat caught in a trap. The reporter said both Eddie and

Amanda were in the hospital with meningitis. Was he right about that? Why wouldn't he be? He had no reason to call her with a lie.

The children were napping. She decided she'd better call the other mothers to let them know what she had heard. Was it true that both had meningitis? How could she know? She pulled her directory of phone numbers from the desk drawer and began to dial Meghan's mother at work.

A car door slammed from the direction of the driveway and then someone knocked at the breezeway door. She hung up the phone before she finished dialing and headed to the back entry. Maybe it was the meter reader. Maybe the UPS guy. Maybe it was Bill Gates or Senator Levin or Prince Charles of England. Such strange things were happening, the visitor could be anyone. She pulled aside the curtain over the window to the breezeway. Davey's mother stood on the step.

"You're early." Rose Marie used her calmest voice, tried to hide the confusion inside her head.

"You bet." His mother's words were bullets, her voice harsh as lye. "I just heard from Amanda's mother that Eddie and Amanda are both in the hospital. I think I'd better take Davey home."

"Davey's fine. He's napping with the other kids."

"Good," she said, abruptly. Her eyes weren't pearly blue and dancing as usual, but, now, were steel gray and deadly serious. "I'll be more comfortable if he stays home for a few days, at least until this all gets settled." She called Davey's name. "Come on, honey. We're leaving early today."

Rose Marie followed them out the back door. By the time she reached the gate, Davey and his mother were already in the car. It backed out the driveway, turned into the street, and disappeared around the corner.

"Sarah, Amanda's also in the hospital." Rose Marie's fingers clutched the phone receiver. "She has meningitis, too. Just like Eddie."

"Oh, boy."

"A reporter from the *Detroit News* called."

"Mother." Sarah's voice was firm. "You shouldn't talk to re-porters about this."

"Don't worry, I hung up on him."

"Umm . . . that might not have been so smart." Then her daughter added, "Is Amanda okay?"

"I don't know. She was a little out of sorts yesterday after-noon and last night her mother left a message that she had a fever and was vomiting." The phone cord stretched out the sliding door, from the console in the kitchen to her hand as she sat in the lawn chair. Meghan and Sawyer were kicking a soccer ball at the target painted on the garage. "I've tried to call Amanda's mother several times today and haven't been able to reach her. I guess she's at the hospital. Do you think I should bother her there?"

"Mom, you need to get accurate information about this. I still think you should call the health department."

"Sarah, why would they know anything about two kids in the hospital? Besides—and I really hate to say this—they can shut down my day care, you know."

Sarah was silent and then said, "Maybe so, but you need to have your questions answered."

"I'll keep calling Amanda's mother. At least, the other kids are healthy as horses."

She reached both Meghan's and Sawyer's mothers and told them about the call from the reporter.

"I still haven't been able to contact anyone about Amanda yet, so I really don't know what's going on," she said to both mothers.

Each asked about her child. "Both kids look terrific," Rose Marie said. "Meghan is in the bathroom at the moment, wash-ing glue off her hands," and "Sawyer's standing next to me. Want to talk to him?"

Now, Meghan and Sawyer had gone, and the kitchen floor was a mess. Rose Marie hauled out the cleaning gear. She had just dunked the mop head into a bucket of sudsy water that smelled of pine needles and lemon peel when the phone rang.

"Mrs. Lustov, it's Gregory Watts from the LaSalle County Health Department. I'm calling to get some information about the children in your day care."

She twirled the mop in the bucket, wondered what he wanted but knew it would be about the sick kids.

"As you know, two of the children who attend your center, Edward Campbell and Amanda Goodman, are in the hospital with meningitis. We're required by law to be sure other children aren't at risk."

"The rest of the kids are fine."

"Good. How many children are enrolled in your day care?"

The strings of the mop head writhed in the water like the tentacles of a jellyfish. Did she have to answer? What could happen if she didn't? Finally she said, "Six, but two of them come only in the mornings."

He asked their ages, asked which children had been at her home since the day before Eddie got sick.

"Are all the children up to date on their childhood immunizations?" he finally asked.

That question again. Rose Marie hated that question. "As far as I know. They were all up to date when they started coming here." She had followed the state law on that, had the parents bring copies of their vaccine records when the kids started.

She sloshed the mop head up and down in the water. Maybe he could help her. "Are the other kids going to be okay?" she asked. "They won't get sick, too, will they?"

"We certainly hope not. That's why I'm calling, so we can work together to be sure no one else becomes ill."

He told her that Eddie's meningitis was caused by bacteria. "*Streptococcus pneumoniae* it's called." He then spelled the words for her. "We don't know what kind of meningitis Amanda has yet. The laboratory results aren't back. The kind of meningitis Eddie has isn't thought to be contagious."

"Good," she said. "That's what Dr. Campbell thought."

"Dr. Campbell?"

"He's Eddie's father."

"I see," said the man from the health department. "Anyway, it's curious that the two children in your day care both have meningitis. We're waiting for more information from the state laboratory."

"Curious," he had said. She wouldn't have used that word. She would have said "terrible."

"Could I ask you a question?" she said.

"Sure."

"How did they get their meningitis if it isn't catching? Something they ate? You can't get it from a dog, can you?"

"For Edward, it's caused by one of the germs that live normally in people's throats but most folks don't get sick from it. He didn't get it from his food nor from a dog. And not from an insect or a cat or dirt. Same with Amanda. That's not how a person gets meningitis."

"Doesn't sound like bad news . . . for the other children, you know."

"No, ma'am. It's not bad news. Mostly, it's uncertain news."

"Do I need to do anything?"

"Not a thing. Not now."

As soon as she hung up, she called Sarah and told her about the man from the health department.

"Good. I'm glad you finally called them."

"Actually, I didn't call them. They called me." She switched the receiver to her left hand and swirled the mop in the sudsy water.

"So, what's the deal?"

"Well . . ." She took a deep breath and squared her shoulders. "Eddie has a really bad kind of meningitis and they aren't sure what kind Amanda has yet. She isn't as sick as Eddie."

"How about the other kids?"

"They're fine." Rose Marie paused a moment, swirled the mop again, and then added, "I guess I don't know about Chris. His grandparents came from Baltimore to watch him."

"What's going to happen Monday?"

"What do you mean?" Suspicion crept up her back.

"Can the kids come back to your house on Monday?"

"Of course they can. The other kids are fine."

"I hope they stay that way. Mother, I gotta go. Let me know what you learn."

Later that evening, long after the sun had dipped behind the maple trees, Rose Marie pumped the rocking chair back and forth, slowly. With the approaching night, the kitchen grew dim but she wanted to stay inside rather than go out to the patio. She couldn't enjoy her garden or the sense of promise that hung in the clear spring air or the chickadees that pecked at the seed in the feeder. She couldn't enjoy anything—not even a glass of white zinfandel. When Beefeater nuzzled his nose into her lap, asking about their evening constitutional, she shoved him back to the floor and snapped, "Not tonight."

She was waiting for the ten o'clock news, hoping to hear something about the meningitis cases and yet hoping not to hear it. She'd run the channels every half hour since the children left but found no reports about Amanda and Eddie. She considered calling Davey's mother to ask where she had heard about it. After further thought, she figured that wasn't a good idea.

She heard a hum. She stopped rocking, tilted her head, and listened to the night sounds. She heard it again. Louder. Then it faded away. Shortly, the hum returned. Finally she saw it, the first mosquito of the season to make it into her kitchen. It flitted against the wallpaper, bobbed and darted its way toward the ceiling, no bigger than a piece of fuzz, no heavier than a breath. She kept rocking. She didn't care if it bit her. At least she wouldn't get sick from it. Nobody would. The health department guy had said the kids didn't get meningitis from bugs.

The ten o'clock news didn't mention anything about the kids. The broadcaster talked only about a threatened strike by the city bus drivers and a fire that burned a restaurant across town. Nothing about meningitis.

Chapter 20

Jake

The elevator slowed to a stop and the doors parted. Inside, Jake moved to the back and a phlebotomist, her blood-drawing equipment in a carrier at her side, exited. A young man stepped in. His hair was tousled as if he'd blown in with a cyclone, his shirttails fluttered against his butt, his pants were deeply wrinkled at the knees. He pushed number three. As the doors closed, he leaned his head against the elevator's wall.

"Well." The young man sighed. He took a deep breath. "Well." Then another deep breath. He scratched his head, rubbed his stubbly chin, and sighed again. "Well, I guess now I'm a dad." A broad grin bloomed on his face.

A new dad. Jake studied him, the fatigue that clouded his eyes, the proud set of his shoulders. The fellow had just crossed that threshold of no return—parenthood. Somewhere in the obstetrics unit, a life had just begun, as happened several times a day. But for this man, it was a monumental, once-in-a-lifetime event. His newborn child, wrapped in either a blue or pink flannel sheet after its long, exhausting journey into the world, would lie sleeping in its plastic bassinette beside the mother's bed.

At floor three, the new father stepped out of the elevator. The doors closed behind him.

For them, it had been the day the green vase broke. That was his and Anna's code for the afternoon Chris was born, the Monday Jake became a father for the first time. Anna had been in labor for several hours, her contractions occurring every ten to fifteen minutes. The obstetrical nurse said to stay home until the pains were five to seven minutes apart.

Anna had paced. Back and forth across the living room floor, from the bay window to the dining room, over and over. With each contraction, she grabbed the back of a chair or the edge of a table, hunched over her bulging waist, and—her face twisted into a grimace—drew in a long tortured breath. Then, shortly, she began pacing again. With one particularly hard contraction, she lurched for the edge of the side table, hooked her fingers in the doily, and sent the green vase they bought in Chinatown crashing to the floor.

"Okay," she said, panting. "That's it. We're going to the hospital."

Jake, gowned, masked, and gloved, had sat on a stool in the delivery room beside Anna's head. Her matted hair was plastered to the sheet, sweat poured past her ears and down her neck. She pushed. She groaned. She took deep, gulping breaths. She panted shallow little puffy breaths. Finally the obstetrician said, "Okay, Anna, with the next push, we'll have a baby."

Her eyes widened. She inhaled—long and deep. She dug her heels into the stirrups, grasped the edges of the bed, and pushed. And pushed. Her swollen face flushed until it grew red as a raspberry and still she pushed. He was afraid she would burst a blood vessel in her head. Or she would starve herself, and the baby, of oxygen. He stroked her hair. "Breathe, honey," he murmured. A low groan rose from the bottom of her chest, like the throttled cry of a strangled animal. She took another breath and pushed again. The baby's head slid out of her and into the gloved hands of the obstetrician.

There, against the arm of the doctor's gown, lay his new little boy. Screaming. Gasping. Arms and legs thrashing. Wet, tawny hair. Blood-streaked skin. His son. He had watched babies being born, had delivered a few himself as a medical student. But, this was different. This wasn't just the birth of a baby. This was the dawn of his son's life. The start of his own new life as a father.

Later, after Chris had been bathed and Anna and the baby moved to a ward room, he held his son while Anna slept. He unwrapped the blue blanket and examined every part of him. So delicate. So perfect. Tiny, pink fingers—clinging, trusting—curled around his seemingly huge, rough pointer finger. "I'm here, buddy," he whispered as he kissed his son's forehead. "I'll always be with you."

Six months ago he had also been in the delivery room when Eddie was born. He was already a father by then, an experienced dad, so Eddie's birth didn't have the same, life-altering effect as Chris's. But, still, it was the beginning of a new, precious life.

The elevator slowed as it approached floor five. Here, in this unit, was another life-altering experience. Although he was a seasoned dad, he'd never before been the dad of a desperately ill child. The elevator doors parted and he walked slowly down the hallway to the pediatric ICU.

His pager sounded. Jake answered.

"Please hold for Dr. Ellis," said the secretary.

He had been waiting for this call. Yesterday Dr. Farley had told him Eddie would get an EEG. He didn't need to explain why. Jake knew. It was to measure the electrical activity over Eddie's cerebral cortex, routine for patients with severe intracranial injuries. It was to determine if Eddie was brain dead.

"Jake? I have the preliminary report on your son's EEG."

He held his breath, tried to read something into the tone of her voice. He wasn't sure he wanted to hear the rest.

Before he could respond, she continued, "Good news. The tracing shows activity, albeit slow-wave activity."

He guessed it was good news. Being almost dead was better than being securely dead. Maybe a tiny bit better.

The bold, black letters, as stark as mud against the white cardboard background, read AUTHORIZED PERSONNEL ONLY. He was a physician, and, of course, authorized to enter. Yet he paused, his palm motionless on the stainless steel push-pad. Part of him wanted to fling open the door and stride confidently inside—man of the world, doctor of the hour. Another part of him shriveled with the sense that he was trespassing. This wasn't an ordinary hospital unit, after all. Here he was a father, not a physician, and his little boy lay in one of the cribs.

The glass door automatically slid shut behind him and a cross-current laden with the usual ICU odors—ionized air, antiseptic, hand-washing soap, clean linen, the plastic from the IV bags—drifted past. At the nurses' station, he rounded the corner where the peach-colored paint, victim of run-ins with gurneys and supply carts and portable X-ray machines, had been chipped down to the white plaster. It looked like a row of open sores.

Across the room, Anna, limp as an empty sack, slumped in her chair, her right hand folded over Eddie's hand. Her left fist clutched a wad of Kleenex against her head. He had begged her to go home last night, to get some sleep. She had refused. Maybe she believed her hospital vigil, sustained by cat naps while folded in a chair, would bring something good, something miraculous. She didn't usually play the martyr, but these weren't usual times. Probably she was angry, too furious to speak. In the past, she had never screamed nor thrown things, never sworn nor made absurd threats. She had an uncanny ability to contain her ire, to modulate emotion with language that was clear and to the point. Several years ago, after he had stupidly poured boiling water into her grandmother's crystal pitcher, she'd wept as she gathered the wet, shattered glass from the kitchen floor. Her only words—spoken like spilled acid—were, "Next time, think ahead." The set of her jaw that afternoon, firm as the floor beneath her knees, was beautiful, inviting. He leaned toward her with a kiss of apology, but she had turned away, saying, "I don't feel very loving right now."

And then there was last Thanksgiving. She had climbed on the kitchen counter to retrieve the turkey platter from the top shelf of the cupboard. He had pulled the bird out of the oven and asked her to fetch the carving knife from the utensils drawer.

Her eyes were daggers, her words gunshot. "You're demanding that I get down from here and fetch you the knife? Right?"

"I asked, nicely."

"Can't you see that I'm up on the counter, unable to reach the damn knife right now?"

"You can get the knife after you're down," he said. A part of him felt vindictive and defensive, another part conciliatory.

"This is our home, not the operating room," she said in a voice that would have frozen the water in hell. "I am your wife, not the scrub nurse."

But, always, the rifts between them were soon over. He would tell a silly joke or pat her on the fanny or speak to her in sad sack tones through Chris or Bullet—"Tell your mommy I really love her"—and she would sigh, soften her scowl, and laugh in her songbird, I-just-can't-stay-mad-at-you-very-long way.

But nothing as serious as Eddie's illness had happened to them before.

He leaned against the counter at the nursing station and watched her, crumpled and haggard, from afar. This form in the chair was not the person he had married. The old Anna had confidence and self-assurance built into her bones. Usually her maple syrup–colored hair swung in a smooth, graceful wave with every turn of her head. Now it hung behind her ears in greasy clumps. When she walked, her clothes used to move over her shoulders and sweep across her backside like flowing water. Now her shirt puckered across her shoulders in sweaty creases.

"Good evening, Dr. Campbell." The ward clerk smiled at him.

He nodded, continued to watch Anna. He had always been proud to be at her side. Male passersby in hallways and on sidewalks, strangers he had secretly hoped to outdo even though their paths would never cross again, seemed to lock their eyes on her, their gazes drawn out well beyond a mere glance.

She straightened up, patted Eddie on the chest, and slumped back into her chair again.

He thought of the way water dripped off the tips of her hair when, surrounded by a floral-scented cloud, she stepped from the shower; the way she rubbed lotion in gooey circles until it disappeared into her cheeks; the way she leaned toward the mirror, dabbing mascara on her lashes.

Apparently, now she didn't care. Two days ago he had brought clean underwear, slacks, and that shirt, now limp and wrinkled. He assumed she had given herself a sponge bath in the visitors' restroom before she put on the clean underwear, but he wasn't sure. Maybe this was yet another way of punishing herself. Or maybe she was letting herself become raggedy to match how she felt.

He walked to Eddie's crib and placed his hand on her shoulder. She shuddered at his touch.

"You scared me." Her voice was thick, groggy.

"Sorry, I didn't realize you were asleep."

"I wasn't asleep." Her empty eyes, now open, stared at the wall.

"Anna," he said, his arms motionless at his sides, "why can't you just let yourself rest for a while? Please come home for the night."

"Quit badgering me."

"Eddie needs you to rest."

"Quit it, Jake."

The photo taped to the metal headboard looked nothing like the baby in the hospital crib. Somehow, back then, the photographer's camera had created an exact replica of Eddie, his animated hands, his buoyant grin, his glowworm face. Even in the two dimensions of the picture, his arms and legs, wrapped in the blue outfit Anna's parents had sent, seemed to spring out of the photographic paper and into the third dimension, fueled by the total body excitement that only a baby can muster. His thin, pineapple-colored hair was parted and combed to one side, a few stray strands falling toward his eyebrows. His fingers clutched an orange and black plastic ladybug that had originally been Bullet's toy. Chris had squeaked it under Eddie's nose the day of the photo and, after Eddie finally managed to grab it, he wouldn't let go.

This was the photo Anna carried in her purse. She undoubtedly wanted it on his bed to show everyone in the ICU that her baby was really a vibrant little boy, that the baby in the hospital wasn't the true Eddie.

The child in the crib was still as a stone, its face no longer laughing, its cheeks no longer dimpled. The endotracheal tube pulled at one corner of Eddie's little mouth, twisting his lips into a sneer, and a gastric tube snaked out his right nostril. The flannel blanket that covered his chest rose and fell to the rhythm of the ventilator. Jake had heard that sound maybe a thousand times during his medical career without really listening. Now, he heard it in a new way—the delicate wheeze, the subtle click of mechanical breathing, the sounds of keeping his son alive.

Before, he had swept in and out of the ICU bays without noticing what was there. Now all the hospital things loomed large, as vivid and contorted as Wonderland must have been to Alice. The stethoscope dangling from an IV pole, the way the blue-tinged walls reflected off Eddie's sallow skin, the lack of privacy and dignity, the urine bag half full of lemon yellow pee and tied to the crib rail, the metallic smell of antibiotics—all of it odious. He reached over the rail and touched his son's head. His fingertips stuck in the globs of electrical jelly glued to Eddie's hair. The nurses hadn't washed it off yet after his EEG.

When would this nightmare end? Ever? Would any day be normal again? Would Anna ever smile? Would Chris have a brother who would climb trees, shoot marbles, race bikes down hills with the wind whistling past his ears?

"Jake," Anna whispered.

"Yes?"

"Stoop closer. I have something to tell you."

He stepped back from Eddie's crib and leaned his ear toward her lips.

"See that guy over there in the running suit?"

"Yeah."

"He wants Eddie's liver."

"What?" That made no sense. She must have scrambled her words.

"Shush, don't let him hear us. He wants Eddie's liver."

"What are you talking about?" He studied her face, tried to figure out what she was trying to say. Wants a liver? Surely that man already had a liver.

Her eyes were hollow, fixed in a faraway gaze. "His little girl over there?" She tilted her head toward the crib across the narrow, crowded room. "The one who looks like a dirty canary? She needs a liver transplant." Anna shot a fierce, hateful glare at the man. "See that pager hanging on his belt? That's so they can call him as soon as they find a donor liver."

The man seemed to be purring as he stroked his daughter's hand, rubbing her frosty pink polished fingernails.

"That has nothing to do with Eddie."

"Yes, it does. He wants Eddie to die so his daughter can have Eddie's liver. She needs a small one because she's such a little girl." Anna tucked a lock of greasy hair behind her ear and then continued. "Eddie's would be about the right size." Her voice lowered to a growl. "Don't let him have it."

"Where'd you get that crazy idea? Did he say something to you?" He eyed the man. Middle-aged. Running suit. Clean jogging shoes. A *New Yorker* magazine balanced on his lap. He looked like an ordinary father, not a ghoul.

"No, but I can tell by watching him." She closed her eyes. "I see the wish on his face when he walks by Eddie's crib. It's like he's measuring Eddie's liver for size."

He looked again at the man. He was humming to his daughter now, and tapping on her nose. Three times. Tap. Tap. Tap.

Anna wore a blank stare. He had heard that kind of tortured logic before, spoken by desperate, crazy patients. But this was his wife.

"Get that notion out of your head. No one's going to take Eddie's liver, because Eddie isn't going to die."

"Are you sure?"

"Yes, I'm sure."

"He'll die sometime."

"We'll all die sometime but Eddie isn't going to die soon." As he spoke, the words, assured and authoritative, bounced through his head as if they didn't belong to him, as if they had floated in from another room. He didn't know if what he said was actually true. But the liver transplant idea needed to be put to rest.

In silence, he reached for her hand. It was limp, as if detached from her body. His finger traced the path of her veins along the back of her hand, over her wrist, and to the spaces in her forearm where they dove deep between the muscle sheaths and coursed, close to the bone, toward her shoulder.

The nurse slid a thermometer into Eddie's armpit, waited a moment, pulled it out, and wrote *37.4* on the vital-signs chart. Then she injected a colorless liquid into his IV line and flicked the reservoir with her fingernail, clearing the bubbles from the fluid.

"What's that?" he asked.

"Antibiotic." She slid the syringe and needle into the sharps container.

"Which one?"

"Ceftriaxone." Her voice was muffled by the empty hypodermic needle sleeve wedged between her lips. He nodded. She pried open Eddie's eyelids, shined a flashlight on both pupils, and charted their sizes on his bedside record.

Jake squeezed Anna's hand. Eddie's pupils must have reacted to the light. A good sign—or rather, if they hadn't reacted, it would have been a bad sign.

"Honey, have you heard about Eddie's EEG? He has brain activity."

"Dr. Farley told me." She seemed vacant. "Tell me what they

do when a baby dies." Her voice was weak, almost hoarse, like sandpaper rubbing against another piece of sandpaper.

"What do you mean?"

"If Eddie dies, what will they do with him?"

"He isn't going to die."

"Tell me what they'll do if he does."

"We're not going to talk like this."

"Tell me, Jake. Where will he go?" Now her words were resolute, spoken as a command.

He took a deep breath but remained silent.

"Tell me, or I'll ask the nurse. I have to know this."

"After the doctors determine that a patient has died"—he spoke of an abstract patient, not of Eddie or even of a dead child—"the nurses pull out all the tubes and wipe off the adhesive tape marks and straighten up the sheets and hospital gown."

He paused. Where were these questions coming from?

She stared out the window. "Keep talking. Then what?"

"Well, then the family is allowed to stay with the deceased as long as they need to. Ultimately the body is taken down to the morgue."

She seemed to listen intently, her eyes half closed. "Where's that?"

"The morgue?"

She slowly nodded.

"In the basement of the hospital."

She was quiet again. She hadn't asked about a postmortem exam. He didn't know how he would have answered that. If Eddie were to die, it might be a coroner's case; by law, an autopsy would be done because he had been critically ill when he arrived in the ER. He envisioned Eddie on the morgue table, dwarfed by the endless expanse of shiny stainless steel. He saw the rubber garden hoses—the ones used to wash down the table when the autopsy was completed—looped on the floor, the jars of formaldehyde, lined up in a row and labeled with Eddie's name and hospital number. The scale where the pathologist would plop Eddie's organs—brain, kidneys, liver, spleen—hung by a chain from the ceiling.

He leaped from his chair, let Anna's hand drop into her lap. Eddie dead. Eddie dead. He ran out into the hallway and leaned his forehead against the wall. He closed his eyes, erased the details of the ICU. The ventilators—gone. The anxious parents—gone. The nearly dead kids—gone.

Voices rang through the ICU like a weird, postmodern chorale, swelling, first, in one corner of the room and then moving in an aural wave to another corner. Someone coughed. An IV pump beeped. A pager chimed. Jake reflexively reached for his belt. It wasn't his.

When he returned to Eddie's cubicle, Anna grabbed his arm.

"What do the parents do?" Her voice was a flat whisper. "Just put on their jackets, walk out the door, and drive home?"

"Eventually, yes." He swallowed and then continued. "That's about it."

"Not me. I'm never leaving Eddie."

Chapter 21
Rose Marie

It was Saturday, and Rose Marie was doing the weekly cleaning. As she swiped the dust rag, which was really an old cotton diaper, over the window frames, she heard the thunk against the porch. Would the paper say anything about it? Would they identify her day care? Identify her?

She pulled open the front door, let out a soft groan as she stooped for the newspaper, and headed to the kitchen. The ink was blurred along the fold. Hopefully that wasn't the part with the story. She wanted to read the whole thing. She flattened the crease of the newsprint against the tabletop with the edge of her hand.

She scanned the headlines of the front page. Not there. On page two she glanced at the death notices and the weather forecast. Not there.

In the middle of the third page the headline read:

Four Area Children Hospitalized with Meningitis

Four? She read it again. Four. Eddie and Amanda and who else? Quickly she skimmed the article for names, her eyes darting across the print, ready to land on the words "Amanda" or "Edward" or "Rose Marie Lustov." There were no names, other than the director of the county health department. Then she returned to the beginning and read, slowly and carefully so she didn't miss anything important.

> Four LaSalle County children have been hospitalized in the past five days with meningitis. Three boys, ages six months, two years, and six years, and a four-year-old girl, are in LaSalle Children's Hospital and St. Andrew's Hospital. The three older children are in serious condition while the six-month-old boy is listed in critical condition.
>
> According to Dr. Myron Klug, medical director of the LaSalle County Health Department, meningitis is an infection of the membranes that surround the brain and spinal cord. The most serious form of the infection is caused by bacteria while a milder form is caused by viruses. Some types of bacterial meningitis can be spread by coughing, kissing, sharing drinking glasses, and other close contact. Dr. Klug said that the six-month-old and the four-year-old attend the same Huron Township day care center, but no link has been identified between these two cases and either of the other cases. The other children in the day care, including the three-year-old brother of the six-month-old, show no signs of the infection, Dr. Klug reported.
>
> Vaccines are available to prevent some forms of bacterial meningitis, said Dr. Klug, and are recommended for routine immunization of children starting at two months of age. The investigation of these cases is still underway, and Dr. Klug said he didn't yet know if the ill children had received the vaccines. Bacterial meningitis is usu-

ally treatable with antibiotics, but serious side effects may occur, such as deafness, blindness, mental retardation, seizure disorder, or cerebral palsy if treatment is delayed. There is no antibiotic treatment for viral meningitis, and children with this form of the infection recover fully.

Dr. Klug emphasized that there is no evidence of an epidemic at this time and urged parents to consult their family physician if their children develop unexplained fever, severe headache, vomiting, listlessness, or stiff neck. The LaSalle County Health Department Immunization Clinic is open Tuesdays from nine to noon at the courthouse; appointments are recommended.

The words swirled across the page, looming large at one moment, fading into the background at another. Her eyes flitted from line to line. She read each paragraph again, and then again. Four children. What was going on?

She warmed a cup of water in the microwave for coffee. At least the other two weren't in her day care. Chris, Meghan, Sawyer, and Davey were well. At least as far as she knew.

She started at the beginning of the article and read it yet again. It seemed odd for Eddie—sweet little Eddie, with the big ears and long, skinny neck—to be called "the six-month-old boy" and Amanda—bossy but imaginative Amanda—to be called "the four-year-old girl." Those words were too impersonal, as if the children weren't really people. Or were insignificant people who didn't deserve to have names.

She tossed the descriptions of the children around in her head several times, amending them to suit her. A six-month-old loveable baby named Eddie. A four-year-old princess named Amanda, who just two weeks ago had declared she wasn't Amanda anymore, because her name was Gretchen. When asked to put the puzzle pieces back in the box, she had turned her head away, lifted her chin, puckered her lips, and announced,

"I can't, because I'm Gretchen." Now she was neither Amanda nor Gretchen, but rather "the four-year-old girl."

She called Amanda's house. No one answered. They were probably all at the hospital. She didn't even know which hospital. After nine rings, she hung up.

She dialed Davey's house. She had to know about the other children. The answering machine responded.

"Please call me if Davey's sick. I sure hope we get to the bottom of this soon," she said into the phone.

No one was home at Sawyer's house, either, so she left another message.

Meghan's mother, thank goodness, answered.

"How's Meghan?" Rose Marie asked, worried about the answer. An army of insects seemed to dance around her insides.

"She's fine. I read the news in the paper; can't tell if I should freak out or not. What's the story about Davey and Sawyer?"

"I don't know. No one answers at their houses. If I learn anything, I'll let you know."

She reread the newspaper article one last time, making absolutely sure her name wasn't in it. She didn't want anyone in town to know that two of the sick children attended her day care. With a sigh, she folded the newspaper and turned on the television to see what the local news would say about the kids.

The first news item detailed the strike by the city bus drivers planned for the next day. Rose Marie fidgeted in her chair.

Then it came.

"Possible Meningitis Outbreak" was written in blue and black letters across the screen. In a breathless, rapid-fire voice, the newsman described the four cases. None of the children's names were mentioned. Her stomach churned as she listened for her own name.

"Two of the infected children attend the same LaSalle County day care." She held her breath. He didn't say Lustov, didn't give her address.

"Dr. Myron Klug is director of the local health department," he said as he thrust a microphone toward a stern man who stood in a parking lot downtown. Dr. Klug repeated a few of the details and explained that they had no evidence for an epidemic in their county.

She turned off the television set and wrapped her arms around her waist. What would happen? she wondered. To Eddie, to the rest of the children? To her?

"The *Free Press* and channel sixteen both say there are four cases of meningitis in LaSalle County," she said to Sarah.

"Holy Cow. Sounds like an epidemic."

"But only two of the cases were in my children, as far as I know. My day care had nothing to do with the other two. I think. The director of public health said there was no evidence of an epidemic and people shouldn't panic."

"Now what?"

"The health department guy said I didn't have to do anything, at least not right now. I've been cleaning this morning. It can't hurt."

By ten o'clock in the morning—after pushing the two Stratoloungers into the center of the living room so she could clear out the cookie crumbs, dog hair, stray toys, and lost barrettes that had been kicked under the furniture—she was vacuuming the carpet. When finished, she shoved the Stratoloungers back against the wall.

"This's going to be the cleanest house in the state," she muttered under her breath. Next, under the couch. She slid the vacuum's upholstery attachment from side to side beneath the sofa skirt, inched it forward with each sweep, and thought about the reporter.

How did he find out about Amanda? About her? Who gave him her phone number? Amanda's mother? Unlikely. Anna? Couldn't be. Who would do that to her?

Next she cleaned the bookcases. Her library, as she liked to call it, contained mostly children's books, which were stacked on the bottom shelves and used too often to get dusty. The book on top of the pile, *Rain, Hail, and Lightning*, was Davey's favorite. He liked to make thunder noises as she read about the storms. She wondered if Davey's mother would bring him back, if the other mothers would pull their kids out as well. Was Amanda in the ICU? Would she and Eddie be okay?

When she finished cleaning the living room, she changed the linen on her bed and scrubbed the bathroom floor with Lysol and a stiff brush, paying particular attention to the base of the toilet. Even though she repeatedly told the little boys to aim *in* the potty, not *at* the potty, sometimes they missed. She couldn't be held responsible for that. She mopped the bathroom floor every night. How much more was she expected to do?

She hadn't heard from the Campbells for two days. Presumably Chris hadn't caught Eddie's meningitis but she needed to be sure. She didn't want to bother Anna at the hospital again, so she called their house, hoping to find her at home. At least, her parents were likely to be there.

As the dial tone rang in her ear, she hoisted herself onto the kitchen stool. Under the table, Beefeater lay curled into an O, his nose wedged between his rear feet. This was one of his favorite places, perfect for snatching fallen food. The curve of the dog's spine, with its row of bony knobs barely visible under his slick Jack Russell hair, reminded her of a rosary. Beefeater lived a charmed life, confident of his next meal, able to sleep away the afternoon without a worry. Besides, he was her automatic crumb cleaner-upper. He kept the kitchen floor spotless.

Anna had never said much about her parents, except that they lived in Baltimore. She assumed Anna's mother would share her daughter's sense of style. She vaguely remembered Anna saying, upon returning from a visit to Maryland when Chris was two, that her parents' home "wasn't childproofed." There was something about lipstick on the dining room wallpaper, a vague reference to what she assumed had been an unpleasant situation.

Although she had never met Anna's mother, she recognized

her voice immediately. It carried the same measured pace, the same remote quality as Anna's. She tried to imagine Anna's mother. Probably trim, like Anna, with sprightly movements. Her hair would be streaked with gray, or possibly pure white, or maybe skillfully dyed, and her face, with Anna's high forehead and narrow, hazel eyes, would be relaxed and knowing, while the folds of skin that ran beside her cheeks would be deeper than her daughter's.

"Both Jake and Anna are at the hospital," Anna's mother said. "Yes, Eddie's still in the ICU."

"And Chris?"

"He's standing right here and would love to talk to you."

"Hi, Rose Marie." Chris's familiar voice sounded like a cherub singing—rather, a worried cherub singing. "Mommy's at the hospital. Eddie's real sick."

"I know, honey. I bet you miss your mommy."

"I want to go to the hospital."

"Of course. Are you having fun with your grandma and grandpa?"

"Grandma made pancakes that said 'C' for Chris."

She smiled as she pictured him stuffing the pancakes into his mouth. "You're being a brave soldier, Chris. Maybe you can come to my house next week, even if your grandma and grandpa are still here."

"Bye." Chris was gone; the dial tone buzzed in her ear. He had sounded healthy, as chipper as ever.

"But Meghan's still fine, right?" she said, watching wind blow through the trees out the kitchen window. Meghan's mother was on the phone, had just told her they'd made other arrangements for Meghan's care for the next week or so.

"We need to be sure there isn't a problem. You understand, I'm sure."

"Well, I don't know what to think. I'm just glad all of the other children are healthy."

"We'll let you know what we decide."

After she hung up, she walked to her bedroom. Beefeater lay on her bed. "Move over," she said and lay down. Sawyer's mother had also read the article in the paper and had called just a few minutes before Meghan's mother. They were all abandoning her. She closed her eyes and tried to think. Her mind was in a muddle. Nothing made sense.

Chapter 22

Jake

Rain pelted the glass pane beside his shoulder. He thought he heard hail. He turned away from the computer and toward the window. It was only rain—thick, lead-like drops driven by the wind. A flash of lightning shot through the room. Two breaths later, a clap of thunder rattled the glass, gently nudged his body. He listened while it trundled off into silence.

Spring storms—the crashing, the thrashing, the wildness—took him back to his youth, to the times when he hid in Buckthorn's cave, when he got lost in the woods behind the school, when he swayed like a bear cub from the top of an apple tree, and when, during midnight thunderbolts, he huddled under his quilt—safe, warm, and dry. There was an odd comfort in those storms. They were always the same. After the flashes and the racket and the blowing, they always stopped and the world became quiet again.

Outside, it was wet and blustery, but inside, in the residents' room where he slumped before the electric blue-gray of the computer screen, the air scratched at his nostrils. It smelled of oily hair, sweaty clothes, stale pizza. X-rays of someone's femur

and a discharge summary from a referring hospital cluttered
the table where his elbows rested next to a cardboard box with
stale bagels, yesterday's sign-out sheet, and a postcard from
Coeur d'Alene, Idaho.

He stared at the words and numbers—the results of Mr. Bender's laboratory tests—on the computer screen. Hemoglobin—
normal. White count—normal. Differential—normal. Hepatic
enzymes—normal. So, why was this guy jaundiced? he wondered, twirling a paper clip between his thumb and index finger.
Maybe his liver was giving out and the enzymes had been elevated earlier but now were on their way down—the ominous
arc of a dying organ. He decided to order additional hepatic
function tests.

The thunder and lightning had stopped and now he felt the
lulling rhythm of the rain. He glanced at his watch. Almost four
o'clock in the afternoon. Things were winding down, both the
storm and the workday. If he finished his patient notes soon, he
might be able to go home early, but first he would check with
Anna and visit Eddie. Fortunately Anna's parents were still
around. He couldn't deal with Chris's exuberance tonight, at
least not alone. He needed a buffer, someone else to absorb a
portion of his son's energy. He'd been up half the night—four
admissions and two open-fracture reductions—and was exhausted.

He stared at Mr. Bender's lab results again, but the numbers
seemed to pass through his eyes, through his brain, and out
again without sticking. Far in the distance, he heard one last
roll of thunder, a grumbly straggler at the tail of the storm.

The rain on the window brought it all back. They were
speeding down Huron River Drive in his friend's ancient El Dorado convertible, the top down, Gary at the wheel, Monica huddled in the middle. It had begun to sprinkle. Gary kept driving
up U.S. 23, toward Independence Lake. Soon the raindrops
were fat and heavy and slapped at their faces like a wet mop.
Finally Gary edged the car to the side of the road to unfold the
convertible's top. Yanking at the rusty levers and pulling at the
unruly canvas, his friend filled the air with profanity.

"Why don't you help him?" Monica had said. She pulled her sopping-wet hair away from her eyes. Her blouse, soaked through, clung to her chest.

"What do I know about convertibles?" he said. "Besides, I have to see a man about a horse."

With that, he stepped into the woods to take a leak. The rain was diffracted by the birch branches overhead. When he returned, the top of the El Dorado was up, Monica sat alone in the front seat, and Gary was wiping his greasy hands on a fistful of wild grape leaves. Jake stopped just short of the car and stared at its top. A piece of faded Levi's was stitched to the roof's black fabric with orange thread. He burst out laughing. That denim patch was the funniest thing he'd ever seen. He bent over and held his sides. He could barely breathe. Finally, weak from giggling, he crawled into the front seat, put his soaked arm around Monica's wet shoulders, ran his damp fingers through her wet hair, and planted a juicy kiss on her wet cheek.

Now, as he remembered the patch from the blue jeans, he couldn't figure out what had been so funny. He could see the mended convertible top clearly and even chuckled to himself as he recalled the peals of laughter, but he no longer understood the humor. Must have been something mystical about the rain and the old car and the evening. And, of course, there was the magic of Monica.

He clicked on the next patient's laboratory results but still couldn't concentrate on the numbers. They swam like hieroglyphics on the computer screen while thoughts of Monica filled his brain. For the past day, she had seemed to follow him everywhere: to the scrub sink, into the john, to the Coke machine. Where was she? Right now, at this very moment, where on the planet Earth was she?

Slowly, as if from the bottom of a bog, the idea bubbled upward into his head. It'd be harmless, he thought.

No, it'd be ridiculous. He twirled the paper clip.

He wanted to know what'd happened to her.

Leave it alone, he thought. He shut down the laboratory results page and aimed the computer's arrow at the Internet Explorer icon.

Just for the hell of it.

Jeez, drop it and go see Eddie, he said to himself. With his finger trembling against the mouse, he aimed the arrow at the stored addresses in the search engine and double-clicked on www.Google.com.

He glanced around the room to see if anyone was watching. A urology resident, his forehead pressed against his folded arms, dozed at the next table. A medical student closed the chart she had been reading and walked out the door. Why be so secretive? he wondered. The residents connected to Google every hour of every day. They looked up the URLs for Cabela's or Amazon, hunted for bed-and-breakfasts in Saugatuck and Traverse City, trolled for stores that sold Rockport shoes. Did they check up on former girlfriends or boyfriends? Probably. In fact, he was sure of it. He typed "Monica Daley" into the advanced search window and hit Google Search.

As the computer ticked through its files, a sense of creepiness folded over him. Peeping Toms are sick, he told himself. They're loathsome, vile. Still, when the list of 540 items popped up, he couldn't keep his eyes off the screen.

Did he really want to be a voyeur? Is that what Jake Campbell had become? Was Chris and Eddie's dad a sneak? Dr. Dunwoody had advised him to be a father but he hadn't warned against being a stalker.

He opened the first link—Monica Daley, a librarian in Seattle. The second Monica Daley ran a women's clothing store in Rochester, Minnesota. The third sold car insurance in Miami. No. No. No, he said to himself as he clicked his way through the list.

Then he found it. Monica L. Daley, MD. Yes, he thought, his fingers sweaty on the keyboard, his intestines twisting behind his belt buckle. Her middle name was Lynn. On the staff of a hospital in Maine. He clicked on her name. Her link in the staff directory popped up. Pediatrician. Graduated from Ohio State University. Residency at Boston University. Board certified. No photo. Clinic phone number for appointments. No office number. He needed her office number.

He searched Google for the American Medical Association. On the site page, he hit the tab that said "AMA Membership List." An error message popped up. "You must log in to access this page."

"Shit," he muttered.

Then he remembered. Dr. Dunwoody had paid AMA dues for all the ortho residents. His heart pounded. He opened his wallet. Wedged between his Blue Cross card and his Western Michigan University alumnus card, he found the AMA membership card, his member number in the upper-left-hand corner.

Soon after he logged in, he found her, along with an office phone number. His thoughts raced. Shut down the computer. Keep going. Go see Eddie. Call her. He reached into the wastebasket beside the desk, pulled out a slip of paper, jotted the number on the back of what turned out to be a pizza receipt, and slipped it into his pocket.

His options collided and fused into a kind of mental quicksand that held him in its grip. He lifted the phone receiver, punched nine, heard the tone of the outside line.

He held the receiver away from his ear. He looked at it and at the number he had written on the receipt. Then he set the receiver back on the phone and headed for the pediatric ICU.

Chapter 23

Anna

It was only five days since she and Eddie left home. Seemed like a month. No, more like a century. Their house still looked the same, two stories tall, murky blue front door, siding the color of putty. The deep taupe trim had always reminded Anna of a snail's shell. She looked up at the roof, squinting her eyes against the cloud-draped sun. The shingles were still shabby; a tiny maple tree had sprouted in the eave over their bedroom. Had she really lived in this house at all? Her memory of the place was like a crooked dream, as if she had known it a long time ago, in another life as a different person. The house seemed very wrong.

Jake had urged her to come home. "Even a short visit would be better than none," he said, his voice tired. She had never heard him beg before.

Even her mother begged. When Anna heard, "Now, dear, be reasonable," she was propelled back to her childhood, back to the time when the next words had been, "practice your piano lessons" or "change that sweaty shirt" or "wear a jacket—the night is cool" or "eat your broccoli."

The final straw, though, came from Chris. "Come home, Mommy," he had pleaded over the telephone. The tension in his sweet voice was like a thorn in the honey.

Jake stopped the van in the driveway. "Here we are," he said.

A Subaru was parked in front of the garage door. She knew it belonged to her because the bumper sticker—faded and peeling off the lid of the trunk—said, "It's my RIGHT TO CHOOSE what happens to my body." She had been eight and a half months pregnant with Chris when she marched in that Freedom of Choice rally, her swollen feet beating what seemed like miles of pavement. Her pelvis was so unhinged in preparation for the birth that she thought she would come apart with each step. After the rally, soaked to the skin by an unexpected downpour, she had ripped the protective backing off the sticker and slapped it on her car. Considering the rain, she was amazed it had stuck at all. Yet, almost four years later, wrinkled and sun bleached, it still clung to the green paint.

"Jake . . ." She took a deep breath, let it out slowly. She needed to place the fragments of her memories in the right order. "I drove Eddie and Chris to the emergency room. How'd my car get home?" In the days and nights she spent at Eddie's side, she hadn't thought of the Subaru even once.

"Your dad rode with me to the hospital yesterday. No, the day before. No . . . I don't remember when. He drove it home."

"Oh." She exhaled into the word. Arranging for a ride, finding the right parking lot at the hospital, locating her green car among the other green cars—the whole process of getting it home seemed an unsolvable problem. Yet, here it was.

"Whose is that?" She pointed to the Taurus beside the Subaru.

"Your folks' rental."

She nodded as she held her head, trying to quell the ache that pounded behind her eyes.

Chris's toy backhoe lay half buried in the sandbox beside the garage, and the old tire twisted slowly from the end of the rope tied high in the oak tree. A child's brown flannel jacket dangled from the groove of the tire. Chris must have left it there and no one noticed. If she had been home at the time, she would have noticed, would have instantly spotted it there in the tire, would have put it back in the closet.

Without thinking, she placed her foot beyond the loose brick on the back stairs, the one that used to wobble when she stepped on it. As she pushed open the back door, the curtain that covered the window brushed against her hair. Somewhere in her sewing cabinet was the leftover material, a piece of dull citron-colored gauze with thin blueberry stripes. She worried about prowlers when Jake was away at night and had made the curtain a week after they moved in.

"Mommy," Chris screamed, racing from the kitchen. He rammed full force into her leg and clung to her as desperately as a shipwrecked sailor grasps a piece of driftwood.

"Mommy's tired." Jake laid a hand on his son's shoulder. "Let her sit down."

Chris didn't move, except to bury his face deeper into her crotch.

She peeled her son's fingers from her slacks and stooped until she was eye-to-eye with him. Cupping his chin in her hands, staring into that bewildered face that seemed to have aged by several years while she was away, she murmured, "Chris, honey . . ."

He wouldn't look at her.

"Honey, I'm so glad to see you. I missed you very much."

He squeezed his eyes shut and shook his head.

She picked him up and pushed his head to her shoulder. His body relaxed against hers.

It had been a good hour with Chris on her lap. Then he became fidgety.

"Honey, I need to go to the bathroom," she said, trying to move him to the floor.

"Come, Chris, sit on the couch." Anna's mother patted the cushion beside her.

"No," Chris said, wiggling against Anna. She nudged him toward his grandmother. He resisted. She didn't want a con-

frontation with him this afternoon. She wanted everything to
be pleasant, wanted her son to be cooperative, wanted her
mother to see him as a well-behaved little boy.

"Let's read about Moira." Anna's mother opened one of his
favorite books, *Moira and the Rite of Spring*, and patted the cushion again.

"You said it wrong," Chris said.

"Tell me the right way."

"*Moyra.* Not *Mora.*"

"Okay, let's read about *Moyra.*"

"No."

He was digging in, taking on his grandmother in a contest of
wills. Her mother wasn't used to a strongheaded child. Anna
had been a very compliant little girl.

Jake lifted Chris from her lap and set him on the couch. "Let
Grandma read to you. Mommy needs a break."

Chris squirmed from Jake's grasp. Quick as lightning, his
foot kicked at the book. It flew from his grandmother's hands
and landed on the carpet.

"None of that, young man." Jake grabbed Chris's shoulders
and gave him a shake. "What on earth is wrong with you? Apologize to your grandma."

Chris whimpered as he tried to pull away.

"Jake, don't hurt him." Anna raised her voice over her son's.
She had never seen her husband physically discipline Chris. She
drew her fingers over her eyes. What weird, awful world was
she in?

"I want my mommy," Chris whined. "You're mean." His eyes
narrowed with hatred as he squirmed against Jake's grip.

She knew Chris would never issue an apology while in such a
defiant mood and no threat could change that. She moved Jake
aside, sat on the end of the couch, and retrieved the book from
the floor. "First I'll go to the bathroom, then I'll sit next to you
while Grandma reads. Jake, could you get my bag from the
car?"

As Jake moved toward the door, Chris stuck out his tongue at
his father's back. She pretended she didn't see it.

When she returned from the bathroom, Chris snuggled against her side and turned his face toward his grandmother. "Moira's a witch," he said. "She lives in a coven. Start here." He turned to the picture of a troupe of Druids dancing around a maypole. "See, that one's Aubrey." He jabbed his finger at one of the robed men. "And there's Aidan."

"Is this about pagans?" Her mother looked alarmed.

Anna took a deep breath. "Well, yeah. He loves it. It's kind of cute." She should have guessed her mother would question the Moira book. It didn't fit with her Lutheran sensibility. "He got it for his birthday, from his friend Davey." She shrugged at her mother. "It's okay, Mom. It won't hurt him."

"Read," Chris commanded.

She had forgotten how comfortable their bed was. Jake had often said, as he sank into the sheets after a night at the hospital, "This is the most wonderful place in the galaxy."

Now, still wearing her stale, wrinkled clothes, she lay under the quilt. Chris curled against her chest like a sleeping cat. Her arms and legs, tight and achy just a few minutes ago, relaxed into the loft of the mattress and she thought how right Jake was about the bed.

Her mother had pulled the window shade to darken the room, but ribbons of daylight streamed past the window frame and puddled on the carpet. Dust motes floated like gnats on its beams. Anna stroked Chris's neck and picked a piece of a dried leaf from behind his ear. She wasn't sure if he was asleep or just playing possum, afraid to move because, with just a little jostling, his mother might disappear again.

She closed her eyes. Against the ebony of her lids she saw Eddie in his hospital bed. What was he doing? What had happened since she left? The nurses had promised to call if anything changed, anything at all. She had already phoned them twice, once shortly after arriving home and again before lying down, and they had assured her Eddie was fine. They had suctioned the usual amount of secretions from his endotracheal tube, his blood pressure was normal. His gases were good, his urine output was fine. Maybe tomorrow they would try again to wean him from the vent.

She knew how Jake felt about Eddie. She had overheard him talking with Dr. Farley about the possibilities—their words weren't clear and they used medical terms she didn't completely understand, but she was able to get the gist of it. Jake thought Eddie would never be normal again. And Dr. Farley agreed.

Why couldn't Jake believe, as she did, that Eddie would be okay? Even doctors should believe in miracles, because sometimes they happened. Deep in her soul, she knew he'd be normal. She could see him as a twelve-year-old, rocketing down a hill on a bike, hovering over a puzzle spread across the kitchen table, swimming the length of a pool in one breath, playing a trumpet. At least he could do those things if he wanted to. And yet, in another place deep in her soul, she knew he might die. The unease that rumbled through her—a wave, a cramp, a seething spasm—churned against her insides until she felt she would throw up.

She rolled over, away from Chris's sleeping body. He lay motionless except for the rhythmic action of his tongue against his thumb. He had stopped that at least a year before, and now had started it again. She stroked his arm, gently so she wouldn't awaken him, sadly because her heart was breaking to see him like this.

A parade of worries trotted through her head. Her mother. The kicked book. Her defiant older son. Her struggling younger son. Her class at the community college. What day of the week was it? When would she return to work? Ever? She couldn't grasp the meaning of ever, couldn't pin it down to a concrete idea. When was ever? Next week? Next month? In an hour? The meaning of never was much easier.

The oven timer pinged in the kitchen below. She had never heard that sound from the bedroom. It had the same pitch as a teaspoon against a fine crystal goblet. Her mind roamed near sleep and her thoughts grew fuzzy.

Smelled like cookies. Her mother must be baking, using her

pans, her oven, her kitchen, her home. Hers and Jake's. Their house, this strange and only vaguely familiar place that belonged to both of them.

And it was Eddie's house, too. His crib was just down the hall, in the bedroom with purple and red balloons painted on the wall. She hadn't gone into his room since returning home. That could come later. Nothing in it would have changed. The foam shapes of the mobile would still dangle over the mattress, his clothes and the clean crib linen would still be in the dresser drawers. Soon Eddie would come home, would be back in his own bed nestled under the blanket Grandma Campbell had crocheted for him. Then the world would be in order again.

Dinner was over and Chris was in bed. She had rocked him to sleep, had felt him jump with one of those nervous shudders that happen during slumber. She hugged him tight, hoping to keep another shudder at bay. Perhaps he was dreaming. About what?

She lay on the couch listening to her parents clean the dinner dishes when the phone rang. It must be Eddie's nurse. She sprang from the sofa and raced to the kitchen.

"Hello?" She had trouble catching her breath.

"Mrs. Campbell . . ."

"Is he okay?" Why was the caller's voice so chirpy? "What happened?"

"Mrs. Campbell, this is Ben from Friends of the Firefighters. We thank you . . ."

"You're not from the hospital?" She was confused. Who was she talking to?

"Ah, no. My name's Ben and I'm from Friends of the—"

"Damn you," she yelled and slammed the receiver down on the console. As she walked into the family room, her mother called, "What was that all about?"

"Jake, take me back."

"What happened? Who was on the phone?"

"Some telemarketer. I need to go to the hospital."

Jake sat upright in his recliner. "Why? Things are fine there."

"I just have to be there." Why didn't he understand? "What if he dies? I can't be here when Eddie takes his last breath."

"Honey, he isn't going to die. The ventilator is breathing for him."

"Stop it, Jake." Why was he trapping her at home when Eddie was so sick?

"How about Chris? Don't you care about him? Didn't you see how grateful he is to have you home? He needs you, Anna. That awful show he put on earlier is because he's unbelievably upset that you've been gone."

She covered her ears with her hands. He was trying to kill her. To murder her with words. She wouldn't let him.

"Are you going to drive me back or do I have to ask my father?" she yelled.

Chapter 24

Jake

Anna was screaming. She was like a lunatic, demanding to go back to the hospital.

"What's wrong with you?" he shouted over her yelling. He tried to wrap his arms around her.

She swatted them away. "Get away from me. Just take me back to the hospital. He's dying. I can feel it." Her eyes were glazed, her mouth twisted into a wicked sneer. He'd never seen her like that. Not sure he'd ever seen anybody like that, even the most demented, panicked psychiatric patient.

Over her shoulder, he saw her parents crowded in the doorway between the kitchen and the family room, their faces masks of fright. He motioned them away. They disappeared.

He needed to get control, needed to bring some sanity to this insanity. "Darling," he said, struggling to quiet his wavery voice. "Why don't we call the ICU? Let them tell you how well Eddie is doing."

"Now, Jake. I have to go NOW." Her voice was getting hoarse.

"You're going to leave Chris? What kind of a mother abandons her son?"

Her face twisted as if he had slapped her. He gasped at the contorted image before him, at the weight of the moment. How could he do that to her? Something had snapped inside him, something huge and dark and ugly.

She sank to the couch, sobbing. "Poor Chris. Poor little Chrisy. Jake, please help me." She was weeping so hard she could hardly speak. "I'm so scared. Eddie's going to die. You didn't listen to me when he got sick. Now you're not listening to me when he's dying."

He slid his arm around her shoulders, tried to draw her to his side. "Anna, honey . . ."

She stiffened. He didn't know what to say to her. He wanted to erase what he had said about abandoning Chris, but couldn't undo the telling. He rubbed her forehead; she pulled away, sobbing.

"Please take me to the hospital."

He whispered into her ear, smelled the clovelike odor of her hair. "We'll get through this, Anna. I know we will."

The rain blew sideways across the hood of his car, the wind so fierce the wipers couldn't keep up.

She had been anxious at home, detached, almost dreamy in the way she drifted around the house as if she didn't belong there. Then she went completely berserk. Her parents had been bewildered—no, surely terrified—when she started screaming. In the end, he'd driven her to the hospital—if he hadn't, she would have asked her father or called a cab; she'd get there somehow. As they neared the main entrance, she seemed to settle down a little. After he pulled to a stop, she dashed out of the car into the rain shower, ran through the door, and disappeared down the darkened corridor. Now he was on his way home through the stormy night that was black as soot.

Suddenly, the red beam of a traffic light glimmered through the inky torrent. His foot hit the brake. The car skidded to a stop. He waited for the red to flip to green, tapped his fingers on the steering wheel. Beacons off the headlights of the cross traffic swept through the raindrops as cars crept, one by one, across the flooded intersection.

A Bob Marley song had just ended on the radio. Now an announcer read the sponsors, Nature Conservancy of Michigan and The Mosaic Foundation of Rita and Peter Heydon, and in his sleepy, nasal voice, reminded the listeners of the time—9:40 PM—and the station—WUOM, 91.7 FM.

A drum beat pulsed against the inside of the car. Voices reverberant as thunder howled the words to the song. The music transported him back to medical school, back to his first date with Monica. The lamps in the bar had been dim, the sound system had throbbed, and she had swayed in the light reflected from the crystal ball that slowly turned overhead. He had been mesmerized by the way her hips rolled beneath her pale pink dress, the way her feet stepped on the wooden floorboards to the beat of the music, and the way her arms—bare except for silver bracelets that jangled at her right wrist—shot into the air as she yelled, "Y . . . M-C-A."

He twisted the volume dial on the radio to the left. Lower, lower. He couldn't bear to listen to that song.

The rain continued to pelt the car. Through the din of the storm, he thought he heard a siren. He turned his head to get a better bead on the sound. It was gone. A moment later, the whine of the siren returned. He stared at the rearview mirror, saw only a curtain of water out the back window. The sound grew louder. He slowed the car. Now he could see it. An ambulance. Coming behind him. He pulled the car to the curb and the ambulance screamed past, its lights flashing through the rain and its rear tires spraying watery rooster tails. Wherever he went, it seemed, medical crises followed.

Thoughts of Eddie raced through his mind. The second baby had been more his idea than Anna's. He believed Chris should have a brother, one close enough in age to be a pal. In his family, there had been three Campbell boys in three years and he was the oldest. Growing up, they were the stair-step kids that raced their sleds through the snow on Forbes Hill most weekends from November through February. They were the three wise men in the Christmas program at St. Matthew's United Methodist Church, stumbling down the aisle in their dad's and uncles' flannel bathrobes, clutching tea boxes or Coke bottles covered with aluminum foil. At home, Jake, Rick, and Luke were the yard crew—one behind the mower, one behind the rake, and one behind the edger—as well as the dish-washing crew—one at the dishpan, one with the towel, and one, the put-away guy, standing on a chair next to the kitchen counter, setting the clean glasses and plates on the cupboard shelf. He wanted the same for his kids: freedom, wild schemes, responsibility, fun.

Anna had balked. "I think we should wait a little longer, at least until you've finished your training," she'd said with a groan when he first brought up the subject of another baby. "Then you'll have more time to spend with us, and Chris can enjoy being an only child for a few more years." She was an only child and seemed to want Chris protected from the intrusion of a younger sib.

Two Easters back, after saying good-bye to their company, after rocking Chris to sleep, after washing the plates and the wineglasses and retiring to their bed, they had begun the famil-iar nuzzling and stroking that signaled love making. He ran his fingertips up and down her backbone. She moved closer to him and buried her face in his neck. His pointer finger drew circles around her nipples. Her knee wedged against the firm-ness between his thighs.

As the heat between them intensified, she had reached into the bedside drawer for her diaphragm. As fast as a bobcat, he grabbed it from her hand, bent it in half, and then let go, launching it into the painting that hung above the dresser on the opposite wall.

"That's so childish, Jake," she said as she scrambled out of bed to retrieve the diaphragm.

"Chris needs a brother. Or even a sister."

"Not yet, he doesn't."

"Well, let's skip the contraception this time and see what happens."

As she stomped back toward the bed—the diaphragm cupped in her hand, the ivory skin of her belly flushed from anger, her nipples pointed straight at him and bobbing with each determined step like corks at sea—a wave of intense passion washed over him. Her fury, her unmitigated rage aroused him even more.

She pulled on her nightgown, lay down with her back to him, and tucked the covers around her neck.

"That ended it for tonight. It's hardly the way to coax me into having another baby."

Now he clutched the steering wheel as the car crawled through the rain. If he could change his wife, he'd give her a better sense of humor, make her more playful. She took most things too seriously, was congenitally unable to see the lighter side of many situations. She was a good mom and in many ways a good wife, but she'd be better at both if she could have more fun.

Then several months later she had acquiesced about a second baby. He wasn't sure why. She was like that at times—completely inexplicable. Maybe it was a hormone-driven, maternal urge. Maybe she just gave up resisting. In any event, she became pregnant right away.

To his relief, once she was pregnant, she seemed delighted to have another child. She rigged up a baby bulletin board for Chris, who was clueless about his impending big brotherhood, and bought children's books to help him with the concept. After the ultrasound confirmed another son, she crocheted blue edging around a set of flannel blankets, saying, "The baby should have a few new things of his own, rather than using Chris's old stuff." She studied lists of names and then settled on Edward, her grandfather's name.

"Poor guy," he had said when she announced her choice.

"Why?" Her head was tilted, her face twisted with wonder. "What's wrong with Edward?"

"Nothing, except it's your granddad's name."

"What's the matter with that? We can't name him after *your* grandfathers. Wayne and Donald are dorky names."

"I don't want to name him Wayne or Donald, either. It's tough for a guy to carry someone else's name. If he's an Edward, he might think he has to grow up to be a successful Baltimore banker like his great-grandfather."

"Is that bad?"

"Yes, he needs to grow up to be his own person, not the clone of a dead relative."

"It'll be fine." She had snuggled up to him and laid his hand on her bulging belly. "Little Edward can be whoever he turns out to be."

It was four in the morning when her water had broken. Thankfully, he was home that night. He had dreamed of swimming in the Mediterranean Sea, in water the temperature of fresh pee, and woke up to find her side of the bed soaked and Anna in the bathroom.

"Jake," she called, that one word spiked with urgency.

"I'm awake," he said groggily. "What happened?"

"My water broke and I'm having contractions."

"Yup." He jumped off the soggy mattress and reached for his underwear. "Let's go."

"Call Rose Marie and tell her we're bringing Chris over."

Anna, the organized. She had arranged for the sitter to watch Chris while she had the baby, irrespective of the time of day or night. What to do with Chris during the birth hadn't crossed his mind until she told him of the plans. Sometimes she amazed him.

Her labor lasted only three hours and was uneventful. That's the way you want it, he thought. Normal. Regular. No complications.

As she was wheeled into the delivery room, he had walked beside the gurney, holding her hand. After she scooted onto the table and dug her heels into the stirrups, he perched on a stool beside her head and smoothed several strands of limp hair away from her damp forehead. She breathed in little shallow gasps and softly moaned in an easy rhythm.

Although he'd been the dad in the delivery room before, he had still been uncomfortable the second time around. His memories from medical school of possible obstetrical disasters were too fresh. Abruptio placenta. Placenta previa. Uterine rupture. Amniotic embolism. Puerperal sepsis. Eclampsia. All very bad.

Sweat oozed from his forehead and ran down the sides of his head. With each contraction, she clutched his hand and let out the scratchy sound of an angry goat. Her fingernails dug into his skin. It came back to him like a nightmare. That awful evening during his junior year on the OB rotation. He'd sat up all night monitoring the labor of a young mother and then watched, horrified, as she delivered a hydropic, dead little boy. That baby's face was so puffy that his eyes and mouth were mere slits, and the yellow-tinged skin of his legs had split open like overcooked bratwursts.

But Eddie's delivery was as normal as the labor had been, ending when his vigorous, healthy son had emerged from his lovely, exhausted wife. Tonight, driving home through the storm, those memories of Eddie's beginnings now seemed as meaningless as the former beauty of a road-killed cat. Now, Anna was crazed. Thank goodness Chris hadn't witnessed her breakdown. He hoped his son hadn't heard any of it. When he returned home, he'd have to face his in-laws, have to explain what had happened. Panic attack was the word he'd use to explain her behavior.

Suddenly the rain ceased beating against the windshield. The car was beneath an overpass. It seemed as if he were traveling through the eye of a hurricane. The car then exited the other side and the rain pounded the hood as fiercely as before. Two blocks farther up would be another overpass, with weedy railroad tracks running overhead.

As much as Jake wished otherwise, Eddie wasn't doing well. They had tried to wean him off the ventilator that afternoon, but whenever the nurses attempted to lower his backup rate or the PEEP or the inspired O_2 level, his blood gases tanked. Maybe that had set Anna off.

What would ultimately happen? he wondered. The ICU docs were so good at keeping people alive—at least keeping their hearts pumping and their lungs trading oxygen for carbon dioxide—that Eddie could go on like this for a long time. If he was still intubated after two weeks, they'd do a trach. Anna would resist a tracheostomy; she would see it as a step backward, which in some ways it would be. He'd have to find a gentle way to explain to her that without it, over time the endotracheal tube would rub raw the lining of their son's nose and throat.

Sometimes Anna was sure Eddie would die. Other times she seemed convinced the high-tech medical interventions would restore him to his former, normal self at no cost. In reality, a million things could go wrong. He could develop hydrocephalus, could have a stroke. He might develop ventilator-associated pneumonia or sepsis. Infection wouldn't be a bad way to die— they called pneumonia "the old man's friend" for good reason. But the ICU docs wouldn't let that happen; they'd flood him with enough antibiotics to sterilize a cesspool and the boy would make it through. As impossible as it was to predict how this would all turn out, it wasn't likely to be good and might be absolutely horrible.

The posts of the Amtrak overpass emerged like astrals out of the rain, lit by the headlights from the cars ahead. His hands gripped the steering wheel. He worked to steady the car as it rushed through the storm into the night.

Of all the tough times in his life—flunking his first anatomy quiz, Monica's abrupt departure, his father's death, failure to get his first choice for his ortho residency—Eddie's illness was the worst, the absolute worst. Anna's decompensation was second worst. Actually, the second worst was his failure to Eddie. He, the doctor, didn't recognize a serious illness in his own child. True, he hadn't been home. True, Anna may have misread how sick Eddie had been. But, still, he allowed his son to spend that whole night getting sicker and sicker.

He felt emptier now than after all those other tough times put together. This was an endless horror with no hope for something better. Tomorrow would be awful, the next day more awful. On and on.

All it would take would be a quick veer to the right. Just a minor turn of his wrists, about ten degrees would do it, thirty if he waited much longer. He glanced at the speedometer. The needle wavered between forty and forty-five. At that speed, it might not be a fatal injury. If he stepped on the gas and moved the needle up to seventy, it would be.

His fingernails dug into the plastic of the steering wheel as he fought against turning.

The car continued forward. The motor hummed. His foot rested on the accelerator. He closed his eyes, gripped the steering wheel, then turned it to the right. The car swerved.

When he opened his eyes, a concrete pillar was straight ahead, illuminated by his headlights. His pulse raced. Reflexively, he jerked the steering wheel to the left. The right side mirror barely missed the pillar. The car shimmied as it skidded back onto the wet road. In the rearview mirror, he saw the rain pelting the back window. The concrete pillars moved farther and farther away.

Now his heart thumped against his ribs and reverberated up to his ears. His hands trembled. What had he almost done? What was happening to him?

Chapter 25

Anna

Her predawn journey from the ICU in search of something to eat was about to end. She had wandered long enough through the dim lobby, through the eerie calm of the canteen. Now it was time to go back to Eddie.

Only one elevator was working, the one on the right. A hand-printed sign was taped to the door on the left. *Out of Order,* it read, the blue magic-marker letters wandering unevenly across the paper. Behind her, the fitful hum of the fluorescent lights echoed in the empty hallway while outside, beyond the glass doors, a cab waited in the rain, the glare of its roof light beaming like a yellow fog lamp into the night. She held a package of M&M'S in one hand and thirty-five cents—change from the vending machine—in the other. Above the right elevator door, the number 6 flickered a smoky crimson color. Then it blinked off.

Number 5 lit up. She expected it to blink off right away, but after two breaths, 5—Eddie's floor—still glowed red. From above, a hollow, metallic sound rolled, ever louder, into the quiet and echoed through the elevator shaft like thunder. She looked toward the ceiling, tried to see whatever had rumbled into the car several floors up. It sounded as if the giant from *Jack and the Beanstalk* were stomping overhead, as if Jack and Jill were tumbling down the hill.

As suddenly as it began, the clattering stopped and quiet returned.

This time of day—before the legions of chattering nurses arrived for the AM shift, before the breakfast trays rattled up from the kitchen, before sunlight threaded its way between the slats of the Venetian blinds—was the best for her. Now that the thunder from the elevator had stopped, the quiet was enormous, holy. She watched the numbers with a sense of anticipation, of serene expectation.

Number 5 blinked off. She heard something. Music. She turned her left ear—her better ear—toward the elevator. It was a woman's voice. Singing. A faint, faraway sound. Number 4 blinked red and the singing—pure, simple—became louder. Closer.

She stepped toward the elevator door and listened for the words. The song was familiar, a hymnlike chant whose swirling tones seemed to reach to the sky as if they were crawling, hand-over-hand, ever upward. She had heard the song before—years ago when she was a little girl. Slowly, the inside of her grandmother's Lutheran church returned to her—the organ pipes aligned like fence pickets, their conical tips aimed toward the floor, their sides perfectly parallel; the marble baptismal font, a faint crack curving around its bowl, beneath the stained glass window; the minister sweeping across the chancel, his white robe flowing like a cloud in his wake.

As number 3 lit up, the singing became even louder. She saw a lonely shepherd on a grassy hillside, his sheep quietly grazing beside a bubbling creek. The words of the song were clear now, the voice strong and confident. "O, Christ, the Lamb of God, that takest away the sins of the world . . ." Her grandmother was singing these words, her face in profile, her eyes shut, her mouth wide open, her fists tightly clinched. "Have mercy upon us." The minister stooped at the altar rail before her kneeling grandmother, tucked a wafer into her mouth, whispered words Anna couldn't hear from her seat in the pew.

Number 2 blinked red. The singing, haunting yet crystalline and louder, rang through the door. "O, Christ, the Lamb of God, that takest away the sins of the world. Grant us thy Peace."

Was this an angel? In the elevator? Maybe she'd come for Eddie. Maybe she was taking him away.

She pounded her fist—her fingers still wrapped around the M&M'S package—on the up button. Why was it taking so long to get to the lobby? The angel would step out of the elevator with him. She'd carry Eddie, wrapped in his flannel blanket, securely in her arms so he wouldn't fall. Where was she taking him? To Heaven? Surely an innocent, sinless baby like Eddie wouldn't go to hell.

Number 2 blinked off. The lobby level was next. The angel came closer, was almost there. Anna took a deep breath and held it. Maybe the angel would have a halo. Eddie would like the halo, would reach for it as he had reached for Anna's pearl necklace. Number 1 blinked on. The singing continued, even louder. "Oh, oh, Christ, the Lamb of God, that takest away the sins of the world. Have mercy upon us."

The shiny metal doors remained closed. Number 1 blinked off. "Oh, oh, Christ, the Lamb of God, that takest away the sins of the world. Grant us thy Peace."

Where were Eddie and the angel going? Away from her. Down. Down.

B blinked on. "Aaaamen." The plaintive chant, now beneath her, called to Heaven, the voice rising like a bird and then falling like a stone.

The thunder returned, roiling from below. Clunking. Rumbling. Then a soft swirling clatter that faded into nothingness.

B blinked off. Were they still on the elevator? Was the angel still holding Eddie?

Number 1 blinked on. The metal elevator doors parted. She searched the inside. Stared into each corner. No one was there. Empty.

Where was he? Where had the angel taken him?

She staggered into the vacant elevator. Her finger trembled, pressed number 5.

As she and the elevator rose, her heart raced. Number 2 lit up. 3. 4. 5. The doors opened and she scrambled down the hallway.

She ran through the door to the ICU, passed a cart loaded with soiled linen that waited to be rolled onto the elevator for the trip to the laundry.

Suddenly she stopped beside the nurses' station. What if the angel had put Eddie in a cart of dirty linen? He might be sloshing around inside a washing machine right now. She shook her head, trying to dislodge that horrible image. She was desperate to see his crib. She couldn't bear to see his crib.

She turned the corner toward his cubicle. The metal cage was still there. The equipment was still there, the monitor, the rows of IVACs, the urine bag dangling from the rail. Inside the crib, her baby lay beneath a flannel blanket, still attached to his IV lines, still attached to the ventilator. She closed her eyes against the tears. When she opened them again, he was still there.

Jake's arms hung helplessly at his sides as he walked toward her. A look of anguish shaded his face. Dark circles rimmed his pink-stained eyes. Two weeks ago, if someone had asked her to describe her husband in one word, she would have said, "strong." This morning, she would have described him—this stranger before her—as "lost."

"Hi," he said. He seemed unsure, cautious. "How're things today?"

"Better than yesterday."

"That's good."

She walked to his side, slipped her arm around his waist, and leaned against his chest. She couldn't stay mad at him any longer. He looked too miserable. His heartbeat, regular and reassuring, thumped under his shirt. She told him about the angel in the elevator.

"What do you think it means?" she asked. "Probably a sign from Heaven. Surely it's a good sign. Not a bad one."

"I think someone was singing in the elevator."

She pulled away from him. "You didn't hear it. I'm telling you, it was an angel."

He stared over her head, remained silent. "No, Anna, it was probably someone taking the laundry cart to the basement. I've often heard them rattle their carts off and on the elevator. The linen lady must have been singing, didn't realize anyone was listening."

She shook her head. "Remember how your mother used to call God an 'organizing principle'?" She stared into his eyes. "Do you believe that? Do you believe there is a God?" She needed him to understand. The singing had something to do with Eddie. It was a message.

He seemed to look right through her. "I don't know what to believe anymore." He sighed, turned away from Eddie's crib, patted her hand. "I have a case in a few minutes."

She sank into the chair. The wooden rockers squeaked as they rolled over the wax on the floor tiles. "Will you bring Chris here tonight? Please?"

He turned back to her, his eyes questioning.

"I want him to come here."

"It'd be too much for him."

"I won't take him back to see Eddie. It's against the rules, anyway."

"Are you sure?"

"It's in the handbook for parents." She pushed her toe into a pile of magazines at her feet, nudged the pamphlet on top.

"No, I mean, are you sure bringing Chris up here is the right thing to do? This is a very scary place. He's had enough trauma to last several lifetimes. He doesn't need any more."

"I'm sure."

He shrugged. "I'm not going to argue about this one, Anna. I think it's a bad idea, but at least Chris will get to see you again." He turned and headed for the door.

She watched his back, the tilt of his shoulders, the swing of his hips in his scrub pants, the way his hair curled over the neck of his scrub shirt. Who was he? She had slept beside him for more than six years. Their clothes hung, nested like teaspoons, in the same closet. Their names were on the same mortgage and checking account. Together they had created two children. And yet she didn't know him. Didn't know if he believed in a God. In Heaven. In the angel in the elevator.

He was a good person. That she knew. He loved his children. Loved her. Was committed to his patients. But, did he have a soul? Would the angel accept Jake into Heaven?

She stared at her son, unmoving in his crib, and listened to the faint swoosh of the ventilator as it pushed air into his lungs. If Eddie died, where would he go? He'd be beyond her reach, far, far away where she couldn't touch him, couldn't see him. Would he grow up there in Heaven or would he forever be a little baby?

Wait. Wait. All she did was wait. For the change of shift, for the nurses—Marcia followed by Natalie followed by Mike followed by Clarissa—to come, and then leave. For the results of endless laboratory tests—a slightly better number here, a slightly worse one there. Wait to go to sleep. Wait to wake up. Here in the waiting room. The infernal room for eternal waiting.

She folded a paper towel in half, then in half again, and then again. With the next fold, she had a fan. She waved it in front of her face—she felt silly—and then tossed it onto the mountain of dirty coffee cups, a sculpture of twisted white foam, in the trash basket.

What was she waiting for? For Eddie to sit up in his crib and cry, "Take me home"? For someone to erase everything that happened the night he got sick, to rewrite a page of history so that Jake was home to take care of him? For Dr. Farley to declare that Eddie would be normal in all ways, as capable as any other kid in LaSalle County of going to the University of Michigan, of reading Shakespeare, of playing the French horn, of running across a baseball field? She leaned against the headrest of the chair and closed her eyes. She saw nothing—the absence of anything, the product of her waiting.

The air, heavy and languid, brushed her cheek. Go away, she thought. I'm waiting.

Again, the air stirred. She opened her eyes. Rose Marie stood beside her, a plastic bag clutched awkwardly in her hands.

"Hi," Rose Marie whispered.

"Hi." She sat up straight and blinked her eyes.

"I brought something for Eddie." Rose Marie held the sack toward her. Toys"R"Us was stamped in green across its face.

"That's very thoughtful of you." She tried to clear her head. In some ways she was pleased to see Rose Marie. And yet, it took effort to be polite to her. What she most wanted was to continue waiting. Alone.

"How is he?" Rose Marie smiled. "How's my little Eddie-boy?"

That voice, high pitched and unnatural, dug into Anna like a nail. Why does she have to talk that way? That's baby talk. Doesn't she realize everything is different now? Eddie doesn't play anymore; he doesn't even breathe for himself. "He's pretty sick." She took the sack.

If she didn't work, Eddie wouldn't need a babysitter and Rose Marie wouldn't be standing here. She herself wouldn't be here. Eddie wouldn't have gotten sick. He wouldn't have gone to Rose Marie's, to that place where slobbery kids spread their germs all over each other.

Rose Marie swayed nervously from side to side. "My house's unbearably empty without him . . . and the other children." Her eyes filled with tears.

Anna's fingers stopped working the sack. "Where're the other kids?" She rubbed her forehead. What day was it? Sunday? Monday? No, Sunday.

"Amanda's in the hospital. You know that, right?"

"Yes, Jake told me." She laid the sack in her lap. "Are any of the other kids sick?" At least Chris wasn't sick. He was home with her parents and healthy.

"No, they seem fine." Rose Marie stared at the floor. "The

parents are afraid to bring them to my house, though. Afraid they'll get it, too, I guess." She dabbed her sleeve against the tear that trickled down her cheek.

She stared at Rose Marie. "I often wonder where Eddie caught this infection," she said.

Rose Marie wiped her wet face with quivering palms. The skin over the backs of her hands was dry and wrinkled, embossed with craggy veins like pale blue tree branches. "What do you mean?"

"Where'd he catch it?"

"Anna . . . do . . ." Rose Marie stuttered. "Did . . . Are . . . are you suggesting he got it from my house?"

"We don't know where. He got it somewhere."

Rose Marie began to sob in loud, lurching gasps. She looked diminished, defeated. Her old brown coat hung from her shoulders like a blanket on a hanger.

"How can you think he got it from my place? Please don't blame me. I love Eddie as if he's my own." Tears trickled down her cheeks. She dug in her purse and pulled out a piece of Kleenex.

"All I know is that Eddie is terribly sick and so is Amanda. The thing they have in common is your house."

Rose Marie stepped toward the door. "I guess I'd better leave."

Anna closed her eyes. She wanted Rose Marie to leave but didn't want her to leave. Eddie loved her, after all, spent hours and hours at her house while his mother—the lady who should have been taking care of him—worked. She opened her eyes again. "Wait. Don't go yet."

Rose Marie turned back to her.

"Do you want to see him?"

"Yes." Rose Marie's voice was thin, uncertain. She was no longer crying.

"You probably won't recognize him."

"No?"

"Well, he's puffy. His head is swollen and he has a breathing tube in his mouth." She rose from the chair, set the Toys"R"Us sack on the seat. "You can barely see his cheeks for the tape. He doesn't move. Or open his eyes."

Rose Marie followed her into the ICU.

Anna pointed to Eddie's crib. He lay, as he had for the past six days, motionless. Tubes ran in and out of him. Machines blinked and squawked beside him.

Rose Marie stopped at the foot of his bed. "Hi, honey," she whispered to Eddie.

Anna could barely hear Rose Marie's words. Certainly Eddie couldn't. Assuming, that is, Eddie could hear anything.

"How does he eat?"

"They pump formula through that tube in his nose. It goes down to his stomach."

"Oh." Rose Marie stared at Eddie for a long time, said nothing.

Now, Anna wished she would leave. It felt as if Eddie were on exhibition, a freak in a sideshow, a statue in a wax museum, and Anna was the docent.

Finally, Rose Marie turned toward her, her eyes glistening. "I'll go now. I hope everything turns out okay."

Something colorful lay against the bottom of the Toys"R"Us sack. Anna turned the bag upside down and a long, rubbery hose fell on the linoleum. It was a toy snake with grass green and leaf brown spots, eyes as blue as the sea, and a yellow stripe that zigzagged like lightning down its back. She picked it up and held the head away from her body so its curving tail dangled toward the floor. Then she coiled it in her lap and closed her eyes again. Would Eddie ever be able to play with this? With anything? She was still waiting.

Chapter 26
Rose Marie

A tangle of invoices, envelopes, second notices, and receipts covered the kitchen table. She slumped in her chair and scratched her wrist with the end of her pen.

Another outrageous Detroit Edison bill. Why was it so high? She kept the house at sixty-two degrees during the night, sixty-eight degrees while the kids were there. She had replaced the ragged weather stripping around the front door. The windows were double glazed. She used forty-five-watt lightbulbs and ran the washing machine only when it was fully loaded. What more could she do? Her hand was hesitant, but she wrote out the check.

She tapped the numbers from last month's grocery receipts into her calculator. $48.43. $14.90. $91.25—why was that one so big? Her eyes scanned the items. Apples, coffee, milk, bell peppers, canned tomatoes. The big beast was $23.39 for a roast. She had made a stock pot of chili with that beef, had frozen six pints for future lunches. She tried to economize on food, clipped coupons from the newspaper, watched for the sales, bought in bulk when she could. One receipt showed three bot-

tles of white zinfandel at $6.99 each. That was important. She
and Beefeater couldn't forego their evening wine.

What if Davey's mother withdrew him permanently? What if
Amanda quit? She folded her checkbook into her purse and
slid the calculator and receipts into the drawer. Out of sight,
out of mind. She wished it all away. But, the worries wouldn't
stay away. If Eddie died or was seriously handicapped, Chris
probably wouldn't come back. She stuck stamps on the envelopes and set them on the counter to go to the post office.
She couldn't make these payments if the kids stopped coming.
It would take months to rebuild the day care.

After the quiet weekend, she missed the kids, wanted their
company. None were there. None. The house seemed hollow.
It almost echoed from the emptiness. Now that the bills were
paid, she had nothing to do but fret. She stared out the kitchen
window at the lonely backyard, at a squirrel that raced along a
limb of the maple tree with a nut in his mouth. He was set, had
plenty of food, for a while, at least. Unlike her.

The nagging thoughts clawed inside her head. She still
needed to know if Amanda had the same infection that Eddie
had, to know if they had gotten it at her house. She needed a
guarantee that her day care was safe. If the health department
was worth its salt, it would do that. Even so, they couldn't make
the mothers bring the kids back. One thing the health department could do, for sure, was shut her down.

She had no choice; she had to get the information. She
found the number in the government section of the phone
book, under LaSalle County, and dialed 7-9-2. Her finger was
about to punch the 4, but she paused. Yes. No. Right. Wrong.
Call. Don't call. Her hand hovered over the 4 for another moment and then she set the phone receiver back on the cradle.
She didn't know what she would say.

She could ask for the fellow from the health department
who had spoken with her earlier. What was his name? She hadn't
written it down. She reran a mental recording of the conversation. His name was blank. She went through the conversation

again in her head. No name. She'd have to talk to whoever answered the phone.

She dialed 7-9-2 again, straightened a curtain in the kitchen window, and hung up the phone. She decided to take a nap.

An hour later, she still needed information, needed to call the health department. She got up from the bed, smoothed the bedspread, fluffed the pillow, and, slowly, walked to the phone in the kitchen. Her chest tightened. Would they give her the information she wanted? Maybe they'd accuse her of running an unsafe center, would rescind her license. Her fingers dallied on the phone buttons. She rubbed the oily smear off 7, coaxed the strand of hair from between 4 and 5. Finally, her hand quaking, she finished dialing the number.

She introduced herself. The man from the health department did the same. She asked if Amanda and Eddie had the same kind of meningitis. He said he didn't know.

"What do you mean, you don't know?" she said. "How can you not know?"

The man's voice was deep and scratchy like a smoker's. "As I just told you, Mrs. Lustov, the laboratory tests aren't completed yet. All we can say is that four children in LaSalle County have meningitis." He paused a moment. Then before she could begin speaking again, he continued, "Three boys have bacterial meningitis caused by a germ called *Streptococcus pneumoniae*. We don't know yet what kind of meningitis the fourth child, the girl, has."

"What if she has the same kind Eddie has?"

"Then we'll have four children in LaSalle County with pneumococcal meningitis."

"You're playing games with me." She slammed her fist on the kitchen counter. "What does that mean for me and my day care?"

"As I already said, we won't know if the kids at your day care have the same kind of meningitis until the laboratory completes its analysis."

"What if they *are* the same strain?"

"Then we may have an epidemic on our hands."

She brushed a dead wasp from the kitchen windowsill into the sink and washed it down the drain. "Would you shut down my day care if it's an epidemic?"

"I can't answer that right now."

"Well, I have to know, because this is my business and I need to know what might happen to it."

"We should have the information by tomorrow or the next day."

"Fine. That's just fine." Her words felt like acid-tipped darts. "What kind of health department is this? These kids are very sick and you guys haven't figured out what they have. My business is going down the sewer and you refuse to help me. The parents are terrified to bring their children to my house. I pay taxes and deserve to get better service from you people."

The man said nothing.

"Are you still there?" She could tell she was shouting.

"Yes, but I can't answer your questions, because we don't have the information yet."

"Well, you could tell me what would happen if they both have the same kind, or what would happen if they don't." Her throat was getting sore. He wasn't listening to her. She clutched the phone to her ear. "You could call the children's parents and tell them my house is safe. You could—"

"I told you I can't answer all your questions right now." He sounded angry. "You'll have to wait until the final laboratory results are available. Good-bye, Mrs. Lustov."

The dial tone hummed in her ear.

She slammed the phone on the hook, then picked it up and dialed her daughter.

"That guy's an asshole," she sobbed. She hated crying to Sarah but couldn't help it. The man had been so ugly to her. She tore a sheet of paper towel from the roll under the sink and blew her nose.

"Mother, you need to settle down. You're totally out of control. Take a few deep breaths and tell me what's going on."

She told her daughter what he had said. "Sarah, the man hung up on me."

"Well, that was rude. I guess you just have to wait until the laboratory finishes their tests. Have you seen Anna or Eddie?"

"I went to the hospital yesterday." Her eyes welled up again and she dabbed them with the paper towel. "It was awful. Eddie looked like a corpse. He didn't move at all, just lay there—still as a stone—with the breathing machine puffing air into a tube stuck down his throat. His skin was gray and waxy. Like recycled paraffin. I didn't dare touch him, he seemed so fragile. It breaks your heart."

"How about Anna?"

"She's a zombie. Very upset. Remember how stylish she always was? No more." Rose Marie shook her head. "I took a toy snake, but Eddie's way too sick to play with it yet."

Sarah's voice softened. "Is he going to make it?"

"Didn't dare ask. Why did this have to happen to us, anyway?"

She called Amanda's house and waited for someone to answer. After the fifth ring, Amanda's mother said, "Hello?"

"Hi. It's Rose Marie. I'm calling to check on Amanda."

"She's doing better but is still in the hospital." Her voice sounded tentative, as if she wasn't interested in speaking with Rose Marie.

"Good. Hopefully she'll be able to come home soon."

"We hope so, too."

Now what should she say? "Um . . . You know . . . I've read the reports in the newspaper and have spoken to the health department. Have the doctors told you what kind of meningitis Amanda has? Apparently they aren't sure if it's the same kind that Eddie has."

"They don't know yet. Amanda still has her IV and they're still giving her antibiotics."

"Have you read the papers or heard the news on TV? Apparently there are four cases."

"Yes, we've been told that." She sounded flat. Was she mad at her? Or maybe just worried about her daughter?

"I've been wondering how the newspaper reporter got my name. Did you by any chance give it to him?" She let out a deep sigh. The question had haunted her for days.

"No. I wouldn't do anything like that." She sounded surprised, puzzled. Perhaps a little offended.

"Good. I couldn't imagine you had, but I can't figure out who did."

"Uh, maybe . . ." Amanda's mother paused. "Maybe . . . My friend Laura's husband works for the paper. I called her as soon as we learned Amanda had meningitis. He might have had something to do with that."

"That's probably it." At least she had an answer. "The reporter was pretty brash, demanding information about the other kids." Why were people so snoopy? Why couldn't they mind their own business?

"That was unfortunate. But, with everything else that has happened, I guess the news would have gotten out one way or the other. They haven't used your name in any of the reports, have they?"

"No, thank goodness. At least not that I've seen. That would be horrible."

After the call, Rose Marie made a cup of coffee and settled into the lawn chair on her patio. The Big Wheels were all lined up against the garage and the sandbox toys were piled in the sandbox. One question was answered—she knew who called the reporter. But, there were still so many other questions. Did Eddie and Amanda have the same kind of meningitis? Did they get it at her house? What would happen to the children? What would happen to her?

Chapter 27

Jake

He felt a tap on his shoulder.

"You've seen the newspapers, I assume." Farley spoke in his usual way, authoritative and fearless, the way ICU docs always were. It was a voice Jake could trust.

"Yeah, read all about it." He liked this guy. Didn't have to second-guess his medical decisions. Farley had, after all, probably twenty-five years of experience in critical care medicine and was the fellow ultimately responsible for whatever happened to Eddie; at least for what happened while in his unit.

"Hopefully the reporters haven't been pestering you."

"They've tried, but my mother-in-law's manning the phones at home and she's a brick wall."

"I'm always amazed with the fear-mongering the press applies to infections . . . Lyme disease, flesh-eating bacteria, West Nile virus, meningitis. A person is one thousand times more likely to be in a car accident than to get any of those rare infections, but . . ."

Farley stopped midsentence. "I made that up, you know. That statistic. But I bet it's close."

They neared Eddie's crib. The closest side rail was down. Jake's knee-jerk reaction was to yank it up. But there was no risk—Eddie wasn't going to roll to the floor, wasn't going to roll anywhere.

Anna sat beside the crib, her head resting on her arm. She lifted her eyes toward Farley with the expectant, reality-weighted look of a mother who seeks a thread of good news from a doctor, yet knows, deep down, he has none to give.

"Our day care lady's been bothered by the reporters," she said. "Now she's scared to death the health department's going to shut her down."

"Oh, brother." Farley shifted to the other foot. "I've spoken several times to their director. He's a pretty sharp guy who has a huge mess on his hands. Even though every parent—at least every reporter—in the state thinks we have a meningitis epidemic here, apparently we don't."

Farley turned away from Anna, toward him. "That fellow from the health department, Klug . . . Myron or Martin or whatever his name is . . . told me just a few minutes ago that all three of the kids with bacterial meningitis—Eddie and the other two boys—have *Strep pneumoniae*, but they are different genotypes, so the cases aren't related." He folded his arms over his chest and then continued. "The four-year-old girl, the one on the pediatric ward downstairs, had a sterile tap. Apparently she received a couple doses of amox for otitis, so it's not clear yet if she has bacterial meningitis or not. Klug is waiting for the enteroviral PCR on her spinal fluid from the state lab."

Anna looked confused. Jake could tell by the twist of her jaw. She wouldn't have understood a thing Farley had just said and would be mad about it. He wanted Farley to talk to her, to use words and concepts she could understand. He was tired of trying to explain medical information to her.

"That girl is Amanda, from Eddie's day care." Anna stroked Eddie's leg. "Did she catch it from him?" Her eyes narrowed. "Or did he catch it from her?"

"Well, that isn't clear," said Farley, turning toward Anna. "Her culture didn't grow any bacteria. It's possible she has the same germ as Eddie, but the antibiotics she received for her ear infection—at first her pediatrician thought she had an ear infection—might keep it from growing in the laboratory. Even if they had the same germ, it'd be impossible to know who gave it to who . . . uh, to whom."

Farley spoke directly to him, again. "If her spinal fluid shows enterovirus, then, of course, the cases aren't related at all and it's an uncanny piece of bad luck that two kids in the same day care came down with different kinds of meningitis about the same time. Since the bacterial culture is negative, if her enteroviral PCR is also negative, then we don't know what kind of meningitis she has."

He studied Farley's face, the wise eyes flanked by crow's feet, the narrow lips. News for his patients—both the good kind and the bad—slipped through those lips with aplomb, very often.

Anna shook her head and looked down at her lap. Suddenly her eyes grew huge and she sat up straight. "What about Chris? Could he get the same thing?"

"Anna, we've talked about that," Jake said. "I told you *Strep pneumo* isn't contagious. Chris wouldn't get it from Eddie."

"I'm asking Dr. Farley." Her steely eyes drilled into him, daring him to interfere.

"Has Chris had the Prevnar vaccine?" Farley asked.

She shrugged. "That, again. I don't know exactly what he's had, except he's gotten everything he should." She leaned against the back of her chair. "Eddie had that vaccination and he still got the infection."

She's so unpredictable, he thought. First she forgets the discussion they had about contagion and now she's invoking second-order logic.

"According to Dr. Klug, Eddie's germ is serotype nineteen A, which isn't in the vaccine." Farley proceeded to explain serotypes to her, saying that the vaccine contained only seven of the ninety types and, thus, didn't prevent all *Strep pneumo* infections—only the most common ones. "Recently, we've seen a few infections with the serotypes that aren't in the vaccine," he added.

"So where does that leave Chris?" Anna scratched at a slub in the crib sheet. "If Eddie had the vaccine and still got the germ, couldn't Chris get the germ even though he's had the vaccine?"

"That's unlikely."

Farley was very tolerant of Anna's inquisition, Jake thought. If Eddie were his own patient, he would have been fed up with this conversation by now. Some mothers just don't quit.

"Unlikely?" Anna murmured, tipping her chin.

She didn't miss an opportunity for a trap, Jake thought.

"Really, really unlikely," Farley said. "*Strep pneumoniae* meningitis doesn't seem to spread from person to person."

"That's what we discussed earlier, Anna," Jake said, again.

"Then how could Amanda get it?"

"Uh . . ." Farley seemed to be thinking. Maybe even he had come to the end of his rope with Anna's questions. "Well, of course, we don't know that Amanda has it."

"It makes no sense." Anna's voice became shrill as she straightened the flannel blanket that covered Eddie's chest.

"Well, it does to me," Jake said. Why was she asking so many questions? She was expecting explanations where there were none, at least not yet. "Chris's fine. If he starts looking sick, we'll race him to the ER, but otherwise we'll just watch him carefully."

Farley patted Anna's arm. "That's a good plan. Understandably, you have a lot of questions. The problem is . . . we just don't know what's going on with these cases right now. After we get all the information, it should make a lot more sense, both to you and to us."

She turned away from Farley. Her brow furrowed. "Are you sure it's okay, Jake?" Her voice was hard. Her glare was fierce. "Are you really sure or are you just saying that?"

"Yes, I'm sure." What did he have to do to make her stop the questions?

"Well, you had it wrong the night Eddie got sick."

"That's the limit, Anna," he yelled and slammed his fist against Eddie's crib. "You're over the line. You also had it wrong the night Eddie got sick and you were there. I wasn't. Remember, Eddie's my son, too, and you blew it that night."

The sound was like a muffled scream. It came from her, from behind the Kleenex she held to her mouth. She was sobbing. He had hurt her deeply. What kind of a husband did that to the woman he loved, to the mother of his children?

"I'm sorry, Anna," he whispered. "I need a break." He turned from Eddie's crib, walked past the nursing station, out the sliding glass doors of the ICU. He couldn't help her now. Let Farley handle his wife for a while; that's his job.

He sat at the desk in the residents' room and dialed her number, the one he had written on the back of the pizza receipt.

A woman's voice answered, "Pediatric office. How may I direct your call?"

He stuttered, speaking in a slightly muffled voice. "This is, uh, doctor, uh, Jacob Campbell from Michigan. I'm trying to reach Dr. Daley."

"Is this about a patient?"

"Well . . . yes." Eddie was a patient. That wasn't a complete lie.

"Name? If you give me the patient's name, I'll get the record for Dr. Daley."

"Oh, she doesn't know this patient. I want her opinion about a patient here."

"Okay, Dr. Campbell. I'll track her down."

In seventeen heartbeats, she was on the phone.

"This is Dr. Daley."

He froze. That voice. It hadn't changed a bit over the past eight years. Its melodic sound, still crisp, still somewhat husky and slightly lower than many women's voices, paralyzed him. He couldn't speak.

"Hello? This is Dr. Daley."

"Hello, Monica. This is Jake Campbell."

"Jake . . . When the secretary said it was Dr. Jacob Campbell, I didn't make the connection."

"I've been wondering about you and learned that you practice in Maine. Thought I'd call and catch up." He sat back in his chair, tried to make himself comfortable, but his muscles refused to relax.

"I'm actually considering a move," she said. "There's an attractive position at a health center in Vermont and I'm thinking of relocating. The pay is good, the hours reasonable." She said nothing about a husband.

"And, you?" she asked. "What are you up to?"

"Actually," he said, "we're having a tough time right now. Our baby—he's six months old—is in the ICU with *Strep pneumo* meningitis."

"Oh, Jake. That's awful." She sounded distressed, unnerved. "Just awful."

He told her about the serotype 19A strain, about the events of the ICU stay. "He may be extubated soon and seems to be holding his own. We don't know about neurologic sequelae, but, as you can tell, it doesn't look real good." Talking to her was like swimming in a calm, warm lagoon. She understood Eddie's disease, knew all the devastating possibilities. He could use their medical language, didn't have to define any of the technical terms.

She said she wished he and his family didn't have to go through all this.

"If you move, what about your family? I guess I'm asking . . . do you have a husband and kids that have to move, too?"

"No. Neither. I'm still running solo. I enjoy my freedom, enjoy traveling with my friends. We—my friends Al and Michael and I—just returned from Tunisia. It was a great trip . . . Hold a sec, Jake."

She must have muffled the phone with her hand. He could hear her talking but couldn't make out the words.

"Sorry for the interruption. Nurse had a question."

"I know you're busy and this isn't a great time to talk. Perhaps we can catch up in more detail later."

"That would be great." She was quiet, then continued. "I've

been thinking of a trip to Michigan to visit my mother—she still lives in the Thumb. I'd like to see you again."

His heart was pounding. Was that what he wanted? Was that why he called her?

Finally, he said, "Thanks, Monica. I'm glad we had the chance to talk. When you're in Michigan, give me a call and maybe we can have lunch or something. I hope all goes well with your move."

"Good-bye, Jake," were her final words.

What could it hurt if they had lunch? Chances were good she wouldn't call on her next trip home. Likely she'd returned to the Thumb during the intervening eight years and hadn't contacted him.

He was very tired. His head ached.

Chapter 28

Anna

Now what day was it? Sunday? Monday? She had lost her sense of the earth's rhythms. The arrival of morning, the coming of night seemed to have no meaning. Time stood still in the waiting room, that bottomless dungeon without windows. She closed her eyes to banish the view but she was still there. The coughing, the scraping of shoes on the indoor-outdoor carpet, the rustle of papers, the squeal of the seat cushions—endlessly, endlessly. They never stopped. Those sounds wrapped around her like a prickly sweater.

She opened her eyes and watched Charlotte step into the room—she held a cardboard cup of coffee in one hand, a bagel in the other—trailed by her husband with a hot dog and a can of Vernors. The father who wanted Eddie's liver for his little girl snored softly on the couch beneath his blanket. These people, as oppressive as sweaty shirts or smelly socks, were suffocating her. What time was it, anyway? Did it matter?

Earlier, as she sat in the chair beside Eddie's crib, the portable X-ray machine had rumbled into the unit. Later—was it two minutes or two hours later?—she had been jolted awake by the sound of the machine being pushed back out between the beds. How many X-rays had the technician taken? One? Four? Thirty?

Even earlier, the nurse had drawn a blood sample from Eddie's IV line, then another nurse emptied his urine bag, recording the volume on his bedside chart. "I'll see you tomorrow," one nurse said when her shift ended. Another had said, "I'm off the next three days—if Eddie hasn't moved to the pediatric ward, I'll see you Friday." Round and round they went.

She should have been accustomed to crazy hospital schedules; that was the way Jake worked—all night every third to fifth night except the month he had been on a pathology rotation; sometimes on weekends, sometimes not. Before Eddie got sick, she longed for regularity and predictability and order but had to adapt to Jake's unscheduled schedule because she couldn't change it. She still longed for regularity and predictability and order, but she wanted it for herself. Now Jake's schedule had little impact on her.

Slowly, she turned the pages of a magazine, watched the colors move first from right to left and then become buried in the pile of preceding pages. Photos of dining rooms, of ski vacation retreats, of greenhouse windows alive with amaryllis blossoms passed before her.

What had happened to her plants? she wondered. She had coaxed the gardenia along since last Mother's Day; the Christmas cactus had burst into a torrent of fuchsia after Thanksgiving. Sunday was her usual plant-watering day. Then she remembered—she had watered them on Saturday afternoon when she was home.

What was today? She had gone home on Saturday. The days melted together—like butter in the sunshine—into a very long stretch of endless time. She glanced again at the magazine in her lap, the January issue, with recipes for beef stew and chicken 'n' dumplings and gourmet macaroni and cheese—hunker-down food for dark, cold winter days. She knew it wasn't January; they had had that month already. But, they hadn't had Easter yet.

Saturday she had been home. Rose Marie had visited on Sunday; she'd come just as the loudspeaker announced mass in the hospital chapel. So, today must be Monday.

She saw a flash of movement straight ahead—the wave of a hand or the nod of a head—and looked up from her magazine. There, across the room in the doorway, stood Chris. She set the magazine on the table beside her and started up from her chair.

The hem of his *Lion King* T-shirt hung almost to his knees. His shoes—the kind that blinked when he walked—stood motionless. A deep frown shrouded his eyes.

Yet, he looked like a prince. A long-missing, now-found treasure. It was like a dream—her son here at last. "Chris, honey," she called, "come here."

"No," he said. She could barely hear him. His body remained still, framed by the doorway.

"Honey, come here," she called again, trying to mold her voice into a kind and welcoming sound. She knew it was a B-movie voice, phony and saccharine. But maybe it would draw him to her.

Jake appeared behind Chris and prodded him forward. The boy's chest arched into the room under the pressure of his father's hand, but his feet remained planted in the doorway. "I don't wanna," he murmured in a whiny voice. His eyes looked past Anna. His face was contorted into an ugly, defiant scowl.

"Move it, buddy." Jake pushed against his son's shoulders.

Chris tried to wiggle away from his father's grip, but his feet stayed put. "NO," he called.

"What's wrong, Chris?" Anna asked. Why didn't he want to see her? "Come here." Why was he being so difficult? He seemed bedeviled. "Show us how your shoes blink."

Chris clapped his hands over his ears and squeezed his eyes shut.

Dark energy, an ominous, threatening force, wove through the room. The usual sounds—murmuring, running water, scraping chairs, slamming doors—were gone, replaced by a cold, expectant silence. The other parents were staring at her, waiting to see what she would do about her naughty child.

"For Christ's sake," Jake said, "what's wrong with you?" He lifted Chris by the waist and carried him to her chair. The boy thrashed his arms and pedaled his feet. His loose shoelace jerked beside his foot like a rat's tail.

Jake set Chris on the floor in front of her. She wrapped her arms around him and drew his tense, reluctant body to hers. "Poor baby," she whispered, kissing his earlobe.

"Don't let him get away with that," Jake said.

She pulled Chris into her lap, turned a lock of his hair around her finger, and let him nuzzle into her chest. The warmth of his body was soothing and familiar. "He's frightened."

"I don't care what he is. We can't let him act this way."

She glanced toward the other parents and then whispered, "Please, Jake."

He sighed and dropped into a nearby chair, his lips drawn into a firm line.

"Tell Mommy what's wrong," she murmured to Chris. "Are you scared about something?"

Chris slowly shook his head.

"Are you mad Mommy left you?"

His eyes narrowed.

She rocked him back and forth, repeating in a singsong voice, "It's okay, Chris, it's okay. It's okay, Chris, it's okay." Over and over. Slowly he relaxed, his arms and legs loosened. He smelled fresh as clean laundry.

While she sang Chris's name, she turned toward her husband. His eyes were rimmed in red, his mouth was now pursed, the hollows of his cheeks were deeper than she had seen them before. She hugged Chris even closer against her chest.

"Jake, please don't be like that."

He said nothing.

"Please."

"Like what?" He refused to look at her.

"Like a jackass."

Jake closed his eyes and leaned his head against the back of his chair.

Chris shifted in her lap, drove his knee into her belly. She groaned and then moved his leg. She heard the sound of rushing water from the other side of the wall—the flush of a toilet. Chris lifted his head at the noise, then buried it against her again.

"This visit hasn't worked out very well, has it?" Jake said. "I told you it wasn't a good idea for Chris to come here."

"Where's Eddie?" Chris spoke into the folds of Anna's blouse.

"He's in the other room." She pointed toward the door into the ICU. "Over there."

Jake's pager sounded. He unhooked it from his belt, squinted at the message, sighed, and pulled himself up from his chair.

"Gotta run. This'll be quick and then I'll take Chris back home. Okay, buddy?"

"Yeah," Chris answered. His voice was timid, quiet.

Back home. Chris would have to go back home. She felt as if she'd been ripped apart. Chris had to go home. Eddie had to stay here. It was a twist on the Solomon story. Rather than threatening to chop the baby in two, for her, the mother was being chopped in two. If there was a Heaven, Solomon was up there in his white robes telling Saint Peter that Anna Campbell was destined to hell.

"Thirty-nine point two," muttered the evening nurse as she pulled the thermometer away from Eddie's armpit. "Wonder what that's all about."

"Huh?" Anna stood at the window, and watched night creep over the hospital grounds below. Someone lowered the window shade in the opposite wing of the hospital. An ambulance screamed down the street and around the corner. She turned toward the nurse. "What did you say?"

"Eddie's temperature is thirty-nine point two."

"What's that in Fahrenheit?"

"Let's see . . ." The nurse stared into the corner of the room, tipped her head first to the left, then to the right. "About one hundred two."

"That's way too high." She scrambled from the window to Eddie's side. "Why does he have a fever?"

"Don't know." The nurse shrugged. "I'll tell the resident on call. I don't think they ordered anything for fever."

Eddie's forehead seemed more flushed than usual. The skin on his chest was blotchy. She laid her palm on her son's leg and felt the heat of his body. She drew her hand away. He was too hot.

A sour taste tinged the back of her throat. She swallowed hard. Maybe the meningitis was back. Maybe he had a new infection. She touched his flushed forehead. It also was too warm. How could anything else possibly go wrong?

For the next half hour, she stroked his skin, trying to rub away the fever. Her fingers tracked the curve of his hip, the mound of his belly, the plane of his chest that rose and fell with the rhythm of the ventilator. She avoided his left wrist so she wouldn't disturb his arterial line. Her touch lingered on the right side of his neck, where the skin was soft as dough and she could feel the reassuring throb of his pulse.

The nurse checked his temperature again. "Thirty-nine point six this time." She wrote the number on his bedside chart.

Anna glared at the nurse, at her raw hands, at the strands of gray threaded through her dull hair. How could she be so blasé about this? He had had a high fever a week ago and it was meningitis. He had almost died. He could still die, and this nurse seemed unconcerned about the fever.

"Why should he have a fever now?" She wanted to grab the nurse's wattly neck, to make her care about the fever.

"Could be lots of things. I'll see if I can get something ordered for it."

The nurse disappeared around the wall of Eddie's cubicle.

Anna dropped into the rocking chair, covered her face with her hands. She felt hollow, empty as a grave. She tried to keep from weeping, was tired of crying. She needed to stay strong.

"Mrs. Campbell?" A woman in a long white clinical coat, its bulging pockets accentuating her hips, turned the pages of

Eddie's bedside chart as she approached his crib. "I'm Dr. Boyd. I see Eddie has a bit of a fever. Looks like it just started this afternoon."

"What's causing that?" Anna's words jerked out in little gasps. She couldn't get enough air. "Is it the meningitis again?"

"Well, I doubt that. Let's see . . . he had *Strep pneumo* that was sensitive to ceftriaxone, so he's been on the right antibiotic." She turned another page. "And he's getting a generous dose."

Dr. Boyd ran her hand over the soft spot on Eddie's head, listened to his chest, prodded his stomach, and tapped below his kneecaps with the edge of her stethoscope. She stepped back from Eddie, twisted her lips, rapped her pen on the crib rail twice, and finally said to the nurse, "We need to check a CBC, a blood culture, urine culture, chest X-ray." She paused a moment and then continued, "We'd also better get a head CT." She glanced at her watch. "Probably can't get one tonight, but we'll order it for the morning, and if he still has the fever, we'll go ahead with it then." She spoke quickly, robotically, as if she were a pilot reciting the checklist preparatory to takeoff.

"Why can't he have it tonight?" The specter of delay flapped around her like an injured bird. "This is serious. If he needs the scan, do it now." Never again would she wait before acting on something that seemed wrong with Eddie.

Dr. Boyd smiled. "We understand your worry about this fever. There are many possibilities, most of them not at all worrisome."

"Like what?"

The young doctor returned the bedside chart to its hook. "Maybe he caught a virus here in the hospital. Or, maybe he's reacting to one of his medications. Or he may have a mild pneumonia from lying so still or maybe a urinary tract infection from his bladder catheter. We'll check a few tests to make sure he doesn't have another serious infection, but I'm not worried about anything bad happening. His ventilator settings are normal, the nurses aren't suctioning ugly stuff out of his trach tube, his heart rate and blood pressure are stable. Basically, his only symptom is a fever."

Anna closed her eyes and shook her head. How could this be

happening? She slumped again into the chair beside Eddie's crib.

"Would you like us to call your husband?" the doctor asked. "We could explain to him what we have planned."

"Go ahead. Page him." Again, he was away, not available when she needed him. "He's on call. He's here somewhere." She held her hand against her head. "Just don't take any chances with my baby."

Chapter 29

Rose Marie

The silence haunted her. Quiet sounds that last week were buried beneath the children's racket now rolled like thunder through the stillness. Beefeater wheezed in the bedroom, a woodpecker rat-a-tat-tat-ted on the neighbor's tree, a squirrel pranced on the roof. Today was the second day of the workweek, the second day in her echo-filled house without the children. Even the walls seemed to miss the kids.

She stared at the crossword puzzle—five letter word for mother-of-pearl, third letter was *c*—and wrote *n, a* and *r, e* in the open boxes on either side of the *c*. She couldn't concentrate. She gazed out the window. The sun ducked behind a cloud; a crow flew across her backyard. She couldn't shake off the worry. How would she pay the tax bill that was due next month? Or the Detroit Ed bill? Or the Shell Oil bill? She had planned to spend next Christmas in Houston with Sarah—away from the bitter Michigan winter for a week or so. The airfare would be at least six hundred dollars. She would probably need to find a new job; her life as a child-care provider seemed to be over. She closed her eyes and slowly shook her head. It all seemed so hopeless.

A sharp ring cut into the silence, startling her. Then another. Cautiously she lifted the receiver. Maybe another of the children was sick. Maybe Eddie had died. That reporter might be calling again, the pushy one who had wanted the names and phone numbers of the children.

"Mrs. Lustov? This is Dr. Klug from the LaSalle County Health Department."

She stiffened.

"Yes?" she said. The children's parents had been scared away, had acted as if her house were teeming with rabies or Ebola or one of those other germy things that kill people—and now another guy from the health department was on the phone.

"I understand you have some concerns regarding the health department and the situation at your day care . . . specifically about the children with meningitis."

She leaned against the kitchen sink and chewed her lip. He was probably calling because of what happened yesterday. Somehow that conversation had gone wrong. When she talked to the other guy from the health department, he'd been a jerk. She remembered shouting at him.

Now she twisted the phone cord around her pointer finger, first clockwise and then counterclockwise, and convinced herself with each turn that her reaction to that other man had been entirely justified.

"Well, of course I'm concerned," she said. "Two of my kids are desperately ill and the parents of the other children won't bring them back here."

"I'd like to explain where we are with this and to answer any further questions," he said. He sounded like an undertaker—formal, low voiced, controlled. She scratched her arm. She didn't want smooth words from him. She wanted the whole nightmare to go away.

"Late yesterday, we received the final report from the state lab on Amanda's samples," Dr. Klug continued.

She held her breath.

"Amanda has the viral form of meningitis, the kind that's mild with no lasting effects. She's doing well and went home from the hospital last night."

"That's good," she said tentatively. Could she trust him?

"Yes, that *is* good," said Dr. Klug. He sounded less formal. "There's more good news. Since Eddie's and Amanda's infections are caused by different kinds of germs, there's no epidemic in your day care, or in LaSalle County, for that matter."

"My other children are safe?"

"Yes."

"Guaranteed?"

"Well, Mrs. Lustov, I can't promise that nothing bad will ever happen to those kids, but I can say we don't expect them to get the serious form of meningitis."

"You 'don't expect.' What does that mean?" Her head throbbed. This might be okay, but how could she be sure? Why did these people talk this way? She wished they would answer her questions directly.

"Although Edward has bacterial meningitis, fortunately he has the kind that doesn't spread to other children."

"As far as I know," she said, "the other children are all fine."

"That's our understanding as well."

"Dr. Klug, if you had a preschool child . . ." She paused a moment. Did she dare ask her question? Would he think it silly? Or inappropriate? What the hell. "If your child needed day care, would you feel comfortable bringing him or her to my house after all this?"

"I'd bring him this very afternoon. Your home isn't a threat to anyone."

She blinked back the tears. She coughed into the sleeve of her blouse so he wouldn't know she was crying and wiped her nose on a paper towel. "Could you call the parents of the other children and tell them that?" she asked, clearing her throat. "They're scared to bring their kids back here."

He didn't answer right away. Finally he said, "I'll have Mr. Watts speak with them. We'll need their names and phone numbers."

That evening, she picked up the newspaper again to finish the crossword puzzle. She filled in several words until she had only one empty square, P☐ RT. The clue read "to snare, in reverse."

A passing car roared down the street, its radio turned up full throttle. She glanced out the window. When she looked back at the puzzle, her mind traced the squares backward, from right to left. TR☐P. That's it, she laughed. The reverse of "part" would be "trap." She wrote *a* in the blank square. She had figured it out. That must be a sign. Another sign of good things to come.

Sawyer would be back tomorrow. When his mother called earlier to ask when she could bring him back—she said she'd gotten a call from the health department—Rose Marie hadn't known how to react. Should she apologize? What for? They were the ones who panicked. She'd done nothing wrong. After an awkward silence, she'd finally said, "I'll be thrilled to have all the children come back. The sloppy-joe mix and Rice Krispies bars are ready in the fridge." It had been the first time she'd laughed in days.

Now the phone rang again. It was Meghan's mother. "We'd like to bring Meghan back to your house tomorrow. Is that okay? Meghan misses you a lot. She keeps asking about Beefeater. She even saved the crust from her sandwich this noon for him."

It was getting darker in the house when she hung up the phone. The sun was heading toward the garage roof and green-black clouds threatened in the west. Thank goodness all the toys in the backyard were put away. The coming storm might be a rough one.

Memories of the children marched through her head. Baby Eddie trying to eat smashed bananas. Chris racing a truck through the sandbox. Meghan sucking her fingers. Sawyer drawing with his left and right hands, at the same time. Amanda the commander. She wondered about Amanda and phoned her mother.

"How's Amanda doing—or is she Gretchen today?" she asked.

"She's still a little tired from being sick, but we'd like to come back to your house next week. Would that work for you?"

"Absolutely." Her sigh of relief must have been audible even over the phone line.

Amanda's mother then said, "Oh, by the way, Amanda has changed her name again. Now she's Ruth, after one of the nurses on the pediatric ward."

Rose Marie laughed again, the third time in an hour. After a week of misery, it felt very good to laugh.

Chapter 30

Jake

The staff room was too hot. He loosened his tie and replayed the last couple seconds of the dictation he was working on. Then he hit the record button and continued. "We plan to see Mr. Holliday in follow-up in the ortho clinic in three weeks. Sincerely, Jacob Campbell, MD. End of dictation."

Earlier in the afternoon, he had stopped by the ICU to check on Eddie. The little guy had developed a fever yesterday and Anna was beside herself with worry. The docs were looking into it, were waiting for the culture results. Other than the fever, everything was pretty stable. He knew a little fever was nothing to get upset about, but Anna didn't know that. She wouldn't listen when he tried to explain that to her.

He was fed up with the whole show. Although Eddie wasn't getting worse, he wasn't making terrific progress, either. He was still on the ventilator. No one knew how anything with Eddie would turn out. And the Chris problem. He was a terror. Wetting the bed. Sucking his thumb. Whining, throwing things, refusing to behave. Worst of all, Anna was not the woman he married. There had always been things about her he didn't understand, but she had turned into a complainer, a demander, a yeller and, yet, in a quick moment, she could suddenly turn into a whimpering lump, incapable of coping with anything.

This was new. The Anna he loved was kind and fair. Even when they disagreed—about the basement tile, for example— she listened to his ideas. She liked the light fixture he preferred for the front hall and thought it a better fit for the small room than the one she had chosen. His Anna was strong, amazingly able to handle a classroom of newly arrived immigrants. She enjoyed her students, could see beyond their bickering. She laughed at his jokes, was quick to see irony in the quirky things around her. She had scolded him for pulling grapes off the stems. "Hey," she had said, lifting the grape skeleton from the fruit bowl and waving it under his nose. "It looks like it's been amputated. You could pull off a whole branch of the stalk rather than ripping off individual grapes." But then it was over, sunshine replaced the storm. Not like now. Now she seemed to fall further and further into the cellar of her sorrows.

Soon he would go home. His in-laws were still at his house, which in many ways was good, but he wanted time alone. Time to do what? He didn't know. He just wanted to get away from it all.

His pager sounded. He yanked it off his belt and read the message.

Dial the operator for a call from Dr. Monica Daley.

Monica. On the phone. He started breathing as if he were running up a mountain. His fingers shook while he dialed the operator's number.

"This is Dr. Campbell. Dr. Daley is trying to reach me," he said curtly, to sound like this was everyday business.

"Hold on. I'll connect you." There was a pause. Then the operator said, "Dr. Daley, you're connected with Dr. Campbell."

"Hi, Jake. I've been thinking about you." She sounded as if she were only three feet away.

"I've thought of you, too, Monica. It was great to talk to you the other day." Why was she calling? They last spoke only thirty-six hours ago. He was confused, apprehensive. He was ecstatic.

"Jake, I'm here. In Michigan."

"Here? Where? At your mother's?" He didn't understand how she had gotten to Michigan so fast. He sank into the nearest chair.

"No, I flew to DTW this afternoon and plan to stay at a hotel near the airport tonight. I'll drive to the Thumb tomorrow morning. I thought perhaps I could buy you a drink."

He checked his watch. Four thirty. His heart was flapping. He could leave the hospital early today. He had written all the afternoon orders on the service patients. The dictations were almost finished. Only two or three to go. He could complete them in the morning.

"Uh, that would be great. Which hotel?"

"The Sheraton. Room three fifteen."

He swerved out the hospital parking lot, sped to the freeway. Traffic going east on I-94 was heavy, slowed by resurfacing on the left shoulder. "Hurry up," he shouted to the car ahead.

He remembered her skin, the soft warmth of her tanned arms with their silky blond hairs. He remembered the strength of her hands as they gripped his wrists. He remembered her laugh, her eyes, her lips. "I can't believe I'm doing this," he yelled out loud. "I can't believe this is real."

He parked the car, marched across the hotel lobby, hit the number 3 button inside the elevator. As he moved skyward, he fingered a paper clip in his pants pocket and stared at the blinking numbers. The seconds passed and he was getting closer to Monica. He walked down the hallway until he stood in front of room 315. She was just beyond that beige door. He raised his hand, paused a moment. Should he do this? Goddamn, yes. He knocked.

The door opened. "Hello, Jake," she said. "Come in."

Her hair was shorter, more carefree than he remembered, her eyes solemn yet wistful. Her red-brown lipstick made her look older, more severe than before. Her hand gripped the doorknob the same old way, with conviction. Her jeans were snug across her butt, her T-shirt loose over her chest. A purple and green woven scarf draped like a saddle blanket over her shoulders. He wanted to set his hand on the back of her neck and pull her to him. Should he touch her? What if she pushed him away? He couldn't stand that. What was she thinking?

He stepped inside. She shoved the door shut and wrapped her arms around him. He smelled her hair, the scent of woods and violets and mushrooms. Different from before.

"It's so good to see you again," he said, stroking her spine.

"Yes, it's been a long time." She stepped back from him. "I ordered a bottle of wine. As I recall, you like merlot."

She poured him a glass and motioned toward the armchair. She poured one for herself and sat on the end of the bed. "To grand old times," she said, swinging her wineglass upward in an arc. "Cheers."

He raised his glass. "Cheers, Monica."

She asked about Eddie. He didn't want to talk about his son— this didn't seem the time or the place to discuss his family—but gave her a brief update. She nodded knowingly as he described Eddie's EEG results, the neurological findings, the lab reports, the vent settings. She understood exactly what he was saying.

He asked about her life.

"Well, it's been a long journey since our days in med school." She sipped her wine, then told him she had begun writing poetry and had attended several Buddhist retreats, the most recent one in Janakpur, Nepal.

"That one was particularly challenging," she said, chuckling lightly. "We walked a day and a half to get there."

"Are you a practicing Buddhist, then?" He knew nothing about Buddhist retreats or the religion itself and was sure his dumb questions filled the air with empty words.

"Oh, no. I go on these things as an adventure. That, and as a personal exploration. It's fun . . . and enlightening."

She spoke of her work. "I'm in a practice with three other pediatricians. As I said on the phone, I may move to Vermont. I think I need a change."

She spoke of her traveling friends. "Last year my friends Lana and Margaret and I rented a villa in Tuscany. For three weeks we hiked the hills, cooked, practiced our Italian, drank gallons of Chianti. The neighbor had a barrel of house red in his backyard and every evening he brought us a liter." She crossed her legs. "Have you ever been to Tuscany?"

"Uh, no." A trip to Italy hadn't crossed his mind. It might be enjoyable, but in the big scheme of things, particularly now, it was the lowest of priorities.

"I highly recommend it," she said.

He finished his first glass of wine. She held up the bottle, a question on her face. He nodded. She poured him a second glass.

There was a lull in the talking. She, also, seemed to be gathering her thoughts.

"Why did you leave so suddenly?" he blurted out. He had waited eight years to ask that question. Now it had been asked. It hung in the air, a demand for an answer, a puncture wound in the otherwise surreal bubble of their being together again.

"I needed a break, Jake. My grades weren't good. I couldn't concentrate on my studies."

That was it? She dumped him because of a rough patch in school? Didn't make sense. "You broke my heart, Monica."

"I'm sorry. I really am. I wish it could have ended differently."

"Or, not ended."

"Oh, I think it was destined to end." Her eyes grew even more solemn.

"I don't understand that, Monica." The conversation seemed to wander like an aimless drunk. Was she being purposefully elusive? "Why did it need to end?"

"As I said, I needed a break."

"You just slammed the door on me. Wouldn't tell me what was wrong. I wanted to help you, but you refused to talk to me. All because you 'needed a break'?"

She sipped her wine and shook her head slowly. Her eyes stared at her lap. "Your life is so serious, now," she murmured.

"It sure is. I have a lot of responsibilities. And some of them aren't going well."

She was silent, seemed to hover just beyond reach. She was speaking on a different plane. It felt as if he was grabbing at smoke.

"Why did you come, now, to Michigan?" he asked. "Why did you call today?"

"I wanted to see you. You sounded so terribly defeated when we spoke yesterday morning."

"Defeated is a good word for it," he said. But still she hadn't answered his question. What was in it for her? Hollow sex? Is that what she was after? Is that what *he* was after? He didn't think so. He thought he wanted answers. Her answers might address the ancient problem of her disappearance, but how about all of today's problems?

"I was very surprised that you called," she said. "It was as if a comet had dropped from the sky."

"I've thought a lot about you over the years." He felt the burden climb back on his shoulders. It grew heavy again. An anvil. "I didn't understand why you left so abruptly. It was cruel. I was devastated."

"Come here." Her voice was soft. She patted the bedspread beside her.

He drained his wineglass, set it on the desk, stood before her, and looked down into her face. She stared back at him, a mysterious glaze to her eyes.

She reached for his hand and pulled him toward the bed.

He stepped back, looked into her face again, into her vagabond eyes. She was a wanderer, a nomad who wouldn't, or couldn't, attach. Why hadn't he seen that before? Back then, he thought they would be a couple forever. Now he knew the impossibility of that. She wasn't capable of being a steady partner. She had been right, after all. It was destined to end.

She pulled again on his arm. He sat beside her. She held his cheeks in her hands and then kissed him, a long, beguiling, twisting kiss. He tasted poison; her lips were acid.

He pulled away from her and stood up. Not that. Not now.

Adrift in a void, he was floating, falling. But she couldn't anchor him. Could anyone? Anything?

"It was important for me to see you. I think I understand it all much better now. I hope your upcoming move to Vermont works out." He opened the door, turned, and said, "Good-bye, Monica."

She had been so important to him—earlier, an island of warmth and comfort; more recently, of hope and longing. They had been a couple for only several months, albeit those were feverish, exploding, sparkling months. He and Anna had been married for six years, steady, priceless, deeply meaningful years. They shared so much: a house and mortgage, mutual goals and memories, inside jokes and common secrets, and, most of all, their treasured children. He and Anna weren't merely additive, they were synergistic, and nothing could replace that.

He stepped out of the hotel lobby into the now silky evening.

Chapter 31

Anna

"Anna, I think we have the answer." Dr. Farley stood before her, his body framed by the confusion of the waiting room. Bags of flesh hung beneath his lower eyelids and chronic worry etched his face. Yet, his eyes danced in the shadow of his brow. He seemed upbeat, almost whimsical as he scratched his elbow through the sleeve of his white coat.

She searched her memory for the meaning of his words and came up empty. "The answer?" she asked. "What was the question?"

"Eddie's fever. We have an explanation." He raised his eyebrows and tilted his head slightly to the right. The faint smile that dawned on this face was that of a supremely confident man. He shoved his hands into his pants pockets and said, "He has a urinary tract infection."

She knew about those, had had bladder infections when she was in college. "How'd he get that?"

"Most likely from the catheter that drains his urine." He rested one arm against the end of Eddie's crib. "See, bacteria can crawl up the tubing and set up a bladder infection."

She looked away from him, didn't like what he was saying. He seemed pleased to have this explanation for Eddie's fever, but she thought it was awful. Germs crawling up the tube into her baby. Growing inside him. Germs, like gray-green mold on old bread, inside Eddie. First they were growing inside his head with the meningitis and now inside his bladder.

He patted her shoulder. "It's not all that bad. Happens all the time. The bacteria—"

She interrupted him. "So, what do we do?" She didn't want to hear any more about germs crawling around inside her baby, no more about the infected catheter.

"Well, the bacteria are most likely resistant to the antibiotic—the, um, ceftriaxone—he's getting for the meningitis. Tomorrow we'll know if that's true, but in the meanwhile, we'll add another antibiotic. And we'll take out the catheter."

"Which antibiotic?"

"Gentamicin."

"Gentamicin," she repeated. At least they had a plan.

"And, I have good news."

His impish grin was disarming. He wasn't taking this new infection seriously at all.

He stepped closer to her and seemed almost buoyant. "We tried Eddie off the ventilator for a while this morning and he did well, so we're going to take out the endotracheal tube."

Take out the tube? She leaned her head against the back of the chair. That tube was how he breathed. The ventilator was his life raft, the tube the safety line. The rhythm of the machine as it blew air into his lungs had been, to her, audible, musical assurance he was getting oxygen. "Are you sure that'll be okay?"

"Well, of course we're never absolutely sure, but he's required lower vent settings for the past two days and seemed to tolerate being off the machine very well."

She studied his face, examined his stance. He stood tall, his eyes rarely blinked, his breathing was steady. No twitches of uncertainty. No sideward glances.

"Maybe you could leave the tube in for a while but let him breathe on his own." She wanted to take baby steps toward this big move. Without the tube he might stop breathing and they might not be able to get it back in again. He'd turn blue. His body would become limp and still, again. He'd die.

"That wouldn't be a good idea." He folded his arms across the front of his white coat. "See, the tube is quite a bit longer than Eddie's windpipe—about twice as long—so a lot of his breathing effort would be used to move air up and down the long tube rather than in and out of his lungs."

She envisioned little molecules of oxygen racing up and down the inside of that plastic tube.

"We've also lightened up his sedation and discontinued his paralyzing medicine," he said. "He's quite the little wiggle bug."

"He's moving?"

"Yeah. Go see him."

The tube was gone from his mouth. His face looked empty, as if the couch had been moved from the living room. She leaned over his crib and stroked his cheek. He turned his head a tiny bit toward her. She laid her finger across his palm and his fingers wrapped around it. His chest was rising and falling under the flannel blanket, without the machine. His nostrils flared ever so slightly with each breath. He was getting better. She could tell. He was really getting better.

Maybe they'd be able to take him home, after all. Maybe he would walk, go to school, sing drinking songs, toss a football. Maybe he'd grow up.

Or, maybe he'd be handicapped, be a baby forever even as he grew taller. What would next Thanksgiving be like? And Christmas after that? No matter. The most important thing was that he would probably be home for all the upcoming holidays.

Chris nestled beside her in the waiting room chair, wedged between her thigh and the upholstery. "When can I see him?" he asked. "Does he cry a lot?"

She answered the best she could. "You can see Eddie later, after he's better. He sleeps a lot, and he doesn't cry much."

Poor Chris, she thought. He was just a little boy, full of worry, full of wondering. When she looked back over his three-and-a-half brief years, a series of adversities—most, thankfully, were small, but a few were bigger—littered the view. His two visits to the emergency room were anxiety-filled illnesses that turned out to be minor viruses. He'd lost his precious teddy bear—the caramel-colored one with a tomato soup stain on its belly—when Jake laid it on the roof of the car and drove eighty miles before discovering it had disappeared. Chris had spent too little of his childhood in the company of his overworked, chronically exhausted doctor-father.

Until now, his worst adversity must have been when Eddie was born. While she was in the labor and the delivery room, he stayed with Rose Marie. She hadn't thought much about it then, but now realized he'd felt betrayed, deserted. He would have sensed a hole in his life while she was away, a huge, gaping abyss. He wouldn't have known what to call that feeling; he hadn't yet learned the "missing" word. And when she reappeared, she'd brought competition . . . the brother.

She thought of the hours of peekaboo she played with Chris when he was a baby—the diaper she tossed over his face, the way his arms and legs stiffened in fear, the sound of his deep, terrified gasp. And then after she pulled away the diaper and called, "There's Chris," how he had collapsed into total body pleasure as his muscles softened and giggles erupted from deep inside him. In that game, her absence had been fleeting. She always returned.

His past adversities were minor, though, compared to his current difficulty. She'd been gone again, now. But he was older. Could he understand it any better, six months after the other absence? But, a three-and-a-half-year-old couldn't rank trouble. Whichever problem he faced at the moment—a lost toy, a denied request, a reprimand for bad behavior, now a sick brother—would be the worst ever. For him, previous hurts had been forgotten, future agonies would be beyond imagining. His world was tethered in the moment.

"Why's he here?" Chris asked again.

She wanted to be patient with him, wanted him to understand. "Because he's very sick. The nurses and doctors are helping him get better." She had told him that several times. He must need reassurance.

"What's wrong with that man?" he called, his voice loud enough to be heard by everyone in the waiting room, including the man with the stump.

"He hurt his leg and the doctors had to cut it off." She watched for his reaction. No horror. No fear. She wasn't sure how to explain an amputation to a child, didn't mention that his father did that to people.

The questions kept coming. "Did you cut Eddie's fingernails in here?" he asked. When he turned toward her for the answer, he knocked his elbow against her still sore breast.

She patted his arm. The fingernails? Of all things to remember about his brother. The first time she had trimmed Eddie's fingernails, Chris had watched with, at first, great interest. His eyes widened as she approached Eddie's thumb with the manicure scissors. When she took the initial clip, he had buried his eyes in his hands and screamed, "Don't cut it off." He couldn't remember, of course, that she had also trimmed his nails when he was a baby.

He squirmed beside her in the chair. "I wanna go home," he whined. "Where's my daddy?"

"Daddy's working. He'll come soon and take you back to Grandma and Grandpa."

She wanted him to be quiet for a while. His voice, earlier angelic and melodic, was now irritating as it rose above the sounds of the waiting room to grab her attention, to demand a response from her. He asked the same questions over and over, even though, over and over, she had answered them. She tried to use words he would understand. Maybe he didn't like the answers she gave. Maybe he just wanted to hear her voice and this was his way of making that happen. Still, she needed quiet; at least she needed a reprieve from the nonstop questions.

She pulled a page of newspaper from the pile at her feet, folded it into quarters with a Lord & Taylor ad on top, and rummaged in the bottom of her purse for a pen.

"Here, honey." She set the paper in his lap. "Fill in all the *o*'s. Remember the *o*'s?"

"Yeah." He made a circle with his thumb and pointer finger and thrust it toward her chin. He then searched her face for approval, begged for it, insisted on it. She tried to smile. He grinned back, seemingly satisfied, and reached for the pen. He took a deep breath, pursed his lips, and began filling in the *o* in "Lord."

A moment later his body stiffened. "Uh-oh," he said. Two short blue lines had escaped the edges of the *o*. He rubbed his finger on the page, trying to make the errant lines go away. "Get the eraser," he commanded.

"You've got a pen and we don't have an eraser for pen ink." She patted his head, felt the silk of his hair. It smelled like pears. Her mother must have given him a shampoo. So much of his life was happening now out of her view. Baths, meals, playtime, excursions to the grocery store. Her mother had taken her place with him at home.

"It's okay the way it is," she said. "You don't have to stay inside every *o*."

Of course he couldn't understand the complexity of her words. He was trying to learn the ways of the world and needed rules. He didn't know yet about exemptions, hadn't learned that certain situations call for exceptions, that some rules may be applied *most* of the time and not necessarily *all* the time. To him, the solid ring around the *o* was an absolute that meant the ink was supposed to stay inside the boundary. Always. Otherwise, why have a boundary?

He looked up at her again, seemed to be checking in with her every few seconds. She nodded and said, "It's okay the way you made it."

He shrugged and started on the *o* in Taylor.

"Almost done, Mommy," he shouted. The newspaper page was pocked with ink dots. Again he stared into her face, searching for something—probably praise, likely reassurance.

"Good job, sweetheart." She patted his leg and spotted Dr. Farley walking toward them.

"Hello, young man. You must be Eddie's big brother."

Chris smiled shyly and returned to his work on the newsprint.

"Would you like to see him?" Dr. Farley asked.

Chris's eyes widened. "Yeah," he yelled. His hand, gripping the pen, stood suspended midair.

She stiffened. "Is that wise? He hasn't seen Eddie. Not since the baby got sick."

"He seems excited about it. Undoubtedly he has all kinds of ideas about what has happened to his brother, most of them much more terrible than reality."

"Okay." She took a deep breath. "Right now?"

"The nurses will let you know when they're ready. We don't ordinarily allow young children into the ICU, but we'll make an exception this time. It'll be a quick visit."

She nodded. This would be one of those elusive exceptions.

Chris was wordless as she carried him through the doors into the ICU. He turned his head from side to side. His eyes darted from gurney to bed to portable X-ray machine to resuscitation cart, all of it foreign to him.

As they approached Eddie's crib, he lifted his chin and said, "It smells funny."

She sniffed, didn't smell anything odd.

"What does it smell like? Smoke? Rotten potatoes?"

"Just funny."

She stopped at the foot of the crib. "Here's Eddie's bed." Slowly, she moved along the crib rails.

He leaned out of her arms and pointed. "Is that him?"

"Yes, honey." She felt sick to her stomach. Bringing him here was a mistake. She hadn't had time to prepare him for this place. She looked at what he saw . . . his baby brother, pale, puffy, and unrecognizable, lying in a metal crib that looked like a jail. Plastic tubes snaked into his body, weird machines surrounded the bed, electronic tracings streamed across the faces of the monitors, lights blinked like robot eyes. Occasional high-pitched beeps sang from the IVACs and the telemetry unit.

He leaned farther out of her arms and poked a finger into his brother's belly. Eddie's abdomen twisted, his left leg bent at the knee.

"Oh, honey, don't hurt him."

"I'm not." He jerked his hand back as if he'd touched a hot burner and stuffed his fingers into the pocket of his jeans.

She pulled his hand from the pocket and set it on Eddie's leg. "Touch him here. I think he's glad you came."

Now she looked at Eddie through her own eyes rather than Chris's. The nurses had wiped away the tape marks from Eddie's cheeks. Even the tubing that had run from inside his diaper to the urine bag on the crib rail was gone. He looked like a human again; his lips were moist and slightly parted, his head lay at a normal angle. Her eyes flooded.

"What's that?" Chris asked, pointing to the IVAC.

"It's the machine that helps him get his medicines."

Again the questions kept coming. "What's that?" He pointed to Eddie's IV line, to the telemetry monitor, to the leads taped to Eddie's chest. She tried to answer the questions accurately, simply.

"Where're his toys?"

"They're still at home. He's too sick to play here."

"Does that thing hurt him?" He pointed to the oxygen saturation monitor taped to Eddie's finger.

"No. It's like a Band-Aid. It doesn't hurt."

"Mommy, can he see me?"

She shifted Chris on her lap. Where did that question come from? She looked at Eddie. His eyes were partially open, but the upper lids hung low, hiding his pupils. She didn't know if her baby could see. She also didn't know if he could hear, or think, or remember.

Chris leaned toward his brother again. "Hi, Eddie," he called. Eddie didn't respond. "When can he come home?"

"Soon, I hope," she said. "Maybe in about a week." Chris wouldn't know when the week was up. He hadn't learned yet how to gauge the passing of that amount of time.

She had no idea when he could go home. Since that first

morning of his illness, she hadn't thought more than four minutes into the future. But now that the breathing tube and the bladder catheter were out, his leaving the hospital was becoming a larger possibility.

Chris stroked Eddie's leg until he squirmed, one of those baby wiggles; his thigh turned right and his chest turned left.

Outside the ICU window, the newly opened leaves of an oak tree stirred in the breeze and fluffy clouds in the west rolled eastward. She thought about Eddie going home. She would carry him through their front door, would sit on the couch in the family room with him snuggled in her arms. He would sleep in his own crib. It would be like before he got sick.

Maybe he would learn to sit again, maybe to walk. Maybe he could go fishing with Jake and Chris, could learn to read and to drive. Maybe he would go to the prom, would marry, and become a father. Eddie's eyes were closed, now. If they were open, could he see?

Chapter 32

Jake

He finally had learned about the real Monica, the vagrant Monica. What about the real Anna? Where had she gone? Was the image before him in the waiting room—the disheveled, beleaguered, terrified woman who was a captive of that chair—the new real Anna? Her hair hung over her face, the skin of her cheeks was sallow. There was a sense of innocence about her, a childlike softness he found alluring, and heartbreaking. Attached? Yes, unlike Monica, Anna was attached. Certainly, she clung to Eddie with the furor of a rabid animal. And Chris? She faced the Devil's choice between her two children. Maybe it was her attachment to Chris that made this ordeal even more difficult than otherwise. She was attached, and, because of it, had been torn apart. How about her attachment to him, her husband? Where did that stand?

She had no idea of her husband's dalliance. Jake knew she had many worries but was unaware of that one. Their little boy snuggled at Anna's side. He, too, was an innocent in the subterranean deceit that Jake now bore. What does a three-and-a-half-year-old know of infidelity? Or, near infidelity. Where was the line, anyway? Did his visit to Monica's hotel room count as infidelity? In his mind, it did, because it was deceitful, something he wouldn't share with Anna. In spite of everything Chris had been through, he still lived in that cocoon of trust. At least, Jake hoped that remained true.

Except for her visits to the ICU, Anna held watch on that throne in the waiting room, claimed it as her own, stored her pillow in the seat and her magazines and snacks on the table at its side. How could she stand it, he wondered, holed up in this windowless, miserable, dank place? Somehow she must believe that Eddie's survival depended on her being there every second of every day. He took a deep breath and headed toward her.

"Hi," he said, bussing his wife's cheek. It was a perfunctory gesture; he didn't feel terribly loving. He wasn't sure how he felt, other than contaminated. "Howdy, Chris. Did you see Eddie?"

"Yeah, he's fine," Chris muttered, squirming against his mother.

"He *is* fine," she said, a thin smile turning on her pale lips. "At least finer than before. They tried him off the ventilator and he tolerated it so they took out the tube."

"Wow." He sank into the chair next to Anna's. He shook his head to clear the jumbled thoughts that hung like spiderwebs on his brain. "That's terrific." He was genuinely ecstatic with the news, genuinely puzzled with himself. Getting off the ventilator was a major step forward. For the desperately ill son of a louse.

"And the fever is from a urinary tract infection," Anna added.

"Oh, well. No big deal. They probably added another antibiotic, right?"

She nodded. "Genta . . . gento . . . something like that."

She pulled herself from the chair and pointed at Chris. "Stay put for a minute."

"Where're you going?" he whined, his face sharp with fear.

"To tell Daddy a secret."

"Tell me, too."

"It's about Eddie and you already know because you saw him."

Chris returned to drawing squares around words on the newsprint, the ones that contained *c* for Chris.

Anna led Jake across the room by the hand. Her fingers were warm, her grip as familiar as a well-worn glove.

"What's up?" he asked.

"I don't want Chris to hear." She sounded tired. "He asked if Eddie can see."

She squeezed his hand and then let it slip away from her damp palm. "Can he see?" Her voice trembled. She grabbed his hand again and stared into his face with desperate eyes. "How will we know?"

Her question seemed to fly out of nowhere; it made several twirly laps around the room and slammed into him as if he'd been hit with a log. Was Eddie blind? It was a complication of meningitis, one of the myriad sterile facts he had learned as a medical student. Now, it was no longer sterile. His son blind? A swell of light-headedness billowed across his eyes, over his forehead, into his throat.

"They'll test Eddie for that," he said. He sat in the chair nearest to Anna. "It's something they routinely do." He wanted to sound confident, hoped what he said was true. Store the blindness notion in the mental file labeled "tomorrow," he told himself. Bury it deep. Make it vanish.

He shuddered and stood up. "I'll say hello to Eddie and then take Chris home. Come with us, Anna. Eddie's doing well. You can leave him for a night."

Her eyes became dull, her lips pursed. Slowly, silently, she shook her head.

In the ICU, Vince Farley strolled toward him and smacked him lightly on the back. "Things are sure looking good in here. As you can see, the tube is O-U-T."

"Yeah, I see. Terrific."

"Dr. Farley . . ." someone called from the nurses' station.

"Coming." He sauntered away.

Jake leaned over the crib rail and ran his fingers across his son's chest. Without the ventilator shoving air into his lungs in a preset rhythm, Eddie seemed at peace. His breathing was quiet, the rolling, in-and-out ripple of a calm sea. He looked natural, like a real baby.

He stood up straight. True, the tube was gone, but what about the rest of it? He wanted to embrace Farley's enthusiasm, but what if his son was blind? Deaf? Severely retarded? Life would be hell—hardly worth living—for a blind, deaf, severely retarded boy. And for his family.

He could examine his son's eyes himself. He wasn't sure he wanted to.

He stepped toward the door of the ICU but then returned to Eddie's bedside. He couldn't leave without knowing.

The baby's eyes were closed. Gently he pried apart the lids of Eddie's right eye, and stared at the globe inside. The pupil looked fine, not too dilated, not too constricted. He pulled the penlight from his breast pocket and waved the beam slowly from right to left across his baby's corneas. The irises constricted but the eyes didn't move. He did it again. They didn't follow the light.

"Vince," he called, trying to steady his voice. "Come over here."

Farley glanced over his shoulder, turned away from the computer at the nurses' station, and walked to Eddie's bedside.

"Look at this." Jake waved the light beam over his son's eye again. Again, they didn't track. "Look." He could hear his own voice—loud and wavering. He swallowed hard.

"Jake," Farley began in a soothing voice, "as you know, visual loss is one of the complications of bacterial meningitis. Now that he's extubated, we can do formal vision testing—visual-evoked responses would be appropriate, considering his age. What you just saw is hard to evaluate." Farley rubbed his chin. "Ahh, you and I both have to acknowledge, however, that Eddie had a very serious infection and we shouldn't be too surprised if he suffers sequelae."

"Yeah." His voice was a whisper. He knew what Farley had just said. It was code for "Yes, he most likely is blind."

"Does Eddie have one hundred percent chance of being blind?" Dr. Farley asked. "Zero percent? It's somewhere in between. As unsatisfying as it is, that's the most we can say right now. We'll give him a chance to recover a bit more and then we'll do comprehensive vision testing."

"Why can't we do it today?" He was almost yelling. Why did Farley have to be so unmoved by this? Why couldn't they just do the test and find out? Now.

"Because the results might not be accurate. Let his brain heal a bit longer. I wish this weren't so difficult, but you have to give Eddie a chance to recover. He's had a major insult."

He bit his lips, leaned over the crib, and stroked his son's head. Such a tiny fellow. Such a precious baby. So much trouble. "You've traveled a long way, little buddy," he murmured. "Keep it up for the rest of the journey."

"Anna, at least walk us out to the car," he said. "Fresh air would be good for you."

She strolled ahead, toward the parking lot, hand in hand with Chris. The rain had stopped and the sun was trying to poke its face from behind a mud-colored cloud. This was the Campbell family as he saw it: Anna and Chris together in the lead, himself in the rear, and Eddie not with them.

Chapter 33

Anna

In her dream, the room was noisy and filled with the smell of coffee. It was rich and heavy, maybe Sumatra, possibly French roast. Moments before, the sun had fallen behind the mountain and, in the last glow of day, they sat around a square table, she and her friends, in a bar or a restaurant in a foreign country, someplace like Morocco or Turkey or Budapest. Haunting music thrummed at her back and everything around her seemed draped in orange and yellow cloth.

"Anna."

Someone was calling her name. The voice came from far away, from beyond the other side of the square table. "Anna." The coffee smell was much stronger.

"Anna, I brought you a cuppa joe. It's fresh."

The friends, the square table, the yellow-orange room faded but the smell of coffee remained. Her arm stuck to the plastic fabric of the chair; the blanket slid from her body and puddled on the floor. The pillow, damp and indented, smelled spicy—the tangy odor of perspiration.

Now the foreign country—the friends, the music, the curry

colors—had completely vanished. She sat in the stifling waiting room where she couldn't see the sun. Charlotte stood before her with the coffee that had filled her dream.

"It's real, not that instant junk." Charlotte held out the foam cup. "I thought you'd want to get up because Dr. Farley was here a minute ago looking for you. When he saw you sleeping, he said he'd catch you later. If it was me, I'd want to know what was on his mind—right now."

"Thanks, Charlotte." She sat upright, pulled the blanket back over her legs, and stretched her arms to shake off the sleepiness. A part of her wanted to go back to the foreign country and to the square table with her friends. She tried to sip the coffee but backed away when her lip touched the steaming liquid. She blew into the cup, sending brown ripples across the coffee's surface.

She tried to remember Charlotte's words. Something about Dr. Farley. Something about knowing what was on his mind.

She jerked upright, knocked her pillow to the floor. Something was wrong with Eddie. She straightened her knees, tried to climb out of the chair. A splash of hot coffee spilled into her lap.

"When was he here? What'd he say? Is something wrong?" Her breath came out in little gasps and her heart thumped against the inside of her shirt. She ignored the hot coffee on her pants.

"Here." Charlotte tossed her a towel.

"What'd he say?" She was irritated at the towel. She didn't understand why it had landed across her legs.

"You spilled your coffee. Doesn't it hurt? It was scalding." Charlotte dabbed the stain with the corner of the towel.

Why was Charlotte being so evasive? She needed to know if something was wrong with Eddie.

She untangled the blanket from her ankles and was scrambling to her feet when Dr. Farley appeared in the doorway.

"What happened?" she shouted.

He seemed relaxed and smiled when he saw her. Above the impish grin, his eyes twinkled like cobalt-tinted sequins. "Nothing happened, except we're throwing you and Eddie out of here."

She shook her head. What was he saying? What was going on?

Dr. Farley chuckled. "I guess you're a bit confused. Maybe still half asleep. Eddie's fine. In fact, he's so fine he doesn't need to be in the intensive care unit any longer. We're transferring him to the ward."

She sank back into the chair, spilling the coffee again.

"For Christ's sake. Look at you." Charlotte clucked and, again, dabbed at the stained pants with the towel.

The first thing she noticed about the pediatric ward was its smell. It was different, less antiseptic than the ICU, more like a blend of milk, eggs, and toast along with cleaning solution and antibiotic, the same bubblegum flavor as the pink amoxicillin she had coaxed into Chris with his ear infection.

She stood in the hallway outside Eddie's new room and waited for the nurses to complete the transfer. Everything about the ward was more vibrant. The walls, rather than the color of aged plaster, were varying shades of pale pink and faint yellow, and the corners, where the colors blended, looked like peaches. High up, near the ceiling, strips of wallpaper with dancing animals and colored flowers—red, blue, purple, orange, and green—edged each wall. Huge, brightly painted panels—circuses, parades, zoos, baseball diamonds, ballet classes—flanked each doorway.

The cacophony of colors and shapes and textures twirled around her, flashing here, darting there. In the room across the hall, a teenager, his leg wrapped in gauze, licked a purple Popsicle. His mother sat on the couch, knitting. No ventilators. No telemetry machines. The IV stand beside the boy's bed had only one IVAC attached to it. She closed her eyes and leaned against the wall, against the picture of a rainbow planted in a pot of gold. This was all so new.

"Watch out," yelled a young voice. She opened her eyes in time to see a boy the size of an eight-year-old zigzagging toward her in a wheelchair. Just as he was about to ram into her, he skidded to the side and, laughing, maneuvered the chair around her. Farther down the hall, a tired-looking man pushed an IV pole that carried a skinny little girl—probably his daughter, dressed in a salmon-colored, frothy princess gown—on its wheeled platform.

"All set, Mrs. Campbell." A nurse scurried out of Eddie's room.

She crept to the crib. Eddie lay on his back. His hair was combed and the sheet was neatly folded under his chin. He looked fresh, peaceful. One IV ran into his left arm but no other lines or wires.

He's free, she thought. Free of the electronic stuff, free of the badness.

As she stared into his face, she had an overwhelming urge to hold him. He had been intubated, catheterized, IV'd, and monitored since his admission. She hadn't been able to gather him into her arms since that horrid morning she drove him to the emergency room. She stroked his head and whispered his name, over and over. The words came out like a song. "Eddie. Eddie." Slowly she pulled down the sheet, lifted up his hospital gown, examined his pale body. His chest moved easily with each breath—no more machine pumping air into him. She touched her fingertips to his mouth. His lips twitched with a sucking motion. It was faint, but still a suck.

"Eddie," she whispered again. "You made it." She lifted him from the crib and lowered herself into the rocking chair. The IV tubing looped over her shoulder; she curled it in her lap so it wouldn't pull from his arm.

This was not unlike the very first time she held him. The uncertainty, the caution, the apprehension were the same. Then his tiny face, now pale and waxy, was red and wrinkled. "You're a new little person, with the big, wide world ahead of you," she had said to her newborn son. Now he had traveled a very bumpy road and was, once again, a new person. She had wondered back then what kind of child he would become, what secrets—and interests, and talents, and habits—would unfurl from him and bloom as he grew up. Would he be lively? Sedate? An artist? A scientist? Adaptable? Committed to routine? Curious? Dull? No, not dull. She knew she wouldn't have a dull child.

Now, looking into his quiet face, she wondered the same things. What would he be like after all this?

He seemed lighter than she remembered, as buoyant as a hollow-boned lark. He lay still on her lap, his head nestled into the crook of her left elbow. He didn't squirm against her as he used to, didn't nuzzle into her breast, now dry from not nursing him for more than a week. Should she start nursing him again? She closed her eyes and shook her head. So many things to figure out.

"Hi. Anna?" The voice sounded tentative.

She opened her eyes and looked into the massive garden of cut flowers that filled the doorway of Eddie's room. "Yes?"

"Are you awake? I don't want to bother you if you're sleeping," said the voice. The flowers moved through the doorway, followed by Elizabeth.

"Where'd you get those?" Anna asked. "They're huge . . . and beautiful."

"Gilroy's. Since they wouldn't let you have flowers in the ICU, I decided to make up for it now. Aren't they lovely?"

Anna agreed. White and maroon oriental lilies. Dusty yellow mums. Sprays of laurel leaves and plum-colored rosebuds just beginning to open. Three branches of contorted hazel twisted like corkscrews from the top of the vase.

"Where do you want them?" Elizabeth turned 180 degrees as she surveyed the room. "How about on this thing here?" She set them on the tray table.

"They're amazing. Are little animals hidden in there?"

"I hope not," Elizabeth said.

She felt Elizabeth's arm slide around her shoulders.

Elizabeth kept talking. "It's good to see you make a joke. What's that loveable bundle in your arms?"

She felt her face relax into a smile. "That's my son, Edward. He just graduated from the ICU."

"Congratulations, Sir Edward." Elizabeth spoke in her most formal voice. She reached for Eddie's right hand and gave it a gentle shake.

Eddie's new room had a real bed. At least a better bed than the lounge chair in the ICU waiting room. She stretched out on the narrow mattress and stared at the ceiling, at nothing in particular. The room also had a phone. No more standing in the telephone closet where everyone in the waiting room could overhear the conversation. It was like playing house. A place of her own.

Elizabeth had told her about her class, about how much the students missed her, how worried they were about her and Eddie. Elizabeth had brought a stack of letters written by her students—in English.

Mis Campbell. I hop youre son gets better real soon.
Sinserly, Ming.

Dear Mrs. Campbell; We miss you a lot. Please come
back now.
I hope your baby will come home from the hospital.
Love, Consuella.

The letters had been a moment from her real life, a step through the clouds of the past week. It felt as if she might be moving back to the real Anna, afloat on a raft edging toward the shore, toward the safety and comfort and familiarity of a dock whose posts were solidly sunk in the lake bottom.

A doctor walked into the room and introduced herself. "Hello, Mrs. Campbell. I'm Ruby Sherman, one of the third-year residents."

She had seen her before. Was it in the ER? In the ICU? She couldn't remember but she recognized the scar. Harelip. Bilateral. She listened carefully to the doctor's speech, heard the minimal nasality. It was a good cosmetic repair with excellent palatal function.

"I've been reviewing Eddie's hospital records and trying to sort out what's next," the doctor said.

"Yes, what *is* next?" Anna asked.

"We generally treat *Strep pneumo* meningitis for ten days and Eddie's ten days are up tonight. That means we need to start thinking about discharge."

She caught her breath. Discharge. Going home. With Eddie. So soon. Too soon?

"Before he leaves, we'll need to test his hearing and be sure he feeds well. As you know, he's had a serious infection and we can't predict exactly how things will go for him."

"How about testing his vision?" She felt herself begging. "Do you think he can see?" This doctor had had a cleft-lip repair, had been a patient herself as a little girl. She would make sure Eddie could see. And hear. And be normal in every way.

"Yes, we'll do both VERs and BAERs—um, that's the vision and hearing testing we do with babies. And he needs to stay on an antibiotic a little longer to complete treatment of his urinary tract infection. We'll use cipro. We can give it by mouth as soon as he can swallow. Are you planning to return to nursing him? Have you maintained your milk? Has he tried nursing since he's been extubated?"

The doctor slipped on a latex glove and stuck a rubber finger into Eddie's mouth. He didn't move. She pulled out her finger and touched each corner of his lips. "Well, he's not sucking very well yet. You can try to breast feed him if you'd like, but we'll have the nurses give him tube feedings for a while."

"He sucked for me." Anna scrambled to the crib. "Really, he did. Here, watch."

She stuck her finger between Eddie's lips. His tongue brushed against the tip of her finger, but he didn't suck. She moved her finger inside his mouth. Still no sucking.

"Well, maybe he's tired. Honestly, he sucked on my finger a few minutes ago."

Her shriveled breasts were limp inside the cups of her bra.

He couldn't suck? Couldn't nurse? He was only six months old. He needed her milk for a while longer. She remembered weaning Chris, remembered the day she gave him the sippy cup. At first he waved it around his head and then flung it to the floor, watching in fascination as it rolled across the linoleum, a trail of milk in its wake. Eventually he came to understand it was fun to drink from the cup. After that, he nursed less and less, sometimes picking up the pace of nursing again when he was sick or hurt. Then he stopped. Just quit—refused to put her nipple in his mouth ever again. It would be different with Eddie. She wiped her eyes on the sleeve of her sweater. Eddie would be different.

Just as the nurse pulled the plastic tube out of its paper sheath, Jake walked into Eddie's room.

"Dr. Campbell," the nurse said. "We're having a lesson here. Mrs. Campbell's learning how to insert the feeding tube."

"They want to send him home," Anna said.

"Great," Jake said.

"Eddie's a little lazy with sucking, so we're going to continue the tube feeds until his suck gets stronger. Mrs. Campbell is learning how to insert it, so at home she can do it herself. I demonstrated what to do and now it's her turn."

"I don't think I can do that. I can't stick a tube into my baby's nose."

"Sure you can, honey. The nurse will teach you how."

She held the tube while the nurse positioned Eddie's head. She set the tube's tip inside his left nostril. It fell back out again. "See, I can't do it."

"Here, let me help you." Jake held her hand while she tried to insert the tube again.

His fingers gripped hers. His sense of confidence steadied her hand, made her less afraid. She glanced at his face. His even, kind eyes told her he wanted to make this as easy for her as possible.

"Hold it steady . . ." he said. "Make it a fluid motion . . . Flex your wrist and let the tube slide into his nose. Remember, his nasal cavity is shaped like a comma so the tube will follow the arc of the comma."

The tube did what he said it would do, slid into his nose easily. It worked well with Jake's help. She wasn't at all sure she could do it without him.

He moved her hand forward while the tube went deeper inside Eddie's nose. Eddie shook his head against the nurse's hand and sneezed. "There, you've got the gist of it. Try it yourself."

She did it again. By herself this time. Again the tube slid easily into Eddie's nose.

"Good. Keep threading it," he said. "There, that's far enough. To the blue mark on the tube." He showed her how to pull back on the syringe, how to push air into Eddie's stomach, how to listen for the air gurgles.

When they finished, Jake hugged her. "Nice job. That was great."

She leaned into him, felt his warmth through her blouse. Would she get through the rest of this?

Chapter 34

Jake

Eddie was about to be discharged from the hospital. That meant Anna's parents would return to Baltimore, and the four of them—Anna, himself, Chris, Eddie—would be together again at home. He and Chris would play horse and rider or read kid books, as before. Chris would build LEGO towns, would learn to put his right cowboy boot on his right foot and the left on the left. Eddie would be a baby, whatever kind of baby he was now destined to be.

He sipped his coffee, room temperature and scum coated after sitting near his elbow for a half hour. Anna had paged him. He downed the last swallow and dialed the number to Eddie's room.

Anna's words quivered as she explained that Ruby had written Eddie's discharge orders. "I don't think he's ready to go home."

"Ruby knows what she's doing. She's a great pediatrician." What worried Anna now? "Maybe *you're* not ready for him to go, but Eddie's ready." She should be thrilled their baby was well enough to leave the hospital. It was her pathologic worry rearing its nervous head, again. He could understand her fears while their baby was so terribly sick, but now Eddie was stable and ready to leave.

He was irritated by Anna's sigh, a long, quiet inhalation followed by a louder, exasperated exhalation that blew like a blast of anxious wind through the phone. She would have struck her dug-in posture; if he were in Eddie's room right now, he would see her lips pressed into a line across the bottom of her face, would see her rigid back and straight shoulders, her elevated chin.

"Look, Anna, it's great that Eddie's being discharged. I'll arrange someone to cover for me so I can drive you home. Start packing. It'll take about an hour for the discharge paperwork to run through the system."

"He's not ready to go home."

"Sure he is. You'll see."

With that, he said good-bye and set the receiver on the phone console. Eddie's discharge meant they could return to their old way of living. Except, of course, it wouldn't be as it had been. It would never be as it had been.

Outside, the noontime sun was tucked behind the clouds; fingers of light struggled to shine through but, in the end, failed as they drowned in the mist. Beneath the blurry sun, buds on the maple tree swayed in the breeze. As he watched, one branch stuttered as it moved. A squirrel? A bird? No . . . Something was odd about the way those twigs flitted. He blinked. Maybe a fleck of dust had blurred his vision. He blinked again. No change. He closed one eye and then closed the other. Still no change. He looked closer at the jerky branch and then spotted it—a warble in the glass, a defect in its surface.

"That's it," he said.

Betsy Bloom looked up from across the table. Those were her Monica eyes, slate blue with yellow dots sprinkled over the irises as if dusted with powdered gold. "That's what?" she asked.

He shook his head, shrugged his shoulders, and said, "A warble in the glass."

"Huh?" she asked.

Now he understood. Eddie being sick, Anna being nuts, Betsy being Monica. Through it all, he had stood outside and looked in at the world through the rippled glass of a disfigured window.

He still hadn't mentioned the Monica visit to Anna, still thought she didn't need to know. She might not want to know. Monica was over. And nothing of significance had happened.

Eddie's hospital room seemed like a party—bouquets of flowers covered every horizontal surface, fuchsia and violet blooms sagged from potted plants, stuffed monkeys and fuzzy bears peeked from behind the foliage, helium balloons bobbed in the air currents.

He stood in the doorway, incredulous. "Anna," he said. "You aren't packed."

She was slumped in a chair, her back toward him. He couldn't see her face.

"Are you going to leave all this stuff here? We need to hit the road." He set one foot into the room. "I've arranged for Martin to cover for me while I drive you and Eddie home."

Slowly, she turned. First her hips, then her shoulders, and finally her face moved toward him. Her cheeks were blotchy, her eyes pink and puffy. Her lips quivered like raspberry Jell-O.

"We can't go home," she sobbed, her voice a whisper.

He crossed the room and hugged her. "Why not?" Maybe his touch would hurry her along.

"I can't take care of him at home. He gurgles and chokes when he breathes. He's going to gag and stop breathing and we don't have the suction machine to clear it out." She was breathless, as if, in listing her worries, she was running a race she could never win. "We can't put the breathing tube back in him at home. We don't have a ventilator."

What's wrong with her? he wondered. He didn't have time for all this. Martin could cover for only two hours.

"Anna, we have to get going."

He watched her shoulders tremble as she turned back toward Eddie. While she sobbed, he could see, through her thin, white T-shirt, the outline of her bra. It was dark—black or navy blue. A fold of her skin bulged along the top of its elastic edges. Before, she would never have worn dark underwear beneath a see-through shirt. He liked her as she had been—coordinated, unjarring, easy on the eye. Would the capable, organized, well-put-together wife he used to have return?

Now she seemed utterly helpless. And yet . . . He stared at the woman he thought he knew so well and thought of his patients, those with bone cancer or multiple fractures or new amputations. Sometimes they needed a buffer against the storm that roared around them, and they needed it from him. At least for a little while. Then, usually, they would rally and find the strength to do whatever had seemed totally overwhelming and impossible. Maybe she, too, needed some kind of protection. Maybe she, too, would rally.

"Honey, you'll do fine. Eddie will do fine. He's a tough little guy who has come through a lot. We need to let him show us how well he will do at home."

She slouched in her chair like a lost kitten, weary and exhausted. He kneeled at her side. "I know you're scared." He took a deep breath. "Honey, I'm scared, too. We don't know what's ahead and that's scary. But, we have to let Eddie prove himself. I know you can do it. And, I'm here to help you. We'll get through the rest of this together, just as we got through the past ten days."

He stroked her hair and ran his fingers across her tear-stained cheek. "Do you want to keep these plants and things? If so, I'll get a box from the trash bin."

She nodded and uttered a muffled sob. Then the room was quiet and she said, "That stuff is Eddie's. He'll probably want it at home."

He was loading the plants and flowers and plushy toy animals into a Pampers carton when Ruby walked into Eddie's room.

"Looks like you're about to leave. Everything's set." She handed Anna a stack of papers. "Here're your discharge instructions—if Eddie develops a fever or, God forbid, a seizure . . ." Her voice trailed off. Surely the young doctor saw the fear that darkened his wife's eyes. "Basically, if you're worried about anything, give us a call or talk to your regular pediatrician. Here's the prescription for the cipro Eddie will take at home. It's to finish treatment for his urinary tract infection. You can get it filled at your neighborhood drug store if you'd like—the pharmacy here takes hours to fill a script.

"And this . . ." Ruby hesitated and then sat in a chair, her eyes level with Anna's. "This's another appointment for the vision and hearing assessments. The tests we did yesterday were inconclusive, so we want to repeat them in about a month." She looked uneasy, avoided Anna's stare. "You don't want to delay that too long, because if, ultimately, they're abnormal, we'll want to get Eddie into a special educational program soon. The sooner the better."

Okay, he thought, Eddie didn't pass either of them. Most likely he's deaf and blind and they'll need to confirm those results. He tapped his fingers against his breastbone, felt as if all the juices had been squeezed out of him.

"Ruby," he said. He glanced at Anna; her eyes were focused on the floor. "You can be honest with us. Eddie can't hear and can't see, right?"

"Well," Ruby began. Her upper lip, bearing the scars from her cleft repair, twitched as she spoke. "It's not as simple as that. The testing couldn't confirm that Eddie can hear or see. It really needs to be repeated. Definitely, children may have hearing deficits after meningitis that improve over time. That's not as likely to happen with visual deficits." She stopped, took a deep breath, and continued. "Look, Jake, I understand that waiting for the final results is tough. Real tough. But we simply can't be absolutely sure yet." She paused, then continued. "In the meanwhile, take him home and love him and talk to him and play with him, and we'll continue our assessment over the next couple months."

He didn't need to explain it any further to his wife. She held Eddie against her chest and wept into the space between his little neck and shoulder. Obviously she understood everything Ruby had just said.

That evening, as his in-laws were packing and Anna scrubbed a noodle-coated saucepan, he heard her scream. He dropped the book he was reading to Chris and bolted out of his son's bedroom and down the steps.

"Mommy . . . Mommy . . ." He heard Chris's terrified words fade away as he neared the kitchen.

"What happened?" he yelled.

She stood, frozen, beside the sink, her face pale as a pearl. Eddie lay where he had last seen him, on a bed pillow on the kitchen table.

"What's wrong?" he yelled again.

"Is he breathing? He was choking."

He studied Eddie, watched his son's chest move up and down, saw the rose tint in his cheeks, a dab of mucus on his lips. He lifted Eddie from the pillow.

"Honey, he's fine. Did he cough a little? There's some crud on his mouth that he might have spit up."

He held Anna's elbow as he steered her to a chair beside the table. He laid Eddie in her lap. "See, honey, he's fine." Eddie turned his shoulder against her shirt and uttered a soft snort.

"Is that what you heard?"

She nodded.

"He's fine, honey. That was a little Eddie honk."

"Mommy." Chris stood in the kitchen doorway in his pajamas and bare feet.

"Come here, lovey," Anna said to Chris and then wrapped her free arm around his shoulders. "I guess I was a little frightened."

Chris turned toward him, a puzzled look on his face.

"False alarm, buddy. All is well here. Let's go finish that book."

*   *   *

Chris's chin was smeared with taco sauce, and shredded lettuce dotted the front of his shirt. "Good," he murmured as he stuffed the last bite into his mouth.

Jake had driven his in-laws to the airport the evening before and now they were alone, just the four of them, at dinner. He had finished eating and pushed his chair back a bit. Almost normal, he thought, surveying his family as they ended their meal.

Eddie lay on the pillow on the kitchen table, between Chris and Anna. His eyes were closed. He seemed to be sleeping, even though he snorted with every fourth or fifth breath.

Anna patted the baby's cheek, said, "Sweet Eddie," and turned his head to the side to stifle the snorts. He opened his eyes and blinked as if to shoo away the ceiling light. His pupils, tiny black dots amid the green-blue of his irises, seemed to catch her face.

Maybe he could see, after all. He seemed to be tracking. His eyes moved as her face moved. Jake leaped to his feet and waved his teaspoon in front of Eddie. Light from overhead bounced off the spoon. Jake moved it slowly to the left. And then to the right. He couldn't tell. He knew his exam wasn't perfect. He wanted so much for his son to see that he couldn't be sure what Eddie's movements meant. They had to wait for the formal testing. Still, he seemed to avoid the light. That must mean the light triggered some kind of response in his retinas. Did that mean vision?

Anna straightened the front of Eddie's shirt. She was such a good mom . . . a very, very good mom. Things were working their way back to normal, to a new normal.

Chris reached over his plate and tickled his brother's foot. Eddie's left knee jerked upward, drawing his foot away.

"Put him in his high chair," Chris said. "Pillows don't belong on the table." This was his officious voice, an echo of Anna when she clarified the rules.

"Eddie can't sit up in his high chair." Jake wished Chris hadn't issued that command. Wished he didn't have to explain Eddie's limitations to his older son.

"Make him." Chris took a sip of his milk.

"It isn't that easy, buddy."

His smart-mouthed son was right, in a way. Eddie couldn't spend the rest of his life on a pillow on the kitchen table. Yet, he needed to be with them at dinner. Ideas began to bounce through his head. High chair. Car seat. Cushion. Oak.

"How about we—you and I—build a new high chair for Eddie? One he can kind of lie in."

Chris nodded, his eyes sparkled.

"And Mommy can paint something nice on it," he added. "Maybe balloons or something."

"Tigers," Chris yelled. "Paint tigers and make them growl."

Anna's eyes lifted from her lap. First she looked at Chris and then at him and then at Eddie on the pillow and shook her head gently from side to side. "Not tigers."

"Then snakes," Chris said.

"How about a cat? And daisies," Anna said.

"Yeah," Chris yelled. "Make him look like Bullet. And make him growl."

"Speaking of Bullet, where is he?" Anna asked. She glanced toward the heat register, then at the cat food bowl on the floor beside the fridge.

"He's around here somewhere," Jake said. "I let him in when I came back from Taco Town. He's probably hiding from you-know-who." He nodded toward Chris.

Anna giggled. It was good to hear her giggle; it sounded like water trickling over pebbles in a creek bed. Not long ago, he had thought his wife might never giggle, or laugh, or even smile again.

Chapter 35

Anna

The sun was not quite above the backyard fence when she discovered they were out of both milk and breakfast cereal.

"I want Kix," Chris called. He leaned against the kitchen doorway, clutching the crotch of his pajama bottoms. His hair was tangled and only three of the six buttons on his pajama top were fastened.

She parted his hair with her fingers.

"Do you have to go potty?"

"No. I want Kix."

Besides no milk and no cereal, there were no eggs. She couldn't make omelets or pancakes or even French toast.

"Go potty and get dressed while I figure out something to eat."

She'd have to make a trip to the grocery store. Day after day, she'd put it off, but now the food situation was a crisis.

Eddie, awake but silent, lay in his new recliner, Jake's invention that looked like a car seat on high-chair legs. The paint had finally dried and just last night she had finished the gingham covers for the cushion that lined the wooden frame. She had made three covers, assuring a clean one when the others were in the laundry. Jake had built it with room to grow, so that Eddie's legs could get longer and his trunk could get taller, and he would still fit in his new seat. When, or if, he had the strength to sit up alone, he could go back to the regular high chair. In the meanwhile, this worked well. They all agreed Eddie needed to be at the kitchen table when they ate.

She thought about the tasks ahead and shook her head at the enormity of it all. She needed to arrange for Rose Marie to take the boys again so she could get back to work. She could feed Eddie immediately before dropping the boys at day care and immediately after picking him up four hours later. That way Rose Marie wouldn't have to deal with the feeding tube. Monday was the target, so she had three more days to iron out the details.

She hadn't driven the car since that horrible trip to the emergency room three weeks ago. She and the kids would go to the store after they finished eating. There must be something in the house to eat for breakfast.

Inside the freezer she found a carton of vanilla ice cream; in the fridge, a wilted head of lettuce, three green onions, and an assortment of half-filled jars—ketchup, mustard, mayonnaise, dill pickles, olives, and BBQ sauce. Nothing of substance.

"Can I have a cookie?" Chris called from his bedroom.

"We don't have any," she called back. "Besides, we're working on breakfast."

"Grandma made some. I want one of Grandma's cookies."

She opened the door to the corner cupboard. Tang. That was a start. Next to the bag of brown sugar stood a plastic container she'd never seen before. Inside were cookies; they smelled like oatmeal and the little brown things looked like raisins.

Her grandmother's words tracked through her head: "Necessity is the mother of invention." That resourceful woman would have been able to cobble together something for breakfast.

She stirred two tablespoons of Tang into a glass of water and set a bowl of ice cream on the table beside a cookie. Ice cream was, after all, made of cream, which was close to milk, and the cookie was close to oat cereal. The raisins were fruit.

Then she called to Chris, "Breakfast's ready."

He wandered to the table and looked at the bowl of ice cream. Then he looked at her. She couldn't read the expression on his face.

Before Eddie's illness, he never would have found a breakfast like this. They would have had plenty of cereal and milk. There were lots of differences since Eddie's illness.

"You found Grandma's cookies," he finally said.

"I did, and figured we could try them out for breakfast."

He smiled and blew a mouthful of air into his brother's face. Eddie squirmed and sputtered.

Chris climbed on his stool at the table. The rays of the morning sun, which had cleared the top of the backyard fence by now and streamed through the kitchen window, lit up his face.

"Ow, too bright." He clamped his eyes shut.

She drew the curtain across the window, shutting out the harsh rays, letting in the filtered ones.

Chris was already strapped into his car seat when she carried Eddie out the back door and into the garage.

She laid Eddie in the infant seat, but his body didn't mold to the padding the way it used to—now his legs were stiff and his spine, rather than bending at the waist, arched backward. She leaned into the rear car door and tried to push him into place. She kneaded his belly to make it bend, tried to fold his knees toward his chest, but his rigid body wouldn't slide into the seat. She took a step backward and bumped against the snow shovel, knocking it off the wall. It landed in an oil puddle on the garage floor. She let out a sigh of frustration.

Chris kicked against the upholstery. "Let's go," he said, a perfect imitation of an impatient Jake.

She couldn't remember how Jake had gotten Eddie into the car for the ride home from the hospital. He hadn't had any trouble that she could recall. But then, she hadn't given that part of going home much attention.

"Chris, settle down," she called. "Quit kicking." She stood beside the open car door and rubbed her sore back.

"Mommy." Chris's call was sharp as an ice pick. "Let's go."

She tried once more to prop Eddie into his car seat. This time a gentle push seemed to coax his body into the right position—his bottom settled into the seat padding, his spine leaned easily against the back. Something had changed in him, something had loosened him up.

"In a minute, Chris." She fastened the straps of Eddie's car seat.

"I wanna get out, Mommy." Chris was clawing at his seat belt.

"Stay there. We'll get going to the store in a minute. Count to thirty."

She fished the snow shovel from the oily puddle and hooked it on the nail in the wall.

"Twenty-one," Chris droned. "Twenty-two."

As she turned back to the car, she caught the smell.

"Twenty-nine. THIRTY," Chris yelled, victorious. Then his voice dropped. "Eddie pooped. It stinks."

She wiped her face with her hands, ran her fingertips over her forehead. How could a trip to the grocery store be so difficult? It wasn't like this before. She reached into the car and unbuckled Chris from his car seat. He clung to her as if stitched to her body, his arms so tight around her neck she could hardly breathe. She rubbed his legs, patted his back, and stroked his hair while she swayed side to side in the damp, earthy morning air that, like her, was trapped inside the garage.

She had no idea how Eddie's illness, the hospitalization, her long absence had affected Chris. In spite of his sometimes cocky talk, he was still a little boy, a child who needed his mother to take care of him, to protect him. The past three weeks must have felt like a hurricane, followed by a tornado, followed by a blizzard for him. Like hell to the third power.

When Chris finally let go of her neck, she set him on the floor and picked Eddie out of his seat. "We'll clean him up and then go to the store." With Chris hanging like moss from the waistband of her slacks and Eddie cradled in her arms, she hobbled back to the kitchen door.

She laid Eddie on the sofa to change his diaper. He had always been a placid baby but now, was more so—no crying, no cooing. His hips splayed apart, his knees were tightly bent and the soles of his feet rubbed against each other. He didn't pull against her, didn't kick at the air, didn't try to flip over while she slid the new Pamper under his little butt. She ripped the backing off the sticky tabs, smoothed the plastic edge against his belly, and remembered the old days—back when she took for granted that Eddie was a healthy baby, back when she took everything for granted. A month ago, she found his rolling around irritating. "Lie still, would you?" she had said, half playfully as she grabbed his leg to keep him on his back. Right now, more than anything, she wished he would flip over while she changed his diaper.

She washed her hands, gave Chris another cookie, and paged Jake.

"Where are you?" she asked when he called back.

"In the clinic."

She explained what had just happened, about the junk food for breakfast, about the snow shovel, about the impossibility of getting to the grocery store. She wasn't sure what she wanted from him. She remembered how, when she was a little girl, her father kissed her scraped knee, made monkey faces, danced around her like a clown. How her tears had turned to smiles when her father had whispered, "After the rain comes the sunshine, Anna-danna-my-dear-bobanna," and everything was good again. But that was long ago.

"It's okay." Jake's voice was smooth as brandy. "Ice cream and cookies won't hurt him. Actually, it's a pretty clever solution to the no-breakfast problem. I can stop for milk and cereal on the way home. What else do we need in the line of groceries?"

"No, we'll go. Hopefully later this afternoon. I just wanted to tell someone how difficult this seems."

"You're doing great, honey."

His voice was comforting. His reassuring words seemed honest. She had to believe they were. She wished he were there, but he would be home later that evening and would help with the children. He had even begun to do some of the cooking. He and Chris. "The Campbell guy chefs," Jake called them.

"Can I do that?" Chris asked as he watched her prepare the feeding tube.

"No, sweetheart. I have to do this." She attached the formula-filled syringe to the hub of the tube and slowly pushed the plunger.

"Does he like that?" Chris asked.

"Do you mean does he like the tube? Or does he like the formula?"

Chris shrugged, staring solemnly at his baby brother.

"Well, he can't taste the formula because it doesn't go into his mouth. I think he likes to eat by the tube, because he feels full when we're done."

When she finished feeding Eddie, she laid him in his crib. "Chris," she called. "Nap time." How could she manage to return to work? She doubted she would ever get into a routine. At best, it would be a new routine, not like before.

Chris argued with her about the nap, whined that he wanted to sleep standing up. "Don't be silly," she said and led him into his room. She lifted him into his bed, handed him Alphie the stuffed alligator, shut the blinds, kissed him, and left.

With both boys asleep, she decided to take a bath. She used to relax in the tub, back when it had been possible to relax. In the past, the warm water that lapped against her skin while she swirled her arms through the soapy liquid had softened tight muscles, quelled hurt feelings, sweetened sour moods.

Naked, she sat on the toilet lid. Goose bumps sprouted on her bare belly as she waited for the hot water to wash through the pipes. She studied her bare feet, the pink of her toes against the brown floor tiles. Toes were funny things, she thought, a row of swollen, fleshy fringe hanging off the end of each foot. It was hard to believe such ridiculous tags of bone and skin belonged to her. Inching her feet apart slightly, she squared her toes with the grout lines. It was satisfying, the sight of her bare feet against the tile grid—evidence that predictability and order still existed in the world.

As she stared at her two baby toes that curled inward, at her bruised right ankle, at the way her second toes were longer than her great toes, she wondered if she was really sitting there. She wiggled her feet, watched them rise and fall against the brown tiles.

"Am I dreaming this," she muttered out loud. "Is this real?"

Six weeks ago she had taken a bath; six weeks from now she would take a bath. As she wondered about former, present, and future baths, time seemed very fluid; days had sloshed into weeks, which would slosh into months. The baths themselves were routine, almost boring in their sameness. It was the surrounding circumstances that distinguished one from the next. Maybe she could magically transform this one into a previous bath—the last one before Eddie's illness—and redo the events that had followed.

Suddenly, the reality of Eddie swept over her—a crushing, suffocating, blinding, inky green truth. She wanted to run, to get away from it, to race to where it wasn't. The room darkened. Her stomach twisted. She shut her eyes, moaned, and grabbed at the side of the sink, trying to escape the inescapable knowing that overwhelmed her—Eddie would never be normal, would never run up a flight of stairs, never blow a chewing gum bubble, never count from one hundred backward by sevens just for the fun of it. He'd probably never count at all. Maybe he'd never talk, never tell anyone he loved her, never tell her of his victories, his worries, his sorrows. Would he be able to hear her voice? To see a beautiful sunset? Maybe he'd just lie like a blob of dough and grow old.

For a while at the hospital, she had thought Eddie would die. At other times she had convinced herself he would snap out of it—that the magic of modern medicine would erase his infection and return him to a healthy baby. None of that was real.

Absolutely none of it. What was real about Eddie was that he would never, never, never be normal.

She remembered the trip to the Upper Peninsula for Jennifer's wedding, the rest stop at the foot of the Mackinac Bridge, the acorn that Jake tossed toward Lake Huron. It had missed the water and landed on the rocks beside the root of a tree. What had happened to that acorn? Had it sprouted? Had the sprout survived? Surely it couldn't grow to be a majestic oak. At best it would be stunted. But maybe it would be a bonsai oak, small and different from other oaks, but lovely. Like Eddie, different from other children, but lovely.

She didn't know how long she stood there at the sink. But, at some point, she tested the bath water. Now warm, it gushed from the faucet and splashed against her hand. She plugged the drain and slid her toes into the growing pool in the bottom of the tub.

By midafternoon, she was ready to try the trip to the grocery store again. She folded three flannel blankets into rolls to cradle Eddie in the car seat.

"Chris," she called, "take these to the garage while I carry Eddie."

Eventually both boys were strapped in.

The shops lining the road flashed past, familiar as the back of her hand and yet oddly different from what she remembered. There was the dry cleaner where she took her woolen sweaters each spring and Jake's suit before every family wedding; the KFC where she used to stop, on the sly, to satisfy a craving for fried chicken and coleslaw; the liquor store that sold the Wild Turkey she sometimes bought as a treat for Jake; the hardware store where Chris had rearranged handfuls of screws from one open bin to three others. The stores seemed to be organized differently, set at different angles, lined up in a different order. That didn't make sense, but something was new about them.

The traffic light ahead turned yellow. She braked, slowing

the car so it came to a stop at the crosswalk just as the light blinked to red. It felt strange to be driving. Her reflexes seemed dull, her instincts rusty. Gripping the steering wheel reminded her of that drive to the emergency room three weeks ago. It seemed like three years ago. From now on, every event in her life would be dated as "*before* Eddie got sick" or "*after* Eddie got sick." Her promotion at work was *before*, Jennifer's wedding was *before*. What would be *after*?

While her car idled at the red light, a cement truck stopped beside her on the left, and a UPS van stopped on her right, squeezing her as if walls along the road were moving relentlessly toward each other, with her in the middle. She looked into the rearview mirror, leaned toward it to see her own face. The woman who looked back was not the same person as *before*. She couldn't remember exactly what the *before* lady had looked like, but probably she had bright eyes, cheeks flushed with excitement, a look of satisfaction on her face. The *after* was a sad-eyed, thin-faced, pale lady who was going through the motions of being Anna. The person in the mirror was the mother of a damaged child whose *afters* she could only guess. She longed for the return of the *before* Anna.

As the light turned green and she let the car creep forward, Chris called from the back seat. "Mommy, play the Christmas tree song."

She looked into the rearview mirror again, at Chris's fly-away, sand-colored hair, at his glistening eyes focused on the scenery as it moved past the car window. "Honey, it's almost summer. We'll play the Christmas tree song next winter."

"Now. Play it now."

She looked at him once more in the mirror. His eyes now stared into the back of her head.

"Okay. I'll get it out the next time we stop."

At the next red light, she fingered through her CDs, pulled out the Mannheim Steamroller *Christmas Extraordinaire* disc, and inserted it into the slit on the dashboard.

By the time the light turned green again, "O Tannenbaum" was playing and Chris was singing.

"O Christmas tree, O Christmas tree . . ." His voice sounded like a golden bell.

Jake had taught Chris a silly, bathroom-humor version of that song, which they had yelled at the top of their lungs last winter, their craggy voices out-shouting Johnny Mathis and the chorus on the recording. Now, Chris sang that newer version of the carol, his head thrown back, his eyes clamped shut, his mouth wide open.

"O Christmas tree, oh, woe is me, before we eat, I've got to pee."

Christmas songs continued to bubble through the spring air. When they were a block from the grocery store, she heard the notes of "The First Noel"—a hymn of epiphany, the celebration of a beginning, the initiation of a new start. She looked yet again in the rearview mirror, this time at Eddie. He was nestled in his carrier among the rolled flannel blankets. And he was breathing.

She glanced over her shoulder to be sure the mirror wasn't fooling her. Yes, he was breathing. From the CD player, the haunting tones of an oboe rose like smoke upward where they were joined by the notes of a violin, sweet as syrup, clear as ice, perfect as a human voice. The sounds of the two instruments intertwined, weaving in, swaying out, twisting together, their overtones ascending, ever, ever upward.

She turned the car into the parking lot of the grocery store and pulled into a space marked with a handicapped sign. She shut off the car motor, slid the keys into her purse, and glanced at Chris, then at Eddie. With a sigh, she opened the door, stood on the pavement, and brushed the wrinkles out of the lap of her slacks.

"Okay, guys," she said to her sons, to herself, to no one. "We made it."

Chapter 36

Jake

On his way home, driving past playgrounds and preschools, Jake marveled at his son's progress. Eddie had been discharged from the hospital almost two weeks ago and, as far as Jake could tell, had been doing well. No seizures. No aspirating. Anna had given up trying to nurse him again but he was beginning to drink thickened formula from a bottle, although they had to bore open the holes in the nipples so the formula could flow more easily. He figured they'd be able to stop the tube feedings by the end of the month. Eddie—all the Campbells, in fact—were definitely planted on firm earth after the horror of his illness.

He parked the car in their driveway. Once inside the house, he called, "Howdy. I'm home." He heard singing from the direction of the family room.

Chris, surrounded by LEGOs, sat on the floor and sang about a dinosaur while Eddie snuggled in Anna's lap. Jake leaned to kiss her cheek. She pulled away.

What now? In the morning when he left, she was sunny as a

goldfinch, looking forward to taking the boys to the petting zoo. This evening she was sullen.

"Someone called for you about an hour ago." Her voice was ice.

"Who?" Jake sank into the couch. From the look on her face—the wrath in her eyes, the sag of her forehead, the tight pucker of her lips—he knew who had called. What on earth had she said to Anna?

"Dr. Daley. Mona or Monica—something like that—Daley."

Jake bit his lip, took a deep breath, wiped his sweaty palms against his pant legs.

"Isn't that the name of the woman from your medical school that you used to date?"

"Monica Daley? Why'd she call? I guess she eventually graduated if she calls herself 'Doctor' Daley."

Anna was wordless. She stroked Eddie's hair, kissed the top of his head.

Jake took another deep breath and wished he were doing anything else other than having this conversation. Sprawled in her chair with her damaged baby in her arms, she was a fragile china figurine about to fall off the edge of a high shelf. He couldn't bear for her to be hurt any further.

Why had Monica called, anyway? She was crazy—now he knew how truly disturbed she was—and she must have said something that upset Anna. "What did Monica want?"

She shook her head slowly, tipped her chin down. She refused to look at him. "She asked how Eddie was doing."

He heard the fan from the refrigerator in the kitchen, heard a blue jay call from the backyard.

"How'd she know Eddie was sick, Jake?" Her words were slow, deliberate.

He watched her fingers twist a corner of the blanket that covered Eddie. Her beautiful, purposeful hands. Her wedding rings, the diamond turned against her left pinkie. Her fingers—they were stiff, as if they belonged to an old lady—pinched the flannel fabric. If only he could hide. He was trapped, had no answer other than the truth.

"It was all a mistake, Anna."

"What was a mistake? Marrying me?"

"No, no. Of course not." Oh God, this was worse than he imagined. "I was desperate, Anna. Desperate for an anchor. That's the best way I can describe it to you. Desperate to connect with . . . well, now I know it was a fantasy." His words felt hollow. What was she hearing in them? He was light-headed, teary, as out of control as an airplane without a pilot. He didn't want Anna to see him that way.

He told her about his call to Monica. "After I heard her voice again, the old stuff seemed to pour over my head. All those questions about what happened to her—why she disappeared—opened up like a gaping wound."

He blew his nose. "Then she called from the airport. She'd flown to Michigan."

Anna seemed to grab every word he said, her face blank, her lips pale.

"I . . . I stupidly drove to her hotel to see her. I needed answers to those old questions."

He wasn't sure Anna was breathing. She didn't move, didn't speak.

He explained everything about the visit to Monica's hotel room. The wine, the invitation to bed, his declination of the invitation, his eagerness to leave. He described what she was like now. "She's nuts, Anna. Probably she was always nuts, but I couldn't see it before."

"Why did you call her in the first place?"

He tried to explain, had trouble finding the words. How could he explain the inexplicable? Anna seemed to be slipping away from him.

"All I know is that Eddie's illness took a toll on me, too. You probably don't realize that. In the crush of the circumstances, I needed . . . well, I needed something. I didn't know what, but seeing Monica seemed like it might offer a break in the storm. It didn't. It was dumb . . . foolish."

He sat on the floor beside her chair and touched her cheek. She pulled her face away.

Chris was quiet, had made a LEGO tower. The family room looked as it always had and yet it was very different, cold, dim, tense. A black force had floated over him, was strangling him.

"I hope you can forgive me. Nothing happened between Monica and me, but I sincerely wish I hadn't called her, hadn't gone to see her."

Anna looked like granite.

"After talking to her for just a few minutes, there in the hotel, I realized what a mistake I'd made. Then I left."

Anna remained still. Was she listening at all?

"Obviously, that visit with her didn't fix anything for me. I really wish you didn't have to know about this. Most of all I don't want to hurt you. Please forgive me."

"Forgive you? I can't think like that now, Jake. I'm going to bed."

She gathered Eddie and his blanket, slowly stood up, and trudged toward the stairs. Should he follow her? Call to her?

"Daddy, look at my tower," Chris said, waving the stack of LEGOs like a wand. Jake kneeled beside his son and, one LEGO piece at a time, began building a tower of his own.

Chapter 37

Anna

He'd broken down, something she'd never seen him do before. He'd wept as he told her about meeting Monica. She didn't want to be in his presence, didn't want to hear the words that trickled from his mouth. She wished he would go away, wished it all would go far, far away.

He insisted they had only talked, that he quickly realized how unstable Monica was, even back when they were dating. For some reason—probably the myopia of youth, he'd said—he hadn't been able to see that side of her before.

Could she believe him? Had they had sex? Did she want to know, if they had? Maybe he'd seen her at other times. Maybe during the orthopedic meeting last fall in Boston. Had Monica come to Michigan earlier and spent time with Jake? Perhaps she'd been in his call room bed those evenings he called to say good night to Chris. Was she with him the night Eddie got sick? Maybe that was why he didn't know how sick Eddie really was.

While Jake spoke, she glanced at Chris who, unexpectedly quiet, was connecting LEGOs. He must have felt the bad aura in the room, known enough to keep from bothering them, but

not enough to be scared. He'd spent the past month in a constant state of upheaval. Maybe he thought this was just the next
chapter in the same terrible tale.

Suddenly, she was tired, more tired than she had ever been.
Her bones were weary, her muscles ached, her head throbbed,
her chest felt as if it were crushed under a boulder. "I'm going
to bed," she told him.

From the dark of her bedroom, she heard Jake usher Chris
up the stairs and into the bathroom. The toilet flushed. They
walked into Chris's room, were talking but she couldn't hear
the words. She supposed Jake was helping Chris into his pajamas, hoped he was being gentle. She couldn't do anything
about Chris, now. He and Jake were on their own.

She didn't know how long it was before she heard Jake's footsteps on the bedroom floor. Had she slept? She couldn't imagine she'd been able to fall asleep. She felt the stir of the
mattress as he sat beside her, felt his hand on her shoulder.

"Anna . . ." His voice was quiet, hoarse.

"I can't listen to any more of it. I need to be alone with this
right now." Why did he call Monica? Why did he go to see her?
So many questions; they rattled through her head like a run-
away train.

She really didn't want to know the answers. If she knew they
had had sex, she'd spend the rest of her life picturing Jake and
Monica together, naked, arousing each other. Every time they
were intimate, she'd feel Monica's presence, like a giant skunk,
in their bedroom. If she had failed to meet Jake's needs, how
would she fix that? Could she? Ever? Would he tell her what she
hadn't been able to supply? She wasn't sure she could believe
him.

"I love you, Anna. Please know that."

She didn't know it tonight. Would she tomorrow? Next week?
Next year?

Epilogue

Spring break is over and the house is quiet, except for the insistent buzz from the laundry room notifying Anna that Chris's towels are dry. He's back at college now, in sunny California, three time zones away. She's still in Michigan, with rain pattering on the deck and thunder roiling in the distance. She pulls the warm towels from the dryer, folds them, and puts them back in his bathroom. She wants it to be ready for his next trip home.

The fridge is a mess but she doesn't mind. It's Chris's clutter, all that remains, now, of his visit. She wipes away the spilled milk from under the vegetable bin and tosses the olive jar—it contains only juice and four pieces of pimento—into the trash. The last of the cheesecake, cloaked in Saran Wrap, sits on the bottom shelf.

Just a week ago they had shopped for the ingredients for that cake.

"How much sour cream?" Chris had asked, turning his head away from the dairy cooler and toward her. Flashing one of his infectious smiles, he held a pint container toward her and then suddenly flipped it into the air and caught it with his other hand. "This size?"

What a clown, she thought. A healthy, fun-loving wiseacre.

That afternoon the two of them made the cheesecake together, as they used to—Anna dictating the recipe while Chris dumped the ingredients into the food processor.

"Where's the vanilla?" he asked, rummaging through her spice shelf.

"Isn't there a bottle up there, somewhere?" She tried to remember the last time she had used vanilla extract. Since he left for college, her cooking had become much less interesting.

"Don't see it. How about almond extract?" He pulled the little brown bottle from the back of the shelf. "Looks about the same." He twisted off the cap and passed the open top under his nose. "This'll work."

He patted the graham cracker crust mixture into her springform pan, poured in the cheese filling, and shoved it into the oven. While it baked, he cooked blueberry sauce.

That night, Chris served his dessert with a flourish.

"Ta-da. The ultimate," he said as he set the cheesecake in front of his father. "You, Dr. Campbell, get to cut it."

Anna brought out the small plates, clean forks, and the silver cake server.

Eddie dropped his first bite in his lap. "Oops," he signed— his fingers weaving through the air like butterflies—to Anna.

"Klutz," Chris signed to his brother.

"Asshole," Eddie signed back.

"Keep it clean," Jake signed to both of them, nodding toward Anna. "There's a lady at the table."

Where did Eddie learn that? she wondered. From Chris? From school? Is that what they teach in classes for the hearing impaired?

While they ate, Chris told them about his new friend, Emmy, at Stanford. He giggled as he spoke. "You'll love her, Mom. She's a lot like you."

"How so?" Anna was curious to hear his answer.

"Well, lively and smart and she reads a lot."

Anna doesn't think of herself as lively or smart. She does, however, read a lot. Maybe someday she'll meet Emmy, who, although unknown to them, is obviously very important to Chris. In a good way. He'll need a steady companion, someone to share the many ups and, hopefully, few downs of his life. And, Anna won't choose her. She hopes Emmy is thoughtful and generous, interesting and ambitious. Anna's job will be to accept her.

Now, standing in front of the open refrigerator door, she cuts a slim wedge from the leftover cheesecake and eats it with her fingers. She misses Chris a lot.

Later that afternoon, rain pelts the back of her jacket as she helps Eddie into her car. She pulls on his sleeve and signs, "Wait." She needs to clear her students' papers from the passenger side. He can't manage both getting himself into the seat and moving whatever may be in the way. He's a one-maneuver kind of guy, she had decided long ago. She tosses the papers into the rear and stands back while Eddie grabs the door frame, lifts his left foot, sets it on the floor mat and slowly lowers his bottom to the cushion. He's awkward, his limbs are stiff. His nerves and muscles betray him, don't follow his ardent commands. Slowly, he pulls his right leg into the car.

"Scoot in a little more," she signs to him and then pats his thigh. He wiggles, inching his butt about a half inch farther inside. Then he turns his rain-streaked face toward her and grins. He's amazingly good natured, contented most of the time, and she's grateful for that. She wants to kiss his cheek, but that would embarrass him.

This is the last day she'll pick him up from school.

"But what if he falls?" she said last week. Jake thought Eddie should ride the school bus.

"He's fourteen," he said.

"Yes, but he's not like other fourteen-year-olds who rattle around on those buses. He's . . . unsteady."

"You're selling him short. Everyone has challenges and should be given the opportunity to conquer them."

"He won't be able to hear the road noise. He might walk in front of a truck that's barreling down the street."

Over and over they pleaded their cases. Jake pointed out that Eddie's friends looked out for him. Anna said his friends weren't always with him. She reminded him that Eddie was "intellectually a little slow." Jake said he was certainly sharp enough to ride a school bus.

Finally Jake said, "He needs to walk more, otherwise he'll have trouble marching down the aisle after his wedding."

Anna shuddered. Eddie's wedding? "I've thought a lot about Chris's wedding, especially with all the Emmy talk. Never Eddie's." Would he find a woman to love him? At least, as the groom, he wouldn't have to lurch up the aisle all alone toward the altar. Instead, he'd wait there for his bride, flanked by the minister and his groomsman brother. Later, Eddie and his brand-new wife would stroll together down the aisle. As she recalled, the bride always leaned against the groom during that walk. She knows she did. But there was no reason the groom couldn't lean against the bride. They needed to be able to lean on each other.

In the end, they agreed. Ed—Jake insisted they call him Ed and she kept forgetting to do that—would ride the bus for three days and then they'd reevaluate.

At home, Anna stabs the power button on the television remote and a soccer game flashes on the screen. She glances at Eddie seated on the couch, stares into his sweet, angelic, not quite yet adolescent face. "What should we make for dinner?" she asks in sign. His smoky blue eyes, the same color and shape as Jake's, stare back at her. He tilts his head, doesn't seem to understand.

"Hey, lovey," she says, louder, even though she knows he can't understand her, no matter how loud she shouts. Sound is a smear of faint warbles to him. She tries it again, signs, "Hey, lovey," making her fingers, her arms, her body glide into the words. "What do you want for dinner?"

His eyes narrow with a smile. His fingers, thin and finely tapered like her own, fly through the air. She's thankful for his fairly nimble fingers.

"Did you say chicken Kiev?" She signs each letter. K. I. E. V.

He nods and utters one of his snorty, burpy sounds—an Eddie chuckle, as Jake calls it. "Chicken, it is," she tells him. "Tonight it's just the two of us. Dad has a big case."

While the chicken simmers in the oven, Anna watches the last of the sun's rays drop behind the dreary clouds that hang like woolen roving beyond the backyard. A budding branch of the hydrangea bush raps against the kitchen window.

The cribbage board is still on the table, beside the deck of cards. She and Chris had played several times during his visit home. They giggled, joked, teased, and, in the end, she won the majority of the games. Now, she sets the board and cards back in the desk drawer. Why does Chris's moving away have to be so hard? she wonders. Hard on her. Not hard on him.

During one of the cribbage games, Chris suddenly announced, "I'm taking a course called Deviance," and then laughed at the look on her face. He explained, his voice growing progressively louder as his enthusiasm ballooned, "It's a soc. course. The social underpinnings of criminal behavior, how economic inequality feeds criminality and domestic violence . . . stuff like that."

She was surprised at his newfound maturity. His world was moving further and further away from hers. He described trips with his new friends through the redwoods of Pescadero Creek Park and to the beach at Año Nuevo to watch the elephant seals; their trips to Half Moon Bay and to the top of the Pinnacles.

"It's best to go up the west slope in the morning, or you fry in the afternoon sun," he said with confidence and authority. In great detail, he explained the thrill of rounding the last pile of stones and spotting the summit ahead and told of his tumble into a pool of muddy water inside an ink-dark cave. Neither she nor Jake had been to any of those places. They seemed as foreign and far away as a swirling nebula, beyond the far reaches of the universe and rolling onward toward infinity. She couldn't sleep that night, tossing over and over in her head his continuing, inevitable, heartbreaking, completely appropriate journey away from her.

In the silence of the family room, she takes a sip of her chardonnay. This is her favorite season, with lengthening days that gently fade into silky nights. Lilac blooms. Tulip blossoms. It's been fourteen years this month but still the fresh spring air ferries back all the memories of that night. "The fork in the road," as the hospital chaplain had said. She remembers Eddie's whimper when she found him. Mostly she remembers the dark. As she looks back, everything seems very dark.

She remembers laying Eddie in his crib and begging him not to wake up. And he didn't. Not through the whole night. Not for a week. He followed her orders and almost died.

The scene scrolls over and over through her mind, as it has a million times. Two million times. It's fainter, now, bubbles up less frequently. But, she can't make it go away completely.

Their wedding picture sits on the desk beside the phone. Jake was handsome, with his sculpted nose, strong chin, thick curly hair the color of walnuts, now highlighted with streaks of gray. Unlike his static eyes in the picture, his real eyes are in constant motion, darting around, searching for things. Assessing, measuring, comparing, calculating.

And, he's successful. Their beautiful home sits on two and a half acres. It's surrounded by trees and there's a pond out back. They have a lot. They don't have all they had hoped for.

She doesn't think of Jake as handsome or successful or rich. Rather, he's the man who snores softly when he sleeps on his back, who spills foot powder on the bathroom floor, who eats the core with the apple. He's Chris's father. Eddie's father. Her husband.

It was also fourteen years ago—a week or two after Eddie had come home from the hospital—that he'd confessed his secret. She was furious, hurt, frightened, vengeful. She felt disconnected from everything she knew. He said he'd been terribly wrong about Monica from the start and that "nothing happened" during their meeting in the hotel. For too long she was unsure she could trust him.

The days went by. Then the months and the years. They laughed, disagreed, worried together, and, during the tender times, confided their longings to each other. They found great joy in the boys.

It was about six or seven years ago—she's lost track of the exact year but it was in the fall, when the evenings were getting cooler—that Jake walked into their bedroom as she was changing the sheets on their bed.

"Here, let me help you with that," he said, grabbing one corner of the clean bottom sheet and pulling it over the edge of the mattress.

She watched as he tugged the fitted sheet over the other corner on his side. He tucked one end of the top sheet under the foot of the mattress and folded a cuff into the other end, pulled pillow slips over two of the pillows and fluffed them with his fist, smoothed the wrinkles out of first the woolen blanket and then the bedspread. He looked unbelievably earnest as he worked, completely committed to the ritual of neatly putting the linens on their bed. Something stirred in her, something good as if a gear, long out of sync, had finally slipped into place. She started to cry.

"What's the matter?" he said, sounding mystified, concerned, staring at the bedspread, wondering if he'd put it on wrong.

"Nothing. Actually, everything's very right." She wiped her tears and chuckled. "For a surgeon, you're very good at making a bed."

The back door slams.

"Anna, I'm home," Jake calls. The coat closet door squeaks open, and then squeaks closed.

He's in the kitchen when he yells, "Where is everyone?"

"I'm in the family room," she says, evenly, quietly.

He bursts through the archway and stops beside her chair. "Ed in bed?" he asks.

"Yes," she says. "It's late."

He sets his hand on her head and bends to kiss her. His lips are soft. She feels the heat of his breath, smells the antiseptic odor of the operating room.

"You must be tired," she says. "It was a long case."

"I'm fine." He squats beside her. "It was a bad comminuted fracture. The poor guy had had an extensive burn on his leg as a kid. I had to cut through his huge scar. That thick, fibrosed skin didn't stretch one damn bit. I hope we ended up with everything put together right."

She leans her forehead against his cheek. It's warm. And comforting. Solid ground in another complicated day.

**Please turn the page for a very special
Q&A with Janet Gilsdorf!**

What motivated you to write this book?

In my professional life, I'm in awe of the ability of parents to accurately recognize illness in their children and to seek medical attention quickly. But, what if they don't? And what if one of the parents is a physician? Parents are hardwired to protect their children, and an ill child brings out the best and the worst in them. I find these reactions fascinating and wished to illuminate them.

Are the characters real people?

Even though the book is fiction and the characters emerged from my imagination, they represent the many parents, physicians, and others I have encountered during my work. Like real people, the characters are imperfect and their limitations make them unpredictable and intriguing. Yet, they are also resilient. While they are not actual human beings, their motivations, reactions, fears, frustrations, and joys are very real.

How can you stand to work with—and write about—sick children?

All children are beautiful and their parents are devoted to them. Working with them—observing their interactions, their worries, their triumphs and failures, their idiosyncrasies—and writing about them is very rewarding. I emphasize over and over to my students, "There are no bad children. Bad things happen to children and they react."

When do you find the time to write in your busy life?

Nights and weekends and vacations. Whatever I'm writing is always on my mind, so I jot down ideas when they come to me at odd times and in unexpected places. I keep a notebook beside my bed and in my car. I jot my thoughts on those flyaway cards from magazines, on white space in the *New York Times*.

What is your next book?

It's a novel about a young woman who defies the cultural norms of North Dakota in the 1960s and goes to medical school. Although my life followed that trajectory, the book isn't about me, but rather a fictional character surrounded by people, places, and circumstances very familiar to me.

How did you start as a creative writer?

After years of clinical practice, I yearned for a way to express my wonder of the parents and children I work with, the interesting—sometimes adaptive, sometimes maladaptive—coping strategies they employ, the lessons in living I have learned from them. About that time, in a stroke of luck (or maybe fate), I was asked to join a writing group. For years I won the most-improved award in the group, because I had such a long way to go. I've attended many summer writing workshops and have come away from all of them with newfound inspiration, commitment, and ideas.

Do you have any advice for a fledging writer?

Follow your heart. Write.

TEN DAYS

Janet Gilsdorf

ABOUT THIS GUIDE

The suggested questions are included
to enhance your group's reading
of Janet Gilsdorf's *Ten Days*.

DISCUSSION QUESTIONS

1. Are either Jake or Anna, or both, bad parents? Why?

2. Who is to blame for Eddie's serious illness?

3. Is Rose Marie wrong to worry about the future of her day care, seemingly ahead of the health of the children?

4. In the throes of Eddie's illness, Jake turns to Monica, his old girlfriend. Why? What does this action do for him? Was he right to tell Anna?

5. Chris, a spunky child, regresses to misbehavior in the face of his brother's illness. Is this realistic? Is it handled well by his parents?

6. Why did the Campbell marriage survive? What might have happened, but didn't, to drive them irretrievably apart? What is the state of the marriage at the end of the book?

7. Should Rose Marie feed her dog zinfandel every night?

8. What is Anna's relationship with her parents? Are they useful to her? To Jake? To Chris?

9. What happens to Anna's reasoning ability? Is she mentally ill? Why does she hear the angel in the elevator?

10. Rose Marie blows up at the fellow from the health department. Is she a mean-spirited person? Is she being unreasonable?

11. The events in the novel occur over less than three weeks. How does time get distorted during this story?

12. Why does the story start with the wedding in the Upper Peninsula of Michigan? What would be gained, or lost, by starting at the time Eddie gets sick?

13. Why is the story told from three points of view? What would be gained, or lost, by telling the story from only Jake's view? From only Anna's? From the perspective of an omniscient narrator?

14. What does the epilogue add to the novel?